Bleeding Heart

a timeless fable about living life with passion

Xavier Saer

"*An inspirational journey into a heart that allows you to experience every aspect of love, heartbreak, glory and triumph. Xavier Saer exposes himself through his main character and takes the reader on a life changing journey that allows us to question every aspect of our lives through another man's adventure. A Beautiful story that is beautifully written with a message that will linger through the generations*"

Leanne Manas,
Award-winning TV presenter.

"*Inspiring journey into the heart of a destiny fuelled by passion and redeemed by love, our ultimate Destiny.*"

Natalie B Becker,
Award-winning actress, presenter, author
and speaker.

You were born an original. Don't die a copy.

John Mason

Published by Heart Space Publications
PO Box 1085, Daylesford,
Vic, 3460, Australia.
Tel 0450260348

Graysonian Press South Africa is an imprint of Heartspace Publications.

Postal: PO Box 4389, Cresta, 2118 Tel +27 11 4311274

For information about this or any of our other books:
pat@graysonian.com or www.graysonian.com

First printed in Australia in 2012

ISBN 978-0-9872816-3-0

Edited by Sumayya Soni - sumflower@gmail.com
Cover artwork by Javier Casella Cabrera - kowalskibros@gmail.com

Acknowledgements

Life, just like writing a novel is a blissful and memorable journey. Alongside my personal path, walk countless souls I need to thank…

Firstly, to The One… thank you! Thank you for allowing me to follow my purpose and pursue my passion. I Love you, my kind and glorious Father.

Sumayya Soni - you are the most wonderful, insightful, and creative editor. I have loved every second of working with you and appreciate your amazing wisdom. I thank you for allowing my dream to be your dream too. This novel and legacy is as much mine as yours.

Vauldy Carelse - my dear friend, I appreciate your honesty, guidance and advice. The time you took to revise the first draft was the catalyst that pushed me to start re-writing. Your compassion and understanding gave my novel its maiden wings. I will always be grateful.

Cathy Lee - your vision and wisdom started it all. Thank you.

Soulla - my angel from Cyprus. Your unconditional Love lives in me. Thank you for believing in my dream. I am as you are.

Craig du Bruyn - the way you look at the world without fear inspired me to look at the world too, with fearless eyes. You awoke the spirit of the ancient adventurer in me and your friendship is invaluable in my life. Thank you buddy.

Mohini - gracias por abrir tu casa. Entre como un extraño y salí como un hijo. Gracias por tu sabiduría y tu amor. Tu influencia en este libro es invaluable.

Regis - mil gracias por compartir tu sabiduría y el amor que tienes por nuestra tradición Andina. Te respeto y admiro mucho.

Alicia Woolf – Thank you for pushing my boundaries and for your wonderful insight.

Mis padres, Vilma y Manolo - gracias por apoyarme en esta jornada tan linda de mi vida. Los amo.

My Indian Mamma, Gauriji Vachher, this first edition would not have happened without you. You are an inspiration and a source of unconditional Love. Thank you!

Sergio Bambaren - thank you for your wisdom and for teaching the world and me, to never stop believing.

To my friends - Silvia, Sunyougtha, Amisha, Lucho, Rachel, Jo-Anne, Nathalie, Christine Angel, and all those countless souls that have in some way or another supported this novel… Thank you.

For all of you who inspire me to seek the light, you know who you are.

I want to give the utmost respect to all the friends that have shown support via my website, blog, Twitter and Facebook pages. Your Love keeps me writing. Thank you for opening your hearts and allowing me to bare mine… without fear.

To those in the journey of the bleeding heart… only *Love can stop the bleeding.*

Author's Note

On a breezy summer's day, I went to visit a friend, an Inca shaman living in Africa to talk about my life and seek her guidance.

During our conversation, she had a startling revelation, an unexpected message, whatever you want to call it… *"I was going to write a book."*

"Who, me?" was my reaction, somewhat surprised.

'That's impossible.'

At the time, I had no ideas floating in my head. I'm a songwriter and I've learnt to tell stories through music in less than five minutes.

'Where would I get the story from?' I wondered.

'What would I write about? How would I fill two to three hundred pages?'

I had no plot, and more than this; I had no experience.

Besides, I have a busy music career that occupies me sixteen hours a day in studios, planes, and on the Internet. I simply did not have the time to dedicate myself to writing a book.

None whatsoever.

Then one balmy August night, while I slept peacefully, I heard a voice.

The voice said clearly, "Wake up and write."

I was far too comfortable between warm sheets so I ignored it.

"Go away," I replied. "Can't you see I'm sleeping? I have a life, you know."

However, the voice just wouldn't stop harassing me.

"There is an empty diary on your desk," it pointed out, "wake up and write. I'm not going away until you do."

This continued for about fifteen minutes.

Eventually, I had had enough. I rose with a massive yawn, dragged my feet to the light switch, collected the diary, and started to write.

I estimated the time to be around midnight.

All the pages of the first three months of my diary were empty – excluding a single page filled with a list of goals for the already-on-the-way year, and writing a novel was not one of them.

It all started then, at midnight.

I wrote the name of the novel first - I don't remember being conscious of the process – but I clearly remember thinking to let the stream take me away…

I was too tired to fight, so I let go.

Names, places, years, twists, and turns flowed out of my common, half-chewed pen onto those empty diary pages.

When I wrote, '*The End*', I heard birds singing outside my window. It was becoming light. I'd been writing for six hours solid.

Then my friend's voice returned….

'You're going to write a book.'

I shook my head, smiled and went back to bed.

This novel is about following your dreams and pursuing your destiny to the end.

Why did it come to me? Who am I to tell such a story?

I've always asked myself these questions… I'm no shaman. I'm no wise man. I don't have a PhD, nor have I written a dozen books. However, the one thing I've always done is to follow my inner voice, the voice of my heart.

Except, almost, for that one August night…

The One (as God is called in the book) speaks to all of us uniquely.

That fateful night, He spoke to me and I told Him to leave me alone; I was too tired. I wasn't prepared to listen.

I told Him *'I had a life.'*

Thank heavens, (excuse the pun), The One is persistent.

I needed a hurricane in my earlobe before I took notice. I have since learned my lesson… and a whisper now is more than sufficient.

I guess He had something to say and He chose me for a reason. I know that one day, I'll find out. Until then, I will feel blessed and grateful… for His choice of messenger.

We all have bleeding hearts.

We aren't born with them - we make them bleed as we grow older.

We make our hearts bleed with our ego, our arrogance, our fear, our hate, and all those negative feelings.

But there is a remedy for a bleeding heart and it's not material.

You can't buy it… and you can't get it from someone else. It is no secret, and it's free.

There's only one thing that can cure a bleeding heart.

That remedy is Love.

This is a story about Love.

Love is everywhere, not just in our hearts but also in our dreams, our thoughts, our choices, our actions, our words.

We can decide to have our hearts bleed forever, or choose the path where there's no more bleeding… *the path of Love.*

I hope that you follow your heart and all your wonderful dreams. They exist for a reason.

Do not be afraid, you're here on earth for a mission. If you listen to your heart, you are listening to God speak. Ask Him what your mission is.

Don't be like me that night… and just… listen.

Before I close, I'd like to say one more thing. Many people have asked me why I spell Love with a capital letter… I tell them that God is Love and I only spell God with a capital letter.

You can choose a life of fear or a life filled with Love. May you always choose the latter.

Believe in your dreams. Believe in you heart. Believe in your destiny. Ah, and by the way… always believe in Love. There's nothing greater than Love.

Yours sincerely,

Xavier Saer

1 The Bleeding Heart

At exactly *11.11* on a Sunday morning, a nurse with a hint of stubble on her chin, declared, "It's a boy, it's a boy!"

The monotonous bell of the children's hospital that announced the birth of all offspring did not ring this time. Instead, it was replaced by the clanks and thumps of the rusty emergency bell down the corridor.

The newborn was rushed to the new doctor, Santiago Salazar, of the well-known Salazar doctor clan, who was napping inside a vacant emergency room. The concerned nurses, with delicate finesse, immediately jolted the doctor awake. Between yawns, he took a lengthy examination of the baby, and realised that all the medical textbooks he had ever read, were of no use in this instance.

"This situation is certainly unique," the doctor pondered, scratching his balding head while looking at the child with interest but without alarm. The serene way he looked at things, especially when surrounded by onlookers, created a deep sense of trust despite his minor squint. But today, behind the arched Roman-like nose and the look of certainty in his oval face, was a man who had no idea what lay before his wandering eyes.

The baby's heart was exposed.

The heart was beating in a gap as wide as a dry mango pip, and as deep as the width of seven silver coins stacked one on top of the other.

Dupp lub… Dupp lub… The pulse of the organ beat with the steady rhythm of a pendulum belonging to a sturdy Spanish grandfather clock.

Dupp lub… Dupp lub…

The baby seemed to experience no pain as he slept in peaceful slumber, covered in a crisp, just-ironed cotton blanket.

His mother was suddenly resurrected from the trauma of an agonising childbirth. With a massive gasp and relentless determination, she tried to stand up, but a nurse, almost twice her size, held her down; the force of a ton of weight bearing on that of a feather.

"Sit down señora… please remain calm," said the bearded nurse with her hands, "your child is fine."

"I want to see him. I want to see my son. Bring me my son!" the mother insisted. The last time she had seen her child was seconds before she fainted.

"They'll return your son after the doctor takes a second look at his… unusual… condition," the nurse replied.

"Nothing to be alarmed of señora, he's in the capable hands of Doctor Salazar and is sleeping peacefully."

"Promise me he's alright, please…."

With a look that screamed of silence, the bearded nurse turned around, and left the room.

After some time, the bearded nurse entered the hushed delivery room to return the baby to his awaiting mother. The distance from the door to her arms felt like a torturous marathon. All she wanted was to see his wrinkled face, smell his unblemished skin, and kiss his little, fluff-filled head for a moment as long as forever.

When a crowd of curious nurses unexpectedly marched into the room, she knew that something was not quite right. Their prying eyes invited a stillness not even a pin-drop could shatter. She had first developed her intuition when she almost drowned by the pier in Puerto Azul, but was saved by a fisherman on a catch-filled boat. Since that fateful day, whenever her left eye twitched, she knew something ominous was about to arise.

"Here's your son señora," the bearded nurse whispered. She had folded the blanket seven times around the newborn to prevent his mother from discovering the pulsating, open heart… at least until she left the hospital.

As soon as the baby was in his mother's arms, the mother rapidly uncovered him from his warm, tortilla-like abode.

Slowly, the folds of the blanket began to unravel.

The sky outside featured the typical linen of clouds that hung above the grey but magnificent 'City of Kings'. In the distance, the fleeting fog allowed some of the sun's rays to soak up Miramar, the gloomy capital city. There was a scent of rain in the air. Through an upper bay-window, the dim light lit up the faces of the curious nurses. The effect made their anxious expressions a little more dramatic.

Alejandra Alegría unveiled the last fold of the cotton blanket… and there, carved into her son's chest, a diamond-shaped cavity appeared.

Silence.

Dead Silence.

A silent tear dropped from the mother's twitching eye into her son's open chest… she did not weep… she did not make a sound… she looked through the window into the half-clear Miramar sky, and saw the most beautiful rainbow the capital had seen in years. The multicoloured spectacle had a violet band that overshadowed the other colours, and produced within her an extraordinary sense of serenity. She interpreted this as a sign that her child had arrived on earth for a purpose, and that one day she would find out what this purpose was. As her single tear dried up, she prayed in the last traces of her silence. Her faith was her bastion, and her complete belief in the Divine gave her the strength needed to accept her son's unusual condition.

She took a deep breath and tucked in her newborn with the rapid but delicate movements that belonged solely to the expertise of an experienced mother.

Hurried, definite steps reverberated like thunder through the long corridor. The sound of leather boots broke the silence, one foot stomping the floor louder than the other.

"Alejandra, Alejandra," a burly and authoritative voice repeatedly called.

"I'm here Amor," she raised her quivering voice to make sure he had heard her, "in the delivery room."

Samuel Alegría stepped in like a raging bull in a deserted ring - his open shirt showing an abundance of moist hair in his dark, muscular chest. A silver dagger with an exquisite filigree-handle protruded from his leather belt. His commanding presence and masculine scent pushed some of the young nurses a few steps backward. He had walked briskly around the adjacent stone-courtyard throughout the entire duration of the childbirth. No longer able to wait (patience was not one of his virtues) and drenched in sweat, he decided to look for his wife. Samuel burst in, bearing the scent of imported Habanos, humidity and unspoken violence.

"It's a boy," pride danced along the pearls of her generous smile, "I gave you a boy."

Samuel looked at Alejandra with a gentleness that did not suit his sun-hardened face, and stood in the middle of the room, eyes wide open, like a salt statue.

On that unusual Sunday morning, holding his primogenital son in his arms, Samuel Alegría, a man with an opinion on everything, did not utter a single word. Moments like these can turn the world to silence.

Moments like this can make any man believe in God.

Seven scorching summers passed through the Hacienda Alegría, just under half a day's walk south from the city of Miramar. The vast sugar-cane plantation rose from the remnants of an ancient swamp, among lush palm-trees and groves of old and graceful willows. On the sun-blistered paths ran dozens of Paso Fino horses, a pedigree breed characterised by their elegant walk and proud stature.

The valleys that ran along the narrow, deserted coastline, received the rich waters of hundreds of rivers falling from the Andes Mountains.

There, the hacienda lay divided into six well-defined properties, cultivated by two shipments of human merchandise. Close to one thousand African slaves imported from Porto Bello, Panama and Cuba toiled alongside two-hundred-and-fifty Chinese labourers from Guangdong and Canton, day after day, under the merciless desert sun.

The handsome hacienda buildings were shaded beneath a tall Spanish arch in white, garlanded with violet flowers, featuring the hacienda's proud name in rusted iron. Shadows from the thorns of acacia trees speckled the stone steps that led to a leafy courtyard, where a distillery and an unpretentious church, erected by the Jesuits in the last century from salvaged pieces of adobe and dark Amazonian wood, were visible. The dwellings possessed aristocratic rooms with open spaces, where curtains shifted softly in the warm, desert wind.

"This all belongs to you," Samuel announced with pride, holding his son in his arms. They explored the hacienda's dusty pathways on his favourite Paso Fino horse, 'Caballero.'

"Look at the size of that black turkey buzzard, Father!" Paco shouted - his finger pointing to the large bird resting on one of the many rows of olive trees that surrounded the property. From an early age he portrayed a vivid imagination and an insatiable curiosity. Everything was a maiden voyage of discovery. That's how Paco's eyes saw the immensity of the world.

"Didn't you hear what I said?" Samuel's face crumpled as his bushy eyebrows met in a frown. "Your mind is always somewhere else… you are always singing or whistling and never paying enough attention to the duties you're going to acquire one day… this is your land! It all belongs to you!" Samuel's eyes hardened with intensity. "The olive trees, the soil, the cane fields, the slaves, even that damned bird… they're all yours," he pointed to his vast expanse of territory, "Can't you understand that, son?"

"Yes I understand, Father," Paco replied, shrugging his shoulders while holding Caballero's reins in his tiny hands. "But I Love music… and I want to sing… I want to write songs and hear the world sing them with me. That is my dream, dear Father."

Samuel pulled back the reins with tremendous force, "Whoa!"

The well-trained animal grunted and froze in the midday sun like a bronze Roman statue waiting for his master's next order. In one swift movement, Paco lay suspended in mid-air like a flour sack, held by his father's log-thick arm. Samuel was born and raised in a violent world, where there was no place for weakness. He never received mercy, and he was not going to give it.

His hand opened suddenly, dropping Paco despite his son's unexplained fear of heights. The mere notion of not having his feet touch the ground would cause Paco an attack of heart palpitations and a dizzying feeling of vertigo, turning his mouth into a dry, chalk-like cavern.

"Listen, you insolent child," Samuel's face distorted; his piercing, green eyes turned snake-like whenever he raged. He was a matchstick that would strike alight at the slightest provocation.

"Can you see where I am?"

Paco had no choice but to nod.

"This is where you belong… overlooking the land that bears your name," he hollered. Bits of dry, white saliva sprayed from the sides of his mouth and stuck to the tips of his sky-pointing, black moustache.

"Our family fought long and hard for you not to taint our surname with your pathetic dreams of music. You are harbouring the dreams of the lower classes - people who have nothing to look forward to and nothing to lose - you as my only child, were born to carry my legacy and the legacy of those who came before you. You will not, and I repeat, will not compromise hundreds of years of achievement for your stupid fantasy of being a singer… is that clear?"

The sun shone above Samuel's head, creating the illusion of a halo. Paco looked up at his father, half-blinded. He didn't understand why he was so unjust. He struggled to understand how someone he loved could be so cruel.

"Yes señor," Paco answered, crestfallen and defeated.

Samuel dismounted Caballero, tenderly seized Paco by the shoulders, and brought him close to his shaggy, moist chest.

"Let's play a game," Samuel said as if nothing had occurred. He had the ability to be a man-consuming beast one moment and a thorny rose the next.

Paco's face lit up. His child-like innocence would always forgive his father's rage in an instant. "What game dear Father?"

"I'm going to kneel behind you. You are then going to close your eyes, and at the count of three, you are going to fall into my arms."

"Don't worry son, I promise to hold you," Samuel assured Paco, "Are you ready?"

"Yes!" Paco replied enthusiastically, his eyes gleaming like two dancing fireflies in flight.

"Close your eyes and don't cheat… now count to three and fall into my arms," Samuel ordered.

Paco closed his eyes, tucked his arms firm at his side, and fell into the steel arms of his father.

"This is fun Father… let's do it again!"

"Twice more and then it's time to go home. Deal?" Samuel added.

"You have a deal."

Paco fell into Samuel's arms again. He was beaming with happiness. On his last attempt, there was nothing to hold him. He fell, head first, onto the oven-hot ground. He lay flat, barely conscious; with the sun boring into his eyes. His father's massive body towered over him and extinguished the painful glare.

"Don't trust anybody… everyone is out to hurt you," he pointed his index finger at his son and shook it viciously as if it was a wooden baton. He would not be weak, and he would not allow his son to be weak. A spoilt child would not survive in a cruel world. And out there the world had no mercy.

"Your pathetic dreams will lead you to the misery and dust of the earth. A man is born to work and provide for his family. A man must sow and a man must reap. A man does not live on dreams alone, nor is his cup filled by pursuing his weaker emotions. You will become what I want you to be. You have no other choice, is that clear?" Samuel mounted Caballero with the dexterity of a man half his age.

"Get up, dust yourself, and find your way home. You'd better be home before sunset. I will not look for you." Samuel tucked his spurs deep into the horse's belly and in a cloud of dust, disappeared in the midst and expanse of the tall sugar-cane fields.

A viscous trail of blood poured from Paco's heart, drawing as a map, rivers of wasted life on his skin. Paco's tears mixed with the floating dust from the galloping horse, forming mud rivulets that travelled down from his cheeks into his mouth.

In his eyes, Samuel had acted unjustly, and Paco hated nothing more than injustice, and so his heart bled…

Paco would bleed every time his heart was in pain. Through the years, a thin, scar flap formed over his heart, hardly protecting it from the outside world. It seemed a mere decoration, compared to the pressure of the blood mounting inside that would rupture it with no visible effort. Paco was used to this, and patiently waited for the blood to coagulate before wiping it clean. He was born with this gift, but he did not see it this way. His heart was open to the world and filled with unfathomable amounts of Love, but he felt that this was a weakness. Samuel's harshness had taught him that the world was cruel and that no one, not even his father, could be trusted.

If he knew, that one can only dream with an open heart. If he knew, that one can only Love with an open heart. If he only knew this and that, an open heart like his… could change the world.

2   The Dream and The Shadow

Hacienda Alegría was renowned throughout Miramar as a sugar-cane plantation of distinction. The constant battle between the fierce heat of the summer sun and the fall in temperature during the misty winters, allowed for a highly concentrated produce. For generations this brought the Alegría family a sizeable fortune. In a refinery propelled by steam and filled with English machinery adjacent to the dwelling house, Samuel produced *Aguardiente* - a strong and intoxicating beverage obtained by fermenting and later distilling the sugar-cane's sap; known for its high alcohol content.

Samuel was obsessed with being the best Aguardiente producer in the capital, which drove him to spend endless nights inside the cramped refinery, immersed in clouds of toxic vapour and untidy mounds of old chemistry books. Obsessively perfectionist and compulsive, he developed a weakness for his own product, often returning home raging like a bloodthirsty beast, ready to release his frustration on his ever-fearful family.

Paco heard the uneven steps of his drunken father echoing from the kitchen. The sound of his leather boots was unmistakeable: a frightening cadence that tasted of rage and tears and crescendoed as it conquered the stairs and barrelled into Paco's no-longer-unbreachable fortress.

All Paco could do was crumble; smothering himself under the flimsy, white-cotton blanket that separated him from the vast darkness, and restrain his breathing. If Samuel entered the room, he'd appear to be sleeping. Although this had worked in the past, his drunken father's reactions were almost impossible to predict.

But on this occasion, Samuel remembered his son's dreams. Tonight, Paco would pay the price for not wanting to follow in his footsteps. Tonight, it did not matter that Paco was only seven years old - Samuel thought he needed to knock some sense into that insolent child for not living up to the Alegría surname.

Paco's door screeched open.

Samuel pushed it aside slowly. It was his preamble. He was going to teach his son a lesson. He was in control. He was the father. He was the bigger of the two. He stumbled forward and stepped closer to Paco's bed; his one foot always louder than the other. His breath reeked of alcohol and the stench of violence.

Paco's heart thumped faster and faster.

"Wake up you piece of rubbish… I know you're awake… I can hear you breathing," Samuel mumbled. His drunken voice sounded throttled; as though he were laughing with a fishbone caught in his throat.

Paco did not make a sound.

He lay still, with a bleeding heart - his eyes shut tight in a *violet* world - waiting for the first blow. Ever since he could remember, whenever he closed his eyes… he saw *violet*.

"Didn't you hear what I said?" Samuel shouted, his arms thrashing wildly in the darkness. He swung his fists at an imaginary ghost. He preferred to live on the attack.

"What do you think you are? Invisible? Do you think I can't hear you? Do you think I'm too blind to see where you're hiding?"

Paco's legs started to tremble; his nerves and bladder could no longer hold in the inevitable.

"I'm going to bend you straight once and for all," Samuel warned, "Music is no longer welcome in *my* home. There will be no more singing, whistling, or feet tapping. Do you hear me?" He continued to punch the invisible enemy that haunted his thoughts, panting like a predator on the hunt.

"You belong to me and you shall be what I want you to be. Your dreams belong to me. I brought you into this world - I raised you! You owe me your life and you will do as I tell you. Is that clear? Now come out of there and face me - you little coward. Face me like a man."

Paco's bed sheet had turned bright red.

He wished he could run but his legs were trembling uncontrollably.

Besides, there was nowhere to go.

A child with a dream-filled heart lay poorly protected by a thin cotton sheet. Inches away and stumbling, drunk in the dark - was a man he loved; set to destroy them early.

Paco closed his eyes and prayed. It was the only thing left to do. He held the bed sheet with all his might. His little fingers gripped it with every ounce of strength he could muster.

'It's too late now,' he thought.

He felt that no one would hear his prayers.

His raging father was already in the bedroom and he believed no prayer could save him. Still, with eyes closed, he directed his voice to heaven. His heart clamoured with faith.

Samuel wrenched off the stained cotton sheet.

Paco found himself in mid-air, facing the wooden floor.

Samuel blinked a number of times, adjusting to the sea of darkness, trying to see his child.

"I'm going to teach you a lesson," he shouted, foaming from the mouth. If he was not Paco's father, then one could swear from the look in his eyes, he was a killer.

Paco closed his eyes tight in anticipation, crossing his arms around his heart; waiting for his father to strike. The flimsy tips of his fingers gripped his shoulders for dear life, clutching every available bone and sinew, protecting the fragile gap above his heart in an act of primitive survival.

Just then, Alejandra jumped in front of Samuel.

"Please Samuel, I beg you! Don't hurt him, he's just a child!" she cried.

"Get out of my way woman, or you're going to get a beating too," Samuel shouted, his breath infused with the pungent smell of Aguardiente and a couple of half-chewed Habanos.

"Please, please, I beg you Samuel. Hit me; just stop hitting your child. He's done nothing wrong."

"I'm going to get those stupid dreams out of his head once and for all," he replied, his green, snake-like eyes contracting and expanding in frenzy.

Paco lay on the floor, his fragile arms still crossed atop his heart. Praying inside a *violet universe*.

"Enough Samuel!"

Alejandra held her drunken husband as tight as she could.

"Enough please! He's scared to death. You know what happens to his heart," she begged.

"I've had enough of his bleeding heart. I'm sick of it. This world is cruel and hard. Yet he chooses to bleed and show the world his weakness," he shouted at Paco, his index finger protruding from his fist again.

"Do you hear me boy? Only the strong survive, so you'd better mend that heart of yours once and for all. Make it hard… Scorch it… Scar it… I don't really care… Fix it or you won't survive!" Samuel screamed – bits of saliva, like killer bullets, spluttering everywhere.

With this, he walked away, leaving Alejandra in tears and a praying seven-year-old child drenched in sweat and the anguish of a bleeding heart.

"I'm so sorry Paco." She held her son against her beating chest. Paco remained unmoved; congealed in his own blood.

He learned that it was easier to shut out the world and fall asleep in a puddle of caking blood. A universe filled with violet welcomed his tired heart. In there, he was free.

Even with Alejandra holding him close, he still felt that she was powerless to protect him.

"I'm so sorry Paco, I'm so sorry," she kept repeating, caressing his wavy, black hair with her soft, slender fingers as if trying to make his pain disappear with each loving but futile stroke.

With his arms still frozen around his heart, Paco fell asleep in his mother's embrace.

The city seemed to be frozen in time, as if a heavenly painter had spellbound every denizen to be still for a minute until he could deliver his last masterful stroke, or until the copper bells of the ancient cathedral turned silent after their long, reverberating serenade. Many kneeled and looked up at a silvery sky that was brushed with smidgeons of blue and gold. Others stood motionless, not moving an inch from where they had frozen when the bells first started ringing; some dressed in their best attires, and the majority covered in their day-to-day rags and circumstance. The *Plaza Mayor*, Miramar's main square, was bursting with young, old, women, men, children, free and enslaved. They were all singing one of Paco's songs, the melody strangely new to him, yet it sounded so familiar and sweet to the ear.

In Miramar, to witness so many different people united in song was, at that time, simply unknown: a runaway dream. The capital was still deeply divided into racial lines, colours, and creeds. There were whites, white creoles, creoles, mestizos, Negros, Indians, Chinese, and any combination of the above. Then there were the Catholics, who were the vast majority, and factions of Protestants, Jews, Voodooists, Buddhists, Spiritists, Muslims as well as those who did not have the time or patience to believe. However, on that unusually half-clear day, with the sky alive and brimming with a carpet of serenading doves and restless seagulls that hovered in silence above the Plaza Mayor, a song united a country; and he was responsible for it.

To celebrate the occasion, the sky had gifted the ever-grey city with a magnificent, violet-coloured rainbow, and a *bright, coral moon* that looked like a polished, silver coin in a wish-filled fountain. But Paco could not move. His hands were tied. He wanted to raise them up to the heavens, because his grateful heart was floating among the scattered clouds, but his wrists were yoked. His heart was in heaven, but his body was earthbound.

Paco woke up with a gasp, holding tight onto his bed sheet. It took him a moment to realise it was all a dream. Everything felt so vivid and real that he found himself mumbling the melody of the song as he tapped his feet to the rhythm. He knew he had to be quiet, and so placed his fluffy pillow over his mouth to make sure his snoring father, in the adjacent room, could not hear him.

Lately the days had been scorching hot and the nights, unusually balmy and warm. He got up from his hand-carved bed, making sure his feet touched the old and splintered-wooden floor without a sound, hoisted his little body up with a jolt and opened the bedroom's single bay window.

Paco unbuttoned the first two pins of his snow-white nightgown, hoping that the magic of the fresh breeze would cool him down.

It felt as if the loving sea was blowing salty mist onto his face, specially, just for him. He took a deep breath from the silent night and filled his little lungs with the sweet smell of the thundering waves crashing onto the rocky shoreline. The atmosphere was infused with the scent of orchards, sugar and seaweed.

Just as he was about to close the window… he saw something. It looked like a shadow – that swiftly disappeared into the darkness.

For a second his heart stopped beating. The miniature hairs on his arms stood up and stirred in the breeze.

'What do I do now?' he wondered.

His first reaction was to wake his father; but an inner voice whispered to him to be silent.

He swiftly slipped into his favourite brown, leather sandals. Snatching the old, wooden latch tight in his little hands, he stole a deep breath. Then he jumped out into the garden, landing close to a row of red roses, and into the stillness of the dead-quiet night.

The bright moon illuminated the surroundings in a bluish light. The leafy trees of the orchards and tall cane-fields swayed back and forth with the whispers of the relentless Pacific Sea breeze.

Paco carefully traced the shadow's path. He felt secure in the hacienda, even amidst the barrage of misleading stories Samuel had created around the African slaves. Whenever his father was away, he made friends easily, and his loving nature gained the respect of many of the household workers who endearingly called him '*Paquito*'. During these times of paternal absence, he befriended two slave boys, and the three spent countless hours playing together.

But Paco was alone now.

Samuel made sure that even when the abolition of slavery was the talk among liberals in the nearby capital, the way his hacienda had operated for years would remain intact. Harm to a family member, even by accident, could mean lynching - and in serious cases, death to the slave.

Not so long ago, Samuel had personally executed five slaves. The slaves had murdered a Chinese cook and hidden his body in an oven after he attacked them with a rusty knife.

Samuel was the law.

Paco took one step after another, tiptoeing like a hunting midnight cat.

The scent of seaweed and molasses invaded the air with palpable sweetness. Ghost-like scarecrows, taller than the cane reeds, waved in a phantasmagorical dance, swaying in the unrelenting wind.

As Paco neared the African slave quarters, he grew more silent with each cautious step.

The African slave quarters were a conglomeration of plastered-mud and cane-reed huts about ten feet tall. They surrounded a small adobe church on an earth-laden square, encircled by a high wall. The closest huts to the hacienda-dwellings were fringed with rows of acacias, alligator pears, and a garden filled with maize, lucerne, pumpkins, and a few other vegetables used to supplement the bleak diet of the slaves. A few pigs and goats lived in peace alongside each other in a semi-circular, reed corral, enveloped by a rich profusion of granadilla vines.

Paco reached a hut next to a blossoming cherimoya tree. It looked slightly larger than the other surrounding huts. There was muttering from within, in low whispers, along with harrowing sighs and mumbles. The remains of a vanishing candle through the speckled window made a visible tunnel of light that flickered like a dancing entity on the mud floor. It was unusual to hear anyone up at this time of night, as life in the hacienda began way before dawn.

With his back to the half-dilapidated wall, Paco made the final three, hushed steps to the window.

Being too short to peek inside, he carefully placed two wooden boxes, which were lying close to the entrance, on top of each other.

Inside, sick and convalescing slaves filled the hut. There was hardly any space to move. Seated in a wood-and-cane rocking chair in the centre was a strange-looking woman singing in a language Paco could not understand. A sulky, symphonic, Oriental sound sparkled like the explosion of a fugitive star in his ears; and in that second, he was hooked.

Her eyes were wise and deep and her Chinese silk-robe, or *Hanfu*, glittered like a sea of miniscule diamonds, shimmering in the glow of the single, dancing candle. Close to her tiny feet lay a cabinet with dozens of pint-sized drawers and secret compartments. The top chest housed a variety of herbs, dry roots, and crushed powders. The cabinet was arranged in symmetrical squares, covered in a resin-like, worn, glass top.

From her modest, swinging throne, she bestowed in orderly turns, various amounts of crushed powders into the mouths of the sick and frail. She sang as she worked and her melodic, whispery tone enthralled Paco into an almost trance-like state.

In the midst of careful whispers, Paco heard a voice he recognised.

On the far right, furthest from the light, he saw a familiar shadow.

With his little nose pressed hard against the window, he witnessed his mother wiping the forehead of a slave possessed of fever. Alejandra stared up at the roof, as if she was having a private conversation with an angel or a visiting saint. She dipped a warm, fever-soaked handkerchief into a bowl of cool water and squeezed the life-saving liquid onto the young man's face and neck, time and time again. In the semi-darkness of the room, Alejandra resembled the Virgin Mary asking God to spare the life of a slave, who rested in her lap like a moribund Jesus.

A perfect mother. That is what Alejandra was; no less than a perfect mother. If someone felt sick, she was the first to arrive with a casserole. And her famous, tantalising casseroles weren't just the perfect remedy for an injured body; her Love-infused recipes would revive the sick, as well as heal even the most tattered heart. Love was an ingredient as important as coarse sea salt and a little cumin in her secret dishes, apart from the way one stirs a casserole, a technique she inherited from her grandmother Ruth (paternal side), who lived to be just over a hundred and could still wax the whole of her lengthy kitchen floor on her knees – while eating an oversized watermelon at the same time. Her expertise and passion for food were not short of legendary. Acquaintances and even strangers would drop in at the hacienda unexpectedly, just to taste her wonderful dishes; then get on their horses, bid farewell and make a U-turn back to the capital. A more gracious host one could not find; even strangers were welcomed as friends.

Petite, well-cared for and wrapped in long, charcoal-black hair exquisitely arranged in a ponytail, she easily looked fifteen years younger. She was the talk of the town in her adolescence, receiving hundreds of written marriage proposals. She single-handedly sustained a small flower shop close to her home during the time when ludicrous quantities of roses would constantly be placed just outside her parent's front door. That is, until one unforgettable starry night, when a foreigner from Miramar with sparkling, green eyes and the bravado of a navy commander, swept her off her feet with a single whisper of, *"Would you like to dance with me?"*

Her faith was her fortress. Alejandra spent hours kneeling at her hand-carved, wooden altar, filled with bee-wax, melting candles and the mandatory figure of the Virgin Mary dressed in a white tunic and a bleeding heart. With her eyes directed to heaven and almost in a state of transfixion, she would plead with God for protection over her family and home with the faith of a veteran nun. "Miracles happen to those who believe in miracles," she often repeated. When she was not delving in spiritual and religious matters (she believed there was no distinction between the two), she was most likely to be found engaged within her pride and joy: an elegant, *'par excellence'*, black-and-white-diamond-shaped-tiled kitchen, which Samuel had especially imported from Paris as a wedding gift.

An exquisite arrangement of fragrant flowers infused her home with a sense of tranquillity, sensuality, and quiet devotion. Returning from a tough day working the immensity of the hacienda, Alejandra made her husband feel as if he had just stepped into their first day of honeymoon. The food-laden table, a vase of fresh flowers, and the servants ready to appease their master's voracious appetite, evidenced her own unbridled dedication and attention to detail. Following her mother's tradition, before she stepped onto the altar on her wedding day, she had already adopted a subservient role in the relationship. Samuel possessed a spark that would ignite in a second; while she played the role of diplomat and diffuser with Elizabethan elegance and panache. Paco however, was too young to understand all this, and only wished she could have protected him more from his father's frequent rages.

With his eyes transfixed on the clandestine hospital, Paco failed to see the monstrous cane rat at his feet. When the hungry animal approached a few rotten maize kernels close to where he stood, Paco panicked - and lost his balance. He fell, shattering the boxes, lost his right sandal and raised a cloud of dust about three-feet high. The clatter created an immediate sense of panic inside the hut.

On instinct, Alejandra extinguished the candle and asked everyone to be silent. The snake-like movement of the dying smoke twirled about in a room filled with nothing but shivering and the rattling of teeth. In a space cluttered with fragments of life, there was no other sound. The darkness that engulfed them was staggering and unbroken.

She was afraid that someone might have found the place where she had spent many nights away from her snoring, drunken husband. When Samuel slept, especially after a night in the distillery, not even an earthquake could wake him. Perhaps tonight, her audacious luck had run out and one of her husband's lynch-men had finally discovered their secret hospital.

Realising his blunder, Paco stood up in a second and stretched his springy legs in a savage run back to his bedroom.

Under the bluish glow of the coral-like moon, anyone might have spotted a small boy, in a white gown, waving his arms like an escaped hummingbird, running as fast as he could towards the sleeping hacienda.

But nothing moved.

Nothing made a sound, and no one saw a thing.

"I saw you last night by the slave quarters Mommy," Paco whispered to Alejandra. He gazed down, looking a tad guilty.

Alejandra looked around her kitchen. She listened for any trace of Samuel outside and realised that they were alone.

"Keep your voice down, my son… your father might arrive at any minute. Let's go to your room so we can talk privately." She took Paco firmly by the hand.

"You're not going to punish me, are you?" Paco whispered, still staring at the floor. He made no effort to retreat.

"No, mi Amor," she responded, "We just need to talk without anyone listening to our conversation… some things are not for everyone's ears."

They left the kitchen and entered Paco's bedroom. It was bathed in warm sunlight that filtered through white curtains. Alejandra was still alert, in case of unwelcome company.

"My son, what exactly did you see last night?" Alejandra kneeled beside Paco, who was now seated on top of his white, hand-carved bed.

"I had a beautiful dream - it felt so real - like I was there. When I woke up,

I couldn't sleep again because my room was hot. I opened the window to get some air… and I saw a shadow running by the orchards. I got scared… but a kind voice told me not to be scared and to follow the shadow."

"You did very well in listening to that voice my child. Now, what else happened?"

Paco gradually lifted his gaze. For the first time, he looked straight into his mother's charcoal-black eyes. They felt like a secure home where all his secrets could be unlocked. He took light, staccato breaths of soothing air.

"I walked to the African quarters following the sweet smell of the shadow. I saw a dim light and peeped through the hut's window… Inside, a strange woman sang the most beautiful song I have ever heard, ever… and then I saw you, curing the sick slaves," Paco explained, still looking deep into his mother's welcoming eyes. "A big, scary rat tried to bite me… and I lost my balance… and my head hit the floor. I was so scared. I didn't want to be eaten alive! I got up in a flash and ran, Mommy. The hungry rat was chasing me like I was dinner."

Her lips revealed a minuscule smile. She pulled his fragile body next to hers and held him as if he'd just been born. Paco felt cocooned in a nest of pure affection. His legs went soft, like gelatine. Only she had the power to melt his fears.

"Listen my son, and listen carefully," Alejandra held Paco firm with intentional softness. "You need to make me a promise… and promises can never be broken - you know that, don't you?"

Paco nodded to show that he understood.

"You need to promise me that you won't utter a single word about what you saw last night, especially to your father. You saw the state of those people… they were sick, abandoned, and uncared for. They came from a faraway land called Africa - against their will – chained by their hands and feet like cattle. They were once free men and women, just like you and I, and every day they're treated like animals by our people," Alejandra's voice almost broke, barring a flood of emotion.

"Close your eyes and pretend for a minute that you're one of them…" she paused, "Do you like how it feels? Imagine if you were not free… imagine if you lived in chains… could you tolerate that injustice day after day? Would you like to walk in their shoes?"

Paco shook his head.

She looked at her son and felt his soul inside her. Their hearts were forged from the same source - the one element forged out of light, which resides within all human beings: Love.

"I know you didn't like what you saw Paco… I know your heart doesn't tolerate injustice… but we cannot go against your father. He's not going to change for anyone. He is the way he is and he loves the way he does. He is merely doing what he thinks is right. He loves us; he just doesn't know how to show it. Both your grandparents and his grandparents brought him up like that – it's how he sees the world."

Paco understood and promised his mom that he would keep quiet, especially around his father.

"If your father finds out, he will personally lynch those men and women Paco. Your silence is of extreme importance."

"Yes Mommy."

"I believe you'll keep your promise my son." The two connected without words.

With extreme tenderness she said, "I am proud of you." She stood up and turned towards the door.

"I need to ask you something Mommy," Paco added in haste. "Anything you want my child," she turned towards her son, "What is it?"

"It's about the strange lady, the one with the herbs and powders and the funny dress," he said.

"Yeees?" she responded, curious. She instinctively knew her son had something in mind.

"Well… Father has banned me from singing and I've been sad Mommy.

I'm not happy if I'm not singing… so… I wanted… to ask you…" Paco's voice began and faltered. The warmth and raw innocence of his tone could melt the coldest of hearts.

"I… want to know… if… I… can… meet… that lady?" Alejandra looked at her son. He had inherited his father's bravado, and she knew Paco wasn't finished. "I want to learn how to sing," he declared with confidence and resolution beyond his years.

They both stared at each other for the better part of a minute, wrapped in infinite stillness, hardly blinking.

Alejandra's first instinct was a firm *no*. Then she reconsidered. If Paco could keep her secret, she knew that she could keep his.

Often a simple decision can change someone's life forever.

She decided to trust her son.

"I will speak to her tomorrow night… but I have no guarantees she'll say yes."

"Please Mommy, please convince her, please, please, please," Paco begged.

"Listen carefully mi Amor… whatever the outcome, keep following your heart, and don't ever let anything or anyone stop you from doing what makes you happy. You are here to do great things. I knew it the day you were born… The One gave me a sign," she said this, with a lump in her throat, "Now go and study before your father arrives… and don't forget our promise."

"Yes Mommy," Paco said in total bliss. He left whistling towards the lounge.

"Paco," Alejandra called him back immediately.

"Yes Mommy?" He answered with a radiant smile.

"Shhh! You are whistling! You know who might be around." Paco immediately covered his mouth with his tiny hands. Alejandra placed her right index finger softly across her lips and smiled.

Several days later, while Samuel was attending a reunion near Miramar, Alejandra presented Paco with the news.

"She said yes," Alejandra announced with a beautiful smile on her face. Her rosy cheeks looked like the velvet petals of an Amazonian orchid. Every time she made her son happy, it filled her heart with endless pages of secret memories. It seemed then, as though life was singing; the atmosphere had turned into a haven, satiated with promise.

Paco did not answer. Instead, he ran towards her and embraced her warm body. He could stay there forever. Nothing in the world felt as safe and protected.

"There's one rule only," she added with natural finesse.

Paco waited for the sole condition of their agreement, "Yes Mommy?"

"You will go to classes whenever your father is out of the hacienda and no other time, is that clear Paco?" She was firm. "If your father finds out she's teaching you music, he will kill her with his bare hands. Her life is in your hands and she's assumed that risk," Alejandra said, seeing in her mind's eye the dire consequences that could arise from a single mistake: if Samuel were to discover the secret lessons, he would hang the perpetrator in a public show of personal disloyalty to himself and his kingdom.

"Yes Mommy, I understand. I will be extra, extra, extra careful." Paco closed his eyes, crinkled his face as if he was underwater and swore to keep his promise with every breath in his body. "I promise, I promise…"

"By the way, she asked me to tell you that she knew you were coming," she said perplexed. "She also mentioned that she felt you at the window that night."

Paco rubbed his chin with vigour, squeezing the dancing folds of skin beneath his lower lip with both his right thumb and index finger. It was an Alegría trait used in moments of deep concentration or universal contemplation.

"She also said that *you had to arrive before she goes home…* I'm not sure what she meant and she didn't bother to clarify, so I left it at that."

Paco, deep in thought, tilted his head to the side, almost owl-like. His lower lip protruded by an inch, and the chunks of skin around his frown deepened like colliding canyons. He resembled a little Napoleon.

"Your father is back in Miramar the day after tomorrow," Alejandra said. "You shall start an hour after he leaves in the morning."

Little Napoleon's frown vanished just as fast as it had appeared.

3 ⬥ Doña Lucia

Lhamo Jia was born in the year of the dragon. She took her first gasp of thin mountain air on a snowy, bitterly cold night inside an impoverished hut, built around a yak paddock. Outside, cloud-kissing valleys raced towards the top of the world, almost touching the star-blown, black sky, and fairytales of bodhisattvas flew from ear to ear, weaving magical stories in the hearts of the people of this faraway land called Tibet.

Tibet was a land lost in time, a forgotten Xanadu. And its inhabitants preferred it that way. They lived from the land and were content with what the land provided. They lived with simplicity. All they wanted, they had; from a quiet prayer to the millions of footsteps left on the muddy paths across the hills by the pilgrims. In Tibet, life sung a daily song of peace and modesty.

Lhamo's parents were devout followers of a spiritual teacher called *Buddha*, a prince who sat under a bodhi tree, a sacred fig tree with heart-shaped leaves, and did not stir until he had found enlightenment.

The day she turned seven, they snipped off her curly brown hair, shaved her head until her scalp gleamed in the sun, and led her by the hand to the gates of a secluded, mud, red monastery, two week's walk from their mountain abode. They explained, as best as they could, that she was a holy offering to the *'Enlightened One'*, and led her in.

Then they left.

She spent the next twenty-four years within the confines of the holy monastery. In that time she grew up as the sole nun amongst roughly one-hundred-and-fifty-five male monks. She received no special treatment.

Lhamo dedicated her adolescence to learning the wise teachings of the Buddha. She studied his philosophy with zestful devotion, often falling asleep with a voluminous sacred scroll as her pillow. If cleaning and scrubbing the man-sized, iron pots used to cook the three meals per day drove her closer to *enlightenment*, she was the first in line to volunteer for the dirty and monotonous task.

During her stay at the secret monastery, Lhamo learned many disciplines from the ancient Buddhist monks, whom she called '*The Elders*'. These included singing, cooking, and the knowledge of curative herbs, plants, and roots. She also learnt the art of predicting the healthy or ill condition of any person by sensing their wrist pulse and smelling their urine - an essential facet of Tibetan medicine.

Nevertheless, her favourite discipline was singing.

Lhamo would roam the green, sky-scraping hills in the dense mist of the morning, singing the highest praises to her beloved teacher. There was a rumour that a watch of nightingales would not move from the branch of a cypress tree, until she stopped singing her melodies. Only then, would they take flight and search for food.

"Why do you sing so much?" the youngest monk in the monastery asked Lhamo. He had been observing her in secret behind an old, twisted tree.

She smiled as if The Buddha had personally asked her the question. She saw the divinity in all beings, "I sing because my soul wants to sing. If I had to deny my soul the privilege of singing, I'd be caging my spirit! Birds are born to fly. I was born to sing."

The little monk gave Lhamo a bright smile. His shaven head wrinkled in a show of appreciation.

On her thirty-third birthday, during the year of the ox, a year that symbolises perseverance, sustained effort and hard work, The Elders opened the rusty gates of the monastery. They placed their hands on Lhamo's shaven head, gave her an extra pair of sandals, and asked her to venture into a sleeping world.

Lhamo was to awaken human beings with Love and compassion. She criss-crossed the treacherous footpaths of the Himalayas, facing fierce wind storms and cataclysmic winters. After arduous months and thousands of steady steps, she reached a land of fertile valleys and living myths called China. During this soul-forging feat of endurance, she explored the soil at the top of the world, as though her eyes were a magnifying glass. She became familiar with it, collecting hundreds of varieties of medicinal herbs and roots and soon learned to identify each bit by sight, smell, touch, and taste.

Wearing her modest smile, she discovered the secrets of rural China, witnessing magnificent sunsets that painted the sky in swirls of pastels, blues and oranges. She visited every countryside village on her path. The incredible journey took her close to twenty years, and dozens of sandals. During her intrepid voyage, she served the sick and destitute, meditated in magical forests - among legends of fairies and dragons, and shed layers of karma and past consequence. Dressed in a fading, ochre-and-fuchsia robe, she travelled with minimum possessions: a palm-sized eating pot, a set of sturdy, metal chopsticks, and her most precious gift – a petite medicine cabinet made of Tibetan cypress that housed her collection of secret roots, healing herbs, and miraculous, crushed powders.

In 1849, Lhamo arrived at the Portuguese coastal colony of Macau, a boisterous port brimming with desperate Chinese migrants looking for work of any kind, no matter how hard or dirty. In the decrepit harbour, close to the waterline, callous racketeers promised them a better life working as contract labourers in the sugar-cane fields of a distant land across the Pacific. Thousands fared the four-month, hazardous ocean trip in despicable conditions – man against man, clutched like newly captured, wild animals, rocking to and fro in the filth of human waste - for the opportunity to send some money to their families back home.

Aside from some ladies of disrepute, Lhamo was the only woman on board. She inspired in everyone who met her, a perplexing and immediate sense of respect.

Her ability to cure the labourers during the ocean-crossing convinced the previously sceptical captain to allow her onto his ship. During the trip, she cured many sick men, and the lonely and desperate voyagers revered her as a woman of higher powers.

In the first few days after leaving port, she encountered a Jesuit priest by the name of Padre Marco dos Santos, who took the sea-faring journey as a means of introducing the men to the teachings of *Jesus*. At first they spoke only with their hands, but on arrival, they conversed adequately - he in Mandarin, and she in Portuguese that closely resembled Spanish (the language spoken at the ship's final destination).

Padre dos Santos taught Lhamo how to play the guitar during the many uneventful days at sea. She returned the favour by teaching the medically-inexperienced priest important aspects of Tibetan medicine, such as disease diagnosis that extended over a thousand years. She also taught him how to use his body as a medical instrument for the purposes of healing and compassion.

One Monday morning, in the middle of the first month of the year 1850, the glimpse of a deserted coastline covered in fog appeared in the distance. The captain rang the previously unemployed ship's horn three times – his recognisable shape, topped by a mariner's cap, floated in the misty weather. Crew and passengers prepared to land after a dizzying, four-month, sea-conquering journey.

The ship docked with a bang as it smacked against a wooden beam protruding from the lop-sided port, rocking the passengers one last time. As soon as all the immigrants had touched solid ground, their heads were shaved against lice. Lhamo insisted that her head was also shaved in solidarity with her sea-faring companions. With the dash of a single slash of scissors, her two long-plaited ponytails fell to the floor.

During the fierce buying negotiations that followed the labourer's arrival, a man by the name of Samuel Alegría, a wealthy and ruthless sugar-cane landowner, contracted most of the ship's human cargo. His well-known bribery of the local authorities brought him fame, fortune, and an oriental army of cheap labour.

Lhamo and two-hundred-and-fifty decrepit labourers dragged their weary bodies through the half-day walk from the capital to the hacienda. They settled in small, blistering-hot adobe huts, similar to those in the larger, adjacent African quarters.

The next morning, on a scorching summer's day, the labourers started to work the cane-fields under the vigilant eye of Samuel Alegría, and his cold-blooded men on Paso Fino horses.

At night, after a cruel day's toil, they gathered in circles around scattered fires to discuss their lives in the inhospitable hacienda.

Buckets of sorrow fell during the first years, and many men aged rapidly as they reminisced of the wives, children, and lovers left behind. They existed, but they were not living. They were barely alive.

In the midst of their laments was Lhamo Jia, brimming with compassion and understanding.

She learnt every person's name, and the men shared their daily triumphs and trials with the saintly monk. In gratitude, a white hut was erected where she could live on her own, as opposed to the rest of the labourers who slept in conditions similar to those inside the ship.

During that time, she waited patiently for the day when the one with the bleeding heart would appear. Unable to pronounce her Tibetan name, he would call her *Doña Lucia*. Under her wings, he would learn many of the lessons needed to fulfil his destiny, and once he grew in awareness and was ready to leave her side, she would finally be free to go home.

4 The Secret Music Lovers

Exactly an hour after the last trace of Caballero's shadow disappeared on the hacienda's horizon towards Miramar, Alejandra led Paco to the farthest adobe hut in the Chinese quarters. The sweet scent of fragrant herbs and just-harvested vegetables swept the air with fresh-farmed delight.

Paco's head moved from side to side, up and down… he couldn't stop staring; it was his first time in the bizarre outlying quarters. He stared at everything, mouth agape, holding his mother's index finger as they walked. He was unaware that such a strange and unimaginable world could exist just footsteps away from his sheltered home. The gap between the lavish hacienda and the crammed oriental quarters did not make him feel comfortable. His sense of justice was developed beyond his years.

Amidst innumerable, mud, brown huts of roughly the same size, there was a single, white hut. It was a washed-out shell amidst a sea of sunburnt adobe and it stood out; also being slightly smaller.

Inside this shack, seated in the same wood-and-cane rocking-chair he had seen back at the slave quarters, was the mysterious woman in the foreign, silk dress.

Paco automatically looked up at his mom.

Alejandra nodded in approval.

Lhamo signalled for Paco to enter with a single, soft wave of her hand. A simple gesture signalled the end and the beginning of an era in both their lives.

Her flowing movements seemed pre-planned somehow, and her motions, coordinated to perfection. Often, after sunset, as the fires blazed, she seemed to walk as though she was not subject to gravity.

"Paco," Alejandra said, "let me introduce you to *Lhamo Jia.*"

There was a look of confusion on Paco's face.

He'd never heard such a strange name before. He was used to names like Maria, Maria Dolores, Maria Julia, Julia Maria, Maria Ana, Ana Maria, and other such names that included the name Maria. Of course, one of his mother's many names was also Maria.

"But you can call her *Doña Lucia*," Alejandra explained, as a gentle smile swept her face.

"It's nice to meet you Paco," Doña Lucia said in a foreign accent.

Paco kept silent.

The wise, slanted eyes above her high, round cheeks and near-perfect skin fascinated him – Paco stared at her like a science project. She looked as if she was made of porcelain, wrapped in luxury, and spun from the finest silk and gold from the Far East. Inside the semi-dark hut, he could see that her *Hanfu* was finely crafted with the utmost care and skill. Occasionally, when one of the silk threads caught the incoming light, her dress sparkled like ancient fireworks on a dark Peking night. The way she gracefully swung, back and forth in her rocking-chair, had Paco in a total trance. Her elegance was breathtaking, close to royal.

Doña Lucia gazed at Alejandra with a look clearer than a hand-written order, and Alejandra immediately headed towards the door and the dusty footpath that winded back to the hacienda.

She waved farewell to both of them.

As soon as she was out of sight, Doña Lucia stopped the chair's rocking motion and leaned close towards Paco, who was fidgeting with a loose piece of cotton on his neatly tucked-in shirt.

"So, tell me about your dream," she said with a smile. It was the first time he saw her smile. Pearly, white teeth adorned her petite mouth. Her breath was almost odourless.

Paco took a step back.

"How do you know about my dream?" He did not hesitate, "I only told my

Mom and *I know* she didn't tell you!" Paco placed both fists on his hips and leaned defiantly towards her; a war-faring stance typical of the Alegría gene.

Doña Lucia leaned closer to her cheeky, four-foot-tall student.

"It's not hard to know what's burning in your eyes, drawn in your palms and written in your heart," she said, "What did you see?"

With a barely perceptible move of her hand, Doña Lucia managed to place her right palm softly on top of Paco's chest – as if a butterfly had landed - something no one, not even Alejandra had yet achieved.

Usually, having a foreign hand touch his heart felt as if someone might kill him. Although this may not seem rational, it was simply Paco's reflex action and a defence mechanism; a primitive act of survival.

His once closest friend, little Luis the Fourth, the son of don Lucho Cuarto the Third, mistakenly placed his hand near Paco's heart, during a game of hide-and-seek at little Luis' sixth birthday party.

Paco retaliated with an automatic fist to little Luis's face.

If Samuel had not picked up his son by both sideburns to seek the forgiveness of his nose-bleeding friend, their friendship would have certainly ended.

Somehow, this time, Paco did not move or retaliate.

For the first time in his life, he trusted... completely.

The woman in the foreign attire and strange accent managed to break all his barriers and touch the place that, until that moment, had remained like the centre of the earth... untouched.

As swift as the hand advanced, it receded.

There were violet sparks everywhere - some even zooming past the shack, like falling stars.

Paco had never felt so at ease. It felt as if all the stars in the Milky Way had descended upon that sweltering mudroom and sparkled just beneath the woven-reed roof.

In that instant, Paco opened up, "I saw the Plaza Mayor filled with lots and lots of people… and they were singing one of my songs… I even remember the song…"

Paco shut his eyes as if a bomb was about to explode. His tiny irises moved from side to side, recalling the dulcet intricacies of the tune, "It went… hum, hum, hum a la hum, hum… something like that." He talked with his hands, depicting everything in detail with the colourful movements of his tiny fingers.

"Then, there was a rainbow… but a different kind of rainbow… very beautiful… it had a big strip of violet that made the other colours look pale. When I saw it, I knew I must have done something good, and I felt happy. I saw doves and seagulls flying in the grey sky. There were also some fluffy clouds floating above us. The moon was shining in the middle of the day, big and bright, like a silver coin… then I closed my eyes and all I saw was violet… *the colour of my heart*…" Paco described his dream with passion.

"That's all I remember," he closed.

"Thank you Paco," Doña Lucia replied, "What a beautiful dream, thank you for sharing it with me."

She knew that every person had a *Never-Ending Legacy* to fulfil on earth - and despite adverse circumstances, one could always rise above these. She also knew that The One used dreams as His canvas – and often enjoyed mixing pictures, colours, sounds and symbols, to illustrate His will to the dreamer.

"There is a place in the world for everyone. There's space for every person to make a difference, from a little difference to a global difference - it is all up to you. The size of the difference does not matter, what matters is the size of the heart that makes the difference. I can already see that you have a heart as big as the universe," she said, looking into his charcoal eyes decorated with big, long lashes. "With the size of a heart like yours, you can touch many lives my child. Use that big heart of yours to change the world," Doña Lucia explained.

"Carry on dreaming my child, and carry on wanting to make a change, a little difference here and a little difference there… the sum of all your efforts creates your Never-Ending Legacy, and this is a reflection of your purpose and mission on earth," she said. "You can turn your dreams into reality. You have the power to create anything you wish in your life, with your thoughts and with your feelings. *You are a creator.*"

"Tell me more about dreams Doña Lucia," Paco asked. He approached her and sat down at her lap, looking intently into her eyes and occasionally reading her lips. He knew dreams were real for those who believed in them, his mother had taught him this.

"There's no dream bigger than yours, my child. Just like no drop of rain is more important than another. Your dreams, just like rain drops, all travel in one direction, and all nourish the most wonderful reality: that without your dreams, and everyone else's, the earth would not flourish and the world would cease to exist…"

"Keep on dreaming. Keep following your dreams. The world is nourished with your dreams."

"Following our dreams is like painting. We receive all the colours in a palette called *life*, but we, as creators, choose what colours to use and how we paint those dreams into reality. With this in mind, what is your dream Paco?" Doña Lucia asked.

Paco did not hesitate, "I want to be a singer and make the world sing!"

Doña Lucia smiled and nodded - his excitement was contagious. "That's great Paco… and why do you want to do that?"

"Nothing makes me happier Doña Lucia… my heart bleeds ever since I can remember. I don't know why, because none of the other children at school have bleeding hearts. They say I'm not like them, that I'm different. And they ignore me."

Paco paused to take a deep breath.

"But when I sing, all the loneliness disappears! I feel happy and I want to tell the world how great I feel! I feel alive when I hear music! My feet start tapping and I can't do anything to stop them! They have a life of their own! When I'm singing, I don't feel alone anymore, and I want to forgive all those who hurt me… I just want to Love the whole wide world," Paco explained; his hands, two hummingbird wings, flapping wildly in excitement. His feet, tapping away like a locomotive.

"I can clearly see that singing is your dream, and I'm here to see that you follow your Never-Ending Legacy… the rest my child, are *just details.*"

"Before birth, every person has music in their soul… it is up to each person to listen and to find that sound. Some listen with half an ear. Others can barely make out that there is a sound… and sadly, most have completely forgotten how to listen for their personal melody, and their hearts are filled with nothing but an empty silence."

"Even when there is nothing but silence, there are people like you who listen with their soul. Every piece of their body yearns for the vibration that moulds their spirit and makes them feel like they're flying," Doña Lucia explained.

Paco listened attentively, mouth wide open, enthralled by her words and the way she pronounced every vowel and consonant with unusual care and attention, despite her foreign accent.

"Every person is born with a gift. It is every person's duty to find what that gift is. You certainly have a gift my child. However, a gift is like a fertile field with nothing growing in it. The ground is there. The water is there. The seeds are there. Both the opportunity and possibility are there too. But only one thing is missing. The most important ingredient of them all… *You.*" She caressed Paco's chin.

"Without you nurturing that field, nothing will grow in it. You have to plant the seeds, water them, nurture them, and not allow anything to grow that might spoil your field… how do you do that, you may ask?"

Paco interrupted, "Yes… how do I do that Doña Lucia?"

Gently, she brought him closer and whispered, "The answer is called *work.*

You need to work on your gifts or they are wasted."

Paco's eyes lit up like two torches.

"If someone special gives you a most beautiful present… will you give it back and say *'no thank you'*?"

"No, señorita," Paco answered, "I'd want to keep it and show it to everyone."

"That's why you need to work on your gifts and all your dreams and aspirations. Water them daily until they flower with the most beautiful plants and fragrant petals, so that one day, you can use your gifts and share them with the world - *si?*"

"Yes, Doña Lucia," Paco answered, filled with excitement. He was ready to face the world. A great teacher is not there to persuade… but to remind.

He understood the simple way she explained ideas and concepts, and his mind absorbed every word she uttered like a sponge. Under Doña Lucia's veiled guidance, Paco's Never-Ending Legacy soon started to flower.

Months and seasons passed in the flourishing hacienda, and the secret music lovers grew closer together in heart and spirit. In every relationship, with time, regardless of age and experience, the two halves inevitably become both student and teacher.

During this time, Samuel's trips to Miramar became more frequent as talks on the abolition of slavery heated up between liberals and wealthy landowners. His increasing time away from home allowed both Paco and Doña Lucia to deepen their sacred bond.

Paco lacked a natural vocal gift, but the size of his heart compensated for this. Doña Lucia knew she had a delicate situation in her hands, and being a dedicated teacher, pushed the child's slim singing range constantly; patiently building a decent set of vocal chords inside Paco's fragile body.

"One of the keys to constructing your Never-Ending Legacy is called *perseverance*," Doña Lucia began.

As curious as ever he asked, "What does perseverance mean?" Perseverance is a big word and it sounded complicated.

"Remember the first time you rode a horse?" she asked.

"Yes, Doña Lucia. I was five years old and was really scared. I'm very scared of heights."

"Tell me what happened."

"Heights make me dizzy, Doña Lucia. They make my mouth dry. They make my palms sweat too. But I remember the more I practised riding, the better I became! Until one day, I was not scared anymore. I remember riding so fast that my father had to let go of the horse. After that, I learned to ride on my own. It was a great feeling." His hands seemed to have a life of their own as they gyrated like windmills in a desert storm.

"Did you ever fall?"

"Yes, Doña Lucia, I fell on the first day. I fell on my face and nearly lost my two front teeth… and father did not help me. He asked me to stop crying."

Doña Lucia kept silent.

She did not judge; her nature was to understand and forgive.

"Riding a horse teaches you perseverance, my child. Your goal was to ride, and gradually, you learnt to handle a wild animal. At first, you were a little scared and that's normal; fear is part of trying something new. Through perseverance, you learnt to control your fears despite your many falls, and that's exactly what you did. Always remember that your falls are as important as your successes. The falls are necessary, because often, we need a little bit of hurt in order to learn and grow. You won't be the same person after conquering a setback. They are gifts of the soul wrapped in the paper of experience."

Paco nodded.

"The biggest blessings are often disguised in the shape of tears," she added.

"As long as we assimilate those lessons and move forward, we keep on growing. Perseverance is the ability to get up fearlessly after a fall… the key is *always to get up more times than you fall*," she explained.

"It's hard to keep going when others want you to fail," Paco added.

"The world is filled with people who will mock you when you fall… they actually thrive and live to see you perish, but don't let it bother you or make you lose focus, my child. The challenge is yours, not theirs. In spite of the ridicule, you must get up, every single time. Persevere, and soon you'll be riding wild horses, while the people who criticised you will stand back and watch from the ground."

"Don't let other's secret fears interrupt your growth. Some people learn to live in fear and prevent themselves from experiencing the best rides of their lives. Once you vanquish your fears, and you conquer the horses that life throws at you… the view is never the same."

Paco stared at his beloved, wise teacher; his heart feeling prouder.

"I've heard from your mother that you're a great equestrian!"

Doña Lucia embraced Paco. It made him feel as if an angel had wrapped her ancient wings around his tiny frame.

"I understand what you mean by perseverance Doña Lucia, thank you. If it wasn't for the times I fell, I'd still be running around the hacienda on the weekends!"

"While we're on the topic of running, it's time for you to run home like a puma my child." Paco looked confused.

Doña Lucia suddenly closed her eyes. She opened her hands and jerked back slightly, as if someone had written an invisible but electrifying message on her bare palms.

"I have a feeling your father will be home earlier today," she said, looking concerned. "Go! Run, my child, run!"

On that windless afternoon, Paco ran home like a child possessed, leaving a trail of suspended dust behind him. As he neared the main hacienda dwellings, he noticed Caballero roped by the porch. The sight of his father's horse wrenched a knot in his stomach.

Samuel stepped outside like a guarding sentinel ready for battle.

"Where have you been Paco?" he asked with sternness - characteristic of his deep, disciplinarian voice. His fists clenched.

"And why are you so sweaty and dirty?"

Paco took a moment to catch his breath. He slumped forward, resting his tired arms on his knees. He knew that lying was not right, but he had to protect the life of his beloved teacher.

"I was playing by the river, Father… and ran back as fast as I could - trying to catch my shadow before sunset." Paco never looked into his father's eyes when they talked. "And I am here before nightfall, like you always wanted."

"You'd better tell me the truth, son. As I've said before: I don't want you near those slaves. They are wicked and dangerous, and need to be treated with an iron fist. They're not like us – don't ever forget that. The moment you show them weakness, they'll try to destroy you. Remember - do not trust anybody. Never show them you heart, it is your Achilles' heel. Is that clear, son?"

"Yes… Father," Paco said in a tone choked with remorse, and walked gazing at the floor as he headed towards his room.

Paco grew in the soft light of Doña Lucia despite his father's ever-watchful eye.

Approaching adolescence, he inherited his father's physical shape and rapidly increased in strength and stature. Due to his newfound vigour, he received three important duties in the thriving hacienda: overseeing the work of the African and Chinese labourers, helping to construct a new dam up-river, and nurturing Samuel's proud, Paso-Fino horses.

During this time, he also took on certain traits from his father's genealogy: a quick temper and an air of arrogance. With Samuel often away in Miramar, Paco also developed a balanced emotional side from the constant contact with his beloved music teacher and his ever-present, loving mother.

Whenever his father was away to fight the liberals in the capital, Paco focused on his Never-Ending Legacy by working on his talent with diligence. As a token of appreciation for Paco's perseverance, Doña Lucia inscribed both their initials on her Spanish guitar, and presented it to Paco as a gift, which he hid among unused childhood toys under his bed.

She pushed his creative boundaries by asking him to write a song per week. He was to do this without excuse. Discipline at school was his foe, but when it came to music, he embraced the art with relentless passion.

His discipline allowed him to receive frequent visits from his muse, resulting in countless songs. But lately, with his thoughts affected by the inevitable increase in hormones, Paco's work centred mainly on the idea of forbidden Love and hopeless romantic conquests. His weakness for women with dark hair became evident when he decided to name his guitar '*Morena*,' or 'brunette'.

"Calm your passions my child… you're far too restless," Doña Lucia said.

"Music helps to calm those young and lustful thoughts. Rest your urges so you can create your best work."

"My *corazón* is on fire Doña Lucia. I can't quench my heart or tame these emotions… they are driving me crazy. All I think about are the beautiful señoritas… I can't single one out… I want them all… I want to sing and tell them how I feel… and kiss them… like a *real* man."

Paco closed his eyes tightly and kissed an imaginary woman, like a man who has been stranded on an uninhabited island for decades, hugging her passionately with his long arms; all of course, without an inch of coordination. Like a real man.

"Paco… control yourself. Music is there to uplift the spirit, not some skirts!"

She gently slapped his hand, "Realise who you are spiritually first and your work will flourish as a flower flourishes after the spring rains. Right now, you're all lust and dust. Make your work permanent and solid like a rock. Don't let it disappear and be forgotten."

"I'll try… but no promises," Paco replied cheekily, his eyes brimming with mischief.

"Don't make the promises to me, but to yourself." Doña Lucia continued.

It was time to start the lesson.

"So, what have you written this week?"

Paco bit his lower lip. He seemed a little embarrassed. He knew his song was not ready to be presented. He felt frustrated; but most of all, he did not want to disappoint his teacher and break his promise. He always wanted to be a man of his word.

"It's just…well… eh," Paco hesitated.

It was time to make a confession. "Whatever I'm writing lately has no… well… rhythm," he said, embarrassed.

"Mmm, I had that suspicion," Doña Lucia replied. "You're *out of balance*, my child."

"What do you mean I'm out of balance, Doña Lucia?" Paco crossed his arms in defiance, and frowned at his teacher.

Doña Lucia gave him a kind look. She dressed her gaze with the colours of understanding.

He immediately uncrossed his arms and opened up again. She needed no words to achieve this.

"Lately, scattered thoughts are pushing you out of balance. You need to re-align your thoughts into balance. Do you know how to do this?"

Paco waited anxiously for the answer. "Yeeees?" he queried.

"*You control your mind, not the other way around,*" Doña Lucia responded.

"Really?" Paco replied.

"If your mind tells you to jump off a bridge, are you going to jump?" she asked.

"Of course not!"

"Good," Doña Lucia answered with a smile.

"In the same light, if your mind tells you to think about girls twenty-four hours a day, will you do that?…"

She left the question hanging in the air.

Paco rubbed his chin and thought hard. She had a point. He didn't think of girls twenty-four hours a day - only twenty-three.

"*You* have the power my child. *You* decide whether to follow your thoughts or not. My question is… who is controlling whom? Are you controlling your mind, or is your mind controlling you? Instead of focusing your thoughts on fleeting fantasies, focus your thoughts on the music and the rhythm of your soul - your true and unique gift – because that's where your power lies and that is where your Never-Ending Legacy resides. Elevate your spirit to the place where miracles happen. *Find your own voice*, my child… *find your own voice*," Doña Lucia repeated, emphasising those four words.

"It all makes so much sense," Paco said, crestfallen. "You're right. Lately my thoughts have been scattered and I've been giving less time to my dreams."

"Why is that my child?"

"My friends keep telling me that following a path in music is a waste of time. They laugh at me when I tell them that I want to be a singer and make the world sing… is that so wrong?"

Paco bared his heart so completely one could almost touch it. "My father is against what belongs to me since I was a child. If he knew I was here with you, he'd kill us both with his bare hands. It feels like the world keeps turning against me. Why keep trying to walk this path then? It's so difficult… with so many obstacles already on my way and so many people urging me to stop… please tell me, why should I continue? Why, Doña Lucia?"

Paco's heart started to bleed. A tiny droplet of liquid-life made a crimson blotch on his shirt the size of a small copper coin.

She understood the quest of a bleeding heart; how following one's dreams was never the easier step to take. Following one's dreams is a path only a few brave souls dare to follow, as it requires absolute courage, perseverance, and resolution.

If Paco only knew that although life is loaded with trials, no one receives more than they can handle. In a dreamer's arsenal, there is nothing bigger and more powerful than *the size of a heart*. A human heart, merely the size of a fist, has conquered oceans, mountains, and continents.

"Ask yourself the following Paco," she said in a tone filled with compassion, *"Could you look back at your life one day and regret not having followed your dreams?"* Doña Lucia placed both her hands on top of her heart. "People who forget about their dreams often end up regretting their decision.

"Following my dreams is just so difficult. What if I just forget about my dreams and focus on something else?"

"You could do that my child, and pretend to the world that you are happy… but only for a while… you couldn't pretend forever. In the silence of your mind, you can never lie to yourself. When you're alone, your heart will demand an answer to the question: *why didn't I take the leap?* Why didn't I find my voice and follow it? When I had wings… why did I refuse to take flight? What kept me back? What was I afraid of?" Doña Lucia posed.

"What if I'm afraid to fly and take the leap?" Paco asked, desperately searching for an answer to his quest.

"I can tell you this much, Paco… *people are not afraid to fly, they are only afraid of the altitude they might reach.*" She was the personification of compassion when she spoke. "My dear child, you cannot let fear rule your life and flatten your dreams. Don't ever let fear make your decisions. Success or failure can only be found in the place that lies between your two ears. Do you remember how you learned to ride?"

Paco nodded.

"Look at yourself now… you're an expert rider."

"I guess you have a point. Then how do I follow my Never-Ending Legacy?"

"When Alexander the Great conquered what was the majority of the known Western World, he didn't know he was going to do this - he went and did it," there was a hint of a smile on Doña Lucia's face.

"*Trust your instincts. Trust the voice of your heart*; it will guide and protect you. The voice of your heart is the voice of The One… He speaks to us all through our own unique voice."

"How do I learn to listen to that voice?" Paco asked.

"Some people need a soft whisper to understand, while others need a hurricane in their ear to comprehend what is required of them. Learn to listen to those soft, silent whispers… they are the louder of the two and will act as your guiding compass in life - if you let them.

Do not let fear conquer your dreams, my child. You were born for this. Do not lead a life without accomplishing what you're born to do. Don't return the gift that The One has so graciously bestowed upon you. Find your voice, work on your gift, and follow your Never-Ending Legacy at all costs. That is your purpose."

Doña Lucia spoke gently to Paco's heart and the bleeding stopped. Her words were soft as silk and her wisdom caressed his heart as though a velvet rose had dried up his pain.

"My child," Doña Lucia continued, "I shall be going home soon, but before I do that, I need to know you are ready to continue your journey without me. A teacher can't allow her pupil to leave home without knowing that her student is prepared for what life may place at his feet."

"What do you mean you're *going home?*" Paco asked.

"I will be returning to my place of birth. The Elders are calling me."

"I don't understand."

"Soon you will, my child."

5 The Out-Break

During the summer, the Andes' rainy season, the newly-built reservoir disciplined the raging river passing through the dry and thirsty hacienda.

Titanic glaciers melted with the rising humidity and descended into the Pacific Ocean as hundreds of rivers in search of the comforting, benevolent arms of Mother Sea.

The placid dam stood where millions of rocks ended their downward battle from the high Andes Mountains in a fierce run west to the desert's fertile plains. The tranquil spot provided a cocoon for tiny river fish to nest, as well as creating a breeding ground for smaller, more dangerous life forms.

During the construction of the dam, the hacienda grew in profits on the back of labour and pain. The living conditions of the workers decreased year after year. Catastrophic acquisitions by Samuel resulted in an increase in the number of both African slaves and Chinese labourers to the extent that both living quarters looked like overcrowded ant colonies.

Some of the recently-imported Chinese carried an invisible enemy that had plundered their mother nation only a few months earlier. Samuel's neglect of essential necessities, including sanitation, caused a viral spread of disease, and soon an outbreak of cholera had infiltrated the hacienda with the bitter stench of death.

"My men are dying like flies with this damn disease Alejandra!" Samuel shouted, his snake-like eyes spitting venom through his dilated pupils. The world could tell the state of Samuel's emotions through his eyes. With a single look, he had learned to speak the language of both Love and hate.

"Let me give you a hand Amor, I can help," Alejandra said. "I will ask Madre Bonita to help us. She's a nurse who can gather many helping hands from the Santo Rosario church."

Samuel looked at his wife, motionless, while the tips of his sky-pointing moustache swayed in a flimsy dance from the breeze entering through an open window. Despite his stern and often lack of emotional connection with Alejandra, he loved his wife more than anything in the world, and one look or a glimpse of tenderness in his voice would be enough for her to understand this.

"Just be careful *my Love*... cholera is highly contagious... and deadly. Save as many as you can." He kissed her forehead and left, leaving his usual smell of perspiration and tobacco hanging in the air.

They did not know it yet, but death had already knocked on their door.

Alejandra spent countless days and nights fighting the scourge with Madre Bonita and the women from the Santo Rosario church. They slept not a wink. Doña Lucia, faithful by their side, dispensed her miraculous potions and powders to the sick and frail with dauntless dedication and compassion. As the outbreak reached its peak and then gradually began to decrease, Doña Lucia fell ill.

It was the last summer before Paco finished school. He was soon to turn nineteen.

During the ghastly epidemic, Samuel kept a close eye on the slaves and labourers, which prevented Paco from visiting his teacher. Samuel also prohibited him from attending school; he needed an extra pair of hands to aid in rebuilding the devastated hacienda.

"Doña Lucia is very ill," Alejandra told Paco. She made sure there was no one around.

Paco turned pale on hearing the news. It was as though a ghost had delivered the message.

"I'm going to see her now, mother," he said, turning his back on her in an instant. The Love and respect for his teacher knew no boundaries. He needed to see her immediately.

Alejandra grabbed his muscular arm before he stepped out the door. His motion dragged her a few feet.

"Not today my son. Your father is watching proceedings from everywhere like a hawk… but he leaves tomorrow morning for Miramar to get supplies for the sick. Be ready," she said with conviction. Paco wasn't being rational. She needed to be firm.

"But I have to see her now…"

Alejandra squeezed Paco's arm with all her might. She looked deep within his eyes, attempting to soothe his aching heart.

"Do not jeopardise all the years she gave you in a moment of ire. Grab hold of your emotions and stop reacting. You will see her tomorrow… now go help your father and avoid suspicion."

The next day, Paco parted as soon as the sound of his father's galloping horse disappeared in the direction of the capital.

He mounted his lightning-fast horse and kicked the animal's belly with all his might. The horse let out a piercing belch and set off at once. The brief journey to the Chinese labourer's side of the hacienda felt like the beginning of eternity. Two tears rolled from his eyes as he rode against the morning wind, leaving a miniscule trail of melancholic salt as they dried on his sideburns.

"Oh, my child, my child, you've finally come," Doña Lucia said. Life had almost left her once-vibrant voice.

She was reclining on a mat entwined with hay and old cotton, covered in an eastern-looking jade mantle. She appeared comfortable, but her body sagged to her right.

"I'm here Doña Lucia. I'm sorry I couldn't come earlier," Paco said. "Father was watching."

"I understand my child. You are here and that's the most important thing," she said in a low, raspy voice; it was the sound of a voice on the path to Elysium. She had never sounded this weak.

Her eyes lay sunken, and the bits of extra skin that filled her Hanfu had dramatically shrunk like baked bread without yeast. Her beautiful coloured cheeks faded to the colour of a stale cherimoya, and her hair lost the lustre that made people believe they were strands of black-pearl's silk. Life was leaving her, but she clutched onto its impermanent reins with the fading tips of her fingers; just for the one with the bleeding heart.

"What can I do, beloved teacher?" Paco pleaded.

He squeezed his right thumb and index finger together as hard as he could in an attempt to stop the inevitable flood of tears by focusing on the pressure. The state of his teacher caused his sensible heart to rupture like a broken dam.

"Don't bleed for me my child... don't cause yourself unnecessary pain. Life ebbs and flows... this is part of the natural rhythm of the universe."

Paco placed in his chest hole the hand-sewn handkerchief Alejandra had given him as a child in order to stop the rapid advance of the bright, scarlet tears. The rainbow-coloured figures of condors, pumas, and llamas sown into the cotton, rapidly turned molten red, like it had so many times before.

"Tell me what to do beloved teacher," Paco insisted.

"Promise me one thing my child," she whispered. Her voice was dwindling fast. She struggled to breathe.

Paco fought the imminent, tumbling tears. He frowned, closed his eyes, and kept squeezing his fingers - anything to prevent Doña Lucia from seeing him cry. He believed crying showed weakness. Samuel had wired his son this way.

"Anything you want, anything..." he replied in a trembling voice.

Doña Lucia observed him with the kind eyes of a spiritual mother.

She lived to serve others and had forfeited the chance of love and raising a family in order to uplift the soul of humankind. If she had ever experienced anything close to the Love of a mother, her only child was at arm's reach, with a ruptured heart and a face filled with broken, inevitable tears. Like her, he could hardly breathe.

"My child, at the end of your days, what determines the story written in your *Book of Life*… are not your words, but your actions."

"What you *do* in this lifetime from now on, will show the world who you are. Build a life that you can be proud of, that others can be proud of too, and learn from the decisions you've made. When the light from earth starts fading and you step into the universal light that shines forever, ask yourself… what would the world have *missed* if I weren't born? What *difference* did I make in my lifetime? How many people did I *touch* with my Love, my mission, and how many other dreams did I *ignite* with my dreams?"

"We are not here to die. We are not here as passengers… but as captains. Choose to *live intensely* my child… choose to take the rudder of the ship of Life and direct it towards your endless sun of possibilities… and during that journey, make sure that your aspirations, goals, and dreams touch as many people in a positive way. To live solely for yourself is meaningless… to live for others… truly enriching. Can you promise me that?"

Paco nodded, unable to say anything. His swollen eyes brimming with all the tears he had never cried. Death had been foreign to him. Until that moment.

Doña Lucia's eyes were closing. Paco held her fragile, slumping hand. He caressed each of her retracting fingers hoping his Love would stop her from leaving him. He would not let go. She was meant to live forever.

With great effort, Doña Lucia unbuttoned the top pin of her Hanfu and gave Paco a necklace, "Here my child." He had never seen it before. The bright, blue amulet sparkled with pink and orange streaks. It looked alive.

"Take this from me Paco… it's a seashell I found among the rocks while collecting herbs and roots in the Himalayas," she whispered.

"It is proof that once the entire world was under water. It also taught me a lesson about perseverance and finding my own voice," she murmured.

Doña Lucia conquered each breath with indomitable strength.

"Millions of years ago, there was no earth as we know it, only an expansive and enormous sea. The Earth lay hidden beneath the waves. However, the dream-filled Earth wanted to see the sun, feel its warmth, and let life grow on her skin. She looked at the sun from beneath the waves and saw the sky and clouds in the day, and the stars and moon at night. In her silence, she longed to be near them, talk to them, and share the space and freedom of the wind with them too. She dreamt of looking at the sea, high from where the clouds were born, and admire the expansive carpet of waves from there… but the sea was so immense, and her dream seemed like an impossible dream.

One day, she decided that to live under the shadow of the sea was not to live at all, and she gathered powers within her that she never knew existed. All her thoughts and might focused on rising up towards freedom.

One morning, she started to rise… and fire appeared from the depths of her heart. The next day, she rose some more. Day and night, she rose higher and closer to her dream of touching the sky. Although she fought long and hard, her task seemed futile, and all her efforts without an inch of hope. Just when she thought she couldn't fight any longer… she finally broke through the mighty surface of the sea.

Waves splashed around her, and for the first time, she felt the warm energy of the sun and the mist from the sea spray on her face. She finally achieved what she had once thought was impossible.

As a reward for her perseverance, the most amazing creatures in the cosmos flourished on her skin. One special day, the Earth received the most beautiful gift from The One: humankind, who later proved to the Earth and sea, that through perseverance - anything is possible."

Doña Lucia gasped for air, suffusing her body with runaway life.

Whispering she continued, "Don't ever give up my child… be like the Earth, find your voice and rise beyond what you think is possible."

"I promise you Doña Lucia," Paco said, his eyes alight with sincerity, and his heart entangled with thorns. "I will keep this amulet with me always, close to my heart, and I will never forget your words of wisdom. Now please rest, you need to get better."

"My child, when I'm not here…"

Paco immediately interrupted and raised his trembling voice. "You're not going anywhere, you're staying with me… I don't care what my father says anymore. I'm staying here until you get well again. I'm not leaving you, ever."

Doña Lucia's pulse weakened.

"My child, before I go, I need to tell you that you're one of the greatest gifts I've been blessed with. You have filled my life with joy… since that summer's day when you allowed me to touch your open heart and shaped it into *your* work of art. You have made me the proudest teacher in the world. You have worked so hard on your dreams and you've shown me the courage that would make any parent proud."

"Stop talking like that please, you're not going anywhere," Paco replied, tears cascading down his face, pooling onto his bottom lip and overflowing, wetting his dark trousers.

"There's no one in the world with your story. There's no one with your smiles. No one with your scars. No one with your heart. No one has gone through what you've gone through. Today, and always, you're the greatest person on earth.

Fulfil your mission on earth, my child… make the world remember you. Create a Never-Ending Legacy with your talents and gifts and never stop persevering. Infuse your songs with positive messages for humanity and infuse your work with Love, because work *is the expression of your inner and outer Love…*"

"I promise you Doña Lucia," Paco continued to hold her limp hand with firmness.

"Your work is like a child: nurture it, give it the best you can possibly give, let it grow in its own space and time, and make sure when it leaves your nest, that it's a reflection of your own happiness and Love. The One chose you for a purpose that will unite enemies and lead a country to justice. Let your heart be your instrument and allow its voice to guide you home. Remember, that no matter how difficult a situation is… *on a rainy night, you can still choose to see stars.*"

Doña Lucia looked at Paco one last time.

She was peaceful. Her ship was waiting in port; ready to take her home. On a trip back to the sky-kissing mountains; the Roof of the World… back to the Elders.

"Treat all your steps as if they were your first. This Life is a journey never to be repeated." She caught her last breath of sweet, escaping air. "The Elders are waiting for me Paco. My ship is here. Keep me in your heart. *I'll be watching you from the stars.* I promise you."

With this promise, Doña Lucia closed her eyes and bid farewell to a world consumed with people that still slept.

Through the power of her unselfish Love, some of the sleeping had been awakened. Her last breath was a holy whirlwind suffused with the scent of roses.

"Doña Lucia?" Paco shook her gently, sensing for any trace of a pulse on her motionless wrist and neck.

His heart began to accelerate "Doña Lucia, please… please don't leave me!"

Outside, the world was racing into darkness. Only a few stars sparkled among the scattered desert clouds.

Paco kept holding his beloved teacher's wrist.

No pulse… nothing.

The thunderous sound of galloping horses shattered the stillness outside.

Two faint glows, barely lighting the immensity of the darkness, approached the white reed hut where an air of serenity reigned, and small stars shimmered, lingering for a few moments before disappearing past the roof and beyond.

Paco lay at the foot of the hay-and-cotton bed, tightly embracing the lifeless body of his beloved Doña Lucia; crying in a pool of congealed blood. Inside the room, the feeling of loss was palpable.

Paco was disorientated from his teacher's passing. He failed to hear the two approaching strangers. His senses were shutdown.

"What the hell are you doing here Paco? What is going on?" Samuel shouted as he entered the gloomy hut.

He hooked his oil lantern onto a protruding piece of wood on the wall with an intense measure of anger. The dangling lantern gave the scene a ghostly appearance as the light swung from side to side.

Paco did not answer.

"I asked you a question, you insolent child. You'd better answer right now if you want to be spared a beating."

Paco looked at his father with hate burning in his eyes – it was a trait inherited from the Alegría side of the family. His eyes were bloodshot and his heart tattered into innumerable pieces of broken glass, each cutting deeper with every palpitation. His cream shirt had turned the colour of the aftermath of a ferocious battle, and his pain was so deep he could scarcely mumble. His trembling right hand barely held the seashell necklace he'd received from his beloved teacher.

"She was my teacher, my mother, my mountain, my pillar, my heart and my life," Paco mumbled, "and now she's gone. Just leave us alone... go!" he shouted. He held his teacher with all his might. He wasn't going to let go. Not for anybody.

"Alejandra, what is he talking about? Explain - now woman!" Samuel grunted, confused.

Her left eye started to twitch.

Alejandra looked at Paco with the immeasurable amount of compassion only a mother can have for her child; but she did not say a word. Paco knew that in the presence of Samuel, she would not answer.

"Let me answer for her, father," Paco replied sarcastically. His sulphurous hate was reaching a boiling point.

"Doña Lucia was my singing teacher since I was seven years old," he said, rage spewing from every pore. "I've been secretly following what my heart desired and what you've been trying to destroy since I was a child… my dreams of a life in music."

Samuel looked betrayed but he rapidly disguised this, regaining his composure. He felt like somebody was strangling him. He stiffened his neck. His muscles tensed like those of a bull, ready to charge.

'How dare my own flesh and blood betray my family's honour for almost twelve years,' he thought. A raging tide of anger erupted from deep within his veins. His fists clamped up like lava hitting the sea. Samuel knew no other way to win a lost argument than resorting to violence; *it was the Alegría way.*

"Did you know about this Alejandra?" Samuel asked his wife. His hand opened, ready to strike her in the face.

She looked at him, and said nothing. She simply stared at Paco. She was as lifeless as the body of his dead teacher.

"You never say anything Mom. You're always keeping quiet. Always lowering down to Father, pretending our lives are perfect. Wake up from the illusion. Stand up and for once, say something. I dare you." Paco shouted; the Alegría ire now consuming him alive.

"I dare you Mom."

Alejandra kept holding up her lantern. She remained motionless, watching her family fall apart, unable to mumble a single syllable.

Her mother taught her to keep the peace, to be second place, and to live a life serving her husband. She learned to be loyal, diplomatic, and perfect in the eyes of the world, even if her inner world was crumbling. She always had to wear a smile; to be the perfect cook, the perfect mother, the perfect lover, the perfect woman. Looking good on the outside was always more important than feeling good on the inside. She was the victim of a victim. She was the product of her conditioning and upbringing.

Alejandra was dying to defend her son – and to finally speak her truth, but in the silences of her soul, there was only a traceless and tacit whisper.

"I'll deal with you later, woman," Samuel told Alejandra. He knew his wife wouldn't say a word. It was time to take matters into his fists.

He turned then to Paco.

He approached within striking distance.

"Now that your dead teacher is not a bother anymore, I'm going to give you a choice," he said, a twisted grin swelling on his lips. "From tomorrow, you will start working for me and the hacienda that has given you everything on a free-on-board basis. I will burn down this place with your teacher in it so that no one will ever remember either existed. Then you're going to go back home, wash the embarrassing blood off your shirt, give me that sissy seashell you have in your hands, and prepare for work tomorrow. If you disagree, you will leave my hacienda tonight, never to return again."

Alejandra interrupted, "Samuel, please!" She begged, placing the lantern on the floor and clasping her hands in a position of prayer at her chest. She looked at her son and went down on her knees.

"Silence, I'm not done, woman," Samuel cut out his desperate wife. "If you refuse to accept my terms, you will also renounce the Alegría surname, tonight."

Paco picked himself up and closed in on his father. He was defiant. Every sinew secretly tensing under his grimy clothes.

"Leave now," Samuel ordered Paco, pointing to the horse outside. For the first time in his life, Paco stared into his father's eyes. He clasped the seashell tight in his hand.

"For your information…" Paco said with a smile dressed in anger… "*I've never been an Alegría.*"

The words were red, merciless darts. They speared Samuel's heart with a violence he could not comprehend, destroying the dream he had for his only son. He was struck with an unexpected scream of pain and disillusion. He did not cope well with either. In the diminished visibility of the hut, Samuel instinctively struck Paco in the face.

Paco's body lifted off the floor and struck the mud wall with such force that tiny fragments of the roof began to fall like dust rain. Samuel's raging anger was prehistoric, out of control and beastly.

Doña Lucia's necklace left Paco's hand. It hit the mud floor close to where Samuel stood. With one solemn stomp of his rugged, leather working-boots, Samuel trampled and crushed the necklace into a scattering of glittering shards. He did not want a single remaining trace of that strange woman.

Paco lay on the floor, semi-conscious; his limbs almost quartered from his frame. Blood trickled from his nose. He could taste its metal burning in his throat. Caught off balance, he regained composure, supported by the increased adrenalin spurring from his infuriated heart.

"*You can take my name, but you can't own my dreams.*" He strapped Morena on his back, staggered towards his horse, and headed for the dwelling-house. He goaded his horse, driving it to charge in an ocean of darkness.

Alejandra watched in disbelief.

No one had ever stood up to Samuel before.

"But Sam…" Alejandra said.

"Don't talk to me Alejandra." Samuel pushed her away with repugnance.

"That taught him a lesson," he said proudly. "He has no other choice but to do what I say; that spoiled child won't leave the hacienda - he has nowhere to go. Besides that, Miramar is half a day's walk and he has no skills to survive in the real world. That little coward doesn't have the guts to leave. One day he'll realise that all I taught him was for his own good - and he'll thank me for it. He'll soon forget that this all happened."

With this, Samuel led his wife out of the electrically-charged hut, and tossed his burning oil-lantern close to Doña Lucia's hay mat. The dried feed caught ablaze. Within minutes, the whitewashed hut had turned into a storming, black-smoke inferno.

Hundreds of Chinese labourers had overheard the incident. They emerged from their dwellings and congregated outside in silent prayer, honouring the life of their holy nun. In the desert where it scarcely rains, a deluge of tears descended and flooded the dry terrain.

A blazing barrage of fire, wood, and flesh ignited the far eastern-side of the hacienda. The charred remains of the reed-and-adobe hut had evolved from a solid foundation into mere specks that dispersed into the wind in less than a glimpse. A brutal reminder of the impermanence of all things…

Thick smoke rose from the remains, and turned wispy, merging with the passing, travelling clouds.

A heart-shaped cloud coalesced above the silent bows and tears of those gathered below; and when the prayers came to an end; it melted into the heavens… from where it once came.

6 Miramar, the Capital

Paco flung his bloodied shirt onto the floor, wiped his chest, put on a clean, crisp shirt, and ran to the kitchen. He tossed some bread in a brown cotton bag, filled a bottle with boiled but cool water, and strapped his guitar with firmness onto his back. Mounting his horse, he headed for the hacienda's portentous entrance.

As he reached it, he looked back at the immensity of it all – the dwelling lights flickering in the far distance, the barely visible night-lamps and scattered fires outside the Chinese quarters, the scent and melody of the rampant ocean. Directly below the entrance that had the hacienda's name engraved in rusted iron, he said goodbye to the place that bore his name. This land had written part of his history. Despite his raging anger, he knew that he could not deny this fact. He dismounted his loyal companion and slapped him with a loud whack on the rear. The horse belched and galloped on instinct back towards the ranch.

Paco did not want to take anything that belonged to his father. He headed in the pitch-darkness towards Miramar, half a day's walk to the north. He knew the daunting task ahead, but his anger made him fearless.

The road to the *City of Kings* zigzagged through vast Marathonian plains of sand, where traces of vegetation and water took refuge from the human eye in order to test the will of those brave enough to cross it. Luckily for Paco, the winding road ran parallel to the sea, and the breeze from the vast expanse of salty water, whispered the way north.

Paco was aware of the dangers he was facing. The path to the capital abounded in under-worked thieves and Cimarrons (runaway slaves coupled with bandit Inca), who plagued the infamous road and were notorious for their swift attacks and merciless killings. Their leader, a man called '*El*

Fantasma', held formidable control over the territory like a renegade phantom. This impressive chief of *banditti* was well-mounted, and his troops of blood-thirsty followers were apparently loyal to the death.

Robbing and killing a boy like Paco would be child's play.

He roamed for hours accompanied by a smattering of travelling clouds and a fistful of flickering stars. From the sandy dunes rising nearby, Paco heard the sound of hooves and the scent of old horses amongst a myriad of arguing voices. He bent down on instinct. Crouching like a tiger in the darkness, he carefully shielded the strings of his guitar with his hand, preventing any unnecessary vibration from slicing the desert's silence. In the proximity of the hushed dunes, the voices were whispers. They were that close. He was surrounded.

Trapped.

Arctic-cold sweat trickled down his temples. His heart lay exposed, beating, close to spilling out of his chest. He could hear the familiar *dupp lub* of his overly-agitated organ. Lying as mute as a fossil on the desert floor, silence was his last-standing friend.

"Great robbery boss!" said a half-stuttering, nervous voice.

"I know *Perro*, did you see his face?" A man answered, growling like a content pig in a bath of mud, "I think he did it right there!"

The bandits burst into laughter.

"When people think they are about to die… they cannot hold it in. I just couldn't kill that coward tonight." Another loud burst of laughter erupted.

The infamous bandit leader, 'El Fantasma,' and his henchmen stood just a few feet away. He closed his eyes and prayed to The One for protection.

"Let's split the takings and go into hiding; that coward probably ran to the police. They might just send a party to find us," El Fantasma ordered.

"Let's go to dune forty-four and carry on with the fiesta. They won't find us there."

El Fantasma clapped his hands twice and the bandits mounted their horses and left in a flurry.

Paco took a mouthful of desert air and wiped the sweat from his brow. He did not move an inch until there was not a sound, except the gentle humming of the sea breeze. Then he sprinted towards Miramar.

A fearless Spanish Conquistador founded Miramar, known in both the Old and New World as *'The City of Kings'*, on Epiphany Sunday, just over three hundred years ago. Lying on the calm shores of the Pacific Ocean, the city extended towards a broad and fertile valley that led up to the glory of the Andes Mountains. A river that followed a tortuous course down from lofty mountain peaks divided the city in two. The local Inca called it, *'The one who speaks'*.

The once-treasured capital of the *New World*, embellished and ornamented in magnificent Baroque splendour, had in recent decades, fallen into a state of degradation and literal decay, especially around its periphery.

As dawn reared its luminous head, Paco trundled into the barren outskirts of the deserted city.

Miramar looked like a ghost town without ghosts. There were the dilapidated, dust-covered remains of houses everywhere, gardens in disarray and corners of abandoned homes now used as public toilets. Wherever he looked, broken walls revealed the layers of plaster that once formed part of dozens of healthy edifices.

As Paco moved away from the outskirts and closer to he city's centre, the capital's buildings became progressively taller and newer. The vague, orange light of the sleeping sun glanced off the city's top-floor windows.

People started their day like every other day. The now-awakened city slowly became a bustling hive of activity. Two-floored residences soon began to fill the landscape en masse, and beautiful balconies embellished the city streets with the velvet, dark tones of polished mahogany. From their small-railed and intricately hand-made portas, Paco felt the eyes of the inconspicuous Miramar women observing him as he sauntered past. As the heat of the day intensified, people opened their windows and doors in an attempt to catch the slightest trace of a breeze. Clothes hung on the morose sweat of the over-active capital's dwellers.

Paco was ravenous. He ate the last piece of stale bread from his cotton bag. Chewing that last bit of sustenance, he felt as if he'd walked for days and that the drama from the night before were just the leftovers of a bad dream, emanating from a previous war-torn life.

The truth is that in half a day, his world had turned upside-down.

There was a Miramar minute, a Miramar second and a Miramar glimpse, where in less than a wink, one realises that time does not exist, only moments.

Paco was completely alone in the middle of a big city where he did not recognise a single soul. The thought of his father hearing that he was in dire straits was enough to resort to begging. He would not allow Samuel the pleasure of his defeat. He would rather starve. He had no idea what he was going to do, but Doña Lucia had taught him to '*trust his instincts*'. He knew his inner voice was the voice of The One speaking, and all he had to do was to listen to the softly spoken, wise words from the heavens.

A smallish man, about a-head-and-half shorter than Paco, dressed in creased, dirty, white pants and an unbuttoned blue shirt, approached him. He walked with both feet pointing out; his left foot at ten o'clock and his right foot at two o'clock and waddled like a penguin to water.

"Do you have matches?" he asked.

"Sorry, I don't señor."

"Well, do you have a cigarette then?"

"I don't smoke. I can't help you with that either," Paco replied. Although he was polite, he was in no mood to talk.

The short, crease-magnetised man stared at Paco as if he was from another planet. He inspected his boots, knees, belt, shirt, and hair from top to bottom, letting out a simian wail and a coordinated head nod after thoroughly analysing each part.

Paco was not in the mood to tolerate queer looks from a complete stranger; especially not after what he had just been through.

"Why didn't you just ask for a cigarette in the first place?" Paco asked irritated.

"It's more polite that way," the man answered sharply, "then it looks like I'm not begging." He continued to stare at Paco as though he was something he was about to purchase in a contraband deal, "You are not from these parts, are you?" He spat something solid, pink, and slimy out of his mouth, missing Paco's boot by an inch.

Paco looked at him with disgust. He decided not to answer.

"We don't see many kids like you around here… you know… upper class, rich parents… walking around the capital with a guitar tied to their backs… mmm… highly unusual." The man commented while scratching his hairy belly and still staring at Paco like a stolen museum piece. Paco was not sure what the man was driving at, but this time he couldn't keep the peace.

"I'm here pursuing my dream. What's wrong with that?" Paco was defiant.

"Dreams of what, rich boy?" The man spat again, aiming for a street dog but missing the curious animal.

"Dreams of music? Of singing? Performing? I think you're in the wrong city kid!" The rotund man clapped his hands loudly a number of times, as if he had just witnessed the world's greatest trick, waking up at least two Miramar blocks. He laughed like a hyena and strutted away penguin-like - from where Paco was standing; shell-shocked.

"What about you?" Paco called after him indignantly, "What dreams do you have? What are you pursuing?"

Paco felt his anger rising, pinching every nerve. He squeezed the top of both thumbs against his index fingers to stop himself from committing his first murder.

"You're in the wrong place, rich boy," the short man said, "Dreams don't flourish here, so you better befriend the disappointments. This is not a city of dreams, and you'd better learn that fast. Dreams evaporate in Miramar in the blink of an eye. Wake up. This is reality - and in reality, dreams lead you nowhere."

"We'll see about that!" Paco was outraged. There was nothing he wanted more at that moment, than to thwack his guitar on the little man's head - so it resembled a Panama hat.

He walked away fuming, although trying to look calm and serene.

A crowd of people stood and watched their engagement, but no one intervened; no one cared an ounce. They watched the episode because they loved the drama, the gossip, and the potential it offered to dramatise the scene at home. They watched because they lacked meaning in their lives.

Paco walked away pretending that the stranger's words did not affect him, but within him lay an open heart, ready to be butchered with words of solace, and sacrificed like an innocent lamb by the city wolves.

He was scared all of a sudden. His mouth felt parched. The taste was a scorched and bitter, foul sensation; a direct punch to the solar plexus. The city had metamorphosed into a ravenous monster, ready to devour him. He asked himself, 'What am I doing here? What is my purpose today? How do I find my own voice in this chaos?'

He had no answer.

'Why did that man aim to destroy the little hope I had when I didn't have much in the first place?' He thought and thought some more. His inner voice was silent again.

Alone in a strange, mammoth city, with no sight of the horizon, Paco felt vulnerable and lonely. His left eye twitched. His shirt clung to his wet skin. He moved further and further away from where the penguin-man had destroyed his dimming hope.

As he approached the city centre, the buildings became more and more opulent and the architecture fit for a ruling king or viceroy. Balconies were aligned with delicate, dark, Moorish lattices. All around him, bold portals defined every street. Beyond every sidewalk and street corner, his eyes met with the seductive glances of the beautiful *Tapadas*; women wearing silken veils that covered their faces except for their playful, arresting, dark eyes. Lost in the ethereal and passionate glances of the provocative, Miramar women, Paco felt a rush of excitement and soon forgot about the bitter episode that had just passed.

The capital was fast and rat-race exciting. The streets exploded with the scent of over-fried street food, spicy, piquant fish, and the aroma of freshly-ground nutmeg, molasses and the distinguishable whiff of horse manure. People hurried past as though plagued by the idea of money escaping them, and Paco noticed more frowns per square metre than any place he could imagine. Shaded beneath sumptuous buildings and decorative trees, the principal avenues of the capital all pointed towards one place: the *Plaza Mayor*.

He had seen this very square in his childhood dream: the violet-tinged rainbow, the white seagulls and doves flying above it, and the porcelain-like moon glowing during the day. The plaza had no pavement and lay coated in fine, grainy sand. In the centre was a greenish-black, iron fountain, with *Fame* spouting water from her mystical trumpet into three basins. Four lions circulated the precious fluid from their mouths.

Before Paco stood the former residence of the all-powerful Spanish viceroys; the *Government Palace*. The rigid and square building had since lost its former glory. Much of its façade now shared a space with small, shabby shops, where illegal activities took place under a dilapidated balcony.

On the eastern side rose the *Miramar Cathedral*, holiest of places for the inhabitants of the capital city, blessed with a beautiful portico and an even more magnificent interior. Adjacent to this lay the *Archbishop's Palace*, its hand-carved balconies possessing a commanding view of the rowdy plaza.

The *Cabildo*, or Senate House, was positioned opposite, on the western side. The city jail and a few squalid shops that traded in old iron were part of the same building. The south side of the plaza encompassed a selection of homes with privileged views that were built next to an array of general goods stores constructed within a colonnade. Thousands of people flowed in and out of the Plaza Mayor daily, chasing their ambitions, money, the survival, and the fame. This was the centre and the heartbeat of Miramar.

He scavenged in his brown cotton bag in the hope of a few remaining bread crumbs. He searched every inch, every corner, and even scratched the whole bottom, but there was not a crumb. Famine was foreign to Paco, and not something he felt he could learn to tolerate. He had no money and nothing to sell, and needed to do something to ease the audible growls of his churning stomach.

After some wandering, he saw a young boy in a tattered jersey that had once been white, selling newspapers at the Cabildo's corner. The kid would befriend the passer-bys, apply a dash of his streetwise charm, and exchange a paper for a penny. Soon his stock had almost disappeared.

'I can certainly match that,' Paco thought.

"Hey kid," Paco shouted to the newspaper boy. He approached him from behind.

"Newspaper?" the kid turned around in a flash. He was fast, sharp, alert, and tiny like a flea.

"No thanks," Paco replied politely. "Actually, I want to know how much money you make selling papers."

The kid flashed a look of surprise. Paco wasn't dressed like a street kid or like someone who wanted to sell papers.

"Well… I get a small commission on the amount of papers I sell. This is *my* corner of the plaza. My corner is my fortress. I defend it at all costs. In *my* corner, I have the *regulars* who always buy from me. I also have people who buy when they don't need a copy: so it's my job to convince them and get the sale. Then, there are those who completely ignore me. I am invisible to them. Then, the worst kinds of people are those that swear at me." The little boy frowned but then offered Paco a smile, "How I see it, is that you win some and you lose some. It's a game of numbers. That's the exciting part of the game of selling."

The kid certainly had a way with words.

"Some people are always angry and I've learnt their mood has nothing to do with me," he continued.

"You certainly have a great deal of patience!" Paco replied. "I'd probably break my guitar on their heads."

The kid smiled; he had street-wisdom written on his face. "I just don't take things personally. What people do or say is a reflection of them, not me."

"I still don't think I could tolerate that," Paco replied. Then his stomach churned again. It hurt to be so hungry. He was desperate and willing to try anything to put some food in his stomach.

"So, where are the newspaper's offices?" Paco asked.

"From the north side of the Cathedral, walk two blocks east and then turn left… they are in the middle of the block," the kid explained, still wondering what a classy guy like Paco wanted to do selling newspapers.

"Thanks for the tip kid," Paco said as he turned away.

"*Don't take things personally, right?*" He said smiling, walking backwards, but still looking at the kid.

The kid smiled back and nodded.

"You got it."

7   'My First Day'

Paco arrived outside the chaotic printing offices of the most popular and widely distributed newspaper in Miramar, *'La Voz'*. Dozens of youngsters appeared from both sides of the street, lined up in order of arrival, received their cargo, and left carrying their bundles in a hurry. It was a human beehive; the perfect painting of organised chaos.

Paco was nervous. He'd never held a job before and had no idea how things operated in the real world. Up until the previous night, he had lived in a dream-like, sheltered existence, and now it was time to grow up, roll up his sleeves, get his fingers dirty, and survive.

"You'd better make me some money kid," a cigarette-laden voice shouted.

"Yes, Señor Barrantes. Don't worry. I'll return a little later to get my second bunch, I promise," a young, fear-stricken kid stuttered, before dashing off to fetch a fresh batch of newspapers to take away. The tightly-packed batch was close to half his total height.

Paco took a few measured steps closer to the dispatch but still kept his distance: the sudden smell of warm, freshly-printed paper and black ink overwhelmed him. There was an incessant whirring and stamping from the countless printing machines. Standing close to the factory was sensory overload.

"What do you want kid?" Barrantes, the human chimney said, looking at a half-frightened Paco; even his attempts at being friendly sounded like a threat. He looked like the kind of man who chewed cigarettes as a pastime.

"I'm looking for work," Paco replied, hiding a slight tremble, "got anything for me?" He gulped, inflating his chest, trying to look confident.

Barrantes inspected Paco by looking him up and down; the same way Samuel inspected a slave before a purchase. He was a sizeable man with dirty, brown pantaloons held together just above his protruding belly with a firm piece of string. His shaggy, curly eyebrows wore a permanent frown and his grey moustache was tainted yellow from constantly puffing nicotine. He had a tendency to lick his lips after every sentence.

"As long as you make me money," Barrantes snapped. "I get plenty kids showing up around here, but they turn out to be nothing but bums… do you really want to sell papers?" He boomed without waiting for Paco to reply. "Then you have until nightfall to sell what I'm going to give you. If you don't, forget about tomorrow, there'll be no job here for you."

Paco felt a rush of immobilising fear lodge in his spine. He had never sold anything before, and above all, greater than the fear of failing, was the fear of rejection. Having what he wanted, when he wanted it, most of his life, he had experienced mostly successes; life had been easy and effortless up until that moment. He did not feel equipped to deal with failure.

Besides this, right now he was dealing with a man who offered him no second chances, and failure to meet his demands would mean starvation. For a fraction of a second, Paco felt like running as fast as his legs would carry him, back to the hacienda, but Doña Lucia's voice kept returning, *'you will never receive a load that you can't carry, my child… find your own voice and get on that horse… and don't ever let fear make your decisions…'*

"I'll take them," Paco said with confidence. "I'm going to sell all your newspapers."

He lifted his chin and swallowed… more than his pride.

"Very well," Barrantes said, licking his lower lip, "we close at seven in the evening… sharp. You'd better be here empty-handed and with two coin-filled pockets, got it?"

"Got it," Paco replied, left eye twitching, palms sweating. He wiped off the excess moisture from his hands onto his trousers and approached his new, cigar-masticating boss.

A muscular, vest-clung loader threw a large stack of papers bundled together in brown string at Paco's feet.

It made a loud thump as it landed.

Paco's eyes widened when he realised the immensity of the task ahead. He looked at Barrantes with an alarmed expression, hitched the papers, strapped his guitar tightly, nodded to his boss, and set out to find a street corner.

He steered his way through the crowded and manic streets, but every well-positioned corner had a vendor on it. The competing newspaper boys gave the new kid in town nothing but threatening glances: a good corner meant the difference between eating or staying hungry, working or begging. No one was going to relinquish their bread and milk without combat - this was the jungle - dressed in concrete, steel, and adobe; and the law was to fight to the death. Paco knew he was strong, could fight and win himself a strategic corner, but he did not want to make enemies this early. So he strolled on, further from the busy city centre, eyes like a hawk, hunting for the nearest available piece of street realty, and a chance at survival.

Ahead of him stood an imposing limestone-coloured building with elegant, tall doors, and a sumptuously-sculpted balcony. The moderately transited corner next to it appeared available, and Paco ran at full speed to lay his claim. Liveried, cigar-smoking gentlemen entered and exited the sophisticated, burgundy-carpeted foyer. Fancy horse-carriages transporting peeking Tapadas stopped to deliver their precious cargo. A man balancing what resembled something between a coffin and a woman's silhouette, whistled his way past a gentleman sporting a dark hat at the portico, and into a velvet-lined salon adorned with polished, brass rails. The place inspired an air of culture and refinement. Roused from his daydream, Paco looked up and noticed a vertical sign tucked above the ornamented stone balcony that he had missed earlier. It read 'State Theatre'.

Once settled on the corner opposite the lavish entrance, Paco decided it was time to start with a deep breath of the capital's worn-out air. Fearing theft, he did not veer too far away from the lumbering batch of newspapers. He was new to the city and an easy prey for streetwise goons, and decided to follow his father's early childhood advice: 'don't trust anybody.'

Samuel's philosophy hindered him from reaching the other corners, and as a result, he missed many potential customers passing by. Only one thing was certain: in less than five hours he needed to sell at least fifty newspapers.

So far in twenty minutes: *nothing.*

An hour passed.

The stack of newspapers remained two feet high.

A fancy-looking man in a tailored, black suit bought a copy, but had to return it since Paco did not have change. Paco almost swore at him in frustration, then swallowed his words instead - just when he was about to spit them in the typical Alegría manner.

It was getting late, and by the second hour, Paco had only sold five papers. Exhausted, hungry and desperate, he sought refuge in the dingy depths of a dark alley opposite the theatre. A foul-smelling rivulet next to the rubbish heap of a fancy restaurant - divided the alley in two halves, just like the river that divided the inhospitable city. His fighting spirit was rapidly waning and all he wanted to do was to sit down, cry, and let the anger bleed out of his heart. At that moment, Paco cursed his luck. He felt like a failure. At his lowest point, his inner voice was wilting.

Doña Lucia had taught him how to fight and persevere, and how to listen to his inner guidance, but he forgot the lessons in that moment of weakness. In a merciless world that didn't recognise his existence, Paco felt alone and betrayed by his upbringing. He thought The One had abandoned him and there was nothing left but to cry; at least the tears were his. Sitting next to a high stack of unsold papers, guitar in hand, he sang the saddest song his semi-defeated heart could muster.

"That's a sad song, son," someone said, "but nevertheless, beautiful." The stranger had an unusual foreign accent. Paco could not decipher where it came from.

Paco automatically wiped the tears from his bulging eyes, cleared his throat with a tenacious gulp, and borrowed a stern voice. In a commanding tone that did not belong to him, he asked the foreigner what he wanted. He believed crying was for the weak.

"I don't want anything young man – I think it is you who is seeking," said the foreigner sitting on the opposite wall near a pile of litter, just a few feet away. The sun was on its journey to the horizon, and in-between the tall walls of the alley, it was difficult to discern someone in the dark, even a few feet away.

Paco did not answer.

"All I gave you was a compliment… and you didn't accept it," the foreigner reiterated.

Something in this barely visible man's voice was soothing… it reminded Paco of the honey tones of Doña Lucia's speech when his heart was broken. He opted to let his guard down.

The foreigner sat in a crouching position, resting his forearms on his knees, with his head in his hands. Paco could not see his face, only the fragments of a fading, grey ponytail, tattered, brass bracelets on his wrists, and a green-and-black poncho.

"What is it that you seek, son?" the foreigner said politely, "if I may ask?" He kept his head down.

His voice was so soothing, there was no way Paco could resist it.

"I need to sell all these newspapers by nightfall and I've only sold a few so far. I've run away from home in order to pursue my destiny and follow my dreams, but the world has only been cruel in return. I'm hungry, thirsty, and alone in this city. I don't know anyone and I'm starting to grow desperate. If I don't sell all the remaining newspapers in the next two hours, I'll have nothing to eat and nowhere to sleep tonight. As you can hear, I'm in a precarious situation, and I just need a break," Paco said in a trembling voice.

Outside, life continued as was usual. People trundled past, tracing their own paths and facing their unique challenges, not aware that just a few feet away, tucked away from the eyes of the world in a dark alley, a life-changing conversation was taking place between two strangers. The world did not stop. It did not take notice. It simply brushed along, like it had always done.

"I see, son…" was the foreigner's reply.

"Is that all you have to say?" Paco reacted angrily, "maybe I should go. I knew opening up to you was a waste of my time." He placed *Morena* with great care against the wall and stood half-way up from the filthy alley floor.

"Maybe that's what is stopping you from selling the papers, son," the foreigner replied swiftly.

"What do you mean?" Paco did not know whether to sit back down again, or remain standing as he was, ready to leave.

"Your anger, your temper, your arrogance, your ego – you're driven by all the things that disguise *who you really are.*"

"What do you mean? Be specific. I have no time for conundrums," Paco replied. His tone was authoritative.

"All these elements form part of the one condition that stops human beings from reaching their true potential - *fear,*" the foreigner said, still not showing his face.

"Let me explain," he cleared his throat. "You can live and work in two states: either in fear or in Love… and right now you're choosing the first. Tell me something son, how are you selling the newspapers?"

"Well, I stand on one corner, close to the bunch, and approach the people that walk near me."

"Why don't you venture onto the other corners?"

"I can't," Paco replied. "I'm afraid someone is going to steal my papers. There is nothing I can do about that."

There was a brief moment of silence.

"You've just said the *magic word,* son." The foreigner's way of pronouncing 'magic' sounded like '*masheik*'.

"What?" Paco was confused, "What magic word?"

"*Afraid,*" the foreigner reiterated. "You're afraid to venture outside your comfort zone because you're *led* by fear," he added.

"Think about it… who is going to steal a heavy bundle of newspapers from a strong, young man like you? Can you see that your fear makes no sense? Who taught you not to trust?"

Paco's heart stopped. One simple question had suddenly stopped the sound of the moving traffic, the foul stench of the rivulet, the movement of the passing clouds.

One simple question.

In a moment of light, he realised that his father's fears were halting his efforts of moving forward - and that's exactly what Samuel wanted - for his son to live in a world where he would never venture outside the family hacienda.

"How you see the world, people and situations is a reflection of what is happening in your mind, a reflection of what's inside you. Look at yourself and see if the world is a place of fear or a place of possibility. When you are feeling good, when there is happiness inside you, everything on the outside looks promising, everything is perfect. Focus on the inside and the outside automatically changes."

The foreigner continued, "Why don't you befriend one of the neighbouring shop owners and ask them to look after your papers? Then you could target every street corner. There are some good people still left in the world, son. You just need to look through the eyes of Love in order to find them."

Paco realised he was not looking at Miramar through his own eyes, but through the eyes of his father… and that was why the capital looked so sinister and suspicious.

"*What do you seek, son?*" The foreigner asked again.

"I want to follow my dreams and fulfil my destiny in the arms of music. I dream that one day the world will sing with me. I want nothing more than that. I've seen it in my dreams and forged it in my heart since I was a child," Paco replied.

"Then use your talents to fulfil your mission – starting *now*," the foreigner said, passionately.

"How do I do that?"

"The answer lies within you, son. Only you will know. I cannot tell you what to do. The only thing I can tell you is this: you will achieve anything if you let your talents and inner voice guide you. They are gifts from The One and you should use them, not leave them to waste. Everyone is different. Some are good with numbers, others good with words; some make things out of nothing, while others lift our spirits, cure our bodies, defend us, give us what our bodies yearn for, and produce what we need in order to survive. In other words, *everyone has a gift to give to the world*. Right now, *you need to use yours*."

"I don't know what mine is!" Paco sounded even more desperate.

"Go back into the world with no fear. You will soon find out," the man replied in a gentle, yet commanding tone. "You're not selling any newspapers here."

Paco snatched Morena and the remaining papers and rushed back into the city chaos. Lost in careless excitement, he even forgot to thank the man who had just baptised his renewed confidence and purpose. He still had no idea how he was going to accomplish the task; the only thing he knew was that if he did not jump into the water, he was never going to learn to swim.

Miramar was brushed with the colours of sunset when Paco approached the owner of a *Pulperia*, or brandy store, on the corner opposite the theatre. The bigger-than-life, friendly, cigar-smoking Italian immediately agreed to look after Paco's remaining stash of tardy papers. With improved mobility and intention, Paco soon targeted the four, evenly spread-out street corners, minimising his stock to almost half - with thirty minutes remaining before seven.

'How do I use *my gifts?*' Paco kept asking himself. He opened a newspaper and read an announcement written in bold letters, "*Tonight at the State Theatre: Opera Premiere with famous Italian Soprano, Signora Fonsetti. Not to be missed.*"

"I can sing," was Paco's intuitive reaction.

'That's my gift… now think properly… how do I use my gift of singing to sell newspapers… think Paco, think…what if I… what if I sing the…' Paco scratched his head in search of a solution.

"I got it!" he exclaimed. "*What if I sing the news headlines?*"

He felt his heart explode in harmony. The decision felt good. If something felt right, this was it. Paco's doubts began to dissipate. All it took was a matter of seconds.

Paco rushed off to collect the remaining papers from his new Italian friend.

"How do you say *thank you very much* in Italian, señor Matteo?" he asked, trying to impersonate a friendly, Italian-like smile.

"*Molto Grazie*," Matteo responded from behind the counter in his deep, Neapolitan accent. He swiftly handed the excited newspaper boy the unsold papers.

"Well, then… molto grazie, señor Matteo," Paco said as he rushed off towards his new corner of dreams.

During the years that Paco had secretly attended his weekly and sometimes bi-weekly lessons, Doña Lucia had taught him the art of musical improvisation. In what an hour ago had been a corner of tears, he sang the morning and afternoon headlines: from the lack of prospective changes in anti-slavery laws, to the anticipated spectacle Signora Fonsetti would deliver that night, to the new park unveiled by the city of Miramar's Mayor.

This pleased the theatre's owner, as curious passer-bys strolled in to purchase tickets for the evening's show. Matteo smiled as he observed Paco work his magic from his Brandy shop. The entrepreneurial young man's initiative had curious onlookers buy his steadily-decreasing newspapers in a rush. Paco's beautifully trained voice enthralled the passing crowds and by five-to-seven, his stock had vanished.

He sold his last paper, strapped *Morena* securely on his back, and entered the dingy alley frantically searching for the foreigner in the green-and-black poncho.

"I just needed to say thank…," he said as he reached the rubbish heap, but the alley was deserted.

With two heavy, coin-filled pockets, he rushed the ten or so street blocks to the newspaper's office before it closed. Exhausted from sprinting halfway across town, he shouted at Señor Barrantes just as he was about to close the depot door.

"Señor, wait!" Paco screamed, bending down with both arms resting on his knees from exhaustion.

"You're damn late," Barrantes answered, licking his lips. He was enjoying the last, nicotine-crammed puffs of a dying cigarette. He threw the butt on the floor and extinguished it with his right shoe.

"*Not bad for my first day*," Paco barely uttered. He was panting, sweat poured down his wet sideburns.

"Don't be cheeky, son," Barrantes replied. He wore a rare smile, buried between his frowning brows.

"Come inside. Let's count your money and see what you've earned."

8 Justice, Freedom and Equality

Single days turned into weeks, and Paco's reputation spread in the capital city, acquiring a large and loyal number of newspaper buyers. He became known as '*The Singing Newsboy*', and was a permanent fixture outside the now-booming State Theatre. Curious onlookers arrived from all corners of Miramar to listen to the latest happenings in their city and the world, sung by the dashing, young baritone.

Luckily, for him, his increased commission from sales allowed him not another moment of hunger or insomnia. He no longer slept inside the San Lazarus church shelter, where the city's destitute, drunkards, and sick took nightly refuge, but in a hostel, where he enjoyed a well-deserved night's rest.

Success, often, also attracts jealousy and mamba-green envy. As Paco's fame swept across the capital's dusty streets, so too did his enemies.

Paco sold the last newspaper from his record eight batches that day, and collected the day's earnings his trusted friend Matteo had safeguarded behind the counter for him. The brass gas-lamps on some of the street corners were burning for at least ten minutes and there was not much walking traffic; it was a typical, Miramar, Monday night.

"Thank you signore," Paco received his monies, "*buona notte* to you. I'll see you tomorrow bright and early," he told his friend.

"Si, Paco," Matteo replied with gusto, "see you tomorrow my friend… ciao!"

The Singing Newsboy had not only increased the walking-traffic to the theatre's corner, but also its profits, and the surrounding traders considered Paco to be their *lucky charm.*

On the way back to the newspaper depot, Paco heard an unusual cry slice the night's fragile hush. It was an uncannily windy night, one could almost taste the scent of the sea. The flames within the streets lamps flickered with the intruding, moist, ocean gust. Shadows passing beneath the flickering lamps, morphed into ghastly shapes that floated along the street floors and walls, leading up to the city centre.

In one of the many, secluded alleys that carved the gigantic city blocks into halves and quarters – he heard a woman in distress.

"Please leave me alone, I said… don't you dare touch me, you savage."

In a murky alleyway, a woman pushed off her pursuer with certain intent. In the veil of darkness, he noticed the distinguishable silhouette of a tall man.

"Leave her alone or you'll have to deal with me," Paco ordered as he entered the desolate alley. He clenched his fists and tightened Morena firmly on his back. When necessary, it was an Alegría trait to resort to violence. Alejandra taught him to defend a woman's honour at all costs. Paco inflated his chest with bravado. When caught in a confrontation he was the replica of his father.

"Can't you see I'm busy?" the tall man replied, laughing. The occasional ray of light from a swinging street lamp revealed a heavily-scarred young man with a missing eye and a mouth filled with brown teeth, typical from chewing tobacco. His breath was torrid.

"You can go," the tall, scarred man pushed the woman aside with an unlikely soft touch and a sulphur-winning smile. She ran away from her pursuer, her dress blowing with a tunnel-like effect in the windy alley, and disappeared into the desolate Miramar streets.

Paco knew then, he was in deep trouble – he just did not realise how deep. The moment felt like an uppercut to the solar plexus.

"What do you want," Paco asked instinctively, "my money?"

The man smiled - his gaze fixed on Paco as though he were an angel he needed to deplume.

"Look behind you," the man remarked laughing; he either had a sick sense of humour, or wore a constant evil grin on his face.

Paco slowly turned around, without shifting his gaze from his adversary.

There were concrete footsteps on the cobbled alley as two shadows approached in stealth. He could feel his heart racing in his semi-open chest, thumping in his ears; cold sweat trickling down his back. The adrenalin swelled in his veins. 'I'm trapped.'

"If you want my money you can have it," Paco exclaimed to the scarred man who appeared to be the mastermind. As expected, he burst out again in diabolical laughter. His smile rapidly crumpled into a sinister grin.

"We're going to teach you a lesson, and then take your money," he replied as he spat on the floor.

Paco loosened *Morena* in one swift move and carefully placed it on a heap of construction bricks. He made sure his beloved guitar would be out of harm's way; even if he was not.

He could not control his reactions in the face of unpredictability, and his legs began to tremble. A tiny rivulet of blood began to trickle silently, from his heart. He tried to make certain the assailants did not notice this; but the darkness helped to obscure it.

His life was hanging from a thread; and he was in desperate need of a shield for his heart. He tightened his fists, ready for battle, but his grip kept loosening from the excess sweat.

He looked up and saw an eternity of brick wall. There were broken windows, but no sign of life within. The alley was silent except for the cat-sized rats slithering among the broken and hanging metal pipes that criss-crossed above them.

The young goons knew the darkest corners of the city better than a veteran plague of city bats, and tonight, they'd selected the perfect spot.

Paco felt a heavy blow to the back of his head and fell down in an instant.

Then it all happened so fast. Down on all fours, and disoriented from the blow, he barely distinguished the six feet kicking him from all sides. On instinct, he covered his fragile heart as tight as he could. A barrage of kicks struck his body. One connected with his clenched jaw and he heard a loud crack, and the grinding of teeth. He bit his tongue. Blood flooded his mouth, throttling him. In an attempt to breathe, he spat some out. He battled for each precious gulp of air as another kick battered his midriff. He was close to passing out… and felt life departing.

Six feet soon turned to eight. "I must be hallucinating from all the blows," he decided. His eyes were buried in a blind, scrunched-up frown from the pain.

Faster than the speed of thought, the scarred criminal fell to the floor like a cold brick, as the unmistakable sound and smell of gunfire echoed throughout the alley.

Paco searched his body, his muddled actions desperately trying to locate the bullet hole - to end the pain, the pouring blood. He crawled up, lying on the dank street floor, and supported his throbbing back against the damp alley-wall.

He touched the gap in his heart – but there was no bullet wound.

The former chaos had in a spark turned into an implausible silence. The sound of moans and groaning and the occasional jarring of bones shifted into the wild, desperate efforts of his breath, wrangling to suck oxygen to his depleted lungs.

An eerie stillness enveloped him, smothering the scene in a murky haze.

There was nothing left but the grey odour of gunpowder, the unconscious robber, and a pair of brand-new, fine, leather boots beside him.

"Are you all right?" a voice whispered.

Paco took some time to gather his wits together. He was still making sure that no part of his body had caught the stray bullet.

"You are not hit," the voice said. It was reassuring and confident, "that was a warning shot."

Paco was caught in a web of shock. His legs were a trembling mass of flesh and bones from the surge of adrenalin, a high from this self-produced drug.

"Come, get up. Hurry… before the police arrive."

The Samaritan held Paco by the left arm and helped him from his position against the wall with one painful tug. The robbers had venomously assaulted every inch of Paco's body. He placed his muscular right arm under Paco's left shoulder, and aided him as he staggered to the end of the alley and into the quiet Miramar streets.

"Don't faint on me kid," the man said, "come to your senses."

Paco was still seeing double.

"You don't want to be here when the police arrive… they are as dangerous and corrupt as the robbers."

"Come on… stay with me…"

Paco had no idea where he was.

"My guitar… and the money," Paco whispered. He attempted to leap from the sofa but the young Samaritan held him back and pinned him down.

"I have them both… calm down and rest," he said, observing Paco with an unspoken, yet measurable degree of sympathy. Paco still looked baffled.

"My name is Patricio de Romana," he smiled, "you were lucky… I was looking for you."

"What happened?" Paco asked, feeling the after-effect of a heavy thump to the back of his head, which had begun to spread south.

"You were attacked by three criminals who wanted something more than your money," Patricio said, "I have a feeling they were trying to intimidate you."

Paco looked bewildered. He waited for Patricio to carry on with his version of the story.

"You're the talk of the town kid… people say you sing with passion, you sell more newspapers than any other vendor, and I can logically deduce that you may have created some enemies on your way up… in other words, some of your peers don't like what you do and they want you out… it's just business," Patricio explained.

Paco gazed at the ceiling as if trying to find hidden answers between the old, wooden beams. He was still new in the city; an innocent lamb. He couldn't comprehend why people would do that.

"You're making more money than the other boys and they clearly want you out of their turf. You're taking away their business. Can you understand that?"

Paco nodded. "Thank you." He paused for a moment to take a deep breath. Every breath was painful. Every breath was a necessary evil. "I'm Paco," he stretched out his bruised arm as a sign of gratitude. It trembled.

"I know. I've heard all about you," Patricio replied.

Patricio had the face every rich or want-to-be-rich Miramar bourgeoisie mother wanted their sons to have: elegant with piercing, light eyes beaming with confidence, a commanding presence - all deeply seated in the classic features of Michelangelo's David. His light-blond hair perched perfectly on his manly crown and his skin was like porcelain.

The way he spoke gave away his privileged background and there was a certain Alexandrian arrogance in his eloquent speech. He leaned back in his chair, holding his chin, and inspected Paco. He had a habit of flicking his voluminous hair into its habitual style with the same hand that supported his chin.

"Why did we run away from the police?" Paco asked. It didn't make sense to him. His fear beat his curiosity.

Patricio smiled, sarcasm imprinted in his eyes, "They are a bunch of no-good, disgusting, worthless, and useless thieves." "Shouldn't we've stayed to tell them what happened?"

Patricio's smile disappeared in a second. It reminded Paco of the way his father's smile would vanish before he wanted to curse.

"Listen Paco, they are *your* enemies… they would have taken your money and left, and if you were lucky - saved an additional beating from them too," Patricio explained.

"They don't care about the citizens they are supposed to protect. It's time for you to realise that they are corrupt and dirty officials whose only concern is their personal gain in the work they do for this damn government… you were lucky I was there."

"Thank you Patricio," Paco reiterated.

"It's okay, don't mention it… simply understand that they are the enemy, that's all… one day you'll see it for yourself. You're still new in this damn city. I hope you don't get to learn your lessons the hard way."

Patricio stood up from a worn, leather chair and walked towards the bolted exit door of the living room. The door looked strangely more secure and solid than an average living-room door. Three sturdy, bronze locks on the upper, middle and lower sections kept the door protected from the outside.

"Please rest tonight. Tomorrow you can leave."

"Where am I?" Paco asked again.

"I can't tell you right now… it's a secret," Patricio half-smiled.

"I'm being serious Patricio, what is this place?" Paco replied authoritatively, "Where am I?"

"I'm not joking Paco," Patricio's smile disappeared in a flash. He needed to assert his position, "it's a long story. Rest, and when you're feeling better, I'll explain everything in detail."

"By the way," Patricio sidled closer to Paco and innocently pointed his finger at his chest hole, "you have a trickle of blood on your shirt right there…"

Paco looked down at his semi-opened shirt and instantly covered his heart, in the same way he did when his father was about to beat him.

"Don't touch me!" he shouted instinctively.

Patricio immediately retreated his hand, "What's the matter?" he said, surprised at Paco's reaction.

"It's nothing, it's nothing," Paco said, exasperated. "I'll talk to you in the morning… good night… and thank you."

Paco woke up just before dawn. His body knew the exact minute when to stop dreaming, open his eyes, and get ready for the day's toil. He lit a used, thin, red candle, washed his face with the fresh water inside a wooden-bucket (that was placed on top of the only table in the room), and attempted to remove the tiny blood spot from his shirt, to reduce the visibility of the blemish with lifelong skill. His attire clearly marked the brutal episode of the night before. Filthy smears from a battalion of shoe stains were scorched into the white and tattered cotton.

The sun in Miramar was still lost in a lazy dream, and even at dawn, the city appeared wrapped in a mantle of darkness.

Holding the melting candle, he opened a door that led into an outside patio. A beautiful, hand-carved, stone fountain stood gracefully in the centre. It was overflowing with hanging, green moss and exotic plants. In a strange way, it resembled a miniature-sized Garden of Babylon. Above him to the right, an intricately-carved, wooden balcony overlooked the stone-encrusted patio from a venerable height.

Paco took a deep breath of fresh morning air. He could feel the blows from the previous night all over his body; a hammer pounding his joints in hellish, five-second intervals.

He was hungry and unlocked a kitchen door looking for something to pacify his hunger. He had not eaten in over half a day.

Inside, resting on a whitewashed oak table in the centre of the room, he found slices of half-eaten, stale bread and a bowl filled with ripe cherimoyas. He ripped open a cherimoya. There was no time to waste. He became an animal, tearing the fruit with his teeth, and shredding the soft, green-and-black skin with his fingers, which were beginning to resemble talons. The juicy, delicious fruit became strawberries and cream, spiritualised; the pulp of the cream-coloured flesh slowly melting in his mouth.

From the kitchen window, he saw three horses in the narrow alley that divided some of the houses in the city. He took another bite of the heavenly fruit, allowing the holy liquid to consume his senses, and closed his eyes in sheer ecstasy.

"How are we feeling comrade?" a familiar voice disrupted his daydream.

Paco jumped back in fright.

He turned around in an instant, cherimoya juice dripping from his lips onto the tiled, patterned floor. Three perfectly-aligned drops of sweet juice adorned the red-and-black tiles near his feet.

"Up bright and early… you must Love your job," Patricio said, edging closer to him.

Patricio had appeared as a ghost; silent, unexpected, and uninvited.

Paco's heart was beating fast, but Patricio's friendly voice was reassuring.

"I need to go back to my post," Paco said, calming down.

"I need to pick up today's papers and return the money from yesterday's sales. The printing manager must be furious wondering what happened to me and his money last night." Paco looked visibly worried. "Now, where am I? You promised you would explain everything when I felt better… and now is the time. I feel better."

Patricio looked at Paco from the other side of the food-laden table.

"You owe me kid… so I need you to promise me something. My security and that of every person who relies on me is at stake. I need you to give me your word and *to us your word means your life*."

Paco did not hesitate, "Yes Patricio, I know I owe you for last night and if it wasn't for you, I probably wouldn't be here today. You have my word, which represents my life. Now, where am I and why the secrecy? Please explain."

Patricio placed both arms on the table and leaned towards Paco. His stance was serious and defiant.

"You're in a secret hideout," he said firmly without the trace of a smile. There was no going back for Paco now. He was in.

"I helped and brought you here because I believe you have what it takes to change the minds and hearts of many people."

"Change their minds and hearts towards what?" Paco replied.

"Justice, freedom, and equality."

"What do you mean?" Paco asked, confused. He had no clue what Patricio was talking about.

"Since our country's independence from the Old World invaders, some of us have enjoyed the fruits that come with freedom. Unfortunately, this is not the case for everyone. The principles and values that hold this nation together shed the blood of countless heroes. A river of life was wasted in the struggle for Independence… and for what?"

"Millions have not received what they fought and died for… now, do you think that's fair?" Patricio's rhetoric was far too perfect to have been rehearsed; it came from the heart.

"No, it definitely isn't," Paco responded immediately, agreeing wholeheartedly.

"Of course it's not fair! It is unjust and unconstitutional," Patricio's fist hit the table. His fist was a five-pound mallet, a judge's gavel, an executioner's guillotine. His body and neck tensed as he leaned aggressively towards Paco like a hunting gargoyle before flight. The veins in his arms almost exploded from the pressure he exerted on the table. He spoke with passion lightly dressed in a veil of anger.

"The heroes hiding here believe we need to build a new nation; a place where everyone is equal, and where every man born under our nation's sun receives the same treatment and is paid justly for the labour they provide. *Slavery is the curse of this nation…* the old feudal system the landowners have enjoyed for so long does not belong in these modern times."

"Elected government leaders have delivered nothing but empty promises to those they should serve, and they are in fact, betraying the majority of the people that placed them in power.

They are traitors and need to be removed from their public posts, tried in court and executed for treason. However, we know this is not possible under our current system… and something needs to be done about it. Failing to take action will make *us* traitors."

Patricio took a strategic breath, "Are you a traitor to the land that conceived you, fed you, and protected you? Are you?" He raised his tone of voice and as he culminated his heated speech, he resembled a Roman Emperor addressing a packed Coliseum.

"Certainly not Patricio, I Love my country," Paco said, feeling a little intimidated but confident in his statement.

"That's why I need you to promise you will never reveal the location of this hideout, do you understand?" Patricio said.

"Yes Patricio, as I've said before, you have *my word*."

Patricio stood up. "Before we leave, I will bandage your eyes. You will only remove the bandage when I tell you to, is that understood?"

"Don't you trust me?" Paco uttered.

"I still don't know you, Paco… you'll have to earn that," Patricio replied.

"Go and get your belongings, we need to leave right now."

Paco ran back to the living room, gathered all his belongings, and met Patricio in the horse-packed alley at the rear of the house. They both mounted a saddled, muscular steed, just as the morning sun was ascending through the dispersing mist.

Patricio bandaged Paco with a long, dark handkerchief. He fastened it so tight that Paco could feel his head throbbing from the pressure it exerted around his temples. The streets outside were empty. Someone unlatched the side gate in haste.

Patricio immediately crashed the iron stirrups on the horse's side. The steed released an automatic wheeze, filled with saliva and vapour, from his muzzle and nostrils. In a cloud of dust, the two disappeared in the direction of the Plaza Mayor.

Totally blinded, Paco was aware of the horse's shoes beating against the gravel road, the bumping guitar against his back, and the thump of his beating heart.

"Take it off," Patricio instructed, pushing his horse to the limit.

Paco hastily untied the blindfold. It was so tight, he was gasping for air. He felt the blood draining from his face.

They were on route to the newspaper's offices, just in time for Paco to collect the new stock and return the profits from the night before. With no previous sense of direction and a horse in full gallop, there was no way Paco could guess the location of the hideout.

"I guarantee your security from gangs from now on," Patricio said, his words leaving his mouth at thirty-five miles per hour.

"How are you going to do that?" Paco asked.

"Don't worry about the details kid… just know what happened last night won't happen again."

"Thank you Patricio, I owe you," Paco said, innocently.

"How can I return the favour?"

Patricio never hesitated - he lived like an attacking hawk.

"Do you want to know more about us?" Patricio asked, "And about our cause and your role in it?" They were less than a few minutes away from their destination and he deliberately slowed down the horse in order to give Paco seconds to make up his mind.

"Yes, I do… I strongly sympathise with your cause Patricio. I've lived my whole life surrounded by slavery and injustice. I believe it's time for things to change," Paco replied.

"We will meet tonight then," Patricio replied. It wasn't a suggestion. It was more an order. That was his style.

"I will be outside your hostel at ten o'clock sharp. This conversation never occurred. Understood?" Patricio often used the word 'understood' as a way of assuring his role as leader and getting others to say 'yes.'

"Don't worry," Paco said, dismounting the horse. They were seconds away from the newspaper's offices. "I know how to keep my mouth shut. I will be as silent as a graveyard."

At exactly ten o' clock, as Patricio had promised, he appeared on the corner, blindfold in hand, his face as serious as a morning's death-sentence. Signalling for Paco to be quiet, he approached the hostel and slid in.

"Always walk about fifty paces behind me on the opposite side of the street. If anything happens, you don't know me. If the police stop you, tell them you've just played at a bar and you're heading home. Is that understood?"

"Yes," Paco nodded.

"As we near our destination I will turn right into an alley - follow me and make sure no one is trailing you. Once we are both inside, I will blindfold you. We'll then proceed to our final location."

The Miramar streets were deserted late at night. Occasional, patrolling police-officers or singing drunks meandered, invading the rare silence of the capital with the monotonous sound of their heels. Rarely did anyone exchange glances. There was some late-night activity near the Plaza Mayor from a handful of bars and the silent escapades of secret lovers, but as one exited the city centre, the perpendicular streets turned solitary as the gas lamps began to grow sparse.

Paco walked the designated distance behind Patricio, trying his best to look inconspicuous.

Patricio turned into the desolate alley.

Paco followed a minute later.

"Are you sure you weren't followed?" Patricio was stern.

"Very sure Patricio, the coast is clear."

"Turn around," Patricio's voice was as sharp as a lance, "time for the blindfold."

Patricio covered Paco's eyes and made sure the streets were deserted before crossing the road. From the far side, a comrade whistled like a night bird, signalling a safe passage. As they left the alley and turned a corner, they walked into a constricted, derelict cul-de-sac and entered the lair via a side door.

Everyone hushed for a minute – listening for any trace of footsteps outside.

All Paco could hear were the bare whisperings of what sounded like three men around him.

"It's safe," one of the men broke the silence.

One of them removed Paco's blindfold. As Paco adjusted his blurry vision, he saw through a haze, the faces of his new comrades. There was no turning back now.

"Follow us," Patricio ordered with a definite hand gesture.

The men stepped deep into the horse alley, past the kitchen and into the patio. They entered the living room where Paco had slept the night before, and into a small room crammed with Spanish and French antiques that exuded an odour of refinement and neglected old-money.

Somebody shut the door.

One of the men lifted a large carpet, revealing a hidden entrance into what looked like a cellar. They used no candles and knew the route perfectly well in the pitch-darkness.

"Watch your head," one of the men warned Paco.

Paco followed them down the cellar stairs. His hands desperately struggling to grip the invisible stair rails.

The last man entered, making sure the carpet adequately covered the secret entrance. He bolted the latch securely.

They met with a scene of dreary stillness.

"Justice, freedom, and equality," Patricio whispered.

Dead silence.

"Justice, freedom, and equality," voices tumbled softly from the invisible heart of darkness.

Someone struck a match and a single candle lit up the cellar. The smell of phosphorus permeated the air. From a single candle, the twenty or so people lit theirs until the room was alight with the flickering fire of youth and newborn patriotism.

"Everyone," Patricio moved to the centre of the room with natural grace and leaned on a small, wooden podium, "I want to welcome the newest member of our ranks… as from tonight, he's one of us; a fellow comrade and a brother. He believes in our manifesto and is here to grace us with his amazing talent.

Paco is both a songwriter and a singer and is currently the talk of the town: I'm sure some of you already know of him. His talent and passion will change people's minds and his songs will inspire a new generation of conscious citizens, willing to sacrifice what is necessary in order to create a country we are proud to call our own."

Everyone stared at Paco.

Some nodded, some smiled politely, and some remained unmoved. The flickering candles ebbed and flowed with the out-of-time inhalations and exhalations of the silent crowd.

"Come forward Paco," Patricio requested that the crowd move aside in order to allow Paco up to the podium.

"What's your surname?" he whispered.

Paco hesitated. He looked at Patricio dumbfounded. It wasn't a trick question.

"What's your surname Paco?" Patricio asked again, forcefully.

Paco panicked.

Patricio grew impatient, "don't make me look like a fool up here Paco, people are waiting," he muttered softly and squeezed Paco's arm with intent.

"It's, it's…" he mumbled. He sounded like a child with an oversized sweet in his mouth.

"It's… Alegría," Paco said half-heartedly in Patricio's ear.

Patricio rapidly regained control of the situation and addressed the wondering crowd.

"Everyone, please welcome… Paco Alegría."

About twenty well-spoken, young men greeted Paco with a light pat on the back or a firm handshake. There was no exchange of words and no applause: silence was of paramount importance. From the rear end of the crowded room, a petite, distinct shadow made its way up to Paco, and with a soft but confident voice broke up the regimented, male monotony.

"Welcome to our family," the young woman uttered. She was about Paco's age.

She smelled of sweet lavender and hyacinth, and her hypnotic perfume took Paco back to childhood memories lying in the flower-filled fields, looking up at the fluffy, racing clouds above the hacienda's winding river.

Mesmerised by her beauty and fragrance, Paco did not realise he was staring, wide-eyed like an owl. "Hello, I'm Paco it's great to meet you… here… well, tonight… thank you… yes, thank you, thank you very, very, very much for welcoming me to your family… I mean this family… I mean, our family now I guess," Paco mumbled his words and gulped as if he had just sipped a gallon of boiling tea through a straw. His heart was beating so fast it almost popped out of his chest and fell into a silver tray, ready to be sliced.

A trickle of ice-cold sweat slowly dribbled from his right temple, which fortunately went unnoticed by the room and the beautiful visitor, but to Paco it felt like a massive swell of salty, burning water was engulfing his entire face and neck.

Attracted by his unusual innocence, she smiled.

"I'm Milagros Del Valle," she said, stretching her slim hand towards his, "I can't wait to hear your work." She looked at him with her cat-like eyes, drawing every ounce of his attention into those two tunnels of charm and grace. Her eyes were so intriguing – almost sinful.

"I'm a budding poet and maybe we can work together… I was thinking… perhaps you can use some of my verses and give them a different life with your music." Her smile could stop a thousand angry hurricanes, he thought. Basking in the soft lights of the candles, Milagros had the most beautiful face he had ever seen. It was as if God had been born at that second.

In a material world, priceless diamonds are all carat and splendour. In his world… she was all eyes. They looked at Paco like two Antarctic glaciers approaching a small, adrift boat in a perilous ocean. To Paco, her eyes sparked the fragrance and chance of a not-so-distant Love.

"I'd Love to," Paco said before she finished her sentence; he was still lost, wandering in her wild beauty but slowly coming back to earth. "Yes, it will be an honour." He coughed.

Patricio rapidly took centre stage once more and asked for silence.

The room immediately grew quiet. He looked at everyone intensely, one by one, making sure that every person was in the palm of his hand. That was his nature: fierce, lethal, and all-encompassing.

"Comrades," he paused, "we live in a large country with a very sparse population, and we can only prosper with a wise and just economic administration. My father and his contemporaries have for years, attempted to develop a campaign destined to modify the political economy led by a few people, to no avail.

I believe we need a *call to arms* in order to restore our nation to the beloved principles of justice, freedom, and equality… the original values that founded our homeland. Throughout history, the most progressive cultures in the world have understood that in crucial times, war is required in order to live in peace."

Patricio fixed his hair and looked at the engrossed crowd with additional intent.

He appeared as a puma would, before the final assault on its prey.

"The Inca, rightful owners of our land and descendants of kings, have been broken by suffering, reduced to hating their tyrannical oppressors, and left worthless and servile by the continuous array of empty promises delivered by this government. The people that are supposed to protect them, further exploit them, obliging them to pay unjust taxes or face expatriation from their lands. The same applies to our brothers from Africa, who were stripped away of their freedom, forcibly removed from their lands, and made to work for no remuneration in our vast sugar-cane fields… Now tell me, where does it all end?" Patricio said, melting ire with every perfectly pronounced syllable.

"The present government is not going to change," somebody replied, "they have too many mixed interests with the rich landowners."

"That is correct comrade," Patricio responded in a second – he believed a true leader never fumbled. "After centuries of exploitation, our Inca brothers have grown unhappy - only excited to drown their misery with drunkenness, while the heartless oligarchy of landowners have profited from their melancholy and pain. In the same light, our brothers from Africa, spread all along the coastal region also suffer from this great injustice. It's time for us to change the direction in which our nation is sailing. It's time for radical change."

The room exploded in quiet chatter.

"So what can we do?" someone asked.

"Comrades, please calm down," Patricio reiterated with a hand gesture. The room automatically grew quiet again.

"There are only a few of us and as you know, we need like-minded people to join our nations' cause. Young, liberal groups are springing up everywhere but they lack something we can provide - passion."

Patricio's eyes drifted warily across the room, leaving his indelible mark in the air, "And this is where Paco's talent comes to the fore."

Heads began to turn towards Paco - the comment caught him off guard, and in the sea of serious glances, he found in Milagros' eyes a home filled with serenity.

"I've seen Paco in the streets, and people relate to him… he speaks to the masses."

Paco felt a rush of heat throughout his body, starting from his feet and spreading upwards, finishing on his itchy scalp.

"Paco, please stand up, I need to ask you something," Patricio ordered.

Paco stood up among the young liberals and tried to look as calm as possible… but inside, an inferno raged as his fragile heart pushed like a locomotive's engine up a Himalayan pass.

"Yes?" Paco replied, his mouth absent of moisture.

"We need to change the minds of the people. Our country needs all you have… are you willing to give it your all? Does our country deserve your all?"

Paco waited in silence for his new task.

He slowly nodded.

"Our country needs a new hymn. We need a song that everyone can relate to… it's time to join our nation in music. Nothing is more powerful than human emotion. We need a song that will speak for us all, a song that will live forever…"

Paco's heart was about to leave his chest again.

'What did I just get into?' His scalp itched yet he did not move an inch to scratch it.

"I know this is no small task comrade, but I firmly believe that you can achieve it. I believe you can create that song," Patricio said.

Paco looked at Milagros once again, and she nodded, small and delicate head movements. She dispersed his fears in an instant.

He immediately remembered his dream of the song. He then thought of Doña Lucia and all her teachings, and of all he had gone through in order to get to where he was now… and he understood the reason: everything he'd experienced up to that moment led him to that second. That very second.

"It will be an honour Patricio, and comrades," Paco said, with no hesitation,

"I will write this song."

Patricio smiled. Paco gulped.

The room nodded.

Life creates a circle of crucial moments that shape people's destinies. The sacrifices Paco had consciously made since he was seven years old, from learning to sing with Doña Lucia to the countless songs wasted and kept, pushed him on to the most critical moment of his musical life… writing a song that would unite his country.

However, life often possesses an interesting duality – on the one hand, many believed Paco could write this song; but on the other, there stood a young songwriter not completely sure he could accomplish such an important task… and of the two sides, the latter mattered the most.

Paco spent the next few weeks immersed in the task of writing a song that would proudly represent his country. 'With so many different people, cultures and tastes… how can I appeal to everybody?' he wondered. 'What was the one factor that would unite the hearts and minds of all people?' Thoughts such as these constantly invaded his mind and caused sleepless nights and endless runs of frustration.

Doña Lucia once said, "When you speak solely with your mind, another mind will understand you. But when you speak with your heart, millions of hearts will listen… and you will change the world." Lost in the obsession of producing the required song, just like Samuel obsessed about being the best Aguardiente producer in the capital, Paco forgot that essential lesson.

Torn pieces of paper lay scattered over the floor of his hostel room. His lyrics grew in anger and despair as he fruitlessly attempted to find the missing ingredient. Falling prey to Patricio's influence and vehement rhetoric, his work took on a highly political twist. Violence and a call to arms became his favourite themes, and he was keen to show Patricio the results of his efforts at the next secret meeting.

But not only was the song on Paco's mind, someone else had also tattooed in him an indelible mark…

Milagros Del Valle.

The provoking looks of the sensual Tapadas that frequented his now-famous singing corner, no longer attracted his attention. The only thought in his mind belonged exclusively to señorita Milagros Del Valle: her scent, charm, and goddess-like gracefulness were driving Paco delirious.

He could not wait for the weekly secret meetings in the hideout, and started to wear a little splash of cologne, behind the ears - as don Matteo explained, in order to impress his romantic dream-girl. For the first time, he caught himself looking at his reflection in both mirrors and windows and started using a new tooth powder, which allowed him to speak with confidence and practise his debonair, *'million-dollar'* smile.

As fervent and religious believers wait for Sunday Mass, Paco waited fervently for the weekly secret meetings to see his beloved. She was his holy host. Each day of the week felt like a year. It felt as if he had to live seven years in order to see her once a week.

His feelings for her were painted everywhere: they hung from the city roofs; melted from the lone street-lamps, howled like a pack of stray dogs and floated like the inconsolable mist wrapping the Miramar morning. His heart resonated like the hooves of horses on a pebbled road, and the shrouded cries of doves under a shadowy tree. She was everywhere; in every living moment, in every breath, in every sound, in every cell.

He felt her in the cool breeze sweeping his street corner, in his music, in the dawn, on the theatre balcony, in the moonlight, in the half-hidden faces of the Tapadas, in a cup of hot tea and even in his room - Paco carved her name in various strategic places so her presence was ever near.

He scratched off a knife carving on a wooden beam inside his hostel room, *'here lies the soul of Luis Gomez, broken-hearted for loving the unfaithful Panchita*

Lopez', and next to it carved an **M** inside a skew heart. He eventually realised that once you see someone's face constantly, even in your cup of hot tea, it was a sure-tell sign… he had fallen in Love.

Early in the mornings, he began singing Love ballads to all the headline news, creating a larger female fan base. Not even an overseas war or large-scaled invasion escaped his heart-felt crooning – he could even make the sinking of a passenger ship sound romantic.

As days and weeks passed, Paco and Milagros grew closer together and spent additional time collaborating. These were straight after the secret meetings, and evoked the envious glances of some of their comrades; not to mention Patricio's disapproving stare.

The last person to arrive closed the latch securely and replaced the carpet over the trapdoor by pulling a string. He then stepped inside the dark cellar.

"Comrades, I've been informed by an undisclosed source that apparently the government has heard of our meetings," Patricio announced.

The whispers in the room turned to deafening silence. The news fell as surprising and unexpected as Judgement Day. Among the uneasy glances, the young men attempted to grasp the hands of serenity, but in their bellies vicious butterflies crashed and burned.

"I don't believe there is a traitor among us. I know each one of you personally and I trust you all, but this is the information I have received from a reliable source at the San Lucas University. Anyone care to comment?" Patricio asked.

"Our support in places of higher learning is rapidly growing thanks to the groundwork of some of our comrades. Maybe somebody is getting too excited and not keeping his mouth shut," one of the young men responded, angry.

There was a great commotion and people stared at each other with suspicion. Everyone had somebody in the room they did not trust.

"Quiet! Please calm down comrades," Patricio remained in control, "this is no time to create division among us… we are surrounded by friends."

The suspicious looks diminished, and were soon replaced by concealed glances.

"We need to be extra vigilant. The next meeting will only take place in two weeks' time. Let's leave the storm to settle. Comrades let us not create unnecessary rifts among us. Our common cause and nation are bigger than our personal problems. Times like these test our loyalty and strength as a movement."

Despite the concern in Patricio's speech, as always, he was in control.

"Meeting's adjourned. Your silence and secrecy are of vital importance. Is that understood?" He closed with his favourite question, which was more of a command.

"Yes," the room replied in unison.

"Half of you must leave through the front door and half through the back. Milagros and Paco… please stay after the meeting. I need to talk to both of you."

Paco and Milagros made their way to Patricio as the other young men left the lair in silence.

The room emptied quickly.

"Yes, Patricio," Paco said while approaching Milagros.

"I wanted to speak to both of you about something that is of concern to me. I've seen the way you look at each…"

A deafening explosion rocked the floors above them and a ballistic symphony of screams and shouts shook the night. It felt like a typical Miramar earthquake, where floors rattled for a few seconds and the earth under foot moved in a hypnotic dance of dust. A barrage of gunfire sprayed bullets, and shouts of death fuelled the air.

"An ambush!" Patricio said instinctively, "they've found us!"

"What do we do?" Paco asked in a trembling voice. Milagros held his strong, muscular right arm.

Patricio disliked her show of affection – it wasn't the time for trivial matters of the heart.

"Follow me," Patricio swiftly replied, "there is a hidden door and tunnel that leads on to a backstreet."

Paco seized his beloved guitar in one hand, and grasped Milagros tightly in the other. The way he observed every inch of her face proclaimed what he felt in his heart; if he died, he wanted his last breath to touch her. She looked back at him, with a look that whispered a lifetime.

Patricio kicked open a secret back door hidden behind a false, silk draping. His flimsy candle flame lit up a spider-webbed, granite passage that reeked of bat droppings. The gunshots continued and the distinct stomping of boots trampled the floors of the hideout. The night reeked with the sound of violence. "Quickly, close it," Patricio ordered. "Close that damn door."

Paco shut the broken door as tight as he could and ran in the wake of Milagros.

It was only a matter of time before the blood-thirsty soldiers would find the latch into the cellar.

In the chaos, Paco had left his anti-government lyrics on the podium; each signed, "*Music & Lyrics by Paco Alegría*".

"I need to get my lyrics," Paco shouted to Patricio, who stopped halfway down the dark tunnel.

"If you want to kill us all… go and get them," he replied, and continued running towards the exit. "Don't be foolish Paco, we need to get out of here," Milagros, still holding his hand pulled an unwilling Paco deeper into the tunnel.

A fragile, rusty stepladder led up to a desolate backstreet corner.

Patricio lifted the heavy, iron latch slowly. He made sure there was no unwanted company. The corner was deserted. But not for long. They all had to hurry.

"I'll see you both in exactly two weeks… ten o'clock in the evening, in the alley behind the bar next to Santa Rosa's bridge," Patricio's speech was hasty, *"justice, freedom, and equality"*.

He climbed out of the tunnel and disappeared into one of the capital's many dark and dingy alleys. No one saw him.

"I'll be back for you Milagros," Paco whispered as he pulled her up onto the street, her dress eviscerated from the tattered pipes and rusty nails inside the tunnel.

"Before you go I want you to have this." She unclipped an enamel seashell necklace and gently placed it on Paco's sweaty palm.

"Think of me," she said, looking deep into his eyes, "I'll be thinking of you… *siempre*."

Paco felt their energies and palpitating bodies become one, and he kissed her. The sound of gunfire did not exist at that moment, only the feel of her soft lips and the scent of her ethereal perfume. Death was a forgotten detail; to kiss the lips of the one you loved for the first time… was the holiest of bonds. No rifle was powerful enough to destroy their moment; no army, and no prison.

They slowly opened their eyes, their faces so close. He wanted to kiss her as if it was his last breath, as if she was the last woman on Earth.

"Come this way," Paco gripped Milagros by the hand and pulled her towards the only escape route available.

Ahead, a young soldier mounted a mule with a wood-and-steel carbine resting on his shoulder, but was distracted by the stirrings on the far side of the street.

"What are we going to do now?" Paco said, "We are trapped."

Before Paco could react, Milagros ran towards the soldier, waving her arms in the air like a witch possessed. She was a voracious puma on the prowl.

"Whoa! Whoa!" She shouted at the top of her voice, frightening the young mule.

Instinctively, the terrified animal shook the startled soldier off its back. He flew into the air and tumbled to the ground, his carbine landing just a few feet away. The head of the young soldier made a loud, solid thump as it hit the unforgiving gravel.

Paco dashed towards Milagros as fast as he could.

The dizzied soldier regained consciousness and stretched out to snatch his weapon.

Paco seized it first, and in one swift move, hit the soldier in the forehead with the back of the compact, wooden butt. The young soldier's head fell back towards the ground, smashing heavily.

"Hurry, take the mule before reinforcements arrive," she ordered.

"You're coming with me Milagros," Paco exclaimed, "or they will kill us both." He stretched out his trembling hand towards her.

"Do you trust me?" Milagros asked.

"What do you mean?" Paco said, "what kind of question is that… especially now."

"Just answer yes or no."

"Yes, I do, why?" Paco replied, shaken.

"Take this mule and go now… they can't touch me."

"What do you mean they can't touch you?" Paco asked, desperately seeking light on his question.

"We have no time for this… if you Love me you will get on that mule now!" Milagros voice broke. A tear fell from her eye gathering speed with gravity as it dashed towards the ground. She did not cry… she exuded holy water.

Paco unwillingly mounted the mule. He looked at her, confused and not wanting to leave.

"I'm the President's daughter," she cried, "they can't touch me."

A squadron of violence-hungry soldiers appeared like a pack of starving wolves around the next bend. They had blood on their hands and they were on the hunt for more.

"Go Paco… please! They are going to shoot you… trust me damn it!" She screamed, feeling scared and powerless.

Paco sat motionless, speechless after her confession.

"You need to escape to the Andes until this blows over. They are going to go and look for you… I know my father's henchmen… they will brand you a traitor and sentence you to death with no trial."

"Paco, listen please… you need to escape now," she continued, growing more desperate with each wasted syllable, "I know you will sense the right time to return. We will find each other my Love… I believe in us… now please go! Goooooooo!"

A shot rang out. The killer lead missed Paco by less than a thread. The projectile left a clear, red mark on his neck from its proximity and heat. The gunman re-loaded.

Milagros slapped the mule in the rear with all her might and it began to move away from her in full gallop. Paco held the reins unwillingly and could only gaze back at Milagros and the approaching soldiers on her right-hand side.

"*Siempre, Siempre,*" Paco shouted as she put her hands up to the nearing militia.

The same soldier aimed his carbine at Paco, who was just under the range of target but close enough to suffer a mortal wound. As the man's finger made a last effort to squeeze the deadly trigger, Milagros pushed the rifle aside. The ricochet hit the ground close to Paco's feet and disappeared into the bridge ahead with a sharp, air-cutting sound.

As he left Miramar and galloped towards the outer city gates that led onto the Andes road, Paco could not stop thinking about Milagros' confession.

He found himself in a precarious position right then: a wanted man, a traitor in the eyes of the government, and deeply in Love with the president's daughter. He was in the heat of an out-of-control, white-knuckle, wild horse ride.

Xavier Saer

9 The Road to The Andes

Paco left the legions of expansive orange and cherimoya trees that flourished on the outskirts of Miramar and surrounded the city's periphery. From there they began to tread the rising slopes of one of the most mystical and colossal mountain ranges in the world: The Andes. Fearing the government soldiers on his track, he drove his tireless beast to the limit.

Paco had never ventured this far outside Miramar. As the vanishing lights of the capital faded in the distance, he felt joy for being alive. 'That last bullet could have killed me,' he thought, 'but I'm alive, and there's always an opportunity to return so long as I'm alive.'

His senses were heightened from barely escaping the killer bullet, and each new breath became a victory over death.

He felt the invisible touch of the mountain wind in his hair, and apart from the mule's galloping shoes, he was immersed in the solemn perfection of silence. Away from the overcast city sky, the stars smiled at each other, and Doña Lucia's bright star from the heavens, winked at her beloved pupil.

As he ventured deeper into the heart of his country, enormous armies of peaks, rose like gargantuan waves of dark granite escaping the freezing heights of The Andes. A sense of majesty and humility grew in Paco's heart as he rode in silence, on the edge of life.

When the song of darkness struck the midnight bell, Paco's eyes began to close.

On instinct he knew that he could not slow down; his escape was a miracle and he could not afford to give his enemies an inch of advantage. Once again, his spurs hit the animal's side with enormous intent, and both melted again into a silent escapade.

During the next few days, Paco encountered dozens of wandering Inca on their way down to the coastal capital. He befriended many of these weary, downhill travellers with music and song, and received everything he required for his journey. Equipped with a comfortable, cosy, red poncho, plenty of food supplies and the vital goatskin water bottle (he had received from the generous people), he slowly pierced the breathtaking corners of the low Andes with vigilance. Paco started to warm up to the idea that the world was also filled with kind and friendly people. Travelling had opened his eyes and heart to this experience. The way a stranger responded, reflected Paco's state of mind.

Paco and his loyal mule climbed higher into the ancient passes of a smiling paradise.

His eyes could not believe the beauty…

On the layered skirts of the heaven-kissed mountains rose the most glorious valleys he had ever seen. Warm sunrays danced gently across fields of maize and fruit trees. Flocks of sheep and goats played in the rarefied air, whilst loving Alpaca mothers protected their little ones. In the heart of this magical territory, he felt like a vagabond explorer on his maiden voyage.

As he approached the largest village he had yet encountered, he saw beautiful Inca girls dancing in the sun in their multicoloured dresses, arms around each other, leading their flocks onto immense, evergreen pastures. A magnificent river raged alongside the almost-ninety-degree escarpments, which longed for the moment when the sun irrigated their fields with majesty and an abundance of light. As he galloped towards the village, some of the girls giggled at the dashing young man on a trotting mule, guitar tied to his back, flashing his charming, *million-dollar smile*.

An elderly lady stooped to fetch water from a peaceful river with a ceramic dish. Llamas with red, yellow, and blue ribbons tied to their elongated necks carefully observed the strange passer-by. Men in knee-long pants and colourful ponchos mended a leaking mud roof. There was an air of serviceable duty with a sense of gratitude. The inhabitants seemed to have so little, but this didn't hamper the abundance of smiles. 'Quite the opposite of Miramar,' Paco thought.

An old man holding his skeletal frame - with two long, crooked branches, crossed paths with Paco.

His face painted a picture of endless years and his abundance of wrinkles etched deep, whispered rivers of tales and canyons of wisdom.

"Good morning señor," Paco greeted him from atop his mule respectfully, "what is the name of this village?"

The old man looked at him; history written in his eyes. He did not speak Spanish, but time and experience had taught him to read the lips of those who did not speak *Quecchua*, the ancient language of the Inca. Everyone spoke the same language - as long as one searched for the meaning behind the words.

"*Kaikay*," he replied, flashing a charming smile. He had no visible upper teeth and his face was wrinkled like a dry sultana.

"Many thanks kind señor," Paco replied, politely.

The old man nodded and gave him another leathery smile. To receive acknowledgement from a man with two wings: one on earth, and one almost in heaven, was a blessing.

Kaikay was a charming, little village with a small plaza and a single, winding road leading both in and out of it. In the centre of the main square rose the statue of an Inca king in stone, his arms holding up an offering to Father Sun. Around it, lying next to each other were dozens of large parasols with women selling wares, fresh produce from the distant mountains, and an array of meals that tantalised Paco's taste buds.

A tiny, lopsided, white church, half-ruined by a long-forgotten earthquake, was the focal point of this amiable place. Paco had no idea what day of the week it was, but the raucous air of solemn festivity, with folks dressed in their finest garments gave it away: it was a Sunday.

Just then, the tarnished church bells erupted, soaking the air-thin atmosphere with joy and music. A small, devout congregation opened the heavy, wooden, double doors with a jolt, and a-thousand-and-one red and white flowers fluttered into the sky.

A handsome couple were welcomed with cheer and song as they stepped out of the overcrowded church. A two-horse carriage, hand-sewn with flowers and straw, awaited them on an unfinished, gravel-and-brick road.

"Long live the bride and groom!" People shouted in unison with the ringing church bells. A little kid with rosy cheeks held on for dear life, his tiny body in mid-air, swinging violently from left to right on the rope of the ponderous, swinging bells.

Paco approached the wedding party and began to sing amidst the noise. His voice broke through the clutter. There was a stirring as the crowd turned their focus to the foreigner in the red poncho, sitting astride his mule, singing, whilst strumming his guitar. Both bride and groom, already seated in the wedding carriage, turned around to catch a glimpse of the curious troubadour.

"Thank you kindly," the groom said in half-chewed Spanish, "my name is Eusebio, and this is my wife Valentina." The crowd erupted in cheer as thousands of small flowers melted into the air once more and then fell back to their feet. A handful of guests started to sneeze.

"We'd like to invite you to our humble home to celebrate this special day with us," Eusebio said. His manner of speech was respectful and formal. Valentina nodded in full agreement and smiled with the kind of smile that says, "*I don't speak Spanish.*"

"Thank you to both of you," Paco responded, "it will be my pleasure to join you… I'm Paco… nice to meet you all." Again, the crowd erupted in frenzy - just as thousands of flowers danced in the atmosphere above the heads of the guests, obscuring the sun and returning to earth sprinkled with joy and a few more sneezes.

"By the way," Paco addressed the just-married couple, "I'm going to write you a song. This is my gift to you."

"Very well my kind friend," Eusebio replied in his broken Spanish, "Follow us to our humble home, and let's hear what your muse has given you on our special day."

Eusebio hit the horses' leather straps and the carriage moved forward. The sense of elation and sincere celebration was palpable: Paco had never met such welcoming and happy souls before. Weeks away and countless miles from Miramar and the Love of his life, he felt that he belonged in the welcoming heart of the mountain people.

As soon as the excited party arrived at the house, three sisters rushed outside, bumping each other on their way out, resembling human avalanches. Each held a jug of a traditional drink of fermented maize called Chicha that spilled onto the floor as they ran. Paco was thirsty and gulped two mugs of the beer-like refreshment, unaware of the alcoholic thrust behind its sourly kiss. Inside the small home, a food-laden table amassed with delicacies from the Andes, painted the occasion in the colours and aromas of festivity.

"Pardon me everyone," Paco tried to interrupt the mood of joviality but no one paid him any attention.

Eusebio shouted a few words in Quecchua, since most of the guests did not speak Paco's language.

The room grew silent.

"I'm sorry to interrupt, but I would like to sing the song I wrote for Eusebio and Valentina on the way here, if I may," Paco announced, as Eusebio translated.

The room burst into deafening chatter.

The three Chicha-bearing sisters pushed the competition aside with their voluptuous hips as they scrambled for front-row seats.

Eusebio asked for silence again.

"Of course, Paco," Eusebio gently replied, "both Valentina and I can't wait to hear it."

"This song is called '*I see God in you*'." Paco took a deep breath, looked at the silent crowd and gently started to strum his mahogany guitar. The beautiful melodic stirrings of the strange instrument mesmerised the awaiting audience.

> *You're the home I seek for shelter*
> *when there is nothing left in me,*
> *in your arms I escape the winter*
> *when there is no one, you keep me company...*

Paco sang with all his heart. The newly-weds looked at each other and smiled, tears welling in their eyes.

And I fall down,
I am humbled,
I am blessed more than I know…
I see God in you,
When you look at me, He's all I can see,
I see God in you,
When I'm by your side, I can tell you why
I see God in you…

In the smile of little children
In the wisdom of an old man by the sea
In your arms I get to heaven
I can find Him in the way you look at me…
And I fall down…"

"I see God in you… I see God in you." Paco closed his eyes as the last chord of his new song reverberated unaccompanied for a few seconds.

There was nothing but silence.

Eusebio got up from his chair and applauded, softly at first, then louder, progressively gathering momentum and volume. Valentina hugged him and the house came alive in an ear-splitting tirade of appreciation and applause. Most of the guests did not understand the lyrics, but Paco's intention to make this a memorable day for his hosts did not need words or translation.

"Paco, I can't believe you wrote that song on the way down from the church," Eusebio commented, still in awe, "how do you do that?"

Paco stood serene, overwhelmed by the response.

Nothing filled his heart more than sharing his gift with the world; he knew this was his mission and he was born for it.

Humbly he replied, "I still don't know. My teacher taught me to immerse my soul in the spirit of music… and swim in it completely. She taught me to think a little less and feel a little more. In many instances, we don't create with our minds but with our hearts."

His host smiled and nodded.

Paco continued, "This is such a special day for you two and I wanted to make it memorable in the best way I can. You've been such gracious hosts to me. It's the least that I can do for you."

Eusebio took Valentina by the hand and addressed everybody, "Fill your glasses with Chicha. It's time to celebrate… to my beautiful wife, to all of you, and to our talented friend from Miramar… God bless you all. Let's eat, drink, and celebrate."

Paco spent the next few hours glued to the edge of the main table making up for what he had not eaten in weeks. The three sisters cooked all the dishes and secretly fought to gain the highest degree of approval from the ravenous, young man.

"Try a little more of this señor Paco," the sister in the tight red shirt said with a smile as wide as the canyon downriver. She flicked her eyebrows continuously as she spoke, "It's my mother's recipe… may *the Virgin of Chapi* rest her blessed, blessed soul."

"No, señor Paco, please try this fine dish, you'll like it more, I promise," the largest sister with the moustache pushed her roasted guinea pig closer to Paco. "It didn't die in vain señor, so try it… it's my mother's recipe… may *the Virgin of Carmen* rest her blessed, blessed, blessed soul."

The third sister, in the almost-exploding, blue shirt, who did not speak any Spanish, moved in even closer, and in a brusque manner, pushed past her sisters with her dishes.

Unable to communicate, she simply started eating her own dishes, "Mmm señor, nice, nice, señor… mmm." Her eyes said, 'This is my mother's secret recipe, only given to me, her favourite daughter, before her death, may *the Virgin of the Hill* rest her blessed, blessed, blessed, blessed soul."

"Eat slowly señor Paco, there's plenty… and have a bit more Chicha, you will digest my food better," the largest sister reiterated.

Paco grabbed a little from each plate in order to please all the sisters and ate to his heart's desire.

A troupe of excited musicians from an adjacent village appeared, and brightened the festivities with melodies from well-known Andean songs.

Paco could not fit in any more food, and began to feel queasy. The sisters lingered at the table arguing as to whose dish he preferred most. They all spoke at once, shouting at the top of their voices, making it impossible for onlookers to understand anything of what they were saying; making sense only to each other. Paco stood up eventually. He could not feel his feet, or the ground, and stumbled from his chair. On the threshold of the front door, he accidentally shoved some guests aside on his way out.

Eusebio helped him to sit on a terrace just outside his humble home.

He had never been drunk before and could not compare it to any other experience.

This was new to him and he had no idea how to handle it.

Eusebio sat next to him.

"Hey Paco, how are you feeling my friend?" he asked.

Paco squirmed, head down, frowning, his eyes lost in dizzying motion amidst the floor that seemed to be revolving as he tried to gain a grip on his runaway mind, mumbling a cacophony of undigested monosyllables.

A crowd soon began to swell around them. The news spread fast. The band stopped playing inside.

Eusebio looked at the three rowdy but concerned-looking sisters who were still arguing as to whose dish Paco had preferred.

"Don't just stand there… bring Paco some food and water," Eusebio shouted.

Like an army of wild elephants, the sisters scrambled hastily inside, fighting to get their own dish to the drunken troubadour first, before the other could get there.

"Eat something. You'll feel better, I promise," Eusebio said.

"I'm so sorry," Paco said, "I've made a fool of myself."

Eusebio patted him on the back. "Don't worry friend. It's a lesson learned. Now you know you can't drink Chicha like its water," he remarked with a cheery smile.

"My head hurts," Paco mumbled, still glowering at the ground. "I feel strange. What is happening?"

"It's not going to last long. Nothing lasts forever," Eusebio said. "Just remember what you learned today. Now let's wait for the water and food."

Fighting to get across the threshold of the front door first, the three sisters got jammed-in together. After some hefty pushing and shoving, the flimsy door frame spat them out simultaneously, each still steadily holding a warm plate of food.

"I know you may not want to see food right now, but you need to eat or drink something," Eusebio said.

"You want some of mine señor Paco?" The sister in the red shirt and trampoline eyebrows asked boldly.

"You preferred this one, I remember," the largest sister interrupted, placing her half-eaten guinea pig at Paco's feet.

"Ladies, Paco will eat when he is ready," Eusebio said.

A few hours and glasses of water later, Paco felt better.

The party was still in its infancy. Guests continued dancing to the band and drinking Chicha under the flickering lights of the dozen or so candles that illuminated the newly-wed's home.

Paco got up, and walked inside, gaze down. The band stopped playing as if electrocuted. "I just want to apologise," Paco addressed everyone, feeling ashamed.

Eusebio did not need to translate.

"No! No." Everyone replied as a synchronised Andean choir. It was one of the few Spanish words they all knew.

Friendly faces glowed in the dim candle light. The people drinking Chicha looked at each other and hastily hid their mugs behind their backs, and out of Paco's sight.

"I'm going to be on my way." Paco hoisted his guitar, still stumbling a little.

"Paco, please stay overnight. This is your home and you're welcome."

"Thank you Eusebio, and thank you Valentina… thank you all. You have made me feel very welcome," Paco said, "but I need to be on my way."

With this, Paco stepped outside, mounted his mule, and waved farewell to the village of Kaikay.

Despite everyone's efforts to reassure him that he was welcome, he felt ashamed and embarrassed. As always, fate was on his side and he was about to meet someone whose life would touch his in many ways.

If he had slept in Kaikay that night, he would have missed this fateful encounter…

 Notas

An hour away from the village, Paco still swayed on top of the mule like a rolling whisky bottle on a ship during a violent storm. The stars appeared closer to the earth, and from where he rocked, they resembled comets flying en route to nowhere.

From the barely visible boulders surrounding the mountainous path, a sweet and mystical melody appeared and disappeared, played by what seemed to be an army of classically-trained Daimones. Soft trills and gentle legato notes meandered through the hush of the petroleum-dark night. Every time Paco halted the mule to determine if his imagination was playing tricks, the haunting melody ceased. Just when he thought he'd lost his mind, the sweet music wafted in again from the vast darkness.

"Who are you? … What are you?" Paco shouted.

The night replied with silence.

"I know there's someone out there. I know I'm not imagining you!"

The haunting melody started again. Absolute darkness was its accomplice, making it impossible to discover its source.

Paco stayed atop the mule, snatched his guitar and prepared to fight music with music.

He waited until the melody started again, before accompanying it with a gentle arpeggio from his beloved instrument. The whispering night erupted with the sweet sound of the two harmoniously blending instruments.

Paco closed his eyes and felt deep in his being the sacred communion in every cell of his body.

Even though he was in a trance-like state from the smooth, melodic vibrations their instruments emitted, Paco jumped off the mule and began to follow the elusive sound.

At times, he felt he could reach out and grab it, but in an instant it would move further away, and bury itself behind a tree or a boulder. He persevered, moving only a few feet away from his rival, determined to see the Andean deity that made a piece of reed croon like a celestial orchestra.

"I can see you," Paco proclaimed to the darkness, his voice echoing in all directions. He was bluffing; the night being too dark for anything but an owl.

He muted his guitar so he could hear the light but definite steps of the vague shadow.

Again, there was nothing but silence.

Paco moved a few steps forward on tiptoe, and heard the trace of a breath.

"Come out… I'm not going to hurt you, I promise," Paco said, edging close to a tree he suspected was hiding the presence.

When Paco was only a few paces away, a small silhouette sprang out, pan pipes in hand.

"Don't come any closer or I'll be forced to use *this* on you," the stranger stuttered, trying to sound threatening.

"What are you going to throw at me, a pan pipe?"

"I have a large stone in this hand. I know where you are," echoed a quavering voice in the darkness.

Paco took a few steps back and tried to focus his vision.

Close by stood a boy wearing a *chullo*, a colourful, woollen cap with earflaps worn by people from the Andes. He was covered in a dark, waist-low, coloured poncho and knee-long, frayed, woollen pants. His diminutive feet were strapped in cross-shaped, llama-leather sandals. He held a set of pan pipes in his right hand and a stone, firm in the other.

He stood with a leg forward and a leg back, ready to hurl the stone at Paco.

His tiny legs were trembling like the branches of a tree in a hurricane.

He wore a determined but fearful look on his face, and Paco instantaneously knew that he would let the small missile go at the slightest move. David from the Andes was ready to battle the Miramar Goliath.

As anxious as he was, the tiny man meant business.

"As I said, *friend*," Paco spoke gently, "I'm not going to hurt you." He slowly raised his arms, "I just need to know two things… who you are and what makes you follow me in the middle of the night?"

"I don't trust you," came the boy's instant response, as stern as an overworked and underpaid executioner.

"Let me take a few steps back, okay?" Paco suggested.

"That's better. Well, you do that, and remember… I know exactly where you are."

Paco took a few cautious steps away from the boy, his arms still up in the air.

In the dying darkness, he managed to take a peek at the boy's face and noticed that his eyes were closed; and after a few minutes of careful inspection they made no sign of opening.

"How can you see me when your eyes are closed?" Paco enquired.

The boy gave away an automatic, deep sigh, but rapidly composed himself.

"Don't you worry about that, I still know where you are," the boy replied.

Paco moved a few steps to the right. The boy automatically directed his aim straight in line with Paco's nose. He then moved his face slightly to the left and the boy's hand adjusted automatically.

"You can't see me, right?" Paco asked. "But I'm guessing you can hear and feel me."

There was no reply, only the sound of two, tiny legs trembling.

"I can smell you too. You need a bath."

"I've been told that but that's not the point," Paco took a whiff of his unwashed poncho. "I know it must be hard to trust people, especially when you can't see who they are," he said, hands raised, "the world is often hard and cruel, and human beings commit the most terrible atrocities to one another, but let me tell you something, not everyone is the same… not everyone is out to hurt you."

"What do you mean?" the boy asked, still standing like an Andean archer without a bow, stone in hand.

"I know you might not see me but I know you can hear me, and I now know that you can feel me too. I'm not here to hurt you. I was on my way to the next village when I heard you – and you spoke my language… Once upon a time, everyone understood that language, but lately people can't hear the music anymore. You, on the other hand, speak the language with such intensity and perfection… I admire you. Only someone with a beautiful, pure heart can interpret the language of music like you do," Paco said.

"My name is Paco and I'm honoured to meet you. What is your name?" He lowered his arms and stretched out his right hand towards the little stranger.

The boy's body language changed in that instant; his legs straightened, and he lowered his right arm, letting the stone drop to the ground. He shook Paco's open, welcoming hand.

"I'm Jose Francisco," he said, "but everyone calls me *Notas*."

"Not too long ago, when this land belonged to the men from the Old World, a silver bridge could have joined our land and theirs… that's how much silver was extracted from these mountains," Notas explained.

The two sat by a river as the sun's first morning rays shone from behind a sacred mountain, or as the Inca preferred to call it, an *Apu*. The birds sang and the crackle of fire warmed the freshness of the dawn.

"My father was a miner, and so was his father and his father before him. When I was seven, strong enough to use a pickaxe, my father led me inside a silver mine, known as the *'Mountain of Death'*. Years passed, and my father fell ill from breathing the evil spirits living inside. Before he died, he made sure he trained me to live and die like a miner too. In our world, you are born to be a miner. There aren't many choices… not mining means not eating. Despite the dangers that come with the job, it is our way of life, and we are proud of it," Notas said, placing his small hands closer to the fire and then directing them over his ice-cold cheeks.

"And then what happened?"

"My father couldn't work anymore due to his sickness… until one day he stopped breathing… death is part of our upbringing and we prepare for it from birth. We understand and respect the cycle of life instead of fearing it."

"His death turned me into the father of the household. Suddenly I had to take care of my mother and my two little brothers. I needed to bring in food," Notas said, looking a little weary.

"Weeks passed and I had no luck finding any ore. We went without eating for days and my little brothers were hungry. We grew desperate. The owners of the mine, three cruel men from the Old World, paid little for our backbreaking work. We needed to survive, so I borrowed some gunpowder… and ventured into the depths of those mountains rich in silver."

"I was fifteen and still learning how to handle the explosive," he said with a slight tremble.

Paco sat in silence listening to the story, absorbing every word. It made him aware of his privileged upbringing and the immense divide between their two worlds.

"I don't remember much after that… all I heard was a deafening explosion. When I woke up, an old piece of wool covered my eyes. I knew I'd never see again… but I was grateful I could hear."

"After the accident, we kept struggling. My mother soon found another man. Unable to work anymore, she guided me to the miner's market every morning so I could play the pan pipes and bring the charity home… but the mine soon closed and the village became a ghost town. I became a burden and when I was sixteen, my stepfather asked me to leave…"

"I have since travelled from village to village following the sound of music and living off the charity of people."

Paco looked at the small boy, seated opposite him, in awe.

Notas was at least two heads shorter than Paco but emanated strength from a sturdy body, squared by powerful shoulders. His face was sun-kissed by the rosiest cheeks Paco had ever seen, and the pupils behind his closed-eyes constantly flickered from side to side as though nature was playing a symphony and they were the baton. On his left eyelid was a small scar, a clear remnant from the accident, which reminded Paco of the scarred flap that scarcely covered his own heart.

He thought, apart from their mutual Love of music, they both had *survival written somewhere on their skin*. Their scars were gifts that said, '*I have lived.*'

"How do you get round from place to place?" Paco was curious.

The fact that Notas moved in the dark of night like a hunting puma bewildered him.

"It's easy," Notas replied proudly, with the beginning of a smile rising from the corner of his left upper lip.

"After I lost my sight, my other senses heightened. When my mother couldn't fetch me from the market anymore, I had to learn to make my way home. On my way back, I played the pan pipes, and soon, I began to hear strange echoes. Certain objects emitted certain sounds… and I learned to recognise that certain sounds paint different pictures and colours in my mind. Each object talks to me in a way only I can understand… trees, for example, have certain sounds and textures I recognise."

"A young tree and an older tree feel different. People feel different too – all around me, nature speaks in a language my ears can hear, my mind can see, and my heart can feel…"

"And your nose can smell," Paco said, a little embarrassed.

"In my invisible world, the sounds from the pan pipes return with hidden messages I decipher. This took me a while to figure out but its second nature now. I refused to give up and discovered that what matters most are not my talents, but my attitude."

"I can relate to that," Paco said. "My beloved music teacher taught me a similar principle… I wasn't born with the natural gifts of a talented singer, and to be honest, I wasn't an exceptional musician as a child. All I knew was that I wanted to play the guitar and sing to the world, no matter what obstacles stood in my way. Under her wings and guidance, she showed me how to persevere, and what really determines the outcome of our goals is how we view, adapt, and react to situations… it all depends on attitude."

"If your heart is set on conquering mountains, you can," Notas added. They both smiled and briskly rubbed their fingers close to the dying coals of the fire. Paco shared some of the remaining morsels from the night before with the boy. "I had no choice but to believe in myself. Others will see and perceive you as you see yourself. If I saw myself as blind and powerless I would be dead by now. I chose to be the most I can be with what I have. It was a choice I had to make."

After eating, they pursued the solitary, winding path leading to the next village on the other side of the green and fertile mountains.

"One thing I miss and I would give anything in the world to see again, is a *rainbow*," Notas exclaimed; his chin up as his eyes gazed into an invisible sky, seemingly lost in his last vivid recollection of a rainbow.

Paco smiled, "In the rainbows we see ourselves, and what it is to be human… our hopes and dreams… and our trials," Paco sighed, remembering the violet-tinged rainbow he had seen as a child, "such simple beauty, such perfection… such awe and wonder… *knowing that after the most savage storm, there is always calm and peace.*"

"As long as we are alive, we can strive to make our lives better; no matter the trials we have to face… that is a rainbow to me."

"Nicely put Paco," Notas said.

"I see them in my dreams… they remind me that The One must be a painter."

"He is," Notas answered, "and a very unselfish one. He gives us nature and all her wonderful creation to admire, day after day for the rest of our lives, expecting nothing back… not even a single thank you."

"We often lose ourselves in our own dramas; close our eyes, and take the beauty of the world for granted, when it's so easy to be thankful for the magic of the universe that lies before us," Paco continued, portraying the wisdom bestowed by his music teacher.

"Saying '*thank you*' to life is worth a million prayers. Every breath we take can be an act of gratitude for the joy of being alive. Make each breath a little prayer." Notas added. "Do we have to lose our sight before we realise we should have been more appreciative of the gifts bestowed upon us?"

"There must be something we can do about your sight Notas," Paco responded on instinct, "a potion, a remedy, a doctor… something… I would Love to write songs with you as we watch a rainbow float above us."

"Wouldn't that be great Paco?" Notas smiled, but he looked pensive all of a sudden.

"What are you thinking?" Paco asked, "You looked deep in thought."

"Well… I've heard of a legend but I can't confirm whether it is true or not."

"A legend? What legend?" Paco's eyes widened – the comment stirred the natural adventurer in him. "People say a mystical *shaman* lives in a canyon two days walk from here, across those mountains," Notas said pointing southeast. Using the direction of the sun, he knew exactly which direction to point.

"Really?" Paco sounded incredulous. "They say he can perform miracles… and that he works for The One. There is no confirmation of the rumours though, and those who have seen him are rare and none live around here."

"What if it's true? What if he exists? What have we got to lose Notas?" Paco grew excited, "Let's find him and get your sight back!"

"It is not that easy though," Notas added.

"What do you mean?"

"There are two tasks that need to be completed before he is to appear."

"Like what?"

"If I tell you, you might get discouraged," Notas replied.

"Try me."

"These are mere hearsay… I cannot guarantee they are true," Notas explained, his closed eyes gyrating in every direction.

"In Miramar, we say, where there is smoke, there is fire!" Paco exclaimed with a smile.

"We've got nothing to lose and I'm in no hurry to go anywhere… are you?" he prompted, "What we have to gain, on the other hand, is great: the possibility to get your sight back. Isn't that reason enough for us to seek him?"

"I understand but the two tasks are difficult to achieve. Only a handful of people have managed to complete them." Notas warned Paco again.

"Well, what are they?" Paco responded in his usual cheeky manner, "Enough of the suspense."

Notas swallowed, held Paco firm by the arm and took a deep breath….

"Well … the first task is, to *trap sound…* and present it to him," Notas frowned.

"Whaaaat?" Paco replied, shocked by the unrealistic expectations of the *first* task alone.

Notas cleared his throat, trying to sound calm and collected, "We need to trap an echo or a sound and give it to him as an offering."

Notas remained unmoved as if he had just asked Paco to pick a flower and give it to the evasive shaman – *that simple.*

In typical Alegría manner, Paco became silent and paced aimlessly just as his father did when he was deep in thought.

He uttered not a word in all of five minutes as he walked around Notas.

"Are you ready for the second task?" Notas interrupted Paco's ruminations.

"Yes, what?" Paco replied, unsure.

"The second task we need to complete is the ultimate… sacrifice…" His words hung heavily in the air.

There was not the trace of a smile on his face. "Giving up one's life to save the life of another," he answered, with all the seriousness he could muster.

Paco gasped.

"I thought the first task was easy. How on earth are we going to achieve that?" He yelled at the top of his lungs.

"I have no idea Paco… no idea."

Paco could see the disappointment in his friend's face, and felt he could not allow him to give up hope.

"Wait a second!" he said, "let's not give up when we haven't even started. We cannot let the fear of failure destroy our objectives and plans. Courage and fear go hand-in-hand. Right now, what we need to focus on is not the fear, but the courage that is inside us. Can I tell you something?"

Notas faced Paco and nodded.

"Every person that has ever achieved what others thought was impossible didn't know how they were going to do it. They only knew there was a way forward and they would be able to cross the hurdles only once they appeared… we must do the same… we must find a way."

Notas shook his head repeatedly. He clearly had no answer.

"I don't know either but we cannot give up and let fear win. We need to believe in the purpose that brought us together. All I know is that our instincts will guide us on our mission. We might believe we don't have the answers, but the answers are already inside us. Our inner voices will show us the way – we just need to learn to trust them," Paco's face was glowing, bathed in the light of his beloved music teacher. "Are you in?" he was obliged to ask.

Notas did not answer, but Paco noticed the inkling of a smile.

They made their way towards the pass where the two highest, snow-capped *Apus* of the region met, the starting point of their journey. From there, in a few days, they would reach the place where condors flew above a canyon, suspended like royal, feathered kites, and where the mystical shaman was presumed to have resided.

After walking most of the day in the thin, cold mountain air, they reached the last village before their destination.

The good-spirited community received them with typical Andean kindness, and warm plates of freshly prepared food. Not many travellers passed through these hidden corners of the Andes.

As darkness fell, the locals grew unexpectedly weary and afraid, advising the two visitors not to venture outside.

"Why is everyone scared? What is out there?" Paco asked an elderly woman who offered them a place to stay for the night.

She took a sip of her piping-hot coca tea; looked at both boys and made sure she had shut the small, single window in her living room securely.

"For over a year, many villages in the surrounding areas have been terrorised by a strange phenomenon… the people that have seen it describe it as *'tall, strong-bodied, dark, and fast as lightning'*," the old woman whispered, staring intently out her window in suspicion. Her restless irises moved from left to right, attempting to spot anything that moved.

"It might be outside listening to us at this moment, so keep your voices low," she whispered, placing her index finger across her lips and blowing a quiet "shhh…."

She took a long, loud sip and continued, "Apparently, it doesn't harm humans," she reassured them, "it prefers our chickens and small livestock… but it also steals dried corn, potatoes, utensils, knives and clothes," she took another slurp of her aromatic coca tea, "some of our men have gone in search of *it*, but found nothing. It disappears into the night like a *shadow*."

She gazed into the dark of night from her window once more, as if something or someone was watching them - and they couldn't see it.

"The strangest thing is that…" Paco anxiously waited for her answer, "this *thing*, this shadow, whatever… replaces what it takes with something else!"

"What do you mean?" Paco asked. "Well… if it takes a chicken, it will leave in its place some wheat, or maize, or perhaps a poncho."

"That's strange." Paco replied in amazement. "So what do you think it is?"

The aged woman took another thunderous sip. Her vibrating vocal chords were not unlike those of an amorous frog. She held her deformed clay cup in both hands and said calmly and with a degree of self-assurance, "It's a *ghost*."

Paco stifled a giggle and made it sound like a sneeze; he didn't want to insult the beliefs of the woman who had so warmly received them.

"Bless you," Notas said. "The lady is right Paco. There's a ghost terrorising the villages."

"Then what were you doing walking outside on the night we met?" Paco asked.

Notas did not look impressed and said, "I've heard and felt it before, and it wants nothing from me. What would it get from a small, blind boy? I have nothing to offer," he replied, "so it leaves me alone."

"I have to see it to believe it," Paco said, incredulously.

The three stayed up talking until the single, feeble, dripping candle, lighting the room, flickered one last time.

Before bed, they asked their host to explain all she knew about the shaman and whether the rumours were true. She did not say much, but one thing was clear – the deeds had to take place where the condors nested; and when the majestic birds took circular flight above the depthless canyon, the shaman was near.

Paco and Notas left early the next morning. They thanked their gracious host, and after a breakfast of fried eggs and hot Andean bread, they proceeded towards a golden summit in the horizon, the highest point of their journey.

By midday, they reached a valley filled with pungent flowers that clothed the mountainsides in shades of yellow and soft orange. Rippling brooks of glacier water painted the valley with flowing strokes of freedom, where flocks of graceful llamas roamed unrestrained in unabashed liberty.

The scenery was breathtaking, and Paco wished Notas could share in the marvels and beauty of the Andes Mountains.

Ahead of them, late in the afternoon, a massive canyon appeared that had only been seen by a few privileged eyes. Its enormity and depth was difficult to describe.

The sun's last rays, faded behind the golden peaks that surrounded the canyon, accentuating the innumerable layers of strata along the gargantuan ravine walls.

Paco looked at Notas and smiled.

"We've arrived… finally."

"Thank you. I needed to hear that," Notas replied with a sigh.

"Trapping sound shouldn't take us more than a few hours," Paco said sarcastically, but his voice concealed a slight current of anger. He was here for his friend, but in his mind, he did not believe with certainty that they could accomplish the first task.

"There has to be a way," Notas said calmly, "he wouldn't ask mortals to do something that might be impossible to achieve. There *has* to be a way!"

"I've been thinking about it for a while and have no solution." Paco seemed annoyed - he often wore his father's expression and portrayed his mannerisms whenever he was about to lose control.

"Calm down my friend, it's getting late and there's no use getting upset now.

We'll start afresh tomorrow and work something out."

Paco got up and walked around Notas like an Alegría: chin up, arms clasped behind his back and with the poise of a strategising bulldog, lower lip protruding.

"He'd better show up," Paco replied angrily, "I didn't come here for nothing. You are going to get your sight back and that is what we're going to achieve, no matter the cost." Like many people, Paco reacted with a measure of angst at the first sign of difficulty. He didn't want to show that he was afraid, and he masked his fear with a veil of anger.

"Paco please calm down, we haven't even started. There is a reason why we are in this together. You have a lesson to learn too. Don't fear failure when we haven't yet moved a finger… weren't those your very words? At this exact moment, we can do little. Let's rest tonight and in the morning, we'll pursue the first task. Agreed?"

Paco understood, but he could not let go the concern that the first task was impossible. He thought that he had brashly jumped into the idea of saving Notas, without a real plan, and it was all a mere illusion. He hated failing, and this placed unnecessary strain on his fragile heart. A heart like his, which does not tolerate injustice, grows impatient when it feels it is unable to help. Paco wanted nothing more than to return his friend's sight.

In his world, failure was not an option.

In his search for the answers, Paco looked to the external world, to all that lay on the outside, to an illusion. He overlooked the internal world, all that was on the inside and was real, and it was this world, his own heart that held all the answers he sought.

As the first rays of light swept the cave they slept in, the two friends were out in search for a means to trap sound. They discussed the various possibilities, but all their efforts proved to be in vain.

"I have an idea," Paco said, his eyes glowing with excitement.

"Yes?" Notas asked in curiosity.

"We can trap sound by capturing something… that makes sound." "You mean like a…" Notas hesitated, not sure what his companion meant exactly.

"Like an insect!" Paco exclaimed, "If we trap a flying insect that makes a buzz, we have trapped sound!" Paco lifted his chin towards the heavens, and felt the warmth of the golden sun on his face as though he had just made a great discovery. It was his 'eureka moment.' Notas stood before Paco, mouth agape, as if his friend was half-crazy.

He did not want to spoil his friend's enthusiasm though, and opted instead to try out the plan.

They had nothing to lose.

"Your ears are highly-developed, so find me a fly, firefly, or a bumblebee," Paco said, still perched high on his humble throne.

"Once we catch the insect, where are we going to keep it?" Notas asked, thinking his friend had skipped this crucial detail.

Paco searched in desperation for what seemed like an eternity, to no avail.

"I have it… my water bottle!" he exclaimed, surprised at his lucky break and his impromptu show of genius. "I will empty it and put the insect inside." Notas half-smiled; it wasn't the perfect start, but at least they had something.

During the next few hours, Notas demonstrated his refined sense of hearing, while Paco ran along the sides of the canyon trailing hundreds of lightning-fast, flying insects. He flapped his arms like the wings of a hummingbird, keeping the same peculiar running style he had developed as a child.

By midday, Paco was exhausted.

The altitude paid a toll on his lungs, and running hundreds of feet alongside the canyon felt like running countless marathons. The young man lay flat on the ground gazing at the passing clouds, arms outstretched, panting.

"I don't know what else to do Notas… please tell me you have another idea?" Paco whispered, catching his fumbling breath. For what felt like an hour, Notas was quiet. Only the wind whispering across the canyon spoke.

"I think I've got it!" Notas shouted.

"Please share," Paco answered in a monotonous tone. He was too tired to be excited.

"Up here in the mountains, there is a cactus that produces a sticky substance that flies and other insects are attracted to."

"So…?" Paco replied. He was clearly not impressed with his friend's idea yet.

"Think a little my friend!" Notas tried to get Paco excited, "flies are attracted to the syrup's bright colour, and once they land on it… they can't fly away!"

"That's when we pick them up and put them inside the bottle." Paco shouted, "you're a genius."

"Look for the cactus with the red fruit and yellow flowers," Notas said, "have you seen any around here?"

"I think I saw some that way," Paco signalled to their left.

Not too far away, an area with scattered boulders and Andean grass overflowed with the precious cactus.

"Take a sharp stone and make incisions on the stumps. Make sure the gum drips onto the ground. We just need to exercise patience and wait," Notas said.

"This better work my friend!" Paco exclaimed, full of vitality again.

Before long, a cluster of flies got caught up in the viscous, white river of cactus blood, unable to fly away. Paco carefully selected a fly, making sure he did not harm its fragile wings. Avoiding a painful prick from the cactus, he placed the buzzing fly inside his goatskin bottle and closed the lid. The sound of the desperate fly within the bottle was clearly audible.

The two looked at each other and started jumping; shouting proclamations of success to the endless canyon.

"Now let's look for the condor's nest," Notas said.

"I… think… I… know… where it… is," Paco answered. Notas noticed the hesitation, "You sound concerned Paco, is everything all right?"

Paco did not answer immediately.

"Well… ahem… I… I… I… am… afraid… of… heights," he mumbled and took a deep breath, "it looks like a small climb though… so as long as I don't look down… I… I… I should be fine."

A short distance walk from the cacti, close to the edge, was a sharp conglomeration of boulders protruding from one of the steepest walls of the canyon. On top of the boulders, they heard the delicate chirp of condor chicks.

Paco inspected his surroundings, making sure there were no condors in the vicinity, and climbed the short distance to the top. His hands were sweaty and his breathing shallow; he had not yet faced his fear of altitudes. Wiping his wet brow with his forearm, he placed the water bottle in position, exactly as the elderly woman had instructed two days earlier. He climbed down to where Notas stood, without looking at the ground, and waited for the condors to appear.

After an hour, not a single condor took flight.

Paco unwillingly climbed up to the nest again. He made sure the fly was still alive and buzzing… it was. There was still no movement in the skies apart from white, cotton clouds charting the direction of the wind.

Paco climbed down again, frustrated.

"What are we doing wrong?" Paco cried, pummelling his left palm with his right fist.

"I don't know," Notas said, "but we can't lose our heads now."

"I bet you he's just a myth. He is not real and all they say about him are just a bunch of lies and stories! The shaman is a myth. Just a myth." Paco hollered down the canyon.

"Don't lose your patience my friend, I bet we can find another way… there has to be another way," Notas said.

"What way?" Paco replied, yelling back at the canyon.

"We have tried *everything*! The moment we have a great idea, he laughs at us, and nothing happens… I'm sick of it!" Paco raged, kicking a boulder over the canyon's edge with his black, leather boots.

Paco and his heart had had it.

In a moment of rage, he removed his shirt and threw it violently to the ground. He grabbed the first stone he saw and hurled it with all his might to the bottom of the canyon, shouting and damning the shaman. His face turned blood red from the desperation of not knowing what to do, and the growing frustration that his friend might be blind forever because he could not decipher a way to reach the elusive master. During his frenzy, he tore off the seashell necklace he had received from Milagros. Blinded by his fury, he prepared to toss it into the endless precipice. When Paco raged, he became a replica of his father.

"Stooooop," Notas yelled at the top of his lungs and lunged himself, arms first, towards Paco. The seashell necklace from Paco's hand tumbled to the ground.

Paco fell to his knees – his heart was bleeding. He could not fight anymore.

He felt defeated.

"You've done what you can, Paco," Notas explained, "stop harming yourself, it is not your fault. Enough now… rest my friend."

"I'm sorry Notas," Paco's voice trembled, "I just want to give you your sight back, that's all." He kept hitting the ground with his right fist and raising small clouds of dust.

Paco hid his face in his dusty hands, in an attempt to mask the inevitable tears of frustration. He snatched the necklace and felt the touch and softness of Milagros. A slight breeze dried up his tears and made contact with the hollow surface of the seashell.

"What was that?" Notas whispered.

"What?" Paco replied.

"I heard a tiny echo next to your face," Notas said, "I'm not imagining this."

"It's a seashell necklace. It belongs to the woman I Love, Milagros."

"Didn't you hear the echo?" Notas said, growing excited.

"You mean the…" Paco's heart started to beat faster.

"Yes, Paco! Whatever you have in your hand is making an echo." Notas shouted.

Paco's face changed. His tears dried up in a second. In the heat of his anger, he had almost thrown his beloved's memento and the prospects of his friend's sight, over the edge of the canyon.

"Let's not get too excited," Notas said, trying to stay calm. "Paco, can you place the necklace exactly where you placed the water bottle?"

"Don't move from where you are," Paco said authoritatively, "we're very close to the edge. I'll be back in a moment."

Paco climbed the fortress of boulders for a third time. He placed the necklace next to the bottle, and climbed down rapidly despite his deep-seated fear.

Paco and Notas stood in silence. They waited.

Nothing stirred.

The warm western winds picked up, and an unusual balmy breeze whistled through the depths of the abyss. Still no movement, only the journeying of some scattered clouds. From the bottom of the canyon, traversing in an upward direction, a large condor appeared, circulating serenely above Paco and Notas. Within minutes, the sky above the canyon was covered in condors.

Paco stood motionless. No words left his mouth. He could hardly breathe.

When he tried to convey what was unfolding, he simply stuttered.

It was all beyond words.

"What is wrong Paco?" Notas asked.

"They are… they, they… they are… they are… here."

"Who is here?" Notas asked.

"The condors," Paco shouted, "The condors are here. It was true! It was true. He really exists. He is no story. The condors are flying above us." Paco shrieked like a lunatic hallucinating on San Pedro's cactus.

Just above their heads, dozens of gigantic condors flew majestically in a perfect circle. Their wings swooshed, cutting through the thin air.

Their wingspans were enormous and in the last hauntings of the orange sun, their dark wings glistened like exhausted ambers. The circular motion was hypnotic.

Paco had no words to describe the sight of such magnificent birds gliding so effortlessly in the wind.

Paco and Notas embraced each other and began to spring about hysterically, lost in the overwhelming sense of triumph. Paco started his *'jelly dance'*, a dance simulating the flowing moves of a jellyfish swept by a ferocious sea current.

Notas did not see the spectacle but sensed that Paco had absolutely no sense of rhythm. His arms were almost gelatinous, and his hips swayed back and forth with no clear direction. Paco's face was at the height of concentration, focused on the feeble dance that possessed no rhythm, no song, no syncopation, and no beat. The hilarious dancer certainly possessed two left feet.

The celebration was short-lived.

In the ecstasy of victory, Notas tripped on a loose stone close to the edge of the precipice.

In one split-second, their sheer sense of joy had turned into a fight for survival.

Notas tried to hold onto the slippery ground but the impetus of the fall pushed him down the slope towards the deadly abyss. His fall created a small avalanche of pebbles and dust, which prevented Paco from seeing where he was. It all happened so fast…

Over the edge of the precipice, Notas's fingernails pulled away from his fingers as he tried to hold onto the crumbling edge. He kept slipping, inch-by-inch, until his lower body hung in nothingness. "I'm coming to get you," Paco shouted, his voice trembling. His heart released droplets of bright blood that began to trickle, growing darker as they mixed with the suspended dust.

Notas' closed-eyes gazed up at his faithful friend, with a smile that seemed out-of-place, "It's my time to go Paco," he sighed, "Let me go."

"Hold on a little longer," Paco said, descending an inch at a time, "… just a little longer."

"I've realised this journey was yours to fulfil… I'm so glad we did this my friend," Notas said. "Find your destiny… my destiny is complete."

"Keep quiet… shhh… just a few more feet to go… we are both getting out of this."

On the edge of life and death, Notas' face lit up. He looked as if he had just seen an angel hovering behind Paco. There was an expression of complete serenity on his face. His smile painted heaven. A fingertip away from death, he understood that everything was working according to plan and what was happening, was happening the way it was supposed to happen.

"Use your talents to change the world. That's your mission. I'll be watching over you," Notas whispered, his fingers no longer able to hold his weight… he smiled at Paco one last time, his eyes still directing the beautiful symphony of life with his unseeing irises, and with this, he let go.

Paco saw his friends' face, illuminated with light and peace, disappear down the precipice; until there was nothing but space.

Their last words were stolen by a sudden rush of silence. An overwhelming sense of solitude interrupted what seconds ago had been a frantic scene. The silence was too much to bear.

Paco slid dangerously close to the edge, but a sturdy arm used its impetus to swing him in the opposite direction. Still engulfed in the surge of adrenalin, he gathered his senses for one last attempt to save Notas. The same muscular arm held him down from the waist and forcefully dragged him back to flat land. Blood from his chest spattered, leaving a trail of red droplets that drew evidence of his pain and shattered heart.

"Let me go," Paco shouted, "Just… Let… Me… Go!"

There was no reply.

"My friend is down there, I need to help him! Please. I beg you. Let me go." Paco begged, battling to go after Notas.

"If I let you go, you will die too. Let him go in peace," a man behind him said calmly.

"If I let you go, I will be responsible for your death, and I don't want your blood on my hands."

"My friend needs me. Please let me go!" Paco kept struggling to get rid of the bear-tight grip of the man behind him. As his strength waned, he fell to his knees, broken. Only then did the man let him go. Tears ran down Paco's face and enmeshed with the river of red life that trickled from his dirty, dusty body.

"Your friend is already watching over you," the man said, "stop being a victim of your emotions… if you want to live."

Encircling above the two men were about two dozen condors, their eyes shining with the last vestiges of the crimson sun.

"Please help me señor, I'm looking for the shaman," Paco whispered and pleaded, still on his knees, exhausted from the struggle.

"What do you want from him?" The strange man asked. He was of small stature, not much taller than Paco's chest, with a clearly-defined jaw drawing the contours of his sunburned but well-aged face. His rainbow-coloured, knitted chullo almost covered his upturned, black, bushy eyebrows. He had a mischievous glint in his eyes, an almost surreal satisfaction in being alive. His soothing voice had an over-pronounced 'r' and possessed a lack of drama and the heightened sensation that every breath was a prayer of gratitude.

His body was as compact as a boulder from *Macchu Picchu*, the sacred temple of the Inca. He stood sheltered in a tightly-knitted, black poncho, garlanded with half-a-dozen necklaces adorned with shells, precious stones and clay objects. His feet lay wrapped in llama-skin sandals, similar to those worn by Notas. Despite his small stature, he possessed a commanding presence.

"I've heard he possesses magical powers," Paco stood up gradually, "and he'd be able to help my friend… he might still be alive. Can you lead me to him?"

"Your friend is right next to you," the man said, nodding his head once as if to greet someone behind Paco.

Paco turned around.

There was no one there.

"I can't see anyone. What do you mean he is next to me?" Paco raised his voice aggressively.

"Is this some kind of sick joke?"

"His name is Jose Francisco," the man said, "but he wants me to call him Notas."

Paco looked perplexed. 'How can this odd-looking stranger know my friend's name?' he wondered. 'Who does he think he is?'

"He wants me to tell you something."

Paco was curious despite his scepticism. "Tell me what?"

"He says that you must go and fulfil your destiny… because his destiny is already complete," the short man said, "one more thing… use your talents to change the world."

"Those were his last words." Paco's eyes filled with tears.

"He also wants you to know another thing…" the strange man in the black poncho smiled.

"What are you grinning about?" Paco said in a threatening tone of voice, typically Alegría.

"He is asking you to please change the way you run and dance," the man grinned.

He was looking at something behind Paco, as if someone was physically there.

Paco was confused.

"He also says… wait a second…" the man paused in mid-sentence… it appeared as if he was trying to hear something.

"… because you look funny."

The small man in the black poncho and the invisible spirit of Notas seemed to be having a private conversation and a chuckle at Paco's expense.

Paco was not impressed; nothing made any sense.

"I'm not laughing at you young man," the man said clearly, "your friend has a wonderful personality and he is asking me to let you know that he is in an indescribable place awash with luminous beings. You mustn't be so hard on yourself. You did what you could… he wants you to know that he is happy."

"But he has just died." Paco yelled, holding a fistful of dust in his trembling hand.

"There is no such thing as death," the man replied; his sense of calm was other-worldly, almost non-human.

"There is no death… death does not exist. It's like walking into the sea, and using the palm of your hand in an attempt to kill the waves… part of the waves might disappear for a second, but in reality you haven't killed anything."

"Nothing has changed – despite all your efforts, the waves of the ocean will always exist, returning minute after minute for all eternity. The form shifts for a brief moment but that does not matter… life shifts, it does not disappear. Do you understand?"

Paco looked more confused than ever, 'who is this little man with an answer for everything?' he thought.

He had no time to waste. "Is there nothing you can do? Where can I find this so-called shaman? My friend might need some help." Paco was growing in frustration.

"No one can bring your friend back to life," the man said in his calm manner, *"he didn't lose any life to begin with."*

Paco lowered his gaze - there was no point in chatting to this man with his strange replies. He started to walk away.

The man interrupted Paco's retreat.

"It's me you're looking for, young man."

11 The Shaman

Paco's eyes opened like two gigantic torches. "Are *you… you…* the shaman?"

"Let me ask you this," the shaman answered, "what is a doctor supposed to look like? Or a sailor, a shopkeeper, a soldier, or a president?"

He took a number of small, firm steps towards Paco. "What people are supposed to look like are illusions you have falsely created in your mind… in that light, what is a *shaman* supposed to look like?"

"Well… I *expected* a warrior Inca priest - tall and strong, with a gold headband crowned with condor plumes and engraved with emeralds," Paco replied, "like they taught us at school."

The shaman remained unchanged. He did not judge Paco based on his comments.

"*I am as I am as I am.* I am no more, and no less. It is *your* perception of me that shifts and distorts me. You can label a rose a cactus, but a rose is still a rose. People can label you, judge you, try to minimise your infinite, powerful nature but it changes nothing. That is, unless you decide to believe otherwise."

Paco remained shocked, thinking, 'How can a man like this command the forces of the universe?' He still had a long way to go before he realised that the body is the outer temple of the soul on earth, and while the body was fleeting, the soul was all-powerful and eternal.

"It's getting dark, young man. How long are you going to stare at me like an owl? It looks like you need some rest… you're kindly invited to stay at my home. Just follow my steps closely, the path is narrow and treacherous." Paco nodded and accepted the shaman's invitation.

The shaman stepped deeper into the open mouth of the canyon. Darkness expelled the last traces of light.

Paco trailed behind his soft, carefully planted footsteps.

After some time, they entered a simple and sparsely decorated cave carved into the side of the canyon's wall. It looked as though a giant had perforated the rock with his huge index finger and left a perfectly oblong cavity ideal for human habitation. The unusually warm bedrock floor sloped slightly downwards, and a scattering of cracks on the wall functioned as storage space. In the centre of the cave, resting on the polished and astonishingly even floor, lay a miniature, square table bursting with crystals, leaves, flowers, candles, and other small artefacts. Dried clusters of pungent herbs hung upside-down from a woollen string secured to the roof. At the back, a corner lay stacked with dry hay and cotton, creating a comfortable resting place. The sage-infused grotto radiated peace and tranquillity.

"Welcome to my humble home," the shaman exclaimed. "Please sit down," he continued, gesturing for Paco to sit close to the petite fireplace.

The shaman took a small, hand-painted, red, ceramic cup, to which he added some herbs, three types of crushed powders, and brought the mixture to boil. He remained silent and attentive during the procedure; it was as if everything he did was ceremonious.

Paco watched him in silence.

"Drink this." The shaman offered the boiling-hot beverage to Paco. "It will do you good."

"What's inside?" Paco asked dubiously.

"Some of Mother Earth's best kept secrets: a mixture of different herbs and roots gathered from the loving Andes and the bountiful Amazon basin. It will make you relax and rest. You've been through a lot. Please, help yourself."

Paco took small sips of the boiling beverage. It tasted unusual to his western palate, but the flavour was bearable.

"What is your name young man?"

Paco gulped the last sip and wiped his mouth clean with his forearm.

"I'm Paco, señor."

The shaman's face changed. It was the first time he had shown any kind of facial expression since they'd met. He almost looked astounded at Paco's revelation.

"Did I say something wrong?" Paco interrupted.

"It's nothing," the shaman replied at lightning speed, composing himself.

Within a matter of minutes, Paco felt himself whisked into a land of slumber, his eyes barely supporting the weight of their lids, and collapsed like lead onto the warm, solid ground.

He peered at the strange man seated across from him, intoxicated in a sea of blurry images, flashing memories and meaningless syllables. Unable to lift himself off the floor, he looked at the blurry shaman one last time and fell into a deep sleep.

Slowly, Paco opened his eyes.

He was lying on the shaman's cosy bed of hay and cotton. His now-spotless, white shirt hung from one of the woollen strings attached to the ceiling. His gleaming, dark-mahogany guitar and possessions neatly tucked against the grotto's uneven wall. He felt completely rested, and his mind, clear and alert. The shaman entered the dwelling wearing his usual calm and content face.

"Good morning Paco," the shaman whispered. He was a picture of contained energy and quiet enthusiasm. Life loved him, and he loved Life back with no uncertain measure.

"Good morning señor. Thank you for allowing me to stay. I feel well rested. I haven't had a good night's sleep for as long as I can remember."

"It wasn't a night Paco," the shaman smiled.

Paco observed the mysterious surroundings – the polished guitar, the clean shirt, and the fresh bed setting. He looked at the shaman waiting for an explanation. He certainly had none.

"You've been sleeping for three days," he explained.

"Three days?"

"That is what I said, young man… no need to panic, your body needed it," the shaman replied. "We often don't listen to the voice of our bodies."

The cave emitted a delightful, early-morning aroma. The shaman offered Paco a clay bowl of warm, heart-renewing quinoa and freshly squeezed milk, which he devoured in an instant with ravenous fervour.

"Savour the moment my young friend… don't be in such a hurry. Each moment is rich and unique because it will never be repeated… can I offer you some more?" Paco nodded, bits of gravity-defying quinoa stuck to the sides of his mouth.

The shaman poured more of the deliciously scented grain into Paco's bowl. The hot milk had a layer of cream floating on its surface. This time, Paco made an effort to taste the nutty flavour of the smoky cereal, and the creamy, luscious texture of the warm milk.

"How did you end up here Paco?" the shaman enquired.

Paco took another oversized gulp. He chewed slowly, once more allowing the mixture to enthral all his senses. He explained how he had left Miramar as a wanted fugitive, barely escaped into the mountains, met Notas after the wedding, and grew determined to search for the shaman in the hope of restoring his friend's sight. A tear welled in his left eye.

"The tragedy is that after all that's happened, I'm still not sure what my purpose is here, señor," Paco replied as he placed the empty bowl on the floor, tiny grains of creamy quinoa still clung round his grubby mouth.

"It feels like I'm running away from the world and I have no place to call home. I'm lost, wandering in the beauty of these mountains with nowhere to go… and no destination. Ironically, I'm welcomed everywhere by the warmest and most sincere people, but I still feel alone. Every step leads me somewhere else, with no direction, with no place to truly rest. I'm a wandering troubadour who doesn't know what he is searching for."

Paco swallowed the last remains of his breakfast and took a minute before he continued, "What I know as 'my life' is back in Miramar, but fate has led me to this canyon and I wish I knew the reason why! I'm also a wanted man and I don't know what is going to become of me. It seems like I have no control over anything anymore. I have no idea where I'll be today… or tomorrow. This feeling of uncertainty is what's keeping me up at night."

The shaman's eyes reflected deep wells of compassion and understanding. They reminded Paco of the way Doña Lucia said so much without uttering a word. They were open books of light and wisdom.

"I can't return home to my father's hacienda… I'm not welcomed there anymore. I miss my mother and I wish I would spend every night in the arms of the woman I Love, but for now, she only lives in my dreams. I've been trying to understand why life happens the way it does… why it gives you so much, only to take it away… why does life have to be so hard? I feel lost in a world that does not want me."

The shaman sat listening. He knew Paco's heart still had things to say.

"They say you are a potent shaman with magical powers… someone who can bring the sight to the blind and who can perform miracles with his bare hands… why can't you concoct something that will help me bring my life back?" Paco's tone was desperate.

The shaman cleared his throat. "Before I answer, I'd like to clarify some of the things you've said," he paused. "It sounds like many people are confused about me and those who follow our ancient traditions."

"What do you mean?"

"People are confused about what we do and who we are - you make it sound as if we delve in magic and the dark realms - when in fact, it is the complete opposite," the shaman spoke distinctly. Every word he pronounced had a specific gesture and turn of his hands. He emphasised their unique meaning by squeezing his fingers, opening his palms, and rotating his arms.

"Shamanism deals with the most powerful thing in the world… do you know what this is?"

"Let me take a wild guess… Love?" It was a wild shot, but it was his instinctual answer.

"Yes, Paco, it is *all about Love*. That is what we work with," the shaman reiterated, "a shaman works with Love and with spirit."

"What do you mean spirit?" Paco asked, as always, in tune with his curious, child-like nature.

"It means we see God everywhere. The spirit can be found in nature as in the spirit of a plant, a stone, a mountain, or an animal, and of course, we also work hand-in-hand with the human spirit." The shaman continued, "And we do this in order to benefit a person, a community, or mankind as a whole."

"How do you do that?"

"Shamans are teachers. *We teach Love in the way we live our lives*, and by repaying the gifts Mother Earth or *Pachamama* gives to us on a daily basis. We teach others how to open their spiritual eyes, so that they can also see how everything is interconnected: the rivers to the rocks, the sky to the mountains, and even the lakes to the fish… don't ever forget how everything is connected, Paco. One day I shall show it to you."

Paco nodded.

"We also live a life of quiet wonder and reverence, working in harmony with creation so we can restore balance to all living beings. One day you too will understand that everything is alive and within you."

Paco listened intently, "Please carry on…"

"In the beginning of time, thousands upon thousands of years ago, a shaman was considered someone who could see in the dark…"

"So you *do* have special powers."

"It is not a special power Paco, what it means is that a shaman can *see* into other worlds and dimensions through what we call *journeying*."

"Journeying?" Paco's curiosity had no limits.

"A shaman journeys between worlds: the real world as you experience it now, and the spirit world that is all around you but cannot be seen with your physical eyes. The good news is that *everyone* has that power. Everyone is a born shaman because everyone has the ability to connect with the Divine, The One, and the All-Encompassing."

"How do you do that?" Paco said, "You make it sound so easy."

"All in due time, my friend," the shaman continued wisely, "just know that a shaman does not need to be recognised or praised for what he does. He works quietly for The One and prefers to remain anonymous. We do not seek praise for our God-given gifts. Whatever we do is for the benefit of the spirit, nature, and humankind."

'I guess you can't help me in getting my life back?' Paco thought, 'I might as well, ask…'

"There is no magic trick or shortcut that I can teach you in order for you to find and fulfil your purpose on earth," the shaman responded, in his dignified manner, "all I can offer is to teach you principles that will convert you into the *Rainbow Shaper of your destiny*."

"What is that?"

"A Rainbow Shaper is someone who uses the *Seven Principles of the Rainbow* to construct the life they would like to live."

"How long does it take?"

"Like anything you want to achieve in life, it is all up to you. The amount of effort you put in is equal to the result you want to get out."

Paco paused and thought deeply. He weighed the pros and cons and took into consideration the repercussions of his negative or positive answer.

The decision felt right.

"I feel I have nothing to lose in learning these principles," he exclaimed. "On the contrary, my life is in a bit of a mess right now and I could use some of your help."

"I'm tired of running away, and if it takes my life to get my world back… then so shall it be. When can we start?" Paco was a man of action. He experienced no satisfaction in wasting time.

"Today if you like," the shaman replied nonchalantly.

"You have a deal. Let's do this." Paco shook the shaman's hand firmly.

"By the way, what is your name, señor?"

The shaman grinned. "I'm glad you finally asked. My name is *Hawan*."

12 ♡ Red, a Life filled with Purpose

"Let me ask you a simple question Paco, *what makes your heart come alive?*"

Paco did not require much time to reply.

"Music," he said. "Music makes my heart come alive with the sounds and rhythms of life. It gives my existence meaning and purpose. When music chose me, I said yes. And now, I'm following its exquisite path of creation. I Love writing songs and making the world sing with me. Nothing else takes me as close to heaven and makes me feel more alive. My teacher called this my Never-Ending Legacy."

"Yes I can see. Your eyes brighten when you speak of your true passion and purpose. Your Love for music is palpable. Your teacher was right to call it that." He studied his pupil with a measure of interest.

"Do you know what the *First Principle of the Rainbow* is my dear Paco?"

Paco shook his head.

"Do you want to give it a try?"

"Well… could it be… whatever it is that makes your heart come alive?" Paco answered, taking a wild guess in response to the shaman's question.

"Very close," Hawan replied lightly. "You said it a moment ago… *purpose…* you said that music gave your life purpose. The First Principle of the Rainbow is to *Live a Life Filled with Purpose.*"

"So am I halfway there?" Paco joked.

"Easy my friend, we only started a few minutes ago," Hawan replied with a light-hearted chuckle.

"In a nutshell… *whatever path you choose…* make sure it has a heart. This principle teaches you that."

Hawan gazed at Paco's guitar idling against the cave wall.

"I see you carry that guitar everywhere and it feels like a precious object, is it not?"

"Indeed Hawan. It's my most precious possession. My beloved teacher Doña Lucia gave it to me," Paco replied with pride.

"It is indeed a beautiful instrument… Spanish made?"

"How do you know that?" Paco retorted in a flash, "How do you know these things?"

Hawan smiled. "That's not important. What is important are the things you mentioned while you slept beside it for three days."

"What did I say?"

"You were mumbling about writing a special song."

"I've tried writing to no avail! Nothing seems to be flowing out of me! My heart is quiet and I am concerned about that silence… it's the first time I've been unable to write a song. What do you think is the problem?"

"Well, what is the song about?"

"I want to write a song that will unite the people of this country. I want this song to resonate in everyone's hearts with echoes of freedom and liberty." Paco's face lit up.

"Do you mind showing me what you've written so far?" Hawan asked politely, not wanting to place unnecessary pressure on Paco.

"Of course," Paco answered. He tuned his guitar, and played the songs he had written during his time spent with the young liberals in Miramar.

The shaman looked bewildered.

"No wonder you're not happy… or your heart," the shaman said.

"I wrote songs about an armed struggle, and now I've realised that this is not the path I'd like my song to take," Paco replied, filled with a touch of remorse.

"It's brave to recognise one's lack of judgement, Paco. It takes courage to say that perhaps you didn't make the best decision. Don't stay stuck in the past though… if your purpose is to unite people in song, make sure *your purpose and work are a reflection of who you are.* Let me explain a little about purpose."

Paco nodded. He waited anxiously for the shaman to begin. He sat cross-legged on the floor.

"Before your physical birth, your soul was called by The One to make a difference on earth with your life, thoughts, words, and actions. If you decide to accept this path, and agree to it with an open heart, you will find your life heading in new and exciting directions. You must remember that often this path feels like it's scattered with obstacles, and even though it might seem a hard and lonely walk at times, don't ever forget that you are never alone… *you will never be led somewhere, or into a situation you cannot handle.* The path of the great starts with thorns and ends with roses."

"So if I'm not walking this path by myself," Paco responded, "who's walking this path with me then?"

"No, you are not," Hawan replied, self-assured. "By your side walk countless angels and spiritual beings that walked this path before you. They guide you at every moment – you can listen to their voices if you choose – and their experience and wisdom are yours to use. The more you let down your thinking guard that says, *'this can't be real',* the more you invite them in. Suddenly, situations, people, circumstances and events will appear masked as good luck or coincidence; but the truth is that you brought them about with your belief in your mission and purpose, your perseverance and belief in your Divine guidance."

"I can think of one of those instances… when a faceless foreigner back in a Miramar alley helped me to complete a mission by asking me to listen to my intuition and use my gifts to accomplish the task," Paco replied.

"…and when events like that occur, it means that you're on the right path. Luck does not exist – luck is no more than the welding of your own perseverance and constant preparation." The shaman spoke with intensity.

"Remember that a life filled with your heart's purpose is magical at every moment. Put all your efforts into following your happiness and purpose… *the rest are details.*"

"This makes sense," Paco said.

"Have you ever felt like you were not following your purpose?"

"Yes, I have," Paco returned. "My father and I have always clashed in that respect. He wanted his purpose to be mine, too. He believed my purpose was to continue running the money-making hacienda our family has owned for generations. However, I knew that wasn't my calling, but he refused to understand this. I felt trapped in his illusion of my life, until one night I decided to risk everything in order to live my truth, and I left my home to follow my dreams in music."

"I am proud of you Paco… that took a lot of courage," Hawan replied. "I guess your father believes we are here solely to accumulate wealth and worldly goods, and that, in his mind, makes one successful."

"That has been the history of my family - accumulating more and more no matter the cost – presenting a happy face to the world to let them know that we are content; but in reality, despite all our wealth and riches, our lives were crumbling, we felt miserable, and our house never felt like a home," Paco replied.

"That is a modern disease of epic proportions Paco, and as we become more advanced as humans and create more things to own, the problem intensifies." Hawan continued, "If humans could understand that many wealthy people are lonely, unhappy, and restless because they believe life is about possessing more and more… Wealth does not bring you lasting happiness. Yet, I'm not condemning being wealthy. In fact, The One wants us to live abundantly. Pursuing only wealth and measuring success by that standard cannot fulfil a person inside for long… as if we'd take anything to the grave. Once we realise that we come with nothing and we return with nothing but our souls, it is too late, and our lives have flown by without having answered the most important call - *the call of our hearts.*

Ask yourself, *what are you without your dreams?*"

"I could not fathom my life without pursuing what I Love the most and what makes my heart come alive."

Hawan smiled. "If your life has no purpose you will face each day feeling like something is always missing. You can bury yourself in work and for a while things might look fine, but you can't lie to yourself. You can accumulate more, change homes, buy a new pedigreed horse every month, and even keep changing spouses, but none of these changes will answer the question you have avoided for so long. Finding a spiritual answer solely with your reason will not work either."

Paco interrupted, "What works then?"

"We need to look with the eyes of our hearts in order to find the real answer. All of us possess inner wisdom – although we don't claim this Divine right because we are afraid to tap into it. The answer we seek lies in living a life of balance and purpose in everything we do. The Inca did just that."

"So, is this ancient knowledge?" Paco asked.

"Yes, it is. When something endures this long, it is something of truth and value. The Inca did not live solely to work; they celebrated the totality of life in every action, which encompassed their spiritual, emotional, mental, and physical being. Life was a celebration, a communion where their souls sang a heavenly song and their spirits danced immersed in gratitude. They knew that living in balance would lift them and those around them to a higher spiritual place of purpose."

"That's how it feels when I'm following what I am supposed to do. I never get tired or bored when I'm playing, singing, or writing music - time seems to fly."

"Work and lack of direction tend to become habits. They sift into your life unnoticed. Then one day you wake up and realise that you are *dying more than you are living*. In addition, by dying, I mean the passing away of your dreams, aspirations, and your reasons to feel alive. Each day feels like you're waking up in a grave and there is no escape.

Instead, wouldn't you rather choose to follow your heart? That is what life feels like when you have a definite purpose. Find what makes you feel alive and immerse yourself in it. Your smile will thank you for it."

"How do we apply this? Life is often hard and sometimes it feels like there is no escape."

Hawan held Paco by the arms, gently. He looked into his eyes as though to instil in him the wisdom he possessed.

"The journey of our lives was not meant to be a road paved with roses. The constant trials that are placed in front of us on a daily basis are there to fuel the power we have in our *faith*. Uncertainty is your friend and an ally, and it will lead you towards a path of inner greatness. The challenging part is learning to trust: trust the universe, trust your instincts, and ultimately trusting what The One has placed in front of you will lead you to greater glory.

From birth, the world teaches us not to trust, to close our eyes to a myriad of opportunities presented to us, and look through the eyes of fear. We need to understand that when faced with doubt and uncertainty, the opportunities for success are waiting for us around the corner. In a way, we have to un-train the way we have been educated and focus only on the positive aspects we might not yet see. There is a greater purpose waiting for us. Choose to shut the eyes of fear and look at new situations through its antithesis: *Love*.

Always remember my young friend: when you are lost in a forest of trees, do not look left, right, back or ahead… just look up, ask for guidance and you will receive it… *Always look up*."

When Hawan spoke, he radiated a delicate but perceptible energy. Paco could feel a slight warmth coming from the shaman's skin.

"What about people like my father?" Paco asked, "He lives to crush my dreams."

Hawan nodded.

"Everyone has a bright, shining and eternal star blazing in their hearts. Some will cover their eyes when they see it… because they can't handle its brightness. Some, will ask, pray, and beg for clouds to cover it… but they are the ones that choose to live in darkness. Others will use a mirror and aim the light from your heart back into your eyes… but they are blinded, not you.”

Paco listened to every word from the wise shaman and captured each lesson with diligence. “No matter what happens, don’t ever close your heart… *the star-filled sky guides sailors back to port only because people like you decided never to stop shining.*”

Paco smiled. He understood that some people would attempt to stop his mission and purpose, but if he carried on shining, he was unstoppable.

“Some people will try to blow out your candle. The good news is that they can’t - they are unable to. Only you can. Only you can dim your brightness. No one can dim your brightness without your permission. Your brightness is a gift. *You are a gift to the world…* don’t ever forget that.”

“You have my promise Hawan,” Paco said, “I feel so powerful – like I can do anything!”

“Keep that feeling. Feel that power within you and radiate it to the world. Learning about yourself is a sure way to find your own inner happiness. *By improving yourself, you elevate others around you.* The happier you become the happier others become around you. Never forget to be grateful in leading a life of purpose.”

“What do you mean exactly?”

“It is simple: Be grateful for everything that has happened to you up to now. You are still here… the fact that you are still alive means *your story is filled with endless possibilities and memories in the making.* You are still in charge of the plot. No one writes the story but *you.*”

“I see,” Paco said, whilst thoughtfully rubbing his chin with his right hand.

“Think of what makes your heart smile. Think of what makes you better. Think of what makes you want to give. Think of what you could do all day, all week, all year, for an eternity. Once you know it, follow it.”

“The universe is there to further your highest purpose. By refusing to believe in it, you will get the same results you’ve been getting so far. On the other hand, the moment you start believing, you will be surprised at what you can manifest with the universe on your side. Do not forget that *The One works with us, not for us.* In that light, what do you have to lose by growing a little faith?" Hawan asked.

"Thank you for this Hawan. I'm grateful to be able to see my life from that perspective. I understand now that I'm here for a reason. I'm here on earth to live a life filled with purpose."

Hawan stood up, walked to the entrance of the cave and took a deep breath of fresh Andean mountain air.

"Always remember this: the first principle of the rainbow is to lead a life filled with purpose and it is symbolised by the first colour of the rainbow, the colour *Red.*

Every single minute following your purpose feels like the birth of a new heart: each moment is exciting, fresh, and possible. Suddenly the world is a fable of limitless possibilities. Do whatever it takes to create a life filled with purpose."

13 Orange, Ayni

Paco thought about the first principle for the next few days.

He spent an increasing amount of time engaged in introspection, accompanied by the freshly cultivated ideas the shaman had planted in his fertile mind. He did not know it, but his muse was already at work, spreading the seeds of inspiration for his ultimate composition. His perseverance and purpose were smiled upon by The One, who never fails to lend a hand to those who help themselves.

During those quiet days, Paco rose with the sun's first rays and observed Hawan performing an unusual ritual. Without fail, the old shaman repeated the same words and sequence of movements. By the fifth day, Paco could no longer hide his curiosity and approached Hawan for an answer.

"Hawan, I've seen you perform the same ritual each day. What are you doing?"

"You're an observant young man," the shaman replied in his gentle voice. "It is a sign of your growing awareness and interest… and it signifies that you are ready to learn."

"Thank you Hawan. I'm all ears."

"What is the first thing I do, young man?" he asked.

"Well… after you rise, you walk towards the entrance of the cave, clasp your hands together on your chest in a position of prayer and bow to the canyon," Paco replied.

"Not quite, my young friend, but very close."

Paco was confused; he thought he had had it in the bag.

"As soon as I open my eyes, all my thoughts are directed towards *Tayta Inti*," Hawan replied.

"Tayta whooo?"

"He is *Father Sun* to the Inca.

Let me explain… First, I clasp my hands together. This signifies harmony and unity within me. Some people believe this is religious, but before man created religion, our ancestors on all corners of the earth followed this simple practice. I then bow my head to the life-giving force of the sun, which allows everything on earth to evolve and survive. Without Tayta Inti there would be no life and the dream of earth would cease to exist."

"In other words, you don't worship the sun as an astral body but honour it as a reflection of the life-encompassing power of The One," Paco suggested.

"Indeed," was Hawan's reply. "What happens next?"

"You then stretch your hands up as if you were reaching for the sky and take a deep breath."

Hawan ambled away from the cave and took a few steps closer to the edge of the canyon.

Paco followed; the wind blowing the two light flaps of his bright woollen *chullo*.

"Here, after saluting and bowing in gratitude to Tayta Inti, I take a deep breath and fill my lungs with the life-giving force of the wind, which we call *Wayra*."

"Do you know that man can go on for a plenitude of days without water, and some weeks without food, but without air… he wouldn't last five minutes?"

Paco nodded. "So I guess you return the gratitude to the life-giving force of the wind, because air allows you to live and carry on your daily path of purpose."

"You couldn't have put it better," was Hawan's reply. "What happens next?"

"You walk to that small rivulet of water descending from the *Apu* and wash your face, hands, and body - always with a smile," Paco answered.

"Just as the sun and the wind have a spirit, we call the spirit of water, *Unu*." The shaman paced in the direction of the trickle of pure, cold mountain water that cascaded down to the depths of the endless canyon.

"Three quarters of our bodies are made of water - just like our planet… now you can see how important water is to us and how we and the earth are interconnected. Water replenishes the life flowing within us. It also purifies and cleans us. I bow in gratitude to Unu, which gives me life, allowing me to be clean, cook, wash, and even swim in it if I so choose."

The two wandered back in silence to the cave, allowing time for Paco to reflect on the simple, yet profound, principles of the daily morning ritual.

"What is the final step?" Hawan asked.

"After you return to the cave, you cook breakfast; again with a radiant smile, and bow to the food present on the table."

"Very observant Paco," was the encouraging reply.

"When I bow to the food, I am actually bowing to the essence of The One growing on earth. The Inca called the earth their *mother* because she nurtured them with her fruits and an abundance of Love. Do you know how to say *Mother Earth* in *Quecchua*, the language of the Inca?"

Paco shook his head. He had no clue.

"*Pachamama*," Hawan said smiling. "Sun, wind, earth, and water are all part of Pachamama, who gives us the ever-flowing gifts we share on a daily basis. Only when all these blessings are acknowledged, can we be at one with nature and unite in *Holy Communion* with The One."

Hawan continued, "The Inca were very wise and knew that their survival and evolution in an inhospitable region like the Andes, depended on their gratitude and reverence to the four elements."

"I guess that is why they thrived and conquered such a vast territorial empire," Paco answered.

"Absolutely, and more than that, this simple ritual forms the basis of *The Second Principle of the Rainbow*, called *The Principle of Ayni*, or *Reciprocity*, symbolised by the colour *Orange*, the second colour of the rainbow."

"Please elaborate," Paco said. "What is reciprocity?"

"It simply means that by giving you receive, and when you receive, you must always give back, and when you give back you will receive, and so on… do you get the point?" Hawan smiled. "It's an endless circle of *today for me, tomorrow for you*, as the Inca so eloquently put it."

"As you care for Mother Earth, she'll take care of you," Paco added.

"It's that simple," Hawan replied, "let me tell you an Inca story about reciprocity."

Paco nodded, his charcoal-coloured eyes transfixed on the mystical shaman - spellbound.

The shaman perched on the warm, rocky floor.

"Not long ago, in a valley not far from where we are, lived two men at the foot of a great and unconquerable Apu. The Apu was so majestic that one side of the luscious valley received very little of the light blessings of Tayta Inti, and so its ground was unfertile and barren.

On the other side, the sunny side of the valley grew the most exquisite fruits and cereals. There were potatoes as large as watermelons. This side of the valley produced, year after year, more than the owners could consume. A very rich man owned the sunny side and walked around the valley bragging to whoever crossed his land about the magic of his crops and the extent of his fortune. On the opposite side, lived a humble man who barely met the needs of his family with the sparse crops his land produced.

On a rainy night, unlike any night in the valley's history, there was a knock on the door at the wealthy landowner's house. The man opened the door to find an old woman standing in the ceaseless, driving rain. Despite her ancient years, she showed quiet vitality and strength.

Soaking-wet from the rage of the storm, she shivered from the cold.

'Good evening señor,' said the old woman.

'What?' was the abrupt reply from the rich man.

The woman took a step forward, 'I am wet and cold. I've been walking for days,' she said, gaze down, 'do you have shelter for me? It's just for one night. I will leave in the morning after the storm passes,' she asked with politeness.

The rich man sneered, 'Go look for shelter on the other side of the valley, there is none here.' He then slammed the door in the face of the visitor.

The woman turned around and walked slowly, struggling to move her tired legs forward in the thick mud, towards the tiny house with a single, flickering light, on the other side of the valley. When she reached the humble abode, she gently knocked on the door.

A meekly-dressed man opened the collapsing entrance to his tiny home, and immediately felt compassion for the stranger.

Again, she asked politely, 'Excuse me señor, I've been walking for days and I would appreciate a little shelter for the night. I will leave at first light tomorrow morning after the storm passes.'

The man did not answer. He took hold of the old woman by the arm and led her up the steps into his warm but modest home. He made her a cup of hot tea; fed her the little food he had received from his fields that day, and made sure she slept in his bed.

Early the next morning, with the storm washed away and the sun out in full splendour, the poor man got up in order to make breakfast for his guest. He entered his room, but found it empty. To his surprise, the room carried the distinct fragrance of a *Kantuta flower*, the royal Inca blossom.

Disappointed, he walked outside hoping to find her.

When he opened the door, he could not believe his eyes. The barren side of the valley was now alive with trees, fields of cereal and potato terraces stretching all the way up his side of the mountain.

Across from him, the lush side of the valley had turned into a marsh. The rich man, down on his knees, cried and pleaded his land back.

Today, the marsh lies on the sunny side of the valley. On the opposite side, which still receives sparse light, grows the most abundant fields under the shadow of the merciful Apu."

Hawan looked at Paco, his eyes burning with the muted intensity of a sacred candle.

"Do you know who that old woman was?" he asked.

"I have no idea," Paco replied, sincerely.

"She was *Pachamama*," the shaman answered.

"Mother Earth!"

"That is correct my young friend."

"Let's look at the story from another perspective… if you knew that woman was Pachamama… would you leave her outside in the cold? Think about it… she feeds you, she clothes you, she quenches your thirst, makes sure you are clean, healthy, gives your lungs the breath of life, holds the soles of your feet as you walk, and gives you more than you need in order to survive, thrive, and evolve. Would you not let her in and thank her for all the blessings she bestows on you on a daily basis? Or would you turn your back on her like the ungrateful man?

Would you not attend to her needs? Would you not *reciprocate?*" Hawan searched for an answer that came from his pupil's soul.

"I would treat her like my own mother," Paco replied. "I see how selfishness and ungratefulness can lead to our demise."

"The Inca were highly-evolved spiritual beings, and they knew that without Pachamama they would not exist." Hawan stood up with the agility and speed of a llama in full gallop. Despite his age, he epitomised the strength of an ancient Inca demigod.

"Stand up. I'm going to take you to a very special place," Hawan signalled with his right hand.

Paco stood up slowly, his knees almost glued to the ground from crouching for so long.

"Wait!" Hawan signalled for Paco to stop.

"What?" Paco replied, surprised by what sounded like a warning.

"Take your boots off."

"We enter holy ground only with bare feet. It will allow you to feel and connect better with Pachamama."

They left the cave and crisscrossed a winding, umbilical-chord-like path that hugged the wall of the gargantuan canyon. They treaded carefully, each step thoughtfully considered. They passed countless downward streams that parted the path with mossy stepping stones, littered with slippery pebbles. One false step could be their last.

Alongside them, condors majestically flew over the bottomless hole, tracing the invisible winds with their solemn wings of feathered plumes.

A few hours later they moved away from the canyon towards a smaller congregation of no-less picturesque Apus, which led into an evergreen valley where thousands of llamas and vicunas roamed elegantly alongside wild horses. The scene unfolding before Paco's eyes was breathtaking.

"Heaven on earth," Paco muttered, awestruck by the surrounding natural beauty.

"This is heaven Paco," Hawan smiled. "The heaven many speak about is right here on earth… right in front of your eyes… as in heaven, so on earth."

"Heaven is anywhere we connect with The One – and witnessing what is unfolding in front of us, I can feel His presence everywhere I look… He's right here with us," Paco replied, hands clasped, absorbing the unfolding earth-born masterpiece.

"Earth is a manifestation of heaven – and Pachamama a manifestation of The One," Hawan said, closing his eyes and feeling the roundness of every boulder and piece of grass touching his feet – two physical expressions of Mother Earth.

They stood contemplating the harmonious interplay of men, nature, and beast.

The Garden of Eden was certainly earthbound.

"As you know, the Inca called Mother Earth, Pachamama. She is our home, the ground you stand upon, the air you breathe, the water you drink and all the wonders that spring up from her bosom. Every second of the day you swim immersed in her loving arms - she is your mother, you are her child, and your life depends on her," Hawan said.

"She is alive isn't she?"

"Yes. As alive and as real as you are," Hawan turned to Paco and pointed to the majestic scene that lay before them.

"Just like you move, breathe, smile and dream, so does Pachamama. Every living being is a manifestation of her life… *she sees through your eyes*… your smile is her smile, and your dreams, her dreams. To hurt her is to hurt yourself, and to Love her is to Love who you are."

"Are you saying that she manifests through the mountains, the trees, the clouds, the animals, and everything that lives on her?"

"Yes… even through *you*! You are part of nature too. You are the trees, the waves in the endless ocean… you are the flight of the birds on a summer's day and the roar of a puma in the high Andes. You live in nature and therefore, you are part of it. With this in mind, there is no '*you*' and '*them*'… there is no separation. *You are everything.* To destroy and misuse her is to go against your very self. She loves you and gives you what you need to survive and thrive… why would you not return her Love? The law of sacred reciprocity is simple: *return the Love given to you in equal measure.*"

"Before today I could not see that," Paco replied, "I have seen so much destruction and separation, especially where I was born. We kept on taking without measure, not appreciating what we had - just like the ungrateful man in the story - that's how we lived… blinded."

"As the world advances, humans have conveniently forgotten to replace what they take in the name of progress. It is easier to destroy than it is to build. It is easier to cut and burn a tree than it is to water it and treat it with care. It is easier to kill an animal than to nurture it and recognise the presence of The One in it… our hearts have turned away from nature as we poison our environment, and so too, our lives. With our hearts contaminated with ego, greed, and blinded by our ignorance, how can we see the future consequences of our actions?"

"How then do we regain that lost connection?" Paco asked, concerned.

Without hesitation, the shaman answered, "Natural harmony starts from *within*. It is simply a realisation, a process of awakening that takes place *inside*."

"How do we open our inner eyes? How do we realise that we are awakening?" Paco asked, maintaining his innocent curiosity and eagerness to evolve.

"All change comes from within. All change has to start with you first. Don't wait for the world to change for you. You must be the change."

"Once you decide that it is your *responsibility* to reconnect with Pachamama, you will feel empowered to take action. The wonderful thing about Pachamama is that she does not judge us – She is like a mother that waits at night for her young son to come home from the fields - she waits for us to return to her, and she does it with open arms. There is no better time to start than *now*," Hawan said.

"How do I return to the arms of Pachamama?" Paco asked, seeking an answer from Hawan; the answer lay dormant within himself, but he did not realise this.

The shaman searched his pupil's face and smiled.

His smile spoke the language of the Universe and Paco's heart understood.

At that moment, Paco's soul immersed itself in the loving arms of nature. In that instant of awakening, his heart connected with hers. His hairs stood on end, as if he had just kissed a lightning bolt - he surrendered.

Hawan took Paco gently by the arm and led him down the hill towards the lush valley below. Paco was euphoric, feeling Mother Earth embracing him with all her Love.

"Become one with her. Rekindle the relationship you both had when you were a child - looking at the world with eyes of wonder and purity. Appreciate her, Love her, and lose yourself in her magnificence. She is all around you, manifesting her infinite power in great and small ways.

Contemplate a sunset and imagine a world without colour - without wind to cool you on a sweltering day – and without water to swim and bathe in… what would the world be like in monochrome? Ask yourself these questions," Hawan spoke with his hands, energising the air around his skin.

"Look at a flower, and see the perfect power of nature as it blossoms. Sit near a lake and listen to every sound. Realise that everything lives in harmony with each other, and that *only perfection truly exists*. The world was there before us and it will be there after our bodies leave it. It gives us her greatest moments: from the magnificence of a rainbow, to the calm after a storm, to the fresh smell of renewed earth when it rains… Her Love is unselfish. And we receive her gifts day after day and century after century without conditions… the least we can do is to be grateful and appreciate her acts of kindness.

Be respectful and interact with all in nature. When we purify our inner atmosphere we radiate this Love to our communities, the world, and back to ourselves. Imagine if everyone did this… we could elevate this planet to a state of *'permanent heaven.'* Imagine if the people from other planets and galaxies spoke of heaven as a reference to our world!" Hawan said, glowing in the gentle and wise spirit of Pachamama.

"That sounds like poetry."

"There is an old Inca saying, which sounds like poetry, and explains simply and wisely, the way they looked at nature and themselves. Do you want to hear it?" Hawan asked.

"Yes señor!" Paco nodded with interest.

"Close your eyes first… and use all your senses."

"Now listen, smell, see, taste, and feel, with the most important part… your heart."

Paco stood next to Hawan, facing the valley, taking all the elements of nature deep into his being. His arms were outstretched, open, and reaching towards all existence.

Wearing a quiet heart, he could smell the humidity in the clouds, taste the pollen dancing in the breeze, see eye to eye with the wild horses, and feel the thunderous pounding of the marching ants beneath his feet. He felt at one with Pachamama and she proudly received her newborn son into her ethereal bosom.

Hawan also closed his eyes, and allowed the words to revere his mother…

Grow your inner wisdom.
Look at a flower and see yourself.
Learn from the moon and start to shine.
Smile at the sun and honour your inner light.
Understand the journey of a caterpillar
and soar like a butterfly.
There is wisdom in the ancient stories of patient trees.
The incessant flow of the rivers can teach you
To break through your personal barriers of fear,
And the depths of the oceans
Prove that under the stormy waves
There is calm and serenity.

Honour the earth like you honour your mother.
Listen to the wind and learn from its travels.
See all creation as a manifestation of you,
Because only beauty exists,
If that is what you choose to see.

Place a bird in a cage
And you kill its reason to live
And its Divine purpose for existing…
In the same light,
Break from your cages
And fly to altitudes you never thought possible.
Look through the eyes of Love
And the world will return your Love tenfold.
This is the law of nature.
Listen to it… not only with your ears,
But also with your heart.

During that moment, time did not exist for Paco. Everywhere, from all corners of the wind, the aroma of God began to arrive…

He became a butterfly's wing and a wave in the ocean. He understood his relationship with everything. His lips needed no words – a code had been unlocked in his heart. With eyes still closed, he radiated the energy of the stirring wings of a fallen angel. He sipped and savoured the milk of Pachamama's Love.

"Open your eyes Paco," Hawan said, "do you understand the second principle of the rainbow?"

Paco gradually opened his eyes, not wanting to say goodbye to the loving arms of Pachamama yet.

"Yes Hawan, I do now," Paco replied with a sigh.

"How do you feel?"

Paco did not need time to think; since feeling doesn't require any thinking.

"At this moment in time I am happiness and I am sadness… I am the wind that rises up the slopes of a valley, and the cold currents at the bottom of the ocean… I am light just as I am shade… I am as fluid as water and as grounded as earth… I am everything, as I am nothing."

"If you want to know how I feel right now, at this moment in time, I am the Universe, as the Universe is I… I am unfathomable… I am eternal… I am Life."

14 Yellow, Think With Your Heart

"What is that strange-looking cross hanging from your neck Hawan?"

The shaman withdrew a cross-like amulet made of a dark, crystalline material from his poncho. All its four arms were short, wide, and equally proportionate. It seemed solid and indestructible.

"This is a *Chakana*," Hawan replied, holding his precious artefact.

"Do you know how old this symbol is? Take a wild guess." He loved to make Paco strive for understanding.

"A thousand years?" Paco answered, feeling that he was way off somehow.

Hawan smiled, holding up and admiring his Chakana with pride.

"Add fifteen thousand years to that."

"That is older than any Egyptian artefact!" Paco retorted. "What does it represent?"

"It means a lot to the Inca," the shaman replied. "Firstly, it symbolises service, and by that I mean selfless service to others."

"How did the Inca selflessly serve each other?"

"When you clothe a beggar, when you feed a hungry child, when you quench the thirsty… you're actually clothing, feeding, and quenching *The One*. Serving others is thus a privilege and a very important pillar in the Inca mentality and way of life."

"What else does it represent?" Paco asked, "I have a feeling we're not finished."

"It also symbolises four of the *basic beliefs* the Inca lived by on a daily basis. These beliefs, deeply ingrained in their society, helped them towards their spiritual evolution. Everything to the Inca was related to something else; in other words, everything was interconnected."

"What are those four beliefs?" Paco was interested, readying his mind in an effort to memorise the information.

"They are *Ama Suwa* or 'Be Honest'; *Ama Qella* or 'Be Laborious'; *Ama Llulla* or 'Be Truthful' and *Ama Hap'a* or 'Be Loyal and Faithful'."

"I'm guessing we are still not done with what the Chakana encompasses?" Paco guessed again.

"You have an unquenchable curiosity!" Hawan said, "That in itself is a pillar for greatness."

Hawan found in Paco an exemplary student, always ready to learn and assimilate what he had been taught, as well as someone who pushed his boundaries with an insatiable thirst for knowledge.

"I'm here for a purpose and I need all the available resources at my disposal in order to fulfil it… and one of them is knowledge," Paco said with pride. "So, what else does it mean?" he asked, wasting no time.

"Two more things," Hawan replied, "first, it stands for the four corners of the majestic empire the Inca built, called the Tawantinsuyu."

"That is a mouthful," Paco replied, avoiding the tongue-twisting pronunciation. "And what else?"

"It also symbolises the *Southern Cross*," the shaman answered, "one of the most visible constellations in the southern hemisphere and an important guiding tool in our next principle of the rainbow."

"Which is?"

"The *Third Principle of the Rainbow* is symbolised by the colour *Yellow* and it's called, *Think with your Heart*."

"That sounds like a misnomer," Paco replied. "How does something like that work?"

"A few weeks ago when you connected with Pachamama you realised how easy it was to find balance in nature. The seasons complement each other, the heat of summer complements the iciness of winter, the dusk balances the dawn, the sun complements the moon, and the same applies to both the earth and the sky… the universe uses both in equal measure in order for the world to work in harmony. We, being a reflection of nature manifested in human form, need our minds and hearts to complement each other in order to experience balance too."

"That makes a lot of sense," Paco said, eager for the shaman to continue.

"However, from the beginning of time we've experienced a battle within us… *the power struggle of the mind versus the heart*," Hawan said, placing one hand on his chest and the other on his forehead.

"I experience it all the time, it's a constant struggle deciding which one to listen to."

"You are not alone Paco. Everyone has experienced it at sometime in his or her life. What we need to realise is that this dichotomy does not need to be a battle. A battle means struggle, and a struggle causes pain and resistance. In order to be free from the pain of resistance, we need balance."

Hawan's hands moved animatedly as he talked. When he grew excited, the various necklaces on his chest tinkled against each other making tiny, metallic vibrations that resonated in Paco's ear.

"How do we strike that balance then?"

"The key is to strive for a balance of both; not a stronger heart and a weaker mind, nor a weaker heart and a stronger mind. My father constantly reminded me, '*Think with your heart.*' He understood that from childhood, the world teaches us to think almost exclusively with our minds and this has turned the balance to the one side, causing imbalance and unnecessary pain. In order to repair this imbalance, we need equal measures of thinking and feeling, and when we learn to do this our choices and decisions will be wiser and more just for our highest good."

"How do we know if we are making the right choices?"

"When we think with our hearts, we are letting both mind and heart do what they do best," Hawan paused and looked deep into Paco's eyes.

"The heart shines with Love - this is what it does best. The mind reflects - this is its strength and duty. When the one shines and the other reflects there is balance. Our thoughts and feelings are a mirror of what is happening in the universe, and our thoughts and feelings can transform the universe into anything we desire. If we think, feel, and act with Love, this is what we will receive in return. If we think, feel, and act with hate, destruction will follow us."

"Simply put, good decisions feel good and bad decisions do not feel so good, in both mind and heart. If we could learn how to make loving decisions more often, humans would live in a constant cycle of renaissance, evolving into lighter beings with each coming generation. By keeping our minds and hearts open to The One, we communicate with the Highest of the High and enter into a communion with all – a fairly good place to make decisions, don't you think?" Hawan asked.

"The One gave us the blueprint to build a ship on earth that can lead us to heaven. The question is… can we sail it? Knowledge or mind alone cannot make that ship cross the infinite oceans. Only when heart and mind work together side by side, will humankind be lifted like a ship into an ocean of endless possibilities. The choice is ours and this is the concept of thinking with your heart," Hawan explained.

"I know how to use my mind, but how do I use my heart?" Paco asked.

"It's already in use. You were born with a heart open to the world. Contrary to what you sometimes believe, it is a gift, not a curse. Living with an open heart shows strength, courage, and conviction. It says to the world, 'look, here is my heart… *I have no fear*'."

"We all get hurt. Pain wouldn't exist if it weren't part of our nature to experience it. What mostly hurts us is not the actual pain but the value we place in it. Life would teach us very little if there were no measure of pain in our lives… and you live with your heart as your emblem and your dreams as your shield. Living with an open heart shows how determined you are to feel alive.

Nowadays, how many people can say that they live steadily in their convictions? How many people can say that they are living their dreams and following their hearts? You are one of few and you should not be ashamed of wearing something more valuable than all the treasures in the world." Hawan took his pupil by the shoulders and looked at him with a deep sense of pride. "Always remember *your heart has no price* because a heart like yours can *change the world.*"

Paco felt humbled by the words of encouragement from his great teacher. For a brief moment, he felt proud of his scar and proud that the hole carved in the centre of his chest was deeper than the canyon outside and larger than the explosion of a supernova.

"I think you are ready," Hawan said.

"I am?" Paco replied, "ready for what… exactly?"

"To test this principle on you."

"What are we going to do? I have a funny feeling about this," Paco said, shaking his index finger at the shaman lightly, but with respect.

"I'm going to get rid of you. That's what I'm going to do," Hawan answered in a serious tone.

Paco immediately lowered his finger.

"You are going to do whaaaaat?"

"Not like *that* my young friend," Hawan smiled, "I'm going to lead you to the *Forest of Illia.*"

"What does Illia mean?" Paco asked somewhat afraid of the answer. If Illia meant *hungry pumas*, that was not a good start.

"It means *enlightenment,* my young friend."

Paco sighed, still doubting.

"What makes you think I can succeed?" Paco's self-doubts surfaced faster than lightning…

"Life throws us obstacles so we can appreciate the straight road. It throws us storms so we can appreciate sunny days. It throws us fatigue so we can remember the energy of youth. Remember, every time you are challenged, a lesson is waiting just around the corner. Your mind and heart are open enough for you to succeed."

"How do I know when they are?" Paco asked, growing butterflies with fire wings that flew and crashed in his gut incessantly.

Hawan smiled. *"You will know."*

Paco paced up and down the cave relentlessly - the Alegría trait. His mind raced with the thought of never returning, lost in a forest where no one could find him or hear his pleas for help. His heart released a silent whisper of hope but Paco's mind refused to hear it.

"We are leaving tonight," Hawan strode out of the cave.

Paco gave his teacher a desperate look in the hope that he might reconsider his decision.

The shaman remained unaltered.

As soon as dusk had enveloped the canyon, the two set out on a path known only to Hawan.

A rope joined both by the hip in case of an unforeseen slip or calamity that threatened to happen in the petroleum darkness of the Andean night. They traipsed in complete stillness. Not a word left their mouths.

Paco's thoughts started to knit their own spider web of self-doubt and negative talk.

Hawan sensed this but remained silent.

Paco needed to endure the test by himself.

Many hours into the walk, the shaman spoke for the first time.

"Can you hear that in the distance?" he asked. His senses were sharp and attuned to the slightest vibrations of the ether.

"You mean the thunder?" Paco replied, unsure.

"The Apus favour you… *it's a positive sign.*"

He said nothing more and proceeded to walk on in silence.

An hour later, he spoke again. "What comes along with thunder?"

"Mmm… usually… lightning?" Paco took a while to reply, still unsure of what the shaman meant; he was like that sometimes, the old and mysterious shaman, a conundrum to be unravelled.

The shaman became silent once more.

Even at a distance of three or so feet in front of him, Paco could barely see the mystical man pressing ahead, so dark were the nights in the Andes without a coral-bright moon.

Far away on the horizon, there was the faint suspicion of thunder. Flashes of lightning unravelled the uneven outline of some of the tallest peaks. In a spurt of sudden light, a perfectly triangular peak distinguished itself among the irregular-shaped Apus around it. Each time a bolt of lightning lit up the sky, it bared the breathtaking, silent beauty of the mountains. Above the peaks rested the Southern Cross and other constellations that were prominent in the southern hemisphere. They were only visible among the impermanent gaps of the passing thunder clouds.

Finally, dawn gazed in on the sleeping planet. As the first hints of sun caressed the weary travellers, Paco noticed how unusual the landscape appeared.

The Apus, dry pampas, and deep valleys had turned to small armies of tree forests. The slight chill of the highlands had also relinquished its fierce claw to the humidity of the approaching tropics. The air was heady. They had travelled downhill for much of the night and Paco felt the pressure of the descent on his wobbly knees.

"Your test starts here Paco," Hawan said, unexpectedly tightening the rope that held them together.

"What happens now?" Paco asked. He had no clue where he was, what to do nor what was coming his way.

"Close your eyes," Hawan said, "I'm going to blindfold you."

"What?" Paco shouted. 'What is it with the world wanting to blindfold me?' he asked himself.

The invisible legions of crickets halted their orchestrated, high-pitched serenade, but continued unabashed a few seconds later.

"*Think with your heart*," Hawan said… that is your test.

"How will I know where I'm going?"

"That is your test, Paco."

Hawan took a piece of wool, knitted in the colours of the rainbow, and covered Paco's eyes, making sure his student had no trace of vision. He tightened the rope again, shortening its distance to just under an arm's length.

"When you follow me, put one of your arms on my shoulder at all times," Hawan ordered.

Two hours later, they entered the *Forest of Illia*, a massive labyrinth of enormous, sky-kissing trees, stretching for hundreds of square miles. This natural habitat was the green-lined lung that divided the high peaks of the north with the beginnings of the Amazon further south. Without intimate knowledge of this vast area, one would get lost in a maze of giant foliage, a mirage of palms, and other low-growing vegetation that stretched as far as the eye could see.

During the time of the *Conquest*, many runaway Inca led small troops of persecuting men from the Old World and carrying muskets and swords, deep into the heart of the forest. The persecutors never left, devoured by insects, the heat, and their half-crazy minds. The forest was an unpredictable predator: dangerous, wild, and merciless.

It was midday when the shaman stopped walking.

Paco's stomach screamed out in hunger. He had also grown thirsty with the increasing heat and humidity in this vast, semi-tropical oven.

The men walked three times around a broad, ancient tree.

The shaman untied the rope. He then asked Paco to remove his arm from his shoulder.

"In exactly one minute you may untie the blindfold," Hawan's voice was a blur amidst a buzzing sea of flying insects.

Paco's heart was beating fast. His temples trickled sweat like a glacier melting in the sweltering Sahara sand. His legs began to quake slightly from the uncertainty of the task ahead and his left eye twitched uncontrollably; he was in an unknown world - a day's walk from the cave… with little remaining faith and no sense of direction.

"Remember everything I have taught you; every word, every lesson – I believe that you can do it. Perhaps right now, you do not believe you can, but *I believe in you.*"

"I'm a little afraid, Hawan," Paco said, serious as death.

"Your inner voice is what connects you to the Divine. It is a whisper that wells up from your infinite depths. It is your guide and your vision. Follow it… it is The One speaking."

"What if it doesn't want to speak to me? What happens then?" Paco asked, yearning for an answer.

There was nothing but the chirping of crickets… and when their invisible ode ceased for infinitesimal seconds… the forest was cloaked in a blanket of silence.

"Did you hear what I said Hawan?"

"Hawan? Hawan?"

Paco ripped off the blindfold and adjusted his blurry vision.

He found himself in a forest with giant trees, some reaching as high as the clouds. Everything looked the same – it reminded him of a monochromatic Minotaurian maze… 'How am I going to get out of this?' he thought.

There were no landmarks to break the monotony… no paths leading anywhere… no gaps… no horizon, and the shaman… nowhere in sight.

He was alone, afraid, and the voice that Hawan had spoken about, silent.

He searched the ground surrounding the ancient tree for any trace of footsteps but everything was covered with fallen leaves and broken twigs. In panic, he ran like a lunatic searching for any semblance of a path, but there was none.

He shouted the shaman's name non-stop as he grew more afraid and insecure in his abilities, but only the song of birds and the buzz of insects welcomed his unheard pleas.

He had never felt so alone and vulnerable in his life.

The day he arrived in Miramar he had been accosted by unfriendly people - but at least there *were* people – however, here in this supposed forest of enlightenment, the only human sign was his palpitating and bleeding heart.

Lost in panic, Paco forgot to think with his heart. In a desperate act of survival, he chose solely to follow his mind and look for visible landmarks: a river leading to a strategic location, a noise that might signal civilization, or a path that would eventually get him out of the homogenous hell of the predatory forest.

However, the more he searched, the more he noticed there was nothing but trees. Hungry and thirsty, he ceased running in an attempt to conserve the little energy he had.

In desperation, he sat on the protruding roots of an ancient tree, defeated.

'Where am I going wrong?' he thought. 'What do I need to do in order to get out of here?' Negative thoughts bombarded and silenced his screaming heart.

'Think with your heart… just think with your heart,' a voice repeated like a broken echo.

"Please keep quiet," Paco told the voice. "I need to get out of here and you're not taking me anywhere."

'Think with your heart. The answer lies there,' the relentless voice kept repeating.

"There are no landmarks, no signs, no people, no rivers, no paths… nothing. For crying out loud… how do I get out of here if I cannot *see* anything?"

'You are *looking* in the wrong places. Think with your heart. Listen to me. Would you give me just one chance?' The voice said, '… *for crying out loud?*'

It sounded like the voice had a semblance of a smile but Paco dismissed it as his own imagination. He was in no mood to deal with the little voice's peculiar sense of humour.

Paco was conditioned to believe that when people spoke to The One it was called *praying*… but if The One spoke back to them… they were going crazy or suffering from an emotional malady.

The day was ending and darkness inevitably fell on the Forest of Illia. The sound of birds soon disappeared and singing troops of insects took the baton and began their own hidden nightingale.

"I'm scared," Paco said.

'You have to learn to trust me,' the voice replied almost immediately.

"Who are you?"

'I'm the voice of your heart. I am the real you, and no… you're not going crazy.'

"Why were you so quiet then?"

'I speak only if you want to listen. Otherwise, I prefer to keep silent. Some people have never listened to me. Most don't know I exist. Some take a lifetime to recognise me when I've been there all along in the quiet recesses of their hearts… and right now, I hope that you are not one of those people.'

"How do I listen?" Paco asked, gazing down.

'First, keep quiet. Close your eyes and shut out all your senses to the outside world. Then you focus on me. Can you do that?'

"I guess I can." Paco closed his eyes and listened attentively to the voice. "I'm here now."

'One, two… one, two, testing… one, two,' the voice said, reverberating.

"What are you doing?" Paco asked, surprised at the voice's peculiar sound test.

'I'm just playing with the volume to make sure that you can hear me,' the voice said, lightly. 'Now that I know you're here, let's solve your problem. Isn't that what you are asking me?'

"Yes, I need to return to Hawan… How do I do that?" Paco was swift in asking – he wanted to get out of there as soon as possible.

'Remember the talk you both had about purpose?'

"Yes I do. Which part?"

'In situations like these, you need to learn to trust in yourself and in The One, remember?'

"Yes," Paco replied, "…when we look through the eyes of fear we lose the myriad of opportunities presented to us."

"Now can you see where you're going wrong?"

"Yes, I'm not trusting! I'm afraid, and I'm not listening! I've been listening solely to my mind… when what I need to do is to think with my heart," Paco replied.

'Exactly. You're beginning to make some sense… finally,' the voice added. 'When you're lost in a forest of trees… where are you not supposed to look?'

"I'm not supposed to look left, right, ahead or back," Paco responded, certain of his memory recall.

'That's what you've done from the moment the blindfold left your eyes.

Now Paco… where do you need to look? Think with your heart for the answer.'

"Up… and the answer shall be delivered." Paco replied immediately.

Paco opened his eyes and sprung to his feet. He lifted his weary eyes up to the night sky. Above the tips of the giant trees stood the Southern Cross, cemented in the blackness of the firmament like a beacon of light.

"That is it."

He realised that Hawan had followed the Southern Cross in order to reach the Forest of Illia. The decision rested well in both his heart and mind.

He adjusted his eyes to the complete darkness of the forest; using his peripheral vision to move forward. 'If we followed the Southern Cross to reach the forest… I need to go in the opposite direction,' he thought.

Paco relentlessly forged ahead through the night, making sure the constellation was always behind him.

By daybreak he had reached the entrance to the forest, exactly where Hawan had blindfolded him a day earlier. He was halfway home and overwhelmed by a feeling of ecstasy and accomplishment.

The return trek to the canyon still lay ahead though, and Paco did not waste time in climbing the path back to the highlands. Many hours into the walk, he arrived at an intersection filled with protruding, human-shaped rocks resembling angels in a yard.

"Just what I needed," he exclaimed, kicking the ground in disgust.

'Is this what you do? Have you not learned anything?' the voice returned.

"Which path do I take?" Paco replied. "I'm hungry and lost again. I need a break… and now this."

'Think with your heart Paco…'

Paco closed his eyes, breathed deeply, and opened his arms to Pachamama. He thanked her for her blessings and asked The One for guidance. He took a number of long breaths to silence his leaping mind. In humble reverence, he asked the voice of his heart to come forth and guide him again.

"I'm here, listening… I'm all yours. Please guide me home. Which path should I take?"

'Heart to Paco, heart to Paco… can you read me?' the voice said.

"Loud and clear, loud and clear, thank you for coming," Paco replied.

'Anytime,' the voice said. '*I am you… so I guess I wasn't going anywhere.*'

"Then please guide us home," Paco asked himself.

'Mmm… okay… might as well… I'm also hungry,' the voice answered lightly. 'Always look for signposts, clues… anything that might trigger a memory,' it said. 'We tend to ignore them when they are right in front of our eyes.'

"What do you mean?"

'On the way down to the Forest of Illia… can you recall any signs?' the voice asked.

"I remember Hawan asking me what element accompanied thunder."

'And your answer was…?'

"Lightning," Paco replied.

'What do you think Hawan was trying to make you see?'

"Mmm, I'm not sure," Paco replied. "I couldn't see much but the flash of some mountain peaks in the darkness. I remember a particular one though, an Apu whose summit looked like a perfect triangle."

There was no response from the voice.

"Are you there? Hello? One, two, one, two… Paco to voice… Paco to voice… can you read me?"

Paco opened his eyes – far away to his left stood the triangular-shaped peak. He instinctively took the left path. The decision also felt correct in both heart and mind as he proceeded forward. Energised by the turn of events, he accelerated the pace towards his final destination.

Hours later, the canyon appeared like a welcoming oasis in the desert.

Just after midday, Paco reached the shaman's cave. Hawan was waiting outside with a warm meal – it smelt like a *dish from heaven's kitchen.*

"I knew you could do it," Hawan exclaimed. His face wore a generous smile, pride sparkling deep in his warm, golden eyes.

Paco raised both hands to his chest in prayer position and bowed in gratitude to his teacher.

"Hurry up. Let's eat inside… the food is getting cold," Hawan said as he led Paco into the warm cave.

15 Green, Munay

With every principle of the rainbow understood, Paco grew more aware and in touch with his heart. His inner peace flourished and this comforted his days away from the one person he could not stop thinking about… Milagros Del Valle.

Hawan noticed how his pupil was at first eager to explore the ancient Andean tradition but as the weeks passed, Paco's mind focused less on the lessons and more on his unquenchable yearnings for Milagros. Every time he thought of his beloved, Paco's eyes would squint slightly and a small smile would rattle and spread along his upper lip, as if he had been softly electrocuted.

"What's on your mind, Paco?" Hawan asked as they both lingered on the edge of the canyon, close to an area abounding with cactus trees.

Paco sighed, his sight lost somewhere amidst the flight of a blue hummingbird and a colourful cactus flower. Milagros' face was everywhere, floating in the freedom of nature and well alive in the middle of the Andes.

"My one and my only Love, señorita Milagros Del Valle," Paco answered letting out a loud sigh, completely depleting his lungs of mountain air; a strong wind could have picked him up and blown him to the other side of the canyon like a plume.

"So what are you planning to do about your feelings for her?"

"I need to go back to Miramar and infiltrate its city walls, be very careful in finding her, ask her to marry me, and escape somewhere so we can both grow our Love alone and in peace," Paco replied.

"I see," Hawan answered. He knew Paco was not finished.

"I would die for her… I would give my last breath for her Love. It would be an honour to die in her arms singing her a song about my undying feelings. She is the only person in the world for me Hawan, the only one," Paco stopped blinking for at least a minute, lost in the sheer ecstasy of the moment. "I could live without food. I could live without water, but I couldn't live my life without her," he said, Cupid's arrow veined deep in his open heart. His eyes were not equipped to see her as anything but perfect.

Hawan smiled at his protégé. "On the contrary, I see you are very much alive."

"I know by the way I *feel* right now that I couldn't live without Milagros."

"Paco," Hawan replied, "I seriously don't see you dying from Love now or in the near future. In the history of humankind, *no one* has ever dropped dead from Love and I firmly believe you will not be the first one. Love does *not do* that."

"What do you mean?" Paco asked, confused, "how could that be when I *feel* this way?"

"I think it is time for you to learn The *Fourth Principle of the Rainbow*."

"Not dying from Love?" Paco naively asked.

"No, the fourth principle of the rainbow is symbolised by the colour *Green*, and the Quecchua word for *Unconditional Love*. Do you know what this word is?"

"No idea señor. Please say it slowly so I can remember it," Paco pleaded.

"Unconditional Love in Quecchua, the language of the Inca, is called *Munay*," the shaman replied, making sure he had pronounced the word slowly and clearly – 'Moo-nah-ee.'

"Please tell me more about this Munay kind of Love," Paco asked, "I like the sound of that… Moo-nah-ee." It appeared as though Paco were already concocting a song in his mind with the holy Quecchuan word.

Hawan rose up. When he was ready to teach he assumed a regal posture, and among the cliffs, cacti, and fossilised trees in the canyon, he resembled a granite gargoyle about to take flight.

"Come, let's walk." Hawan reached out for his pupil with his right arm. He lifted Paco from his position on the ground without any visible effort.

"Munay, the Love the Inca taught, practised, and spoke about is not object focused. Do you know what this means?"

"I think I have an idea but please elaborate," Paco answered. He had no idea, but Hawan knew this.

"What it means is that Munay or unconditional Love does not depend on anyone or anything for its existence."

"I see," Paco replied disappointed as he vaguely began to understand the concept.

"Are you saying that the Love I feel for Milagros only exists because Milagros exists?"

"Yes," Hawan replied. He was always honest without being hurtful.

"Munay is not the kind of Love most people learn about. Munay is not sentimental or based upon a person. This Love is not a means to an end – it does not lead to marriage or relationships. It is an all-encompassing Love – in other words, *Munay is an end in itself.*"

It was difficult for Paco's mind to comprehend such a concept. Since he was a child, he had learned that Love was dependant on others, but he respected the shaman and was naturally curious to listen and to learn more of his ancient wisdom.

"Tell me more Hawan, this sounds interesting. I would like to understand and experience what a Love like that feels like."

The shaman drew closer to the edge of the canyon. Every time he looked pensive, his bushy eyebrows moved with a life of their own.

"The Love people are taught often creates neediness and addiction in a partnership. One of the partners is always getting more, and of course, one is getting less. The Love the Inca taught and practised was a Love that existed *for no other reason but to Love.* It is a Love that starts with the Love for oneself, because when we express the Love within us, we recognise the Love in others. This portrays the true essence of who we are."

"So the Love that most people learn is closer to… an illusion?" Paco asked.

"Yes Paco, it is not real Love. Unfortunately it is a fantasy that we create so we can feel good and believe we are worth loving because we do not feel good about who we are. In other words, *we do not Love ourselves enough.*"

Paco looked at his teacher in silence and realised that the Love he felt for Milagros was certainly not Munay. Does the Love he felt exist because it inspired him to write great songs? Does the Love he felt exist because his ego needed to know a beautiful woman reciprocated his Love? He understood that his Love focused on three ideas: a possible marriage, the exciting discovery of both their physical bodies, and the feeling of accomplishment when people discovered he was seeing a beautiful, desirable lady.

He had never been in Love before, so how could he know what Love truly was? How could he Love someone he knew so little about? Was the feeling of Love always that intoxicating? He suddenly understood that what he felt for Milagros did not encompass the Inca principle of Munay.

"When you connect Munay to your heart, you learn to Love for no reason… *you Love because there is nothing greater than to Love for the sake of loving.*"

"When you do that, you stop thinking of the reasons why you need to Love and you realise that loving is needless of words or reasons. The experience of loving itself then becomes sacred and empowering. Love has no expectations. If we Love expecting something back, we are no more than beggars."

"Love only wants to give. If we Love for the sake of giving, we will never beg again. Love has no conditions. Loving unconditionally entails living in the present moment, because if your thoughts are in the past or worrying about the future, you cannot concentrate on the one thing you have power of… the Now. Only in the now can you be happy to Love. Only in the now can you be truly free to Love. Only in the now does Munay exist," Hawan explained.

"Can you see what unconditional Love truly is? Do you now understand Munay?"

"Yes, I'm starting to see what the Inca referred to as unconditional Love," Paco replied, slowly growing in light and consciousness.

"The principle of Munay means more than that," Hawan remarked lightly.

"We are not done yet."

Paco grinned.

"So tell me, what else is Munay?"

"Munay is also living in a constant state of Love. It is Love for creation and the Universe - in other words, the Cosmos."

"A heart filled with no Munay is like a flowerpot with no earth for the plant to grow. Without Munay, there can be no roots, no leaves, no flowers, no seeds, and ultimately, no Life."

"I experienced it the day I felt Pachamama for the first time in that beautiful valley, remember?" Paco added.

"I remember, Paco," Hawan replied. "Munay is waking up and appreciating the wonders of the world around you, from the small things like a falling leaf in autumn, to the mountains and horizon-less deserts. They all form part of creation, and The One lives in all."

"I clearly remember how I felt part of creation. Few times in my life have I felt so close to The One," Paco said, closing his eyes and travelling back in time to that glorious moment.

"In addition, there are so many other aspects of Munay," Hawan continued.

"Do things with Munay and the earth will be generous to you and your legacy. Treat others with Munay and you will receive Munay. Be Munay as you are Munay. These simple lessons appear throughout the world. Just as a condor is designed to fly, you are designed to Love. A condor's life would have no purpose if it could not fly."

"That is very wise Hawan," Paco exclaimed, "and simple to understand."

"Yes, it is young man. The simplest teachings often carry the most profound truths. When you live your life according to this principle, Love ultimately becomes an expression of who you are."

Hawan took a handful of earth. He caressed the soil with the Love a father has for a child. "Your every word and action will be guided by the way you feel Love inside. This will manifest into every aspect of your life and being. Life will attain a magical quality because of the way you feel. Living in Munay is not an easy path: not every person will treat you the same way you treat him or her, but always remember that *a candle loses nothing by lighting another candle*. Carry on bringing your light to the world and let nothing and no one dim your brightness."

"I guess you are saying that we need to learn how to Love others unconditionally," Paco replied.

"Even those that caused you harm… no exceptions."

"That is so difficult to do," Paco answered quickly, "how is that possible?"

Hawan released a soft smile; he appreciated Paco's innocent curiosity. "Tomorrow we're leaving."

"Please don't tell me you are going to leave me in another forest?" Paco sounded like he was joking – but he was not.

"I think this might be a more difficult test for you than the last one," Hawan replied.

"Nothing can be tougher than escaping the Forest of Illia!"

"This challenge will test not only your mind and your body, but the way your heart has felt for years." Then the shaman added, "It's not easy to change something that has been hurting for so long."

"If I can survive the Forest of Illia," he said, "I think this is going to be child's play."

The shaman looked at his pupil and nodded. "I'm glad you feel that confident. Get ready for another challenge tomorrow."

The next day the two woke at the break of dawn to receive the first rays of Tayta Inti, or *Father Sun*, in a ceremony called *Inti Raymi*.

Hawan waited for the rays to break through the almost-impenetrable morning clouds before he blew his ancient, pink-and-white seashell and honoured the life-giving power of the blazing deity.

As soon as his breath entered the shell, the deep, echoing sound of the instrument journeyed through the canyon like the sound of a thousand wolves.

Before the last blow ceased, the morning sky was blotted with enormous condors. The men hung back in silence, each wearing a poncho against the chilly winds of dawn, and stared intently at the immense ball of fire rising East, between the Apus.

Hawan had taught Paco how to look straight into the rising sun safely and receive its energy and life force. Paco had never experienced a sunrise as beautiful as the one that morning. Hawan offered corn beer and fruits to Pachamama and bowed in reverence. Master and pupil each sent a prayer, in their own language, to Tayta Inti.

"What did you experience?" Hawan asked.

"I've never seen such a spectacular sunrise," Paco replied, "no wonder the Inca revered the sun as a living entity, which is a tribute to The One, after all."

"Tayta Inti is a living being, alive as you and I - *conscious, benevolent, and wise.*"

"He makes me feel so insignificant," Paco replied.

"Don't say that," Hawan interrupted. "Our minds, bodies, and souls are part of the infinite mind of The One and His creation. He is an endless ocean of Love and you are a part of that ocean. Whether you are a drop of salt water in it, or a wave, you are still an important part of it. Just because you are a drop does not make you insignificant. Drops of water like you and I, together, make the force and power that is the ocean. The power that is in that ocean is within you. So don't ever feel small. Instead, harness it!" He explained firmly with his hands.

"Thank you, Hawan. I just feel sometimes that I'm not big enough or worthy enough to change the world."

"Listen my young friend," Hawan's hands reached for his pupil's body and healed his doubts with a simple touch, "With the size of your heart, nothing is impossible. Throughout our lives, we listen to voices that tell us we are not clever enough, tall enough, thin enough and even worthy enough. You must realise these voices don't come from you. Only you are responsible for feeding them and giving them power."

"I had no idea. I thought those voices were my own." Paco replied, surprised.

"As children, we look at the world through eyes of innocence. We believe everything adults tell us. If someone told you that you were not worthy, you accepted it as the truth, and for years, you kept repeating those same words until you believed they were your own. We all need to realise what those negative voices say, is not true. That is why this next challenge is so important."

"What do you mean Hawan?"

"We are travelling to a special place where you are going to let go of those self-limiting thoughts. There, you are going to forgive and learn to Love again those people who created them."

"Where are we going then?"

"*The Lake of Gratitude*," Hawan replied, "are you ready?"

"Ready as I can be. When do we leave?" Paco replied confidently.

"Get your things."

The two embarked from the canyon and into the highlands of the Andes. The terrain was treacherous and the path, a constant uphill battle. Paco's lungs were stronger after living at an altitude for a number of months. He followed the steady footsteps of the altitude-borne shaman in quiet resolution.

"Centuries ago, the men from the Old World arrived here with their cannons, muskets and horses. In a few short years, they decimated the Inca Empire with the kind of violence the *Children of the Sun* had never experienced. They brought an armoury of diseases with them, often deadlier than their swords, raping and pillaging cities and villages until a glorious empire fell to slavery and misery. The atrocities committed against the Inca reduced their nation from the millions to only a few hundred thousand. In order to preserve the Inca wisdom and way of life from the genocide, the last king ordered his wisest Keepers of Knowledge and most beautiful Inca maidens to escape to

The Place in the Clouds. The Inca archived their knowledge via oral tradition, and these priests and maidens needed to maintain the Inca way of life at all costs, so their wisdom and knowledge would never disappear.

In the cold and misty conditions, the war-faring intruders were easy prey for guerrilla attacks by the fierce, last Inca-warriors that accompanied the fleeing knowledge-keepers – and luckily, they were left alone. Many tears fell during those sad days of flight… the brave priests and maidens knew they would never see their loved ones again. Families were broken and destroyed – all for the sake of keeping their culture and traditions alive."

"That is a sad story Hawan, I feel for those people," came Paco's response. "But how does gratitude and Love fit into the story?"

"You're curious and always thinking ahead Paco, it is a great quality," Hawan replied as he walked up the inclined skirt of a treacherous mountain.

"When the beautiful maidens first arrived at The Place in the Clouds, they sat by a nearby pond and cried from dawn to dusk for the injustices they'd suffered at the hands of the cruel Old-World invaders. Many tears of hate and sorrow fell into that pond, and as the legend tells, the pond eventually became a lake of tears. One day, the most beautiful maiden had a profound realisation. She discovered that crying for what had happened in the past didn't change anything. With a compassion-filled heart, she helped the other maidens to let go of the past too, until they decided to forgive and Love those who were unjust and cruel to them, their families, and their broken empire. On that day - the only day the lake has ever seen the sun - Tayta Inti turned them into angels, so they would never again shed a tear.

Today, where angels tread, there is a *Lake of Gratitude.* This lake is filled with the rivers of acceptance, forgiveness, and unconditional Love. But its main source of water is its most precious; a waterfall that flows with the maiden's tears, because they never wanted the people they loved to cry those tears."

"That's a beautiful story Hawan. Thank you for taking me there. I feel privileged walking in their footsteps."

"The kind of Love they *first* showed for themselves and then, their people, is the kind of Love that will bring about the change needed to transform the world. And when that change happens, sons and daughters, mothers and fathers, families, cities, towns, countries, and the world… will change too."

"I can see that now," Paco replied.

"Now is your time to face what you need to face in order to free yourself and change the world," Hawan exclaimed. "*Always start with you first. The Love you have for yourself is the most important Love there is.*"

Paco nodded quietly and tightened his red poncho – as they climbed higher and higher, the temperature dramatically decreased. He had no idea what was coming and how he would react. He only knew that it was time to face his demons and liberate himself from the self-limiting thoughts stalling his destiny. It was time to slay his dragons.

After climbing for hours in the poor visibility of the clouds, they arrived at an aquamarine lake fed by a bright, crystalline waterfall. Peaceful llamas surrounded the lake, feeding in the barely visible slopes that steeped down into its tranquil waters.

"I guess this is it Hawan," Paco added. "It feels serene."

"Yes, we are finally here," Hawan replied. "Do you know which of the four elements never lies?"

"I have no idea."

"Water. Water acts as a mirror… the reflection you see is always the truth. Go to the water's edge and see what you find."

Paco ran to the tranquil shore, removed his poncho, knelt down, and looked at his reflection.

"I see a great-looking, young man winking back at me," he joked.

"Look deeper," Hawan shouted from the edge of the hill. His voice was serious.

Paco looked more intently, but again, nothing but his face reflected on the still water.

"Ask the lake what is stopping you from Munay," Hawan shouted.

"How do I do that?" Paco replied, still looking directly into his reflection.

"Repeat '*Hanpuy*,' loud and with intention," the shaman shouted back.

Paco started to shout, "Hanpuy, Hanpuy!"

"Louder Paco… much louder… mean it." "Hanpuy, Hanpuy!" Paco shouted, pushing every bit of air out of his depleting lungs.

Suddenly, Paco's reflection began to change. His hair thinned out a little. His face hardened. It grew a moustache and hard-looking, snake-like green eyes. He rubbed his eyes vigorously to see if it was an illusion. To his surprise, his father's face stared right back at him.

"Argh!" Paco yelled in horror. He jumped away from the water, landing on his back on the hard ground.

"What are you scared of Paco?" Hawan shouted.

"It cannot be, it just cannot be," Paco whispered to himself. He clawed the ground as if the world had suddenly turned upside-down.

"Go back to the water," Hawan said, "look at what is stopping you from Munay."

Paco slowly leaned forward to look again at his reflection. His father's face almost jumped out of the water. "You are a good-for-nothing Paco. You were born to work for me and the hacienda that bears your name. That is your destiny. You will do as I say. Your life belongs to me."

"Nooooo!" Paco slapped the surface of the water with all his might, causing waves to ripple in all directions. "You will not control my destiny father… I hate you. I wish you were dead. I hate you." Paco screamed, slapping and punching the water's surface uncontrollably. After a few minutes, exhausted from the emotion, he paused to take a breath.

His father's face was still on the surface, his snake eyes churning with the contours of the flowing water. By now, Paco's shirt was completely drenched in blood.

"By running from the truth, you will not make it go away Paco," Hawan said as he edged closer to his frightened pupil. He perched near him on a rock, close to the edge of the lake.

"Nooooo!" Paco continued punching the water until most of his strength had waned.

"You cannot fight hate with hate… you are only destroying yourself. Can't you see that?" Hawan placed his arm around Paco.

"He's not going away Hawan," Paco panted on his last whispers of breath.

"Remember what the maidens did?"

"I just can't do that." Paco's answer was immediate.

"You are where you are supposed to be Paco; otherwise you'd be somewhere else… use this opportunity to face your fears and grow as a person. Choose this moment to evolve. Take this chance and embrace it wholeheartedly. What is the use of running away from reality? It will always catch up to you. You can only win by facing your fears. Remember that you are the closest being to The One in all creation. To Love you is to Love The One. Always start by loving you first. Loving and forgiving yourself is the greatest gift you can give to you. Don't you think you deserve that?"

"It's just so damn hard!" Paco shouted back, trembling from the freezing water.

"How much longer do you want to suffer? How much longer do you want your heart to bleed? How much more pain do you want to endure? How many more tears do you want to cry before you awaken? Open your eyes. Awaken."

"My heart has been bleeding my whole life. What difference does another pint of blood make?" Paco replied. Dry saliva soiled his mouth.

"Do you want to suffer until the day you die? What kind of life would that be? If you don't forgive your father, you cannot fulfil your destiny!"

"Why should I forgive him after all he's done?" He lifted a stone and clenched it as hard as he could. He wanted to squeeze the water out of it, his anger was so intense.

Hawan looked at him with compassionate eyes. "You need to forgive your father because you are no longer a victim. The moment you let him go, you will free yourself. Forgiveness is the highest expression of self-Love Paco."

Paco nodded, wiping the angry tears from his eyes.

"Leave behind those emotions that have no positive place in your life. Forgive those you need to forgive not because they deserve it, but because forgiveness is about self-Love. *The greatest gift that you can give the world is to Love yourself.* You do not want to keep hurting yourself by carrying your anger around. Now please lean into the water again, and from the bottom of your heart, look at your father - not as the person that hurt you but as the person you chose before your birth to teach you this lesson in unconditional Love. Break free from the chains of pain and hate that have bound you for so long. This is your time to experience true freedom - and your challenge today is to let go of all those negative emotions and replace them with Munay. Only Munay can set you free."

"I know it seems difficult, but you are bigger and stronger than this challenge. You can do it Paco… learn to Love yourself with no conditions and stop carrying that garbage around. Show yourself and your father Munay," Hawan held Paco by the shoulder and gently led him back in the direction of the water.

Paco's tears fell like rain into the lake – just as the maiden's tears had centuries before.

He ripped the thin, scar tissue from his chest and looked at his beating heart through the open gap. As the mental and physical pain intensified, his heart poured blood into the lake. 'Only I can stop this. Only I can stop the bleeding,' he thought, 'only I can heal my pain.'

In a moment of awakening, Paco decided never to bleed again… for no reason, or any person.

He removed his shirt and washed the blood from it in the freezing water. Thin rivulets of the crimson liquid vanished into the depths, washed clean by the invisible hands of the Inca maidens. Hawan moved away from Paco and silently observed his courageous pupil.

Paco leaned over the water's edge. His father's face soon resurfaced, frowning as it always did when he looked at Paco.

This time, he looked angrier than before. "You are good-for-nothing," he said.

"That is not true father. I forgive you," Paco replied.

"Carry on Paco," the shaman encouraged his pupil.

"Your dreams are fickle, useless, and childish," Samuel shouted, pointing his right index finger.

"No father. My dreams are what give me life… they are a part of me and no one can destroy them. They are gifts given to me by The One before birth. They are part of my mission. They give my life purpose and it's my duty to fulfil them and utilise them. From now on, your words no longer carry any force in my life. From now on, you no longer have any power over me, dear father. *Only I decide* what my destiny is."

"I do not belong to you but I have to thank you for bringing me into the world. Please understand that I *chose* you as my father. My soul *chose* this experience so I could learn how to Love with no boundaries, no conditions, and no limitations. I Love you father, and now, I let you go in peace," Paco's chin sank into his chest.

Paco grew weaker from the huge loss of blood. He was struggling to hold his body up and soon started to crumple.

This was Paco's lesson and Hawan did not intervene.

"I Love you, I release you, I forgive you," Paco repeated, incessantly.

"You are not worthy Paco, you are useless. You are a good-for-nothing son," Samuel kept repeating.

"I Love you, I release you, I forgive you," Paco mumbled, weaker this time.

With every word uttered, Paco lost more and more consciousness. With every loving word, Samuel faded back into the lake's depths until the sound of his voice finally disappeared.

Paco closed his eyes. His arms surrendered to his weight. He took one last breath and sank head first, into the depths of the lake. He dropped like a stone into the depthless, watery hole, leaving a trail of blood as he plunged deeper towards the bottom. He felt he had forgiven his father and that perhaps now, it was his time to die. He wondered if the reason he had arrived on earth was to learn how to forgive and Love his father. Maybe, once he achieved that, he would follow the maidens to higher realms.

Although his lungs screamed for air, he felt the peace of unconditional Love, a feeling of peace beyond understanding. Paco realised his life was worth that single moment and he welcomed death with a smile. He was ready to go.

"Take me home," he asked The One, "Take me home Father."

From the depths, a single arm held him like a mother holds a child. Soon, a dozen arms engulfed him. He opened his eyes despite the murkiness, and in the freezing depths, saw a dozen maidens suspended in mid-water gently holding him. A current of warm water unexpectedly brushed his skin as a foreign light conquered the darkness.

Blinded, he saw the brightness of the sun.

Hawan jumped into the water as soon as his pupil's body rose aided by the invisible hands of the maidens. With a single, swift move, he pulled Paco back to dry land.

"Thank you Tayta Inti, thank you," Hawan declared to the sun that broke through the impenetrable clouds for the second time in hundreds of years. Thick, fluffy clouds formed a halo around the lake, and in the unnatural light, the shaman held his pupil close to his chest. Covering the freezing boy with his red poncho, he shed a single tear for returning the precious life of his pupil.

Paco slightly parted his eyes. Water gushed out of his nose and mouth as he steadily regained consciousness.

"Paco, Paco," Hawan said, consumed with excitement… "Your heart."

"What's happened to my heart?" he barely had the strength to mumble.

"It's stopped bleeding," Hawan cried, "your heart is not bleeding!"

Paco lowered his chin. The gap on his heart was as dry as a desert stone.

"We did it," Paco managed a frail whisper. A trace of a laugh escaped his bluish lips.

"No, Paco… You did it." Hawan smiled at his exhausted pupil.

"I'm proud of you. It's easy to be hard. It's easy to live with a heart of stone. It doesn't take much effort to hate. It's easy to go through life deciding not to feel and not to smile and to carry on with a heart that is not open. Those who decide to Love when it is hard to Love, those who decide to say thank you when they have everything, those who humble themselves in victory, are the ones that have the courage… those who decide to smile when the world around them is frowning… those are the ones who have the courage. To live with an open heart is not easy."

"Now look at you, a courageous young man with a heart as open as a canyon… that will never bleed again.

Paco's soul danced in sacred communion with the maidens of the lake. He experienced an awakening of immense proportions, just when he thought it was all over. "I did it," he said to himself, "I did it."

"Let's go home," he said to Hawan, with the touch of a smile.

Hawan nodded at his pupil. Paco squinted in the blazing sun.

"In a while my young friend," he said, "in a while."

16 Blue, The Present Is A Gift

During the next few weeks, Paco felt lighter, as though a dark fog had evaporated from his soul. In the mornings, he helped Hawan fix an ancient Inca irrigation system that ran alongside the terraces where they grew their vegetables. In the afternoons, on a deserved break from the backbreaking toil, he retreated to the edge of the precipice and attempted to write the single piece of music that might one day unite his country.

Lost in a myriad of mediocre ideas, Paco battled to get inspired. His mind wondered incessantly: jumping for a few minutes to Milagros, returning to the song, then rapidly off to a past fight with Samuel, then back again to Milagros and at last, to the song once more. By the end of the night he had nothing to show. Paco grew frustrated with the process and it was not long before Hawan noticed Paco's mood after his song-writing sessions.

Early one morning, the shaman decided to discuss with his pupil, the reasons behind his lack of focus and unstable humour.

"Let's talk," Hawan said to Paco. The cave lingered with the sweet scent of fresh-roasted quinoa and burnt sage.

"Yes, Hawan," he answered with a hint of frustration.

"I have noticed that before you go to bed, you arrive from your song-writing sessions in a bad mood. Your energy is palpable and your aura, dimmer and darker. What is it?"

Paco instantly opened up to his teacher.

"I'm not able to get inspired and it's driving me insane. I've always written with minimum effort, but lately, I just can't get into that *zone*. My thoughts are scattered – sometimes with Milagros; other times stuck in why I cannot write this song. Occasionally, I'm floating in past conversations or events that haven't yet occurred. Am I making any sense? Does this sound familiar to you?"

Paco asked in desperation,

"It does. What else is on your mind?"

"Well… I am focusing on the reasons why I *can't* write this song… in other words, I keep reminding myself of the reasons why I've failed in the past. My mind keeps taking me back to all those sour-tasting moments of failure and I don't understand why. It's so frustrating. I can't create when I'm frustrated. Paco grew more annoyed with every sentence. He kept moving his hands like windmills in a dust storm. "Does that explain it in a better light?"

"Let me tell you a story Paco."

"I'm listening señor." Paco took a deep breath and counted to eleven.

"In a secluded Andean village lived a lady who kept thousands of small glass bottles filled with the breaths from the moments of her life. She labelled the bottles with the date and time of each experience. Her collection had two types of bottles: the clear, see-through bottles, and the dark bottles. The clear bottles stored her fondest memories and moments. The dark ones held the times she'd rather forget.

As the years passed, she created more dark bottles and consequently, her dark bottle collection grew. One day, as happens so often in our country, a huge earthquake struck the sleeping village, destroying her humble home and her entire collection of bottles. She thought her life was over when she saw her memories in tatters, but to her amazement she was the same person. The moments inside the bottles already formed a part of who she was. Seeing the dark bottles shattered on the floor helped her to realise that she had given them far too much attention and meaning."

"What does the story mean?" Paco replied, slightly confused.

"It means that life is a collection of memories and experiences. In many ways, we are a product of those - *but*… we are also responsible for creating our own memories and experiences. Through our powers of creation, we can decide on the colour of the bottle we want to create. In that light, *let go of your dark bottles*. Their lessons and experiences are already within you, so don't keep storing them. You have already succeeded in learning their difficult lessons. Instead, focus on creating more clear bottles. Conquer the present moment and make a conscious decision *right now* to create more positive and happier memories. In your case, this means nurturing a more conducive space for creating."

"I can see how I've been jumping back and forth between the past, the present, and the future with no clear direction," Paco exclaimed.

"This is where *The Fifth Principle of the Rainbow* comes in. Care to guess what it is Paco?" Hawan asked, hoping his pupil would get this one right… finally.

Paco closed his eyes and thought of the answer. "Well… could it be… not living in the past?"

"You are not far off," Hawan replied. "That is one of the factors that encompasses the fifth principle of all Rainbow Shapers… represented by the colour *Blue*."

"Which is…?"

"The Present is a Gift," Hawan stated.

"Huh?"

"Each day is a novel gift," Hawan said, "the most important day of your life does not exist, because each day is… you are reborn every morning as you wake up, so use every day as a platform to evolve, Love, and be grateful because there could be no tomorrow."

"I'm still not getting the point."

"Stop for a moment," Hawan ordered. "Sit up straight and close your eyes for a minute… look at the picture of your life behind you. Go from your earliest memories to about five minutes ago. Take your time." Paco closed his eyes. He reminisced on the most important events.

"At this very second," the shaman said, "can you change anything?"

"No, I cannot."

"Open your eyes Paco," Hawan indicated. "Right now, in this second, you are unable to change any of those moments - so smile, and be grateful. Every experience you've ever had served a purpose and got you where you are today… to this very second. This second is all you have. There is nothing else but this moment. You can't change the past. *The only thing you can change is the Now…* which is this very moment you are experiencing." Hawan radiated wisdom, "Savour it. Design it. Build it. Reap it. Conquer it… It's all you have, and ultimately, it's all you can change."

"That makes a lot of sense," Paco replied, "I can see where you are going with this. Can you please explain a little more about what it means to be living in the now, and why the present is a gift?"

"Every day offers us an opportunity to create memories. This is living in the present: choosing to make each experience unique and memorable. Have your tea, but taste it like it was the last tea on Earth. Savour the moment and life will become unforgettable."

"Living in the present moment or the now has a magical quality. When we do this, we get to enjoy life to the fullest. Actually, many of the bitter episodes we keep re-living in our minds would have never occurred if we were living in the present when they happened. Let me explain. Do you remember having said something in anger and later regretting it?"

"Yes, many times," Paco replied with certainty. His short and flammable temper had drawn him into many situations he'd rather forget.

"If you had this awareness at the time, do you think you would have reacted differently?"

Paco thought for a moment. "Absolutely, I would rather have bit my tongue than speak in anger."

"That is a great start," the shaman said. "Now go back to your school days and think of an exam you did poorly in. You studied the night before. You were certain you knew the material. You then had an argument with someone and it stayed on your mind. You took that feeling to the classroom and it negatively affected the way you performed during the exam. Does it sound familiar?"

"It sounds more than familiar." Paco said with a cheeky smile.

"It's not hard to guess whether you were living in the present moment or not. Another question," Hawan always spoke with his hands, "did worrying or re-enacting the conversation that made you angry serve you in any way?

If you'd said to yourself, 'at this moment in time I am finished thinking of the argument. I will deal with the problem later in a calm and thoughtful manner. Let me now concentrate on what I need to do right now' - do you think you would have fared better?"

Paco replied without hesitation, "I'd have to agree with you Hawan. I would have done much better if I had focused my attention solely on accomplishing the task. I don't doubt it for a second."

"We can all enjoy the present moment in many ways… having a meal is a simple way to experience the present moment. Most people live at such a frenetic pace, they eat on the run - often forgetting that what enters their bodies nourishes the energy needed to get them through the day. You don't even taste food anymore. Next time you eat, make sure you are seated and relaxed. After thanking Pachamama for the blessings you are about to receive, take the first bite of your meal in silence, making sure you taste every morsel. Close your eyes if you have to, chew slowly, and experience the flavours of the food in your mouth. The One gave us an extraordinary machine equipped to taste thousands of different flavours and most don't use it to its full capacity. Eating is a privilege and a ritual you need to start honouring again. Do you see how living in the present encompasses many aspects of your life?" Hawan asked.

"Yes, I can but it all seems so tiring. I mean, how do I monitor my thoughts and actions at every single moment?"

"Have you ever learned anything meaningful without effort?" Hawan asked. "Go back to the time when you were a baby. Picture yourself in your first year of life. See yourself crawling and growing in awareness, watching adults stand on their feet. Your little heart tells you to stand up and walk as big people do. One day you decide to try. You gather the little strength you have on your tiny legs and push yourself up. You hold onto a chair and decide to take the plunge. You attempt your first steps. Your hands leave the chair. With a little impetus, you take the first step, then the second, third, but not before falling face first onto the floor. If you had decided at that moment never to walk again because you'd failed, you wouldn't be walking today," Hawan explained.

"Something we need to learn from babies is their lack of fear and their willingness to succeed. Only through constant trial and error and a lack of fear, you learned to walk. The same principle applies to your mind. At first, it might seem useless to grow your consciousness, just as trying to balance on your two legs seemed futile. With a little discipline and continuous trial and error, it will grow into a habit. Before you know it, it won't take much energy to be constantly aware of your thoughts. This simple example serves to show you how anything life-changing requires a little effort, some courage and especially, s the absence of fear."

"My beloved music teacher Doña Lucia always reminded me of this lesson. I remember learning to ride a horse and failing constantly. Having out-ruled fear, I started gathering the little wins, until eventually I conquered the animal. It sounds like a very similar principle Hawan," Paco answered.

"It is. This simple principle applies to many aspects of our lives."

"How else do I learn to live in the present moment?" Paco asked, growing not only in curiosity but in understanding.

"You mentioned earlier that you came from Miramar, the country's bustling capital."

"Yes. The hacienda I grew up in is a half day's walk from Miramar."

"Going back to your last visit, can you recall the daily routine of its citizens?" Hawan asked. "Can you see them rushing up and down the busy streets, blank stares on their faces, looking tired and exhausted when it is only nine o'clock in the morning?"

"Of course I do. That's the look on most of the faces in Miramar," Paco replied, picturing the haggard-looking expressions on the faces of many of the capital's dwellers.

"Many rush from one point to the next, not enjoying the moment. They walk in a trance, unaware of their surroundings, the song of birds or the warmth of the sun. Their minds control them. Worst of all, while rushing about, they keep re-living past experiences and conversations that most likely have no positive effect on what they are about to do. Let's not forget that not only physical exertion makes us tired - mental juggling takes as much energy away from us as well. Imagine how much more energy you would have if your mind was steady and anchored in the present moment.”

“How do I know when I’m living in the present moment?” Paco asked.

Hawan got up and strode outside. It was an overcast day with the first brushstrokes of rain.

“Come with me Paco. Let us take a walk to that viewpoint.”

Teacher and pupil headed shoulder to shoulder towards a dark-granite outcrop protruding east, close to the cave’s entrance.

“Now close your eyes. Don’t open them until I ask you to do so. Quiet your mind. Take a deep breath… inhale… once more… inhale deeply. Let the energy from our beloved wind Wayra fill you with life. Empty your mind of thoughts and only listen to my words. Now…” the shaman allowed Paco to be with himself, “*smile.*”

With eyes closed, Paco smiled. He saw violet everywhere, just as he had since he was a child. On that rock facing the bottomless canyon, for an endless moment in time, there was nothing on earth but Paco and his smile - no thoughts, no worries, no past conversations or future concerns. Paco was one big smile in the present moment. He was one big smile with feet. As he breathed deeply, he felt his body radiate intensely with life force.

“What you are experiencing is the present moment,” Hawan continued, as Paco’s smile grew wider and wider, “that is your essence – *the real you.* When you leave the earth, your essence remains. It is eternal. Continue to keep your eyes closed and feel the essence of who you are as you breathe in and out. The space between your thoughts… the consciousness of being alive, of just being you… your true self… that is the present moment. That is the only thing you can change. That is where your choices lie. That is where your power lies too.”

“How does it feel?”

Paco did not answer for some time. Completely engulfed in the experience, no words were necessary.

“I’m speechless. It feels so peaceful and yet, so powerful. I wish I had known about this earlier."

"Everything happens when your soul is ready. Your soul has called for it, and this is your time to experience and cherish it." "I feel like I am in control of my thoughts, my emotions, and my body. It truly feels empowering."

"When you are aware of the present moment, your vision is clear. You can be who you truly are and receive both the answers and wisdom required to make the best decisions. In the present moment, you stop being a machine that reacts. Your mind is lucid and your actions, effortless. Do you feel like you have more time to think clearly now?" Hawan asked.

Paco nodded.

"When your thoughts are scattered and travelling at the speed of light, you miss most of the view. If there was a wall ahead, would you have enough time to make the best decision and avoid hitting the wall? That is how our minds usually behave. We are continuously and obsessively thinking, reliving the past or worrying about the future so that we miss the mark - and we hit those walls, often at full speed. When you live in present time, you think more clearly because your mind is at ease."

"When your mind is at ease, you see the full picture. Your judgement sharpens. Situations come into true perspective. Only when you escape the repeating thought patterns in your mind, can you take the time to enjoy all that's around you, including yourself. Only then can you be. In this lifetime, there are not many things as rewarding as just Being. *Just being you.*"

Paco kept his eyes closed. He wore a smile that portrayed a new, deep understanding.

"This is I!" Paco shouted with enthusiasm, "This is who I really am. Hawan, thank you… this is a life-changing realisation."

"You brought this into your life Paco. I'm just the pointer. You can open your eyes now," the shaman replied, proud of his pupil.

Paco looked bedazzled. In a cursory moment of light, he realised he was more than his body, more than his thoughts, more than he was taught to believe. He was a soul. He was energy. He was an eternal spirit having a human experience, where the present moment was all there was. It was his newfound point of power.

"Every moment is perfect. Every moment just is. Everything you're going through is designed to *shape your soul* in this journey. What you do at every given moment is creating the story of your life. Will you write a great biography?"

Hawan allowed his pupil to enjoy a moment of profound realisation. He calmly observed Paco's joy dancing in his heart. The lesson was not over, though.

The shaman continued, "More important than your relationship with Milagros, me or anyone else, you need to have a relationship with the present moment, *The Now*. This is the key relationship in your life. If this relationship doesn't work, none of your other relationships will work either. You have to decide what kind of relationship you choose to have with the Now. Will it be one of misery or one of joy? Will the Now be your friend? Will it be your worst enemy? It is all up to you. Everything in life you want to achieve is your choice."

"I choose to befriend it and promise to work on it daily until I am fully aware of the present at all times," Paco replied, invigorated with new zest, he grew more resolute in his decisions the more time he spent with Hawan.

"I'm glad to hear that Paco. Remember, everything you want from life is a choice. What the future holds for you depends on the state of your consciousness today.

Now let's discuss your song-writing dilemma."

"What do you think is my problem?" Paco asked.

"Every time you get angry or frustrated when you are unable to write, you place yourself in a negative state of mind. This will only push you away from the creative state you need to be in. Choose to enjoy the process of writing. Choose to relax. You need to be gentle with yourself and become a friend to the process. What is the point in getting angry? What is the point of becoming frustrated? You will only chase away all your positive intentions. Try to stop thinking about the results and start enjoying the process. *Be positive to the point where it becomes such a strong habit that you don't know how else to live.*"

"When you live in the Now, it feels like time does not exist, and that is when your creativity will really flourish."

"Song-writing is one of your passions. Have fun when doing it. We are here on earth to have fun, not suffer like some people make you believe."

"That makes so much sense Hawan," Paco said, "I remember writing my best work when I was feeling great. In other words, those songs came from a joyful place in my heart."

"*Joy is found in the Now.* All you have is this moment Paco. Why would you want to be somewhere else? Think of the past for a second. Is it here?"

"No, it's gone," Paco replied.

"Then, is the future here?"

"No, it's not here either."

"Think about this… carefully… when is the only time the future arrives?" Hawan asked, caressing the Chakana he wore with pride around his neck.

"Mmm… interesting question Hawan… I guess if I could jump forward to the future, the only way to create it is with my thoughts and actions today, so my answer is… that *the future can only arrive in the Now,* in the form of the present moment."

"You have it."

Above them, a water-charged storm from the warm Amazon tropics moved in and collided with the freezing Andean air. In a colossal clash of titans, an army of massive clouds raged through the canyon screaming deluge. The canyon immediately fell to a massive shower of rain.

"Let's get inside Hawan," Paco shouted, hastening back towards the cave.

"Remember to enjoy the present moment," the shaman replied. Paco stopped in his tracks and looked dumbfounded. "Grey, cloudy days remind me of how infinitesimally blue the sky is," the shaman said.

"What is there not to enjoy about a little warm water on your skin?" Hawan wore a smile from ear to ear. "Enjoy it Paco. Open your mouth and taste it. Feel the trickle caressing your face… it's a miracle of nature."

Paco closed his eyes and opened his arms wide, whilst leaning back so his face was directed toward the heavens. He threw his head back to receive the full effect of the downpour. Tiny droplets of the rushing deluge took refuge in his welcoming body and flowing hair. It was the first time in his life that he had not run from a thunderstorm – instead, he embraced it as a thirsty camel worshipping water in an elusive oasis.

In that moment it was only Paco and the rain.

"Raining reminds me of guests throwing rice at a married couple," Hawan said. "*When it rains, nature wants to remind us how much we're loved.*"

Paco kept his eyes closed and felt the unique way each raindrop danced and jumped, seemingly with joy, on his skin. Pachamama whispered with happy tears… "I Love you, my son…"

"Every moment is perfect. Every moment just Is. Everything you are going through is designed *to shape your soul* in this journey. What you do at every given moment is creating the story of your life. It is *up to you* to create the memories of your lifetime. Will you create one Now?"

"Yes señor," Paco replied, "another perfect moment."

Hawan smiled as he watched Paco attempt the '*jelly dance*' in the rain. His dancing style wasn't pretty. He remembered Notas mentioning that Paco had an unusual way of running and dancing - and he was right… Paco's style of dancing could make a stone or tree burst into laughter. He twirled as if he was made of gelatine and twisted like a desert snake zigzagging down a hot dune. His arms waved to a beat only he could hear and understand. He bit his lower lip slightly, his eyes totally focused on the revolving floor around him. In his mind, he was the master of rhythm, the Duke of the Dance floor.

"Hey Paco," Hawan said.

"Yes, señor… you like the way I shake my skeleton?" Paco replied, his eyes fixed on the stony ground. "A heart afraid of failing never learns to dance like this."

Hawan rested his arms on his hips as the wild rain fell even fiercer. He was smiling, his two bushy eyebrows sagging from the downpour.

"I think it's marvellous," he replied. "Just dance Paco… at this moment you don't need a reason… it's just you and the rain… *so just dance.*"

17 Indigo, Selfless Service

The daily weather in the Andes was unpredictable, unlike the change of season, which was easier to forecast. The nights became chillier with the approaching winter, and as the leaves turned caramel and withered, Paco grew in wisdom and vision.

His heart opened like a lotus, and he began to understand his unique mission in the world. He also developed an inner sense of calm and peace, which made Hawan a proud teacher. Forgiving his father in the Lake of Gratitude and understanding the other principles of the rainbow, had allowed him to grow closer to his truth and venture deeper into his real self. His Never-Ending Legacy was beginning to materialise.

With the advent of winter, the two men began to gather dry pieces of wood from the nearby forests in order to create a healthy reserve for the cold season. Large quantities were gathered, tied, and lifted up the treacherous incline back to the cave. During this arduous task, Paco took note of the never-failing, teeth-bearing smile the shaman wore like pearls on a glimmering crown. Hawan seemed to enjoy every moment of the work.

"Excuse me Hawan… I have a question that has been floating in my mind for a while."

"Feel free to ask me anything," Hawan replied, halting his climb to the cave.

"We've been gathering, stacking, and lifting heavy pieces of wood for days on end. I've tried to see the positive side to it, but apart from having fodder for the approaching winter, I do not see any other benefit."

"Would you care to explain why a man of your age smiles at such unpleasant toil?"

Carrying a heavy load of lumber on his back, Hawan turned around to face his curious pupil.

"It's time to move on to The *Sixth Principle of the Rainbow.*"

As always, he gave Paco a chance to guess the principle.

"Mmm… 'Smile while you work'?" Paco retorted, taking a wild shot at the conundrum.

Hawan grinned. "It has to do with work, so again, a close guess."

"The sixth principle in order to live like a Rainbow Shaper is called *Selfless Service* and it's symbolised by the colour *Indigo*."

"Selfless service?" Paco responded. "How does this relate to carrying endless loads of heavy wood?"

"The Inca lived by a principle called *Llancay*. This means going beyond what we consider work. To the Inca, work was an *innate expression of who you are as a person*. This way, what we label work becomes Love and service. Remember the principle of reciprocity?"

"Yes, very well," Paco responded.

"In relation to this, the Inca knew that working solely to elevate one's self was limiting. On the other hand, practising work with Love and selfless service would allow us to grow further as individuals as well as expand the consciousness of everyone around us. Are you getting the picture?"

"I think I do," Paco replied, still warming up to the idea.

"You see, many times we live our lives like we own a store," Hawan said, using hand movements that were coordinated to perfection.

"What do you mean?"

"Often, we only give or do things in order to get something back. We focus on how much we are going to get for it and who is going to pay the bigger price. If something does not benefit us, we simply don't do it. If that's our sole purpose, yes, we can accumulate many material benefits… but how can we enjoy what we have if we have no one to share it with? Selfishness will not create friends for you. By opening our hearts to others and giving freely of ourselves, we create reciprocity and grow in unity with life."

"Is that why you smile while you work?" Paco asked, setting his heavy load of wood on the ground.

"Yes, Paco," the shaman replied, "A meaningful life is blessed with attributes such as service and sacrifice. When I carry the load, I think of whom I'm serving at that moment and how I can give more of myself without expecting anything back. The stacks of wood we're setting aside for winter will keep us warm, and allow us to share special times together until such a moment when you decide to part ways. Our work will also grant us many hours of talking and discussing in the comfort of a warm cave. These moments are priceless, and that's why I smile. I try to see the bigger picture. I'm not just carrying a load of wood: I'm creating memories through the winter."

"Now I am starting to understand you." Paco exclaimed.

"The Inca understood that humankind needed to evolve. This was an important principle in their lives. They knew they were on earth to evolve and progress. Think about it, what is the point of staying the same - unchanged, and horizontal?"

"I couldn't imagine a life without growth," Paco responded. "So… do we evolve by helping others?"

"Yes, we do. One of the many ways to evolve is through selfless service," Hawan added, "tell me Paco, what qualities would you eradicate in humankind?"

Paco placed his foot on top of a timber stack like a pensive conqueror and rubbed his chin vigorously in the Alegría manner.

Before Paco had an opportunity to answer, the shaman continued, "Let me put it this way… if you had the power to click your fingers and instantly eradicate some of the worst qualities we have as a planet, what would they be?"

"That isn't a difficult question to answer," Paco replied, still rubbing his chin.

"I would eradicate suffering, injustice, egotism, hate, jealousy, racism, greed, and violence."

"What would you replace these qualities with?" The shaman asked without delay.

"First on my list would be unconditional Love, reciprocity, humility, unselfishness, tolerance, laughter, and service."

"You missed one word before service," Hawan added, and smiled.

"I meant selfless service!" Paco smiled back.

"Do you remember that selfless service was one of the many meanings of the Chakana?"

"Yes, I do Hawan," Paco answered, "I think you said that clothing a beggar, feeding a hungry child, and even quenching the thirsty, was clothing, feeding, and quenching The One. Selflessly serving others is thus a privilege."

"Excellent," the shaman replied. "The greatness of the mighty Inca Empire just like the future greatness of our planet relies on this kind of service. Do you know what is so wonderful about service?"

"Please tell me," Paco said, foot still atop the load of wood.

"By applying selfless service, the negative qualities in humankind are replaced with positive ones; not just in each of us, but in everyone. This is our planet's road to salvation, and without it, the world will not change, evolve, or progress."

"I see how selfless service elevates each person touched by it and consequently the planet," Paco added. "It explains the greatness of the Inca Empire."

"If you want to see a better planet, a better country, a better community and a better you, it has to start with you Paco. There is no other way. The more you elevate yourself spiritually, the more you elevate others around you. It's a perpetual circle. If you decide to serve, for no recognition and for no reason other than to serve, life will reward you and give you what you desire. By serving, you rule – although for this to happen, one has to do it with a *pure heart*. Remember that you are the world, and the world is you – everything is connected. One of the keys to the success in any undertaking is to stop doing it for you, and start doing it for others. By helping others, you are helping yourself. Can you think of a time when someone helped you, expecting nothing in return?"

"Back in Miramar, when I first started to sell newspapers on the street, the owner of a Brandy store, señor Matteo, offered to keep some of my unsold papers," Paco replied. "He asked for nothing back."

"Did you two become friends?" Hawan asked.

"We became best of friends."

"The moment you serve someone with no ulterior reason but to be of service, you win that person forever," Hawan said.

"Thanks to señor Matteo's efforts, I became the most successful newspaper boy in Miramar," Paco exclaimed.

"That is true, selfless service young man – when someone elevates you to a higher place of being with their open and helpful heart."

"He was an angel when I needed it most," Paco replied.

"That is something we all are - angels."

"What do you mean?" Paco asked.

"We are angels - we've just forgotten about it," Hawan said, "selfless service reminds us of our power as angels. Let me illustrate this point. When you perform a random act of kindness, clothe someone you don't know, or you help anyone to succeed just because it makes you happy… you are *being an angel!* Angels do these wonderful things. It doesn't matter who does it - what matters are the purpose and intention behind the action."

"I guess the purpose is to be of service for no reward," Paco replied.

"It is my young friend," Hawan said, "When you serve selflessly, you build a corner of heaven on earth. What is also amazing is that all the travelling you do only takes place from your head to your heart."

"What do you mean?"

"What I mean is that you don't have to come down from heaven to do the work of an angel. All you have to do is open your heart, listen to the inner voice that asks you to serve, and take action. That is it. You don't need much thinking to take action now. You can also use all the resources you have collected with your mind; use your education, your working experience, your intellect, and even your wealth, and apply them with your heart to uplift the planet as a whole. Just like Pachamama gives us her boundless gifts, day after day with no expectation of return, we can do the same."

"It sounds so easy to give a hand to those in need," Paco added.

"It is," the shaman replied lightly, "look at your hands."

Paco opened both hands and did not see anything peculiar.

"Close your hands. Make a fist. Now look at them… they look menacing, dangerous, unwilling to be opened… in other words, they look hard, don't they? Paco looked at his fists, turned them around a few times and realised they couldn't do much but hurt.

The shaman continued, "If your fists are closed, you cannot give or receive."

Paco nodded.

"See that yellow flower?" the shaman pointed to a beautiful daisy a few feet away.

"Try and grab it with a fist."

Paco kneeled to grab hold of the flower with closed fists but it escaped him.

"It's not possible," Hawan remarked. "Now open your hands and look at them… look at how magnificent your hands are - designed to be open in all their magnificence. Designed to build, create, and heal. Once your hands are open, they can now receive as well as give… a big difference. Your two hands when used for selfless service become the hands of The One."

"Now imagine millions of human hands all working together, helping each other… When that happens, The One will smile proudly at his most beautiful creation."

"If all humans decided to be angels to each other by practising selfless service, there would be no one left without a human angel," Paco added.

"Let me tell you a story about being an angel. It happened about thirty years ago," Hawan said.

"During the recent *War of Independence*, countless brave soldiers from all over South America travelled to our shores in order to liberate us from the shackles of the men from the Old World. During the war, a battalion of young volunteers secretly docked at an unknown location along our coast, planning to reinforce some of their troops huddled at a strategic location further inland.

The soldiers, inexperienced to our desert conditions got lost, having mislaid the meeting point with their principal battalion.

The relentless sun and the lack of shade pounded them for days, and in a final attempt to survive, they chose three of their fittest men to go and seek help."

"The three men walked for miles in the fierce heat, when suddenly they spotted a dark speck in the distance that did not belong in that desolate and dry landscape. They rushed to the spot, and to their surprise, found a small, deserted water well. The three desperate men lined up in order of rank.

The highest-ranking officer reeled up the rope that led down the well, not knowing if they would find life or death. As the sound of something solid banged against the walls of the well, they were lucky to find a tiny bucket, the size of a single glass and barely enough for one person, but it was filled with fresh, cool water.

The first officer brought the bucket to his lips. He tipped his head back and gulped all the water without a single drop of liquid missing his mouth. They reeled in the bucket once more. While the second officer glugged the water down in gulps, the third, selflessly ran back to his missing friends to let them know they had found water and led them back to their survival."

"From this true story, it is not too difficult to spot who the angel was," Hawan said.

"I believe you have that quality in you Paco. I believe you would run to help everyone before you helped yourself. Do not ever lose that quality. In the world we live in today, it is a unique quality and it signifies strength. If only more people were like you, no one would be thirsty or hungry."

"Just imagine Paco… for a second… what our world would be like. If everyone did this, we would bring the kind of transformation that would change our world forever."

"That's a beautiful thought, but can we really do it?" Paco asked.

"A new world is not only a reality… it is already on its way. In the silence of our mind, it knocks on our door… and it is up to us to open the door and let it in."

"I have learned that if you want something to happen, it is up to you to make it happen," Paco added.

"The surprising thing with positive change is that it doesn't occur at once and by the millions… but by a slow process of osmosis, one person at a time," Hawan said. "Start with you first. Be *that change*. Live it and personify it. Your life will be blessed for it. Isn't that a reason to smile?"

Paco lifted his heavy load of wood and placed it on his back in one swift swoop.

He looked at his teacher and gave him a smile of gratitude.

With the approaching sunset, the two men carried their heavy loads of selfless service up the slopes to the cave again… and they simply, smiled.

18 Violet, All Is Unfolding Perfectly

"I have another question," Paco stated.

A quarter of the cave lay occupied by layer upon layer of dry branches, all horizontally stacked carefully alongside each other, in rows and columns, creating a tower that almost brushed the ceiling. The shaman had just finished a cleansing ceremony and the air was pungent with the scent of sage and ash; rolling puffs of smoke lingered in mid-air.

Hawan gazed at Paco with a look tattooed with the word 'proceed.'

"You've always looked so calm and present, Hawan. No situation has ever been bigger than your peace of mind. Paco said in deep reverence to his teacher, "but only once have I seen you change that look. It happened the day we met, when I told you that my name was Paco. If I may ask, why did you look shaken when I revealed my name?"

Hawan seemed to be levitating from his seated position in the centre of a storm of smoke clouds, as though he were not subject to gravitation. In his usual calm, deliberate manner, the shaman fixed his black poncho and stood up, dispersing the nebulosity around him.

"You took me by surprise," he replied with utmost sincerity.

"What surprised you?" Paco replied, "My name?"

"Yes, your name, and the fateful series of the events of that day."

"What is so unusual or interesting about my name Hawan? And what happened before I arrived?" Paco asked.

"Well… your name is a Quecchua word that means an *initiate of the Andean tradition and way of life.*" Hawan replied, bowing his head to Pachamama, "and that is what you have so proudly become."

Paco sat in silence as his teacher proceeded to explain.

"For years, I have communicated with the Spirit. It speaks loudly and its message is clear. During those years, it showed me the attire of a Paco - the colour of his bright poncho and the multicoloured weaves of his chullo. The day we met, they matched yours. When I first saw you, I doubted the voice of the Spirit. I dismissed it as mere coincidence. Then you revealed your name and its thunderous roar shook my incredulous heart. In that second, I learned to listen and believe without doubting its voice again. The Spirit also told me that the arriving Paco had an important mission and that I'd be responsible for sharing its ancient wisdom for the benefit of our country and humankind."

Hawan approached Paco and knelt before him; the master bestowing a deep sense of humility in his student. He took Paco's hands and looked at his pupil, his eyes brimming with a deep sense of gratitude.

"It is I who need to thank you Paco," he said.

"Thank me for what, dear teacher?" Paco replied, taken aback by Hawan's show of respect and humility.

"When I realised, I did not fully listen to what the Spirit had told me…" The shaman had to clear his throat before proceeding, "I acknowledged that I didn't trust its voice completely. Your arrival taught me to believe without a shadow of a doubt that, everything in my life was unfolding as it should."

"I really did that?"

"*You* taught me The *Seventh Principle of the Rainbow*, symbolised by the colour *Violet*. Now it's your turn to discover its miracle," Hawan answered.

"Take one last guess at the name of this principle."

Ever since Paco was a child, whenever he closed his eyes, he saw *violet* - the colour that overshadowed the other colours of the rainbow in his dreams. Now, as he closed his eyes, the same intense violet appeared, just above the place where his eyebrows met, and in an unexpected burst of enlightenment, he heard it.

"*All is unfolding perfectly*," he replied swiftly.

For the first time, Paco's answer was correct.

Hawan embraced his pupil as a giant bear would that latches onto its cub. The two had never been this close before. It felt as if the beginning of the end had begun to unfold in one simple embrace. They remained holding each other, proud master and pupil, enjoying the moment.

"Walk outside with me," Hawan signalled for Paco to follow.

Outside the cave, they witnessed the spectacle of more than a dozen condors gliding above them, temporarily blocking the rays of the sun with their enormous wings. Their flight gave the impression of a tornado of wild plumes and dark silhouettes that caressed the space above them. They were as silent and graceful as angels in prayer.

"They are just majestic," Paco exclaimed.

"They symbolise to the Inca all that is Divine and pure," Hawan replied. "They also represent the Upper World called *Hanaq Pacha*."

"Tell me more about this upper world of the Inca," Paco replied, gazing in awe at the condors above him.

"The Upper World is inhabited by celestial citizens, angels and guides, like your teacher Doña Lucia."

"How do you know?" Paco effused, "Can you see her?"

"Her energy is always around you, and she is smiling," the shaman replied.

"Thank you Hawan. Please let her know that I think of her daily."

"She can hear you right now, so please speak to her directly, you don't need a go-between."

Paco closed his eyes. He silently thanked his beloved Tibetan teacher for the wisdom and Love she inspired. They felt each other's energies and connected in a place where words are inadequate luxuries.

"What else happens in the Upper World?" Paco asked.

Hawan felt Doña Lucia's divine presence and nodded. It was time to proceed with the last principle of the rainbow. Her strong energy reassured Hawan that she would be behind Paco; especially during the last and most difficult task.

"The Upper World is a place of no boundaries. The universal power reigns supreme and all beings are part of its Divine light. It's the place where every human should strive to journey towards and finally reside. No words can describe its beauty and peace. It is symbolised by the eternal, the infinite, and on earth, the condor."

"Why does the condor signify such a magnificent place?" Paco asked.

"Hanaq Pacha is a place where there is no fear… and *where fear is absent, only Love reigns*. If a condor feared, it wouldn't be able to fly. A condor has to trust completely in its ability to fly or it would crash and die. Just like a condor sees life with a clear view from the heavens, see your life without fear and with no judgement from your highest place of being. As you learn to soar higher, you'll start shedding some of your weight and you'll see your life from a wider and clearer perspective."

"With new wings and awakening eyes, you'll start to see how life is unfolding perfectly before you. You'll understand your past and you'll start designing your future, because your wings are steadily holding you in the present moment. When you learn from the past, live in the moment, and take the necessary steps to design your future, you will experience the *joy of being*. You will feel more alive and be able to fulfil your mission and purpose with renewed strength and vigour. Like Doña Lucia says, you'll be able to fulfil your Never-Ending Legacy."

"The key is always to trust and believe that everything is working in your favour. It's not easy to completely trust that a Higher Source is directing your flight with you, but once you do, you will be soaring to heights you never thought possible, and that is the challenge."

Paco looked at his teacher. He rested both hands on his hips, and tilted his head to the side, in one last attempt to declare that he was ready for whatever the shaman, or the world, could throw at him. Hawan knew exactly how to interpret that look – it was Paco after all – determined, curious, and confident.

"I'm waiting for you to tell me what's on your mind," Paco said cheekily, "I'm more than ready." He was beaming with self-belief, having surpassed the other challenges. 'Why shouldn't I be confident?' he thought.

"Are you still afraid of *heights?*" Hawan asked.

One word was enough to bring his Royal Highness straight down from his floating throne of bubbling confidence.

Paco turned pale. His palms started to sweat profusely and his heart began to speed as his mind raced to the challenge of facing his worst fear… and one he had not yet conquered.

"I know you can do it," Hawan replied, trying to calm his pastel-faced pupil by encouraging his instinctive, competitive nature. "Your fears are just thoughts you give power to. And just as you feed power to a thought, you can starve it of power… and change it at will."

"My fear of heights is something I've never conquered!"

"I haven't even told you what you have to do and you are already in a panic," Hawan said, "this is your time to learn how to trust in the Divine."

Paco shut his eyes. The easy violet that surrounded his inner sight calmed him slightly. He breathed with intensity, and attempted to anchor his thoughts in the present moment, subduing his natural fear of heights.

"Ok, I am ready," he said, "what is the last challenge?" He breathed out like a dragon before dying.

"Do you remember the perfect, triangular peak you saw on the way back from the Forest of Illia?" Hawan tried to be as gentle as possible, even though he knew it might not work.

Paco felt his legs give way and rapidly took a seat on a solid boulder, his back to the canyon. He covered his face, ashamed to show his teacher the feelings of terror wrangling inside.

Hawan continued, "That holy Apu is called *The Peak of No Return* and one can get up…" Paco interrupted his teacher in mid-sentence, "…but one can't come down? … Is that it? Please tell me that isn't so."

Hawan did not reply. His eyes gave the story away…

Paco's heart knew the answer too.

"How do you then get down?" Paco asked.

"I'm the only person who's ever conquered the Apu," the shaman answered, "but I cannot tell you how I achieved it – that is something you will have to find out for yourself."

"Thank you Hawan, that really helps." Paco grated, terrified, moving his arms with a high voltage of emotions. He got up from the boulder and pranced around the edge of the precipice in typical Alegría manner.

"Do you feel like you've already lost?"

"I feel like the world is coming down on me and clipping my wings when I'm just about to take flight… why this, and why now? Why can't life just get easier? Why do we always receive the most difficult tests at the end?" Paco remarked with frustration.

"Why are you suddenly losing faith Paco? Have you not learned anything? Have you already forgotten about the *Forest of Illia* and the *Lake of Gratitude*? Your success was conceived the moment you believed you were capable of winning."

"Yes, I remember that… but this… Now I have to face my worst fear. In addition, the only person who knows how to succeed will not help me. Is there anything else I don't know?"

"The only way to get down the peak is…" Hawan paused, "… if you trust that everything in your life is unfolding perfectly at that moment."

"What?" Paco shouted, bedazzled.

"That's it," Hawan replied and began to stroll away. "I will leave you with your thoughts. I trust you will find an answer."

"Thank you, I appreciate that," Paco answered.

"Before I go," Hawan stopped. "I need an answer by tonight."

"Why?" Paco was surprised by the lack of time the shaman had left him in order to make such a pivotal decision. "Can it get any worse?" he thought aloud.

"The peak can only be climbed the day before a full moon… which is tomorrow. That is why I need your answer by tonight," Hawan remarked. "By the way, Paco…"

"Yes Hawan…" Paco continued to shake his head with a resolute 'no.'

"I know you can do it," the shaman uttered as he strolled away.

With sunset approaching, he grew more and more confused. The rumble of thunder shattered the Andean silence in a flash. Soft droplets of cold rain made their way down to earth, and reminded Paco that he was still alive. He felt the energy of Doña Lucia surrounding him, whispering her last words in colours of velvet and rose.

'On a rainy night… you can still choose to see stars.'

He looked up and glinting between the water-laden clouds was a lone, bright star in the almost-night sky.

"Doña Lucia!"

Paco knelt down, the ground as his pulpit. With both hands on his heart and the lingering rain on his skin, he knew it was time to face the last challenge. Calmly, he walked to the cave and said, "It's time."

Hawan lifted his gaze from the broth, "Good. We get up at dawn. Please have an early night."

The two men departed at the crack of dawn the next morning on their way to The Peak of No Return. It was a cold morning but a hearty breakfast nimbly warmed Paco's spirits.

He was exhausted after a sleepless night pestered by the pirouettes of his restless mind. He had many concerns attacking his heart and was eager to get answers before the final climb.

"What must I do when I'm about to face an obstacle I believe I might not overcome?" he asked. "My mind keeps repeating the impossible."

"Impossible is fiction. Impossible only exists in your mind and anything that exists in your mind can be changed at will. Firstly, there is nothing you cannot overcome; and secondly, there's no point in developing a negative mindset before a challenge. In any case, why do we look at obstacles as negative experiences? If something or someone moves you away from a comfort zone, why don't you see the positive in it? Mistakes happen only in situations when we learn nothing. If an experience allows you room to grow and evolve, it must be a positive experience."

"Take this challenge as an opportunity to expand. A new challenge is always a chance to improve your already-working wings, so see it as a goal you need to accomplish or a lesson you need to learn. By thinking you cannot overcome it, you have lost the war before the battle begins."

"That is what my mind keeps repeating," Paco replied, "so what must I do?"

"Many successful people throughout history set out to achieve their dreams with very little in their pockets. They only knew one thing: they would achieve whatever was in their mind at all costs. Their vision was already a reality. That is the attitude you must take in order to overcome anything - never give up! If you have the will, nothing is impossible. The universe has a solution for everything… except one thing: your perseverance."

"When it is time to act, remember to opt for the most positive choice. Whatever the outcome, one thing is very important: acceptance. Accepting that the result is part of your greater plan will open new doors that will lead you closer to your destination. On the way there, enjoy the process of evolving, unfolding and learning to trust that whatever you are going through is always in your best interest. That is the key: learning to trust."

"Do you mean I must learn to trust that The One will guide me?"

"What you need to understand is that you are part of a universal plan. What this means is that you attract into your life the necessary experiences you need at the exact point in time they are supposed to happen."

Paco looked confused. "Please elaborate," he said.

"Earth is a place where your life is tested. This is a testing ground for all human beings. We are here to learn how to move to the next planes of existence. In that light, all that you experience in life is geared towards your evolution. If something or a situation wasn't for your highest good, it didn't happen. Everything in life you can either accept and evolve or deny and wither. It's all your choice."

"Think back to the challenges you have conquered so far: they were exactly what you needed to experience in order to get you where you are today. In other words, they were *perfect*. You can argue that they were difficult, challenging, and one almost took your life, but still, they were always perfect. *They were all perfectly geared for your evolution.* This is not an easy concept to understand Paco."

"You have the answers to all the questions in your life. You may not believe this because you were taught that answers came from outside of you. You are the book. You are the wisdom. You are the key. All you have to do is learn to remember. The answers have always been within you."

"Do not forget what you've learned about reciprocity, your purpose in life, unconditional Love, how to think with your heart, selfless service, and how to live and empower yourself by living in the present moment. Every lesson created the person you are today. You have grown in leaps Paco. Your belief in The One and in yourself got you out of the Forest of Illia. Why have you so soon forgotten?"

"No, I have not, but… this is something that might be beyond me," Paco replied.

"Consider every obstacle you encounter on your evolutionary path a blessing, whether you perceive the experience to be positive or negative. If you are experiencing it - it must be for a reason – there is a universal plan you are part of, so flow with it, be effortless. It takes considerably more effort to swim against the current than to let it lead you forward on your journey. Stop wasting energy resisting it," Hawan said.

"Right now, it feels like I'm swimming against this massive current and I have no power over it."

"The magic about it all is that even though you are part of this exquisite plan, you still have a choice. If you decide to swim against the current, you are welcome - no one will stop you. Doing that though, might eventually tire you and defeat you. Remember that what you do and what you think is always your choice."

"Every human being has free will and the power to choose – and that empowers us. Your choices today will attract the exact experiences you need in order to evolve and grow, and these choices will have a hand in determining your future path. It's all up to you Paco. Are you going to approach this task with a weak mind or are you going to give it your all and know that when you do this, The One will take care of the rest?"

As he said this, Hawan put his arm around his shoulder.

"The One never gives us more than we can handle. So remember to keep on pushing, keep on conquering, and keep on smiling, because *the load you have right now is never bigger than your heart.*"

Paco believed in his teacher's wisdom, but he still harboured some doubts.

"You told me once I get to the apex, there's no way of coming down. Is that true?"

"Yes, it's true. The peak has small openings along the rock walls. Hands fit perfectly during the climb. On the descent, those apertures are too small for a foot to enter and so a descent is not an option - unless you have a death wish. People have attempted descending in the past but none of their bodies have been found. It's your choice whether you decide to do that or not Paco."

Paco's heart began to beat as fast as a hummingbird's heart on an escape flight.

"What must I do when I reach the top? How do I learn how to get down?"

"Just like you found the answer back in the Forest of Illia, you'll find the answer at the top of The Peak of no Return. The answer is within you Paco, so trust."

"You have taught me to trust and although I know it will be difficult, I will do my best to overcome my doubts." Paco said with resolution.

"This is not about what you do or what I did, but about *who you are*. The battlefield of owning your dreams is won the moment you decide to conquer your fears Paco."

Hawan paused and turned around to face Paco.

"Let me ask you something… what changed your mind yesterday and convinced you to face this challenge?"

"The voice of Doña Lucia," Paco answered, "it was so clear – she said that even on a rainy night I can still choose to see stars. That touched me and changed the course of events."

"She means that in the face of adversity you can still choose to see the positive, grow the belief in your abilities, and listen to the guidance of your inner voice," Hawan explained. "The One will do the rest."

"Yes I understand," Paco replied, "but once I'm up there what must I do?"

"I cannot answer that for you Paco. When I was up there I didn't have the answer either. I found the answer within me. All I can say is that you must always choose the path of Love. Choose the path that leads you towards it. *Don't go against yourself.* Don't miss the mark. The more you opt for the path of Love, the more blessings you will receive. Remember where there is only Love… there is no fear."

"If you focus your energy and effort into something, by law of The One, it will increase. The more energy and focus you place into feeling good, creating positive thoughts, increasing your self-belief and self-Love, the more they'll return to you. *If you want to fly, you can.* Focus on flying and you will. You already have the wings."

The two men arrived at their destination. The Peak of No Return rose from the canyon's gentle slopes to a height where rock and sky almost joined hands. The coral-like moon framed the sky. It was a dry, sunny day and the weather was perfect for climbing. This calmed Paco's nerves a little.

From the base, they could see the trail of small apertures on the rock's face that allowed a climber to ascend. The openings eventually disappeared, engulfed by the height of the holy Apu.

"It is time Paco. Are you ready? Your *Never-Ending legacy is calling.*"

"No one can ever be ready for this señor, but here I am willing to give it my all."

"Some words of advice: keep on climbing. Do not stop, and do not look down. You have five hours to summit before sunset. Never give up. Some people give up knocking at the ninety-ninth door, when the hundredth door was the one meant to open. Listen to your inner voice and trust that The One has a plan that is unfolding perfectly for you. The beginning and end point of every successful journey is the same: gratitude. *Remember, if you want to fly, you can…*"

"I believe in you Paco. You have always proved yourself worthy of any challenge. I know you will succeed."

"Thank you," was all Paco said. He was putting on a brave face. "Thank you for your kindness, your wisdom, and your friendship. I will never forget you."

"Don't speak like that, young man. It sounds like a goodbye. I will see you later, I believe in you. *Now go and conquer,*" Hawan replied.

Paco gave his teacher one last look, and began the climb.

His hands fitted perfectly in the rock apertures and his cat-like agility and musculature allowed him a swift pass onto the higher sections of the peak. Within the hour the shaman had lost sight of his pupil; but for the next four hours, he still felt Paco's heart, thumping wildly against the merciless rock.

As a result of his fear of heights, Paco never looked down, and calculated each move with serene precision. He paused every time the task seemed overwhelming and closed his eyes. The serene, violet universe nursed him again into the present moment.

Hours into the climb, as the shaman had foreseen, he saw the last section of the peak, culminating in a sharp point about three-feet wide and just big enough for one person. A current of adrenaline exuded from his constricted nerves. The sweat from his stiff hands and fingers left vanishing trails of salty water on the porous rock.

As sunset approached the canyon, Paco hastened in his attempt to summit before the sun reached its resting post. The bright, almost-full moon smiled at the world below her.

'Another twenty feet and I'm there… I can't believe it.' Paco thought, as the orange-tinged world below him sparkled in splendour. If this was his last day, the world was certainly beautiful.

Finally, after five gruelling hours of climbing, Paco reached the triangular summit's peak. He was sweating profusely and his heart was thundering in his semi-open chest. He could feel the heat and the colours of the sun's light, meandering through the clouds and sky, as it encapsulated all his senses. The dizzying silence, the view, the height – it was all beyond words or expectations. In desperation he grasped the small apex with both arms. His gaze fell down the escarpment, and he came to the numbing realisation that at that moment, the possibility of a descent, was non-existent.

Despite realising that he could not descend, a strange sense of serenity and achievement flooded his being.

'What do I do now?' he thought. 'How do I get down?'

He observed the hundreds of magnificent Apus in the surrounding areas. He was clearly the only person on a summit.

'Who would be crazy enough to climb a peak before sunset?' he thought, and in that fraction of a second, he felt alone and helpless at the height of a desolate world.

'On a rainy night… you can still choose to see stars,' the soft voice whispered.

"I need to believe," Paco reiterated, "that everything happens for a reason. I need to trust that The One has a bigger plan for me, and it entails me living on the ground, not dying up here… there has to be something I can do." Paco felt at peace.

"The One gives me free will to choose my thoughts and actions, and these in turn, define my destiny," he proclaimed in the silent space of his mind.

"I need to believe, with no trace of fear. There must be no place for fear in me; only then will Love reign."

Although Paco's mind was calm, his arms and legs were quivering uncontrollably.

He made his first attempt to get onto his feet and conquer the apex… but to no avail.

The wind was picking up. His white shirt blew like the broken sail of a ship in a savage sea storm. As the sun's rays disappeared, stealing all the light from the Andes, Paco attempted to stand at the top of one of the highest peaks in the region in almost-complete darkness.

"Let me try one more time, I can do it… I need to trust," he whispered, "I need to trust… I need to trust."

With a little added effort and still holding on tightly to the apex, he attempted to summit once more. His foot slipped as he pushed with all his might. He barely managed to grab hold of the apex with his left arm – a fall would be a guaranteed high-altitude funeral.

Sweat poured from his forehead. Yet, no fear poured from his heart…

"*All is unfolding perfectly*… this is a test I need to conquer and I will not give up until I'm on the ground again," he said. Engulfed in sheer determination, Paco looked at a ruby-red Tayta Inti disappearing on the horizon. He silently thanked Pachamama for all her gifts.

The breathtaking view, the wafting wind, the smell of earth and sky and the opportunity to stand atop a majestic mountain, humbled him.

The feeling of being alive was an intense sensation reverberating in his chest.

He closed his eyes and thanked The One for his amazing life and the opportunity to grow and evolve through this, his most difficult test. He asked for additional strength on his next attempt to summit the peak, and gratified his heart with a sense of trust that contained no space for boundaries or fear.

He looked up to infinity and his heart spoke to The One with utmost sincerity and reverence. He had a direct line to the heavens. "I know I have a destiny to fulfil and I am part of a unique universal plan you have in store for me. I place my Never-Ending Legacy in your hands. Thank you for my life. Thank you for allowing me to experience this amazing journey on top of the world with all your creation around me. You are everything and everything surrounding me is part of me. I am made of you. Because I am made of you, I can do and accomplish anything. If I give it my all and place my trust in you, I know you'll give me the wings to fly. In your hands, I am invincible and unconquerable. In your hands, my arms become wings. In your hands, nothing is impossible. I believe I can achieve anything, because behind my thoughts, choices and actions, I find your power. I will not fear any height or obstacle and I will be brave because I trust in you, and thus, I trust my own abilities. With you on my side, I will conquer my fears and I will create the life that I've always wanted. On a rainy night, I still choose to see stars, and right now, I have the wings to fly… if I want to fly… I can," Paco uttered as he looked at the coral-like moon twinkling above the earth.

In one effortless swoop, with renewed faith and strength, he pushed one last time and finally stood up firm on top of The Peak of No Return.

In one moment, the choices you make will dictate how you write your Never-Ending Legacy.

Paco opened his arms, threw his head back and fully trusted in the perfection of the moment. There was no fear in his heart. In a fearless heart, Love was king.

"If I want to fly, I can… if I want to fly, I can," he kept repeating as the night began to engulf the world in icy darkness. His eyes were closed as he sailed into the calm, violet sea of The One.

"If I want to fly, I…"

Without warning, Paco's feet lifted off the apex. For what felt like hours, nothing made sense. Something remarkable was happening. He refused to open his eyes, deciding instead to relish the sensation of being airborne and experiencing the glory of that perfect moment.

'*All is unfolding perfectly…*'

A rush of wind caressed his face and hair. With arms still wide open, he gradually opened his eyes. Everything was speeding past him, even the clouds. They were so close he could kiss them.

'Have I died? Has The One turned me into an angel?'

Paco felt a tight grip around his arms. Something was cutting the air around him. He looked to both his left and right - two massive condors held him, one on each side, and in that perfect moment, he was flying.

"I'm flying, I'm flying!" Paco kept screaming, relishing the experience, tears of joy flowing from his eyes and falling onto the earth like drops of holy rain.

From the place where the clouds smile, he saw the beauty of the world gleaming in splendour below him. All of a sudden, hundreds of giant condors from nearby peaks joined him in flight. The prophetic words of his teacher had become true: 'if you want to fly, you can…'

From the ground, Hawan witnessed the remarkable sight of the courageous, young man flying with hundreds of condors.

He too, remembered the feeling of flying when he had conquered the peak - as if it had happened yesterday. He kneeled to thank The One for his mercy and kindness. There are few greater moments of pride in a teacher's heart than the instant when the pupil becomes a master. Gliding down in circular motion, the condors approached the shaman and gently placed Paco on the ground beside him, before retreating again into the darkening skies.

The two embraced with joyous intensity and respect, awash with the unfathomable glory of the heavens. Above the two, a single, smiling star sparkled more brightly than all the other stars in the sky. The coral-bright moon was its witness. As the condors disappeared with the growing darkness, a shaman and his pupil knew that nothing was coincidence… and that their time together had inevitably come to a glorious end.

"Is my time in the Andes over?" Paco asked.

"What does your heart say?"

"It says that my time here has been invaluable, but I need to go and fulfil my Never-Ending Legacy."

"Then do that my young friend," Hawan said, calm as always.

A majestic, dazzling butterfly hovered around Paco a few times, and peacefully rested on his shoulder. He smiled while it fluttered its wings, proud and exquisite.

"The One personally painted this wonderful creature with His hands, as He does with every being in creation. It must be a sign of blessings to come," the shaman exclaimed, studying the rainbow-coloured butterfly that afforded Paco a little affection.

"Really?"

"Yes Paco, in the Andes, it's a sign of *prosperity in your mission*," Hawan replied as the butterfly flitted away with the current of a tender wind.

"Your time here is over for now… a butterfly always returns home with Love like the green returns with Love to the exhausted leaves after a cold winter."

"Nature is like Love: it allows the butterfly to follow the path it needs to traverse, and as such, Love, like nature, does not harm. It knows it's in a butterfly's nature to fly. The instinct of Love does not harm itself, because it understands its purpose. Just as the butterfly escapes with the northern winds following its call, it also returns to its source, where it belongs."

"A butterfly never forgets its source - from time immemorial it has travelled with the butterfly… and you see it in the shape of its wings, in its body, and its freedom. A butterfly is what it is because it realises that it comes from where it does."

"A butterfly's colours paint the history it has flown: the bright colours depict the smiles. Its dark shades and scars say to the world, *'I have survived, there's life in me.'*"

"A butterfly is like nature. Nature is wise. Nature is the voice of The One murmured in the flow of a river, the shade of an ancient tree, or the flight of a butterfly. Speak to the wind and let your wishes and voice resonate on all four corners of the earth… the world will hear you."

"Now go home with Love… it is calling you," the shaman said exquisitely.

"So I guess this is goodbye," Paco said. Although his heart agreed, a part of him wanted to remain with the shaman and carry on learning about the ancient Andean tradition. The two had become closer as the last challenges unfolded, and Paco felt he was leaving a large piece of his heart back in the canyon.

"In the Andes we do not say goodbye," Hawan replied. "We say, until we meet again."

"And so it shall be… until we meet again Hawan… and thank you," Paco bowed, his hands clasped together on his heart, and hastened a few steps away from his teacher, who was attired in his hallmark black poncho.

Hawan blew his ancient seashell until the echoes of the sea resonated along the walls of the ancient canyon. From the Apus, a large Condo of condors invaded the firmament and bid farewell to the visitor… until such time when their paths should cross again.

"Not everyone's purpose is to build an empire or change the world. Your purpose can be raising a great family or being of service to the community. The size of the purpose doesn't matter, but the size of the heart behind the purpose is what matters. Write *the history of your soul* and don't forget your home in the small corner in the Andes. You will always be welcome," Hawan offered as Paco began to pack his belongings. "Whenever you look at yourself, remember me… *I am as you are.*" The shaman's last words went up to heaven… like all prayers do.

"So long Hawan," Paco called from a few feet away. "I will always carry this place here," he said, pointing to his heart as he disappeared from the shaman's sight. He made his way along a winding road that journeyed through the cliffs and canyon.

In the Andes, Paco grew his wings; it was now time to spread them and fly.

As Paco made his way from the canyon, the view changed with every step towards Miramar.

What he did not know, was that the view was going to change faster and more perilously than he had ever thought imaginable.

19 Dead or Alive

After spending invaluable months with the shaman in a magical part of his beloved country, Paco traced the long, westward road back to Miramar. 'In a few weeks,' he thought, 'I'll be in the loving arms of Milagros… perhaps things have returned to *normal* and I can enter Miramar without having to hide.'

In two days, he would be back in Kaikay. He would see Eusebio and Valentina again and share his stories and adventures, as well as stock up with the essential provisions required for the return voyage to the coastal capital. The Andean scenery was breathtaking as he sauntered down to Kaikay… he felt Pachamama's presence everywhere. The special time spent with the shaman had opened his heart to the glory of the world.

As Paco approached Kaikay, a small child darted past him at full speed. The little man was certainly in a hurry.

"Hey," Paco waved his arms and signalled for the child to stop. He was curious to find out how far he needed to journey to arrive at the sleepy Andean village.

The child slackened as his feet sandpapered the gravel and came to a standstill.

"How far is Kaikay?" Paco asked politely.

The child stared at Paco with a look of horror, and in a flash scampered away as though Paco had been a ravenous puma in search of a meal. He disappeared in the opposite direction, leaving in his wake a dispersing cloud of dust and a scattering of tiny pebbles.

Around the corner was the village of Kaikay, just as he remembered it. There were small adobe houses surrounding a crooked church steeple that had been left askew after the blow from a merciless earthquake many years ago.

Pieces of paper nailed to the trees alongside the road announced the arrival of another wedding… or if he was lucky, an Andean festival, and the time to celebrate with friends again.

'No more Chicha this time,' he thought, and smiled at the barely memorable happenings of that fateful wedding night.

On the last curve just before entering the awaiting village, Paco made his way over to where a massive oak tree stood. Stapled to the tree were numerous papers that bristled in the breeze. Some of the papers were yellowing and smudged - having suffered previous spells of rain, but a more recent notice had been pasted in the centre. It held the sketch of a young man.

The flyer advertised, "*Hefty reward… Paco Alegría. Traitor to the nation: wanted dead or alive.*"

Paco froze.

The bubble of happiness that had been holding him aloft in his heart - burst. It dissipated in less than a second, turning into a state of panic and disbelief. His eyes were transfixed by the flyer, lost for an eternity. His pencilled face on a sketch stared back at him: cold, dead. Days, hours, weeks seemed to pass, while icy sweat trickled down his temples and his mouth shrivelled like a desiccated grape. The back of his neck was hot.

'Why would anyone want me dead? For what?' he thought, still aghast at the news.

He began to jog his memory… he remembered then, having forgotten a collection of lyrics back at the cellar on the night of the massacre – each sheet had been marked with his signature… it was in that flash that the realisation struck him. His words of revolt and revolution had converted him into a traitor in the eyes of the government. Milagros had warned him the night he escaped to the Andes.

The panicky child scurrying away was a sign of looming trouble – and he was at the centre of it… right now.

His senses were startled and suddenly, out of nowhere, a primal survival instinct governed his every move.

Kaikay was not a safe haven anymore, but a deadly trap.

Nobody could be trusted.

'Where is everyone?' he thought.

The village was as a cemetery is at midnight; silent and lifeless. The feeling of desolation seeped through the gaping doors; it was as if a tyrannical hurricane had broken into every home, forcibly removing all the people and vanishing them into nothingness..

Kaikay had adopted, for the first time, the impression of a ghost town.

He heard a commotion.

Silent as a puma, Paco immediately crouched down and edged closer to the voices. From his position, concealed behind a shoulder-height stack of wood, he observed the dwellers collated in the centre of the plaza.

A dozen horsemen, dressed in grimy, white pants, brownish ponchos, and clutching short carbines and rusty swords, surrounded the terrified villagers.

The visitors appeared callous and bloodthirsty - some were shoeless – their spurs fastened to their bare, cracked heels. On their heads they donned broad straw hats, and their deeply scarred faces told stories of lives as ex-highway robbers and lawless rascals.

Paco realised he was looking at what were once free men; men who had forfeited that freedom due to their heinous crimes. As an alternative to jail, they'd opted to work for the government as a renegade force that traced escapee prisoners, traitors, or any person wanted by the authorities. The *Montoneros* in their muscular horses and mules contained the terrified people from Kaikay within a circle in the centre of the plaza. From the motley gang of Montoneros, a single figure emerged, dressed in military regalia, bearing a polished and magnificent sword that glittered in the sun. He walked with a distinct air of arrogance - his chin pointing skywards as though everything was on trial.

He asked the villagers a tirade of questions.

They shook their heads.

"I was told that the man I'm looking for, Paco Alegría, passed through this village a few months ago," the military man announced. His eyes bore fiercely into the eyes of each villager as he attempted to spot a liar in the crowd. He had trained under the tutelage of a few surviving generals from the War of Independence, graduating at the top of his class. His arrogance confirmed this.

His sense of intuition was highly developed and before receiving orders to search for Paco, he'd worked as an unsolved murder investigator with the infamous and ruthless La Costa police, Miramar's port.

He walked among the villagers, a wolf in regalia, attempting to sniff out any guilty sheep, "I trust my sources. If you know what's good for you, you will hand me the information I need… so don't waste my time! I don't like how you lazy people use your time here in the Andes. In Miramar, we get things done fast… so you'd better cooperate."

He stepped between the trembling villagers, a shark in a sea of alarmed, panicking anchovies.

"I'm Sergeant Guevara of the national forces," he proclaimed, with pride. "Who is going to tell me whe-re-my-li-ttle-prey-is-hi-ding?" He pronounced each syllable perfectly as if he was singing a song in staccato.

There was not a whisper, nor a sigh. For a couple of minutes no one moved in the plaza.

Eusebio gazed at Valentina. His look clearly spelled, '*do not say a word.*'

Most of the villagers understood the unspoken consensus of not giving away any information to Guevara.

The sergeant grew increasingly frustrated with the uncooperative people from Kaikay, and climbed the statue of the Inca in the centre of the plaza. He hated wasting time.

"You… in the green poncho, come here," he pointed his finger at Eusebio. "Hurry."

Eusebio kissed Valentina and moved forward through the crowd.

"Yes, Sergeant Guevara."

"Are you a community leader?"

"Yes señor sargento, I'm one of a few."

Guevara took off his right glove and struck Eusebio in the face with tremendous force.

Eusebio had no time to react and fell to the floor, concussed.

Valentina ran to her husband. "You pig! You heartless pig!" she cursed in Quecchua.

A Montonero dismounted his horse and grabbed her by her long, black hair before she reached the enraged, sneering sergeant. He threw Valentina to the floor.

"You'd better tell your people to speak up or I'm going to cut you into pieces like a sacrificial lamb, do you understand?" Guevara barked at Eusebio, making sure that everyone had heard him.

"We haven't seen Paco, sergeant, please do consult again with your sources," Eusebio replied as he wiped the dripping blood from his fractured, battered nose.

In one swift move, Guevara kicked Eusebio with the point of his boots in the mid-riff, sending him stumbling backwards.

Eusebio squealed. His pain was evident, almost unbearable.

"Don't lie to me you insolent worm," Guevara was furious now, "I know you are lying."

As fast as lightning, he placed his right hand on the sword's hilt and prepared to unsheathe it.

"I'll make a dying example out of you," he roared as the sword left the scabbard, and the crisp sound of metal brought the tense plaza to total silence.

"I'll confess, I'll confess," Valentina yelled in Quecchua. She ran towards her fallen husband; her face swathed in tears.

"Please stop… mercy, please…"

Sergeant Guevara did not require translating to gather that he had a confessor.

"We have a repentant… well done, at least someone has some common sense. There is always a way to make someone talk… isn't it wonderful?" he exclaimed, lost in his inflated sense of arrogance as he sheathed his sword.

"Do speak. Someone translate. I don't have all day," he said, pointing his chin towards the sun.

"Paco arrived the day we got married a few months ago," she muttered as Eusebio translated. "He left the same night on the eastern path out of the village. We haven't seen him since… I swear that is all we know… we have nothing to do with him. He only said he needed to go… I swear it sergeant. I have told you everything, please leave us… I beg you," Eusebio gasped for air as he translated his wife's confession.

Guevara seemed smugly pleased with her answer. He knew she was telling the truth.

"When you place a sword on someone's throat… somebody always tells the truth," he laughed.

Again, he directed the crowd, this time waving the sketch with Paco's face on it, "if you see Paco Alegría, you better let me know, or this will happen to your brother, husband, father or child… no one will be spared if-you-de-ci-de-to-har-bour-my-fu-gi-ti-ve," he bellowed in his overly-pronounced manner.

"I will not stop until I seize my prey. My Montoneros will live here and in the adjacent villages until I find him. Make sure you treat them well or they might hurt you," he said, and paused… "They are not as polite as I am."

The Montoneros laughed like a pack of frenzied hyenas.

Paco slid back towards the fringe of the village to search for a place to hide. It felt as if he was being drawn into a war play, without a script. He was clueless on what to do, who to talk to, who to confide in. He only knew he had to run - and hide.

"Now go back to your small, meaningless lives and spread the word… I want Paco Alegría," he added, "*Dead or Alive.*"

20 The Ghost

Paco tiptoed towards a cluster of boulders and lone trees that gazed over the village like silent sentinels. He found refuge in its safe distance. From there, he had a privileged view of the plaza and the whereabouts of the guarding Montoneros.

Ferociously hungry, he waited patiently for nightfall in an attempt to reach Eusebio and the much-needed supplies, before disappearing towards Miramar.

The sun vanished behind the glorious Apus as night fell. Paco decided to wait some time before attempting to reach the slumbering village. Hours later, as peace descended with the growing darkness, he circumnavigated the eastern section of Kaikay and observed Eusebio's home, lit by a single candle, from a relatively secure vantage point.

The lone light was extinguished and he cautiously made his way forward. A few feet away from the shack's wooden entrance, a neighbour's dog began to bark, setting the night alive. The precious silence Paco was seeking, had been shattered.

He immediately retreated, seeking partial safety in the darkness, in anticipation of a Montonero's sudden appearance… but no one moved. Eventually, the dog ceased its barking and the night fell once more into fragile silence.

A granary protruded from the outskirts of Eusebio's home, offering a relatively safe passage inside. 'That might be my way in,' Paco thought. Minute by minute, he moved a little closer, making sure he was dead still, a dead man walking. He moved so silently and so precisely, the watchdog was unaware of his almost-invisible presence.

By midnight, the granary door lay no more than a few inches away. He reached out for the door handle as a treasure hunter, reaching his trembling hand towards the elusive Holy Grail…

From the depths of darkness, and as silent as a ghost, a muscular arm stifled him and prevented him from screaming.

Paco took a big gulp of air.

It felt as if a monstrous wave had engulfed him, and this was his last breath of life. He clutched onto that last bit of air with all his might.

He was swiftly lifted off the floor and lugged a dozen feet away from the granary like a sack of potatoes. The neighbour's dog split the night's silence again with ear-shattering howls.

The granary door opened with abrupt force.

"If you say a word, you're dead," a voice warned. Somehow, Paco recognised the peculiar but familiar accent. He decided to heed the warning. He had no other choice. He was in mid-air and unable to move.

A single Montonero heaved open the door and stepped out of the granary, carbine in hand. Wiping the sleep from his eyes, he let out a tremendous yawn amidst the unceasing racket of the dog's barking and the constant screeching of frightened chickens.

"Can you see anything out there?" an irritated voice from within the granary enquired. "Go and see what it is."

The lone, barefoot Montonero marched a few determined steps until he stumbled and hammered his shin on a barely visible boulder. A loud crack resonated.

He shouted obscenities at the night, damning the Andes and all its creatures, holding his shin up and hopping on one foot.

The barking of the dog intensified. The Andean winter night was like any other – pitch-dark and cold. The only other sound to break the still air of the late night hours, apart from the loud dog, was the chirping of troubadour crickets.

"Nothing here Pedro," said the cursing Montonero still hovering in pain, "probably a small fox or a wild dog looking for some chickens… I'm going back inside, it's freezing cold."

The stranger still suspended Paco in mid-air, without any sign of fatigue. Paco's feet remained airborne.

Once the dog had ceased barking, the night became hushed once more, and Paco was finally earthbound.

"Don't panic," the stranger said, "just turn around… slowly… and quietly." Paco nodded. "Don't panic, I'm not going to hurt you."

Paco took an uncomfortable step forward and gently turned around. His heart pumped incessantly. His breathing was short and shallow. He had no clue what to expect.

He stood under the low roof of a typical Andean home. In the darkness, Paco could only see a pair of pants and a leather waistcoat on top of a dusky, woollen jersey that seemed to float at the height of the roof. The stranger's body was not visible in the darkness.

Then he remembered the rumours of the fierce, fleeting ghost that terrorised the villages. Paco froze in his tracks: a mammoth creature was stationed just a few feet away. Panic-stricken and immobilised by fear, he murmured a quiet prayer.

The ghost took a step forward.

Paco was confronted with the face of an African man. He was built like a demigod, and his skin was as dark as the darkest of nights, but he wore the warmest of smiles. Paco relaxed with that smile.

The man stretched out his massive hand, and in a soft whisper, introduced himself.

"I'm *Manolete El Negrete*… but you can call me *Mano*… it's great to meet you," he said. Paco couldn't even mumble. "You must be the man they're looking for, Paco Alegría."

"Why did you save me?" Paco asked.

"I saw your face on a sketch in a village two days south-west from here, and if the government thinks you are an enemy, then you are a friend of mine," Mano explained, piercing the blanket of darkness for any movement or suspicious sound, "but I also wondered about your name."

"My name?" Paco was taken aback. "What has my name got to do with anything?"

"I thought you might have ties with the Hacienda Alegría," the giant replied.

"That's my home!" Paco shouted. "Shhh!" Mano immediately attempted to cover Paco's mouth, but his hand was so large it covered the whole of Paco's face. "You never know who is around – you have to be more careful!" Mano whispered.

Paco nodded.

"I know who you are now," Mano said, "you are that kid that used to play with my nephews by the river when you were just a boy."

Paco smiled; for a moment, his mind returned to those long, lazy summers back in the hacienda – where, against his father's wishes, he had played with some of the slave boys close to the winding river's meandering shore.

"Those were memorable times," Paco exclaimed, laughing, his soul suffused with childhood memories long gone.

"What are you doing here then?" Mano asked, returning the conversation to a serious tone.

"Long story," Paco replied. "I will explain to you one day. Right now, I urgently need to return to Miramar."

"If you are heading there, I will go with you," Mano replied. He didn't need time to deliberate his decision. "I know the safest route back to the capital. I desperately need to see my child… it has been almost two years. It's time to change that."

"We must leave immediately. If I take you to Miramar safely… could you do something for me?" Mano asked.

"Yes, of course, what is it?"

"When we make it back to the hacienda… could you talk to your father, well, about me… and… my… freedom?"

Paco looked surprised at the unusual but plausible request.

"I'm sorry Mano. There is nothing I can do about that," Paco was honest. "The day I left the hacienda, I renounced my surname. Samuel does not consider me his son anymore. He gave me an ultimatum, which forced me to leave."

"The only way I can return is down on my knees, a defeated man, ready to take my post running his slave trade for the rest of my life – and that is something I will not do. I will never go against my principles and beliefs." Paco was decisive in his answer.

"I understand, Paco," Mano replied with disappointment. "Well then, we have much to talk about on the way to the coast."

"Yes we do," Paco smiled. "Let's go."

Before dawn, the two men made it to one of Mano's many hiding places. It was alongside the single road that ran towards the many, scattered mountain villages on the way down to Miramar.

Inside a tiny, poorly-lit cave, Paco told Mano many of the stories created about him by the Andean people.

"I escaped the hacienda in search of the money to guarantee a better life for my unborn child." Mano told Paco, "We didn't receive any money for our backbreaking work, and so I had to do what I had to do."

"I have the spirit of a free man. My heart told me to escape. I couldn't go any longer against the voice of my heart," he told Paco, who listened to every word attentively, "even when escaping the hacienda meant lynching and death at the hands of your father."

Paco knew he was telling the truth – Samuel had murdered many runaway slaves in order to intimidate the remaining slaves at the hacienda.

"A life in chains is no life at all… *no creature in the world is born with shackles, so why should men live in chains?*"

"I started as a highway robber, lured by the idea of a quick return, but realised I could not steal. Stealing was wrong. As soon as I'd collected some money, I secretly planned to leave the gang and seek a job in the capital."

"One April morning, the Miramar police busted one of our robberies. They killed most of us. I was lucky to escape unharmed," Mano said. "My destiny changed that morning. As a wanted man, I had to make a forced flight to the Andes."

"Out of fear of the repercussions from the local authorities, who strictly forbade charity to runaway slaves, prisoners or robbers, the mountain communities could not help me. Fortunately, some kindred souls took mercy on me, as I walked helpless and starving from village to village."

"What happened then?" Paco asked.

"More dead than alive, I decided I had to '*borrow*' food and other essentials in order to survive. As I gathered strength, I decided to travel only at night. Many Andean people, who had never laid eyes on a man of colour before, inaptly described me as a *ghost* – this suited me just fine." Mano released a burst of innocent laughter.

"I didn't feel that stealing was right but I needed to survive. As I became more familiar with the terrain, I built small shelters away from the villages where I stored my precious, life-sustaining takings. If I took a chicken from a home, I'd replace it with maize from another home…"

"I did not consider this a rightful act but it was better than taking and not replacing something of the same or relative value," he said.

Paco listened for hours to the remarkable stories of survival told by his brave, new friend.

After sharing their tales, both men went to sleep in order to have enough strength for the long trip to the capital.

They made their way down to Miramar solely at night, spurred by Paco's desire to see his beloved, and Mano's longings to see his child.

Paco trundled a few steps behind his giant friend with no exchange of words, except for the occasional whisper that signalled danger ahead.

During the day, they rested in one of Mano's many hiding spots, and this afforded them much time for conversation and the exchange of ideas.

"How did you end up in my country Mano?" Paco asked.

Mano took a deep breath before answering. "I came from a land of glory and myth… my father was the wise ruler of a large kingdom." Mano spoke like a royal warrior, a million stars glimmering in his eyes. His Spanish was exquisite, surprising for a man not native to the tongue.

"During my father's reign, the land prospered. We bathed in milk and honey and our women wore gold from head to feet. In our kingdom, no one went hungry - my people did not know what hunger was. Our land extended from the sea up to endless savannahs where animals roamed free. Food was plenty. Our kingdom, to us, was the closest place to heaven."

"My family ruled from the capital - that was close to the sea - in the southern part of the elephant continent called Africa," Mano explained, whilst looking at the tranquil blue sky outside the dark cave. He gazed back at Paco, "One day, we saw one of the many ships that sailed across our bay, suddenly steer in our direction."

"The ship, led by a Captain Moore, docked in one of our tranquil beaches. Many men descended from boats onto our shores. My father was a man of peace and welcomed the foreigners with food and song, a tradition we had honoured for generations… but the men carried the stench of liquor and savagery."

"I was young at the time - I trusted easily. I offered the captain a pot of our traditional beer. He drank it; then threw the pot on the ground… and it all started," Mano said, lowering his head; pain etched in his eyes.

"What started Mano… if I may ask?" Paco responded, cautious.

"That day, our lives changed forever… Captain Moore and his cruel men murdered my father and forced us into slavery. They forced the men to wear chains or they would kill our women and children. We had no choice; we had never experienced such violence."

"Even in war, there are rules… but those men showed no mercy… and so we boarded their ships in order to save our kingdom and families. Then they sold us like cattle to different proprietors."

"Us, children of kings and God, now subdued to live a life of animals… can you imagine how we felt?"

"One stormy morning, they led us inside an older galleon and sold us to men who spoke a different language. They lacerated our backs with their whips because we didn't understand their orders. We travelled the seas for weeks, perhaps months on end. We were tied in chains, my feet against my neighbour's feet, and my hands tied to his hands in a space so small we could barely breathe. Many died on the way - some of disease and some of sadness - our pride stolen from us and replaced with rusty, metal links."

"What those cruel men forgot is that we are made of Africa, the Mother Land, and we are fruit of her soil, made from the same force that forged the mountains that rise from the sea… and that force is within us… and allowed us to survive. We promised each other to survive so the world would hear our story and these atrocities would never happen again."

"After months at sea, we arrived at a place called Cuba and settled for a scorching summer."

"At our new home in a vast sugar-cane plantation, they chose me to represent my people. Soon, I learned the foreigner's language. A year later, a violent hurricane struck the island, and many of the plantations were lost. We left Cuba and headed further west. We travelled to a place called Hispaniola, then to Panama and finally here, where your father bought us like cattle at a slave-trade fair."

Paco felt ashamed. 'If people like my father didn't buy slaves, there would be no slave-trading business,' he thought.

He wanted to apologise on his father's behalf, even though it was not his fault.

"We were the last lot of slaves to arrive in this so-called 'free' country."

"At least my children's future will be slightly brighter. Today I am here, with no chains, wanted by the authorities and your father for seeking my freedom."

"Freedom belongs to me as it belongs to every human being. I was born free and I shall die free. My hands and feet were made without chains, can you see?" Mano furiously rubbed his hands across his scarred arms and lacerated feet in a desperate gesture of liberty.

"If they only knew what we can achieve when we are not chain-bound." Mano proclaimed.

Paco nodded in silent respect.

"Before Africans left en masse to work the sugar plantations of the New World, the men from the Old World used them as voluntary expeditionaries, and in some way, as unintentional colonists. We fought alongside them in the conquests of Puerto Rico, Cuba, Mexico, and in countries as far down as Chile. They knew us as *'The Black Conquistadors,'* " Mano said, proud of his glorious and valiant ancestry.

"Please tell me more," Paco asked, enthralled by the unfolding facts. "This is something we didn't learn at school."

"Many Black Conquistadors fought side by side with the men from the Old World and were granted their freedom by proving their valour in the field of battle. Colonists wrote back to their families, describing their situation in the wild and uncolonised New World. In these letters, they described Africans as indispensable to the empire and worth their weight in gold."

"Even in this country, we formed a pivotal part in the conquest of the Inca Empire. Not many people know that thousands of Africans were part of the colonist battalion that subdued the last great Inca king, Atahualpa. Actually, one of the first four men to lay his eyes on the holy city of the Inca, *Cusco*, was an African..." Mano's eyes flickered with a degree of honour.

"We fought against indigenous warriors all along the Americas. We suffered and gave our lives and limbs so we could improve our worth in a foreign and unforgiving world. We died so we could regain our freedom. We are the natural-born warriors from the elephant continent. We are proud of our ancestry and history. We are made of sand, gold, and forged with pride. We are made of Africa."

"That is amazing Mano, I never knew that." Paco exclaimed, looking at his companion with admiration.

"Would you not do the same for your freedom?" Mano asked.

"Yes, my friend… and brave prince… I would. I would die for my freedom," Paco responded, honouring his new friend.

"*Freedom is in the mind*," Mano said, "they tied my body in chains, but *they never conquered my mind*."

"I can see why you are a Prince," Paco replied.

"My people need me Paco… they need you… and I need you," Mano whispered, staring without hesitation into Paco's eyes. He was dignified in his approach and speech.

"What can I do?"

"Help us get our freedom!" Mano shouted. "*We shall be free!*"

Paco understood a decision of this magnitude meant going against his father, but he knew it was time for things to change. His family's hacienda was forged from misery and death. Its land built piece by piece with the hands of children who were torn away from their mothers, husbands separated from their wives and entire families destroyed for the sake of profit…

His heart spoke: it was time for the injustice to end.

It was his time to stand up for truth.

It was time to follow his mission and Never-Ending Legacy, no matter the price. In spite of the consequences, he had to do the right thing.

The time was Now.

"You can count on me," Paco responded without hesitation.

"*We shall be free*," Mano said. "*We shall be free.*"

21　I Shall Be Free

A week later, the twinkling, far-flung lights of Miramar appeared in the distance. The salty scent of the Pacific Ocean swirled with the citrus aroma of ancient orchards – it reminded Paco of home. His heart began to beat faster as the city lights neared - so close he could almost snatch them and play with them in his hands.

He wondered where Milagros was at that moment… and wondered which of the tiny lights in the monstrous city ahead, emanated from her window… and whether she was thinking of him.

"The sun will rise in a few hours. We need to find shelter," Mano said. "We'll make the last stretch back to the hacienda as soon as the sun sets."

The flat, deserted coast provided only sporadic places to hide. The Andean topography was benign, offering shelter among its caves, valleys and rocky outcrops, in direct contrast to the undulating monotony of sand dune upon sand dune as one neared the vast, blue Pacific Ocean.

"A fugitive experiences only a relative sense of escape," Paco told his companion, "but not freedom." Mano nodded. "A man accused of treason is the loneliest man in the world," Paco proceeded, "one could equate him to a ghost without a house to haunt. He has no home. He has no shelter. A man accused of treason has no flag, nor country. The only thing he has is his breath, and even that is on the run."

'Freedom is fragile. Savour it each second. It's like the last drop of honey on earth," Mano replied. "You are free, so treasure it. There is nothing sweeter than the fragrance of freedom and being alive to relish it."

"To freedom," Paco cheered.

Before sunrise conquered the night, they spotted a desolated Waka, a sacred Inca temple found throughout the coastal and mountain region. Both men decided to set up camp. During winter, gentle dew fell on the desert plains from an almost-permanent stratum of low-levelled clouds.

Mano was happy to taste the tiny droplets of water on his cracking lips.

"Aah… a *Garua*," he said, 'I've missed you," savouring the almost-invisible dew drops descending from heaven.

"The taste of home," Paco added with a bright smile. "By the way, I have something to tell you."

"What is it Paco?"

"For the last few days, I've had a song in my head and I needed to thank you for giving me the inspiration," Paco said. He placed Morena on his chest and softly strummed a few notes within the sacred Waka.

"Did I really do that?" Mano replied, surprised, "What did I say?" The big man was proud for having inspired something, anything.

"*We shall be free*," Paco answered.

"I remember that… back in the mountains a week ago."

"Well, I've turned your phrase into a song called '*I shall be free*,' and I want you to tell me what you think," Paco asked. He was a little weary for his song's first show of public criticism.

"It would be an honour, please go ahead."

Paco started to strum the chords, eyes closed, lost in the melody and rhythm of the instrument, as though every note he played, was meaningful. He started singing…

It's a long way back home,
It's a dark, restless fight
When your freedom's at war,
My hope's wearing thin
But it won't fade away, fade away…

Nothing's going to shackle my dreams
Nothing's going to tie them down
No one's going to lay their hands
And stop me from believing…

When the chains that hold me back
Finally break to my attack
I shall, I shall be free.

When I find my destiny
I rewrite my history
I shall be free.

I'll take the chains that hold me down
And I'll turn them into a crown
I shall be free.

When I finally make the choice
I will find my own voice
I shall be free… I shall be free.

Paco opened his eyes and saw his colossal friend holding back tears… as if an arrow had touched his heart… Paco instinctively knew that he had created something of infinite value and beauty.

"Thank you Paco," Mano exclaimed, swallowing the lump in his throat, "That song speaks to me, my people, and every person in this country and the world that ardently feels slavery should be abolished forever… *This is our hymn!*"

Paco hid his face in his hands, trying to hide the inevitable wave of emotion, and shook his head slowly from side to side in complete disbelief. "Finally," he said to The One, looking to the heavens, "*Thank you, finally…*"

Every experience since he was born had brought him to this moment; the lessons in Love, life and purpose… all led Paco to that glorious instant… *when he became music*, and his soul joined The One and melted into a piece of harmony, rhythm and melody that would change his country forever. As every experience flashed before his mind, he acknowledged them in silence…

"I would do it all again," he said to himself and smiled, knowing that every second of his life was worth it - and worth praising.

He remained looking up to the sky, the soft Garua caressing his skin, "Thank you for a life so blessed and so filled with happy memories."

He felt The One holding his hand.

"I know I don't thank you enough," Paco murmured, "but I just want to tell you that I never forget you. You're always in my thoughts. I don't need to seek you in a building because I find you in my heart. I find you in nature. I find you in my guitar. I feel you everywhere and especially, *I find you in me.* Thank you for making me who I am, with all my strengths and weaknesses. I am proud of my mission and I am proud of what I am becoming… Thank You."

That moment of connection to Source was worth a thousand lives lived. In a desolate Waka, with a warrior Prince moved to tears, he realised that The One was to be found everywhere, as long as you still had a beating heart.

Late that night, the two managed to infiltrate the sleeping hacienda. The dangerous dogs that guarded the perimeter behaved like newborn puppies as soon as they recognised the scent of their returning master and howled at the moonless night like a nostalgic pack of wolves.

After a brief walk, both men reached the slumbering African slave-quarters and discreetly approached Mano's old hut. In the centre of the square, an almost-extinguished fire was a sign that the slaves had had a tardy night.

Paco knocked gently on the heavy, wooden door.

An elderly woman opened. She gasped as soon as she saw Paco.

"Master Paco… what are you doing here?" she asked, surprised but elated to see the prodigal son return.

"Good evening Maria," Paco replied politely. "I need you to please stay calm and not cause a stir. Ask everyone not to light any candles and please call Juana."

Maria turned around as instructed and began to head inside.

"Pardon me Maria… one more thing."

She turned around.

"Ask her to bring her child… I have a surprise."

Maria observed Paco incredulously with her sleepy eyes and followed his instructions.

Juana approached the door a few minutes later holding a tired little girl by the hand.

"Good evening Juana," Paco said.

She looked at Paco as if he had risen from the Dead. Paco's calm and unassuming manner was very unlike his old self, and it took the young mother a number of minutes to digest what she was witnessing.

"I have a surprise for you," he said.

"Yes…?" Juana replied, not knowing what Paco meant; at the slave quarters, there weren't any surprises that were welcomed, especially after midnight.

"She is so beautiful… what's her name?" Paco asked.

"Her name is Manuela. I named her after her father Manolete."

A shape moved in behind Paco, kissing the darkness with his colossal shadow.

Maria gasped immediately. Although she could not see the stranger's face, her heart did not need translation.

"Mano… oh my God, it's you Mano!" Her voice gasped for a breath of air, drowning out two years of not knowing whether the Love of her life was alive or dead.

"Oh Mano, my sweet Mano…" Paco moved away from the doorstep and the lovers embraced, little Manuela still holding her mother's hand, in awe of the gigantic man towering beside her.

"This is your daughter Mano… I named her Manuela, after you."

Mano stood frozen, like a giant, silent oak in the doorway, staring at his daughter. It was a strange sight to see an African warrior melt like candle wax in a furnace - he was so tall it seemed to take an eon for him to kneel to the floor. Few people can decree they have seen the face of God… That night, Mano saw it in his daughter.

"I'm your father Manuela," he said in the gentlest voice - he could separate the quills of a feather with his tone, "I'm your father my Love… I am Mano."

When Paco lifted his gaze, a curious crowd had formed around them. They could not afford to make any mistakes now.

"Listen everyone, please return to your beds. Be quiet please," Paco ordered. "I've got something to tell you."

The slaves returned to their bunks in silence.

"As many of you know by now, I am no longer welcome in this hacienda. Tonight, I have returned against my father's wishes. For your safety and mine, I need you to maintain secrecy… no one must find out that I'm here. Mano and I have returned because we want slavery abolished in this hacienda. You were born free women and men and it's time for your work to be remunerated like everyone else, according to your time and effort, not the colour of your skin."

In the pitch-darkness of that quarter, Paco's words ignited a little light in those weary hearts.

"Furthermore, I'm joining forces with colleagues back in Miramar. We are going to make sure the government adheres to the guarantees of freedom they have promised you for so long. We've kept quiet for too many years… but we will no longer be silenced."

No one spoke, but the hasty winds of hope and the unspoken roar of liberty, stirred the room like an earthquake.

Paco looked at his friend standing proud beside him.

"Mano is an example to all of you… a man who represents true freedom in both heart and mind. In exactly three days, thousands of people like you will join us in the Plaza Mayor to demand their freedom back. We need you to be there," Paco pleaded with every heart.

"Spread the word; slavery is a thing of the past. Join us and claim back your freedom. Other haciendas will join our cause. Our strength lies in numbers. The time is now. Do it for you… but especially for your children," Paco spoke with relentless passion. Those who knew him could hardly recognise his newfound strength and sense of conviction.

"How much longer do you want to live in chains? Is a life in chains worth living? Is this what you want for your children, and your children's children?" he appealed to each heart. "I trust you will all be there. I trust you will follow your heart's calling."

Paco signalled for Maria to come.

"My darling Maria… please let my mother know I'm here as soon as my father leaves for the sugar-cane fields. It is imperative that you do this in a calm manner," he held her gently by the shoulders. "Please sit her down - you know how excited she gets sometimes."

Maria nodded – she had worked for the Alegría family long before Paco was born and knew Alejandra since the time she had been a young woman.

"I need to see her urgently. I'll be hiding in these quarters. Ask her to come as soon as possible. I need to write a couple of very important letters. Ask her to bring some writing material," Paco instructed.

A new day dawned and the hacienda was a hive of activity, the norm for a typical morning. People rose before sunrise in order to work the fields at first light, but on this particular morning, one could sense a palpable energy with the rise and fall of the scythes.

Paco's brief speech had moved many hearts, and the sound of freedom spread like wildfire throughout the slave quarters. The return of Mano also uplifted the community - they saw in him the qualities of the hero they had always longed for.

An aged slave woman sat with Paco in the abandoned quarter – while time dragged on, waiting for Alejandra to arrive.

By noon, there was still no sign of Alejandra and Paco grew increasingly preoccupied with the silence.

An hour later, hurried footsteps approached the hut.

Paco slid under a tattered bunk bed. There was a faint knock on the door. The elderly woman answered the door.

"Who is it?"

No one replied.

Paco's heart drummed at a thousand beats a minute.

The weary door burst open and Alejandra stepped in. The walls within the quarters were painted insomnia-yellow. Beneath the jagged ceiling, laced with weather-beaten cracks, were dozens of hoary spider webs.

However, within the empty quarters, she witnessed only the old woman in a chair.

"Good day señora," Alejandra greeted the elderly woman, "pardon my rudeness…" she said, "I'm looking for my son Paco."

The old woman tilted her head to the right – to indicate where her son was.

Paco slid from under the bunk bed and rushed towards his mother's embrace.

Not a million and one roses in bloom could replace the familiar fragrance of his mother's perfume – it was the unforgettable scent of home.

"I've missed you mother," Paco said and gripped her so tight - they became one in a long overdue embrace.

"My son, my son," she took a step back and placed both hands on his cheeks.

"Handsome as always," she said lightly. "You're alive, the Lord is merciful."

Paco felt every ounce of his mother's Love.

But now was not the appropriate time for nostalgia.

"Time is not on my side mother. Just know that I am healthy, happy, and in grave danger from both father and the government. I'm sure you're aware of my situation…"

She nodded her head in agreement. "Some people told me that you might be dead but my heart always denied it… a mother always knows."

"Mother, I only discovered I was a wanted man a few weeks ago. I have so much to tell you… we will have to leave this conversation for a more appropriate time. Did you bring the paper, plume, and ink as I asked?"

Alejandra opened her cotton bag and placed the writing material on an almost-collapsing table.

"Dear mother, what I'm about to do might go against what you believe, but if you open your heart, I sincerely hope you will understand," Paco said, gazing deep into his mother's eyes.

"In three days' time I'll be marching in the Plaza Mayor in an attempt to banish slavery from our country forever. I know this means going against my father's way of life, but I have to follow what my heart says." Paco paused for a second. "Soon after my arrival in Miramar, I met young revolutionaries who became loyal friends. They will mobilise our ranks in the capital… I need you to please give them the letters I'm about to write." As he said this, Paco looked for any suspicious movement outside.

"The first letter will go to my Love, señorita Milagros Del Valle…" Alejandra looked at her son in total disbelief.

"Are you referring to *the* president's daughter?"

"Yes mother," Paco replied nonchalantly, without wasting time.

"The second letter is for Don Patricio de Romana. Ask Milagros to deliver his letter at once. Time is of the essence in the success of this mission… the march will take place in exactly three days' time," Paco reiterated.

Alejandra looked at her young son - she could hardly believe how much he had grown in such a short space of time. He was so determined, so suffused with purpose and with a strong sense of self.

"My son… my beloved child," she said, "these long months without you have been the most difficult in all my years… I wasn't certain if you were alive or dead… and if you were alive, if you had a roof over your head, something to eat or clothes to weather the cold. Often, my heart reached for yours and it instinctively knew that you were still alive, waiting to return one day. A mother never tires of waiting, and every night, I kept a warm plate of food in case that was the night you decided to return…"

"I have since realised how wrong I was in not standing up to your father. I nearly lost you and I never want that to happen again. I believe what you are doing is right… it is time for change. The world cannot continue this way, with people mistreated and abused because of their colour or race. Our family has built an empire on other's misfortunes and we have irrigated our fields with blood and tears… I want to wipe my hands clean… my silence has caused so much suffering to others. I can't live a double life anymore," she proclaimed, her eyes blazing with tears.

"My dear son, just know that you are my greatest accomplishment and nothing in the world shines with more pride in my heart than you. From today, I don't want to be away from you. You might be surprised, but I don't want to fail you again. You can always count on me."

"I will depart for Miramar with your letters today, and I assure you, they shall be delivered. I'm proud of you and of the man you have become."

Paco bowed and kissed his mother's forehead.

He steadied the collapsing table and wrote the two letters. "By the way, dear mother," Paco interrupted Alejandra before she closed the door, "give Milagros a message for me."

"What is the message my son?"

"Tell her I say *siempre*," he replied. "She'll understand."

Alejandra smiled warmly at her son and stepped out in a hurry.

Not far away, Samuel worked the fields, unaware of his son's return.

Travelling at full gallop and accompanied by her two trusted escorts, Alejandra reached the Presidential Palace in the afternoon. Two mean-looking armed guards, holding lances and dressed in red and blue regalia, barricaded all from entering the palace.

"I need to deliver two letters to señorita Milagros Del Valle. It's an urgent matter. Can you call her for me, please?" Alejandra politely asked the guards.

"Señorita Del Valle is not allowed any visitors," the elderly guard firmly responded, standing motionless and looking straight ahead, avoiding eye contact.

"It is of extreme importance… please señor," Alejandra begged.

"Those are the rules madam," the same guard said. "The police quarters are around the corner. They will deliver the letters for you. We cannot move from here."

Alejandra stepped away from the presidential gate. She knew she was not going to win that battle. She did not trust the police either, but after some deliberation, she opted to watch the comings and goings of the palace staff instead.

Within a few minutes, a young maid ventured outside the gates and headed for the food market around the corner. She skipped on the road like an energised flea. Her head bounced up and down with each trampoline step.

Alejandra followed her.

"Excuse me señorita, can I ask you a question?"

"Yes madam, how can I help *you?*" the maid abruptly turned around and responded in an overly-friendly manner.

"Do you know señorita Del Valle?" Alejandra asked, with a polite smile.

"Yes madam, I'm her personal maid," the young lady answered with a shiver of pride, elongating her spine and straightening her back.

"Can I ask you a favour then?"

"Of course madam, what do you want me to do?" she answered, excited. She loved surprises - or anything that added a little spice to her tedious routine at the palace.

"You know how some young men are… deeply falling in Love, but shy to express their real feelings… especially when we are referring to the president's daughter…" she paused for a second. Alejandra's opening lines had already captivated the attention of the maid.

"My son, being the timid young man that he is, wrote a few poems for señorita Del Valle and he doesn't have the courage to give them to her personally… so… he asked me for a small favour," she paused, "would you be kind enough to deliver these *two secret Love poems* to señorita Del Valle?" she asked firmly.

"Today? As soon as possible?… now?" Alejandra tilted her head and smiled with such grace, not even The One could have refused her demands.

The mortal maid stood no chance.

"Of course, my señora. It will be my greatest pleasure!" she sprang a few inches off the ground in excitement and snatched the letters from Alejandra's hands with such intent that she almost tore them in two. She then placed the crumpled letters close to her heart and sighed.

"One more thing," Alejandra said before hurrying back to the hacienda, "please tell señorita Del Valle my son says… *siempre*."

The young maid blushed then, turning as red as a ripe plum and gazed around the market in suspicion - as though somebody had been eavesdropping on their conversation.

She seized Alejandra forcibly by the arm and drew her deep into the stalls. Her two escorts swiftly approached, but with one shake of her head, they retreated immediately.

The maid whispered, "Are you Paco's mother?"

"Yes… how did you know?"

"*I know everything*," she whispered, closely resembling a government spy. Her irises moved left and right, inspecting everything and everyone with suspicion.

She seemed proud that the president's daughter trusted her with all her secrets.

"When you said *siempre*, I knew. Can I trust you?" Alejandra asked.

The maid nodded non-stop, like a starved squirrel eating a walnut.

"These letters are very important - a matter of life and death," Alejandra reiterated, placing extra pressure on the maid. "She needs to receive them today… make sure the guards in the front do not see them… hide them under some groceries. The letter with the word siempre is for Milagros. The other letter needs to be delivered to Don Patricio de Romana no later than tonight… is that clear?"

The young maid kept nodding her head, excited to be in the midst of such high drama.

"I need to go back home now… please get the groceries and hurry back to Milagros," Alejandra pleaded.

Milagros opened the letter titled, '*Siempre*' at once.

She bolted the door and told *Dolores*, her faithful personal maid, who stood at the door like an overexcited lioness, not to let anyone in for whatever reason – not even for a palace-consuming fire.

As she read Paco's words, she wept at the foot of her bed, which overlooked one of the corners of the Plaza Mayor.

"Paco is alive, Paco is alive," she murmured as tears fell in un-expected gratitude.

Milagros soon managed to calm herself and control her emotional outburst. Now all she needed to do was think up a feasible plan that would get the other letter to Patricio before nightfall.

She wasted no time. Dolores was called in.

"Dolores, I need you to help m…" before completing her sentence, Dolores pounced on the bed and nodded her head up and down as if her hair was on fire.

"Yes my lady, I will," she answered, placing her intertwined hands under her chin and fluttering her eyelashes.

Milagros raised her eyebrows, surprised at her strange, over-enthused maid, "I haven't even told you what I need you to do Dolores," she said annoyed.

"I'm ready my lady… I'll do anything for Love," she deflated, whooshing all the air out of her lungs, while she contemplated the grey sky through the dust-filled window.

Milagros knew she had a madcap on her hands - but she also knew she could be trusted.

"I need to deliver an important letter to Patricio. Wear your *tapada* outfit, and make sure your silken veil adequately covers your face, got it?" Milagros instructed. "I don't want any suspicion raised when you leave the palace. I'm going to use you as a decoy."

"Yesssss my lady." came her quick, high-pitched reply, like that of a schoolgirl.

"Be ready in five minutes. Then I need you to come back before the hour. I have to leave before sunset," Milagros ordered. She clapped her hands lightly to get her excited but dependable maid out the room and into the street as fast as possible.

Dolores rushed down the front steps of the palace draped in her tapada outfit.

The two guards spotted her and in typical South American manner, whistled.

"Come talk to us beautiful lady," the young guard shouted. "You make the sun shine," the elder guard hollered. "The twenty-four hours of my day are divided like this: nine, dreaming of you and the other fifteen… thinking of you," the young guard added.

Dolores turned her head in the opposite direction, snubbing their advances.

The guards chuckled as she hastily disappeared into the crowded streets of the capital.

Dolores returned a short while later to more whistles and advances before entering the palace.

"I'm here my lady," Dolores rushed into Milagros' room.

"I need your clothes. I'm going to dress like you and deliver the letter," Milagros explained, "Hurry up. Undress!"

Milagros dressed promptly in Dolores' outfit, adjusting her body shape accordingly with extra stuffing to simulate her maid's curvaceous figure. She waited for sunset, when the change of guards took place, before attempting the risky escapade.

As the guards exchanged posts, Milagros, posing as Dolores, rapidly exited the palace and headed towards Patricio's home, making sure no one trailed her footsteps.

Paco's letter rested deep in her bosom, close to her heart. She reached Patricio's home and knocked three times with intention.

After a few long minutes, he opened the door.

"Hello Patricio… It's Milagros," she whispered, hidden behind the tapada veil.

Patricio appeared surprised at the eccentrically dressed visitor.

His eyes shot left and right - the street was deserted.

"Come in," he whispered, and led Milagros to a private room within his opulent home.

"What are you doing here?" he asked. "This is bold… it must be important."

"I have a letter from Paco," she whispered, her voice was barely audible.

"From whoooo?" Patricio took a second to realise his friend was alive.

Milagros turned around and removed the letter from her bosom.

"Here it is," she said, now facing him. "It needs urgent action."

Patricio tore open the letter. He smiled when he read his friend was safe and had returned from the Andes. Milagros seemed anxious to know the content.

"He wants to meet me outside the city borders tomorrow morning," he replied. "He needs us to move our ranks and join him in an anti-slavery protest at the Plaza Mayor in three days' time," he said with a sharp intake of breath.

"Let's start moving," Milagros replied, "what are we waiting for?"

Patricio took a few hesitant seconds to make up his mind – he did not like to appear indecisive.

"I'll be there," he replied, confident as ever.

Milagros nodded. She had already made up her mind.

"I knew I could count on you. Now, I need to leave."

Patricio escorted Milagros to the front door. She placed the shawl and veil over her face so only her left eye was visible – the typical look of the Miramar tapada - and she stepped outside.

"I'll see you in three days' at the Plaza Mayor at the designated time," she said in an earnest tone.

"I'll be there Milagros," Patricio replied. "By the way… I'm glad he is back."

She revealed a furtive smile and merged into the darkening streets of the capital before disappearing from his sight.

"I can't get your song out of my head," Mano said to Paco, "Please teach me how to sing it?"

"Of course, it would be an honour," Paco replied. He strummed the guitar as an angel would, gently caressing the nylon strings as if brushing the hair of a newborn child.

"Let's keep our voices down Mano," Paco whispered, "my father's lynch-men are known to appear at the strangest of times."

The slave quarters remained in darkness.

In an empty corner and in hushed tones, Paco and Mano sang *'I shall be free'*. Soon, everyone had joined in the singing, the yearning for freedom burning alive in their hearts, feeling the same emotion Mano had felt the first time he heard the haunting melody.

Over the next few days, the rest of the slaves sang their new song of freedom while cutting the sugar cane. Samuel's men noticed. They wondered from whence the mysterious song had been born, but took no further notice.

Patricio was to meet Paco on the city's periphery as arranged, the morning after receiving the letter. The dilapidated buildings provided a perfect setting for the friends to reunite in secret, away from the bustle of the capital. There, they could chat freely without the danger of a curious police officer or an onlooker singling Paco out as the man from the notorious, well-known sketch that had been distributed far and wide all over the city streets.

Alejandra had secretly organised a champion racehorse to transport Paco to the secret meeting. Paco arrived at his destination sooner than he anticipated. At the rendezvous-point, Paco waited impatiently for Patricio. Concealed behind the shade of a large straw hat, it felt as if every second multiplied itself by three. At the designated time, from the direction of the city centre, a rider galloped towards the building.

He approached Paco at lightning speed.

"My dear friend," Paco said, "I'm so glad you've made it!"

"What did you expect?" Patricio replied, "I wouldn't miss hearing about your adventures in the Andes for anything."

"I have so much to tell you," Paco replied, with his open smile.

The two dismounted their horses and embraced. They tied their horses to a pole that protruded from a broken adobe home.

"Tell me all about your escapade Paco, I can't wait to hear it."

"I wouldn't know where to start my friend… I had the most incredible experience of my life, but I'll leave reminiscing for another time. Right now, I'd rather discuss our plans to march in the Plaza Mayor."

"Go ahead," Patricio said, looking interested but not giving away too much excitement; always - in complete control.

"The day after tomorrow we will lead the people working in my father's hacienda into the Plaza Mayor. I have received confirmation from one of their leaders and they are ready for action. We will leave quietly at midnight in order to be here in the morning. It is time for the people of Miramar to witness that this feudal system has no place in our so-called democracy anymore," Paco said, passion burning in his eyes.

"We will achieve our objective no matter the cost and no matter the effort… I believe that our support is also growing rapidly in universities and I know you can rally all our forces to participate too… *justice, freedom, and equality*, remember?"

Patricio smiled casually. Then, all of a sudden, he shook his head.

"*My dear Paco*," Patricio said, "the night of the massacre, I saw my life flash right before my eyes and it forced me to do some serious thinking about my future," he crossed his arms staunchly.

Patricio looked defensive. His eyes stared at Paco with the whirlwind of arrogance that sweeps some who believe that whatever wrongdoing they are about to commit, serves a higher purpose.

"While you were away, many things changed. People regarded our murdered comrades as martyrs - but as you know, in our country, very few own the most and the newspaper's owners did not make a fuss of it. Unfortunately, the massacre didn't make it to the front page, so by the following week, people forgot and things were back to normal. Of course, many citizens were shocked by the atrocity - but in the end, the government has been committing atrocities for generations, and I guess time makes people a little more desensitised to them." Patricio exuded arrogance with every word.

While he spoke, Paco got the feeling that he did not quite know who this person, standing before him, was.

"As you probably know by now, when you signed the songs you left inside the cellar, you signed off your liberty as well as your death sentence. You instantly became a traitor to the nation, which means conviction with no trial - treason forfeits your right to any defence."

"In case you don't know, talking to you in public makes me an accomplice and a traitor and I don't want to die yet. I also need to inform you that while you leisurely walked the mountains, your face appeared in every newspaper in the capital. They branded you a traitor of course, paid by the rich landowners who'd like to see anyone fighting against their way of life, well… *dead*." Patricio smirked.

"Now, let's talk about me…" he suddenly turned menacing. "Soon after you escaped, the government offered a secret pardon to all the survivors of that fateful night. They were five of us in total, not including you, of course, and after some discussions, which involved my politically-influential father and the fathers of the other so-called liberals, we all came to an agreement." Patricio spoke in his habitual, over-grandiose manner.

"The agreement benefits me and my family, but I won't go into detail now, since I don't have the time. For your information, your sudden appearance has also made me a couple of Reales richer; well actually, many Reales richer, so I need to thank you for this."

His words tasted like a poisoned challis – bitter and treacherous.

"What?" Paco gasped in total disbelief. For the first time, since the Lake of Gratitude, his heart shed droplets of blood; it could not handle the feeling of absolute betrayal.

Patricio waved his right arm twice.

In less than a minute, five soldiers on horseback arrived. Paco froze with a blank expression on his face; all he heard was the laboured breathing of the horses close by.

Patricio took a few steps back.

"Your plan in two days' time is unfortunately not going to work Paco. No one would have joined us; it would have been futile my friend. Now please excuse me, but I have to go and claim my reward. Thank you for returning,"

Patricio smiled, as cold as dusk in the Antarctic. "Take him away," he added with a single arrogant wave of his right hand.

Paco did not struggle, he was too stunned to fight; his betrayed heart kept bleeding.

A guard tied his hands and torso to one of the horses – they would parade him in the city centre as a traitor.

"By the way Paco," Patricio said before mounting his horse, "public executions take place two days from the day of capture. What a coincidence! May God bless you… and good luck!" With this, Patricio mounted his horse and rode into the boisterous streets of Miramar.

Paco bit his lower lip and shook his head in utter disbelief. He was broken-hearted - he couldn't hear the birds singing or the soldiers jabbering.

As the soldiers made their way into the centre of the capital - Paco was made to trail the horses. He looked and felt like a zombie: lifeless; an almost-dead, walking shadow.

They soon marched into the busier sections of the capital, where the occasional yellowing sketch with Paco's face appeared, nailed onto lamp poles or random walls. People recognised him immediately as the streets simmered over with curious onlookers. Many remembered him as the newspaper boy from the theatre's corner and called out words of encouragement, but Paco was so heart-broken, all he heard was mumbling.

The soldiers, dressed in their best attire and mounted atop their muscular horses, looked proud and commanding, dragging a sacrificial lamb but giving the impression that they had captured a fierce man-eating tiger.

Paco felt abandoned and alone.

He closed his eyes and took a deep breath, 'one of my last breaths on earth,' he thought, '*I'm going to make it last.*'

Tied and displayed like a wild beast, Paco lifted his gaze and studied the growing street parade as he proceeded towards the Plaza Mayor. People stared and rejoiced; ravenous onlookers at a blood circus.

*"It's a long way back home…
It's a long restless fight, when your freedom's at war…"*

Paco burst into *"I shall be free."*

He sang from the deepest part of his being, and his heart stopped bleeding.

He thought of Doña Lucia, Notas, and Hawan - and every lesson he had ever learned – and sang with all the life and the fight still bundled within him.

'You can kill me,' he thought, 'but you can't kill my voice… my voice is the voice of a nation that is still learning to speak.'

Paco was singing as loud as he could. The boisterous streets turned silent.

People stopped what they were doing. They opened their windows, and listened.

They lifted the sills of their balconies and halted their calesas, and watched the young man - tied to a horse like an untamed animal, cry out the tune he had co-written with The One.

When music comes from heaven, one only needs a heart to hear it… and the people of Miramar heard, and understood. Buried beneath their stone and steel facades, stirred a beating heart.

"Shut him up," the elderly soldier with a bushy beard said, "just shut him up."

The youngest soldier yanked Paco from his horse and shoved him closer towards him. Then with his pointed leather boots, he delivered a brutal kick to the ribs.

Paco closed his eyes and suppressed the imminent scream of pain that surged through his body. He took another decisive breath and carried on…

"I shall be free…
When the chains that hold me back,
Finally break to my attack…"

The onlookers began to lash out obscenities at the soldiers, "Let him go, let him go!"

The cries grew louder as they approached the chaotic city centre.

Hundreds of curious onlookers, harried workers and passing traders caught up in the Plaza Mayor froze when they heard Paco's singing. When the soldiers reached the municipal jail next to the Presidential Palace, they threw Paco into a filthy cell piled with criminals, highway robbers and murderers. The soldiers shut the cell gate and left amidst the disapproving glares of the booing crowd.

A massive, mean-looking man with a noticeable horizontal scar across his neck stood up, and staggered towards Paco; his hands tucked deep in his pockets – a man nobody wanted to cross.

As he got closer, Paco became aware of his discernable stench.

"Are you the young man from that sketch? The infamous Paco Alegría?" he asked, running his tongue across his brown teeth, most of which were missing.

Paco gulped, pretending to be calm and in control. He didn't show any fear; in prison, fear meant death.

"Yes señor," he replied, steadily and with pride… "I'm Paco Alegría."

The big man looked at him intensely before saying, "That's my seat over there, take it."

"Your summary trial was concluded earlier today," The local councillor explained, "the state had witnesses and evidence of your treason charges."

"They approved your execution in two days' time."

Paco did not stir.

"Any particular place… for the execution… you'd like?" He made death sound like the planning of a birthday party.

"Can I talk to a lawyer?" Paco pleaded in desperation, "or anyone who can help me?"

"Son," the councillor replied in a state of almost non-existence, as if he did not have an ounce of emotion in his body, "treason against our nation has no remedy in our current system," he declared nonchalantly; trying to sound as academic as possible. "The law clearly states in article forty-five, paragraph b. of 1828, that… a person charged with treason beyond reasonable doubt is due for public execution, two days after his or her conviction. I'm sorry son, the law is the law," the councillor elaborated, picking his nose and looking more interested on what was on the tip of his finger than in Paco.

"So… any particular place you'd prefer?"

Paco remembered his childhood dream – the Plaza Mayor teeming with thousands of people, hundreds of birds flying above it, and the ever-grey city sky painted with the bright-coral moon that looked like a silver coin in a fountain… he couldn't forget the beautiful moon. 'Is this it?' he thought, 'Is this my fate and where my destiny ends?'

"The market is a great place," one of the prisoners interrupted with enthusiasm. "I'd like to die in the market surrounded by the smell of fresh beef, cabbage, and watermelons before I hear those gunshots."

"I'd prefer the *Alameda*," another one interjected, "the view of Miramar from up there is the last thing I want to see before those bullets tear my flesh into pieces…"

"I don't have all day son," the councillor added, silencing the prisoners.

Seconds felt like ponderous minutes.

"The Plaza Mayor señor," Paco answered at long end, honouring his dream.

"Great choice," the councillor replied immediately. "Traditional and classy. Superb taste, son."

The councillor certainly loved his job. He grew visibly excited at the prospect of any execution - taking part in something 'historical' as he called it, made him feel important - it was something he would, one day, tell his grandchildren.

For the councillor, choosing a place to die was as informal as deciding whether to have his eggs scrambled or fried for breakfast.

He knocked twice on the cell's rusty bars to exit.

A police officer opened for him.

"I have a last request councillor," Paco burst out before the obnoxious man left.

"Yes, son," the councillor replied.

"I'd like to see señorita Milagros Del Valle."

"You mean…" the surprised law man replied, "as in *the* Milagros Del Valle?"

Paco nodded firmly.

"I'll see what I can do about that," he said, stepping away from the cell with a wet smirk, shaking his head from side to side.

"I thought I had heard it all…" the councillor lingered near the door before leaving.

'What some young men fantasise about…' he thought, and trundled away.

Early the next morning a soldier approached the cell, hammering his metal baton along the sides of the prison bars as he marched, disturbing most of the sleeping prisoners. Two of the older inmates did not wake up. They snored so loudly not even an earthquake could have interrupted their slumber.

"I have a visitor for Alegría," he said.

Paco's heart almost jumped out of his chest gap – he was finally going to see his beloved; months of waiting soon to be over. He didn't care what he looked like or how bad he smelt - he just wanted to kiss her lavender skin and get drunk in her cat-like eyes.

To see Milagros for just one second was worth at least a thousand two hundred deaths in a row.

The door swung open. A young woman he'd never seen shyly stepped inside.

His heart sunk to the depths of the darkest, deepest ocean.

"I'm looking for Paco Alegría," she said nervously. Her scent invaded the room and clung to the bars of the cell. All at once, the desperate prisoners - as a collective, took a whiff of her feminine perfume as if it was the last pocket of oxygen on earth. Her sweet scent even revived the two dead-beat, snoring prisoners.

Most of the men had spent months in prison, anxiously awaiting their trials. As a result, their appearance was noticeably unkempt.

It was not difficult to spot the newly arrived Paco.

"Good morning, I'm Paco," he stood up confidently and approached the bars of the cell, "who are you and what are you doing here, señorita?"

Dolores fixed her untidy hair. She looked strangely flirtatious, as the reeking but still dashing young man approached her.

"I'm Dolores," she said, "Milagros' personal maid… her father strictly forbade her from leaving the palace. Unfortunately, she's not allowed to see you…"

"But it was a last request," Paco uttered, devastated.

"When President Del Valle heard you were caught, he locked Milagros in her room and placed guards around it, day and night," she replied, "she's not allowed to go anywhere."

Paco hung his head between two rusty, grimy cell bars.

Often, Dolores felt she was living Milagros' life. She frequently fantasised how life would be in her shoes. She almost reached for Paco's hair and caressed it. But of course, she wouldn't; she was just a young and pure-hearted dreamer.

"Anything I need to know?" Paco asked Dolores.

"Yes," she replied attentively, fidgeting with her hands. "Your face is on the front page of all the local newspapers. The whole city knows about what's happening… tomorrow."

"Dolores, listen," Paco said firmly, "anything I need to know from her?"

Dolores covered her mouth with her hand. She felt silly. "Milagros says… *siempre*," she added, "She says she will Love you. Siempre…"

"Siempre, siempre, siempre!" Paco slammed the bars in frustration. "What is the purpose of *forever* if I can't see her now?" he cried.

"I'm so sorry," Dolores replied, "is there anything you'd like me to tell her?"

Paco drew Dolores closer to him through the bars. She gasped for a second in panic, but enjoyed the two-second, high-voltage drama.

Paco whispered something in her ear – and then she departed, with a shudder.

'I was born to die on a Thursday,' Paco thought.

He remembered the talk he had had with Hawan about death. He remembered the part where Hawan had mentioned that one is not able to kill a wave, because life shifts, it does not disappear – and suddenly, he was no longer afraid.

He realised that they could not kill his dreams. Even with his body confined to a prison cell, his mind was still free.

'*Freedom is in the mind,*' he thought, remembering Mano's words back in that small cave in the high Andes. 'I shall be free,' he said to himself.

The prisoners slept. On the last day of his life, he arose at sunrise to express gratitude to Tayta Inti for all his blessings. 'I've lived a life of purpose…

I'm proud of my decisions and I'd repeat them again if I had the chance… I have followed my Never-Ending Legacy with no fear and I have *no regrets*. I'm not afraid,' he thought, amidst the dreams of prisoners as they dreamt of freedom in the recesses of their restless minds.

Paco did not sleep during the last night of his life… Milagros was constantly on his mind.

"I wished I'd spent more time with her, but even during the brief time we spent together, I learned what it is to Love, and that is enough. Many people go through their lives without finding true Love… I can proudly say I found it."

"In her Love, I experienced The One. In her Love, I savoured His essence, and soon, I'll taste more of His eternal nectar… I've learned to Love completely, unconditionally and with no expectations. I can now go in peace. *I'm not afraid…*"

A set of keys unexpectedly unlocked the rotting, wooden door that separated the stench of the prison-cell from the police room. A senior police officer entered. He was impeccably dressed.

"I see you are awake," he said to Paco.

"Still alive señor," Paco replied, "I'm enjoying these last moments. My life has been wonderful." The officer snubbed Paco's words.

"The execution will take place at nine o'clock sharp," he said, "You have a few short hours, son."

Paco nodded. Some of the prisoners began to stir.

"In case you're religious, you have the right to a priest," the officer said.

Paco bowed. "*Love is my religion.* Thank you for the genuine offer señor, but I'll pass."

"Very well… may God be with you," the officer replied. "I'll see you in a couple of hours."

"It shall be so."

The officer knocked on the cell door and left.

Some of the awakening prisoners heard the conversation. They took turns shaking Paco's hand. In the Miramar underworld -where they came from, this was a sign of respect and solidarity.

The big man stood up. He had a distinguishable, unsettling morning breath. "I can understand *our* punishment," he said, "we've done wrong," he addressed everyone, "we've stolen, plundered and murdered... but you... you've stood up for all of us, the people of colour and broken rights, and they are taking your life away for seeking justice," he thundered in the direction of the police room.

"You dirty government swine!" he banged the prison bars with his giant hands.

"Calm down," Paco said, "no need for violence, señor."

He placed his hands on the big man's shoulders and gently sat him down. "It is what it is," he whispered. There was a strange look of serenity on his face. For a brief moment, he resembled Hawan or Doña Lucia.

The big man looked perplexed. "Aren't you afraid?" he said, "They are going to shoot you in a couple of hours!"

"They can shoot me, but they can never kill me."

The big man looked even more confused.

"What is your name?" Paco asked calmly.

"I'm Big L."

Paco looked at the man with half his front teeth missing, with Love and compassion – behind his unpleasant appearance was a heart dying to redeem itself.

"*The biggest blessings often come disguised in the shape of tears,*" he added, and smiled at his new friend. "Thank you for your concern Big L. I'd like to spend these last two hours quietly."

The big man nodded and the cell plunged into silence.

The two hours were up faster than a summary execution. The cell lock opened again to reveal the senior police officer accompanied by three young soldiers dressed in full military regalia. Big L immediately raced towards the cell door and held it shut - preventing them from entering.

"You'll have to kill me before getting to him," he hollered, foaming from the mouth and heaving the door against the hostile soldiers.

"Big L, sit down please," Paco sounded authoritative - but the big man maintained the struggle.

Paco stepped up to the big prisoner and hugged him.

Big L eventually surrendered.

The soldiers thrust the door open and seized Paco by the arms.

The big man was teary-eyed as he hugged Paco for the last time. "This is so unfair," he kept repeating, "this is so unfair…"

"It's part of my life and mission," Paco replied. "Thank you Big L… The light and the good you see in others, is the light and the good you already have within you. There's much light and good inside you."

As Paco walked away, the prisoners stood up in a line, their left hands placed atop their hearts, as if the national anthem was playing in full musical glory; and paid their last respects.

Somebody opened the door to the police room.

The rowdy crowd could be heard then – a multitude of people had gathered to witness Miramar's favourite newspaper boy see the last minutes of his life. The capital was a carnival of angst, anger, blood, and morbid curiosity.

The cruel whip of sunlight slashed Paco in the eyes, tearing away his vision as he stepped into the busy streets. He was a gladiator battling the brightness of the arena, stepping out after a few days of captivity in a dark dungeon.

The plaza took a gargantuan and coordinated gasp as the soldiers led Paco to a pole placed slightly askew, in the centre of the sardine-can-packed square.

While he was away in the Andes, the press had made a dragon out of Paco. When the crowd noticed the helpless singer in chains, they realised they had been misled, once again.

"Another life wasted," an elderly woman said to her son, "these barbarities only happen in our country and no one has the guts to do anything about it. It's very sad. I can't watch this." She immediately turned around and walked away from the maddening crowd.

The entire episode was a bizarre sight for the almost-permanently overcast City of Kings. Unlike a typical winter's day, the sun had separated a blanket of horizontal clouds, impregnating the city in warmth.

A light, renegade Garua fell from a smattering of rebellious clouds. Enmeshed with the sun, the rain took on the form of minuscule diamonds cascading from the heavens. It was the perfect weather for a rainbow; but none appeared.

Miramar was not this exciting every day: people of all races and colours hurtled down to the Plaza Mayor to witness the spectacle. Dozens of curious seagulls soared in excitement above the heads of the crowd.

The autochthonous pigeons crooned their morning song, the *cu-cu-liu*, waiting to feast on the remnants of the human circus.

The moon, just as Paco had envisioned in his dreams, was suspended just above the Cathedral, affixed as a beaming coral painted in the sky.

The soldiers tied Paco to the pole. "Do you want a bandage over your eyes?" a soldier probed. "No," Paco replied. "I'd like to see the moon."

A soldier bound Paco's hands behind his back. Paco felt the bite of the rope rip some of the skin from his wrists. He felt the hate of the pull and the tear of the flesh. He did not utter a sound; it was too late to be concerned about such trivialities.

He looked for a familiar face in the crowd but did not recognise a soul.

Not a single soul.

The senior police officer in the unwrinkled uniform mounted a small podium a few feet away.

"Ladies and gentlemen… silence please… calma, calma…" he cleared his throat, attempting to look dignified and in control. "The city of Miramar and the government of our country have found Don Paco Alegría guilty of treason."

The crowd mumbled and booed.

"A trial took place two days ago and the evidence against Mr Alegría was unyielding and unequivocal. Our law states that a person found guilty of treason is liable for execution two days from the final verdict, no exceptions. Mr Alegría…" he turned to Paco, "*do you have any final words?*"

Paco looked up at the silver-coin-like coral moon – it was so bright that it seemed alive – and that's how he felt inside… *alive.*

He lowered his gaze. Thousands of eyes fell upon him.

He took a deep breath… and his voice broke through the restrained breaths of the crowd.

> *"It's a long way back home,*
> *It's a long restless fight*
> *When your freedom's at war…"*

The restless Plaza Mayor turned to geographical silence.

Paco's voice broke through the mixed mutterings and gossip of the multitude.

A country heard Paco's heart and soul melt into music…

> *"When the chains that hold me back, finally break to my attack*
> *I shall, I shall be free*
> *When I find my destiny, I rewrite my history*
> *I shall be free…*
> *I'll take the chains that hold me down, and I'll turn them to a crown*
> *I shall be free*
> *When I finally make the choice, I will find my own voice*
> *I shall be free… I shall be free… I shall be free…"*

At exactly quarter-to-nine in the morning, as had happened in Miramar for hundreds of years, the colossal bell from the Cathedral tolled, inundating the city with a heavenly metallic timbre that had not changed since the capital city was founded.

The bell proclaimed the raising of the host during the daily morning mass, which was saturated to capacity by the faithful, praying for mercy on Paco's soul.

During those seconds, as it had occurred for over three centuries, Miramar came to a halt. Time in the capital turned immobile and decrepit.

In that instant, there was not a sound; except for the clanging of the ancient bells melting with Paco's cry for freedom and justice.

A whole city fell to its knees. Coachmen halted their moving carriages. Horses and passerby's froze like salt statues - not moving an inch. People stopped whatever they were doing, and knelt.

The city collectively and in quiet, said a prayer.

If horses could pray, they prayed too.

Thousands of silent petitions journeyed to heaven, guided by Paco's song of freedom.

In a few more seconds, the bells would cease and the singer's time to live would end; but for those few seconds - a *song of hope* would grace the final moments of his life.

As was customary, after the cathedral's third and last bell had sounded, other bells from belfries all across the capital burst into song. The sight belonged in a painting by Velasquez: people of all races and colours on their knees, their prayers guided by a young man tied to a post... a divided country finally united in a prayer for peace and the end of slavery.

A song written by a human heart and guided by the hand of The One, had silenced an entire city, uniting a country for the first time.

Light rain unexpectedly descended on the crowd giving an eerie feeling to the proceedings. Paco never stopped singing.

Rain mixed with tears. Prayer mixed with song.

Hate and injustice rose to forgiveness, and minds conditioned to apathy, driven to change.

A rainbow appeared behind the cathedral; as if The One had painted it with His own hand, or as a symbol.

"Look, a rainbow!" someone yelled. Thousands of eyes witnessed the first rainbow in almost twenty years – and it was beautiful… a violet streak lightly overshadowed the other colours with its peaceful hue.

The moment felt like it did not belong on earth.

Many people turned away from the plaza – their hearts changed. They had seen enough. Some people sang 'I shall be free' quietly, while others sang aloud with Paco - all hands on their hearts.

The bells went quiet.

The senior police officer gathered the soldiers and ordered them into line; and to be ready to fire.

The young men rapidly scrambled into position.

Paco sang louder than ever, his heart taking a heavy beating from the flushing adrenalin.

His body shivered in cold sweat.

"*Prepare!*" the officer commanded as loud as he could. The crowd had joined Paco in song and the officer needed to holler the firing orders.

There was no quarter from Paco… '*I shall be free*' grew louder and was sung with greater resolve. The proximity to death had amplified his senses.

Paco could smell the sweat of fear that clung to the soldiers, hear the whisper of prayers in the cathedral. He could taste the glimmer of hope in some of the witnesses, and touch the silver lining of the clouds above him. He could feel The One saying, "hold on my son, hold on…"

He squeezed his fists as tight as he could and prayed for strength, and a quick death. 'Life is sometimes hard and unfair and tough. And it hits you right between the eyes when everything is going along just fine,' he thought as he stared at the four steady rifles. 'But that is the nature of Life. Not God.'

"*Get ready…*"

From the four corners of the Plaza Mayor, gargantuan choirs of voices broke and conquered the tense atmosphere. The noise was so deafening that a young soldier brought his rifle down in alarm.

"Keep your positions!" the officer ordered. The threatening legions of voices grew closer and louder…

"*I shall be free…*"

"*Get ready…*" this time the experienced officer's voice revealed a mild tremble. Every muscle in Paco's body tensed, every sinew stretched, delaying the moment of death.

Still, "*I shall be free…*" rang out from thousands of voices like a legion of avenging angels cascading from heaven. People ran away from the centre of the Plaza towards the neighbouring shops, in panic, overwhelmed by the vociferous song that reverberated like thunder from the four surrounding corners.

As if orchestrated by the hand of The One, thousands of slaves entered the square led by Alejandra and Mano. All held hands.

They surrounded the execution pole - holding rusty scythes, wooden pitchforks, and broken chains. Some of the women carried their babies. As far as the eye could see, there was an ocean of people yearning and demanding liberty.

With the added voices of the singing slaves, the atmosphere was electric. Their pleads finally broke through the walls of the Presidential palace.

Despite fear of reprisal from the invading crowd, the senior officer was ready to give his last command – it was his job and he would die honouring it. Behind the cathedral, the violet rainbow rose in splendour and intensity.

Birds flew unnoticed across the coral-like moon – a perfect replica of Paco's childhood dream.

Paco understood that every moment in his life was perfect - even that moment - tied to a pole with four rifles pointing… two at his head, and two at his open heart.

During those last seconds of his life, his heart did not bleed. He understood that nothing mattered, except Love; without it, everything else was meaningless. *Love was the cure for a bleeding heart.*

Paco lifted his gaze to the heavens. He knew he could depend on The One for anything, because *when one sees a rainbow, the storm is over.*

He then looked at his mother and Mano singing, and smiled.

In that moment he was fearless; he became the human embodiment of Love, and as he sung with all his might, his heart finally healed… and for the last time, he closed his eyes – and the world was once again, **violet**.

Xavier Saer

Footnote

Two years later, after the city of Miramar witnessed a young man sing with all his heart while tied to a pole - under a coral-bright moon and a violet rainbow, slavery was finally abolished; first in the capital, and then spreading to all corners of the new nation.

The newly elected president ended centuries of injustice with an ink scribble anointed on a page in the amended constitution. That is all it took: a single signature.

But behind the law, the smiles, the tears and the new breath of freedom, hung the life of the boy with the bleeding heart, which will never be forgotten.

The endless fields of cane, strewn along the coastline, never again saw a sheath's edge nor cut a single cane without remuneration. Feet and hands were free of chains. Children did not inherit their parents' shackles.

Over a hundred and fifty years later, a song called '*I shall be free*' is still sung and whistled by the children's children of the bygone slaves. And once in a while, when the sound of the cathedral bells toll, Miramar stops for a moment, and prayers return to its source: back to the place where only Love reigns, and all bleeding hearts are healed.

About the Author

Xavier Saer was born in Peru with the Inca culture and wisdom on his doorstep. Before he was ten, he had written his first novel, a two-page thriller titled, '*Journey in a time machine.*' It would take him over twenty years to write his second novel.

Xavier is an internationally published songwriter and recording artist with Universal Music/Markon Records. His work has received two South African Music Award (SAMA) nominations. His website, *www.xaviersaer.com*, has logged millions of hits since inception.

Xavier has been interviewed on many of South Africa's TV shows and his music played on major English and Afrikaans radio stations. He has featured in ad campaigns for Peroni, Sun International, SAA, 7Camicie, Miller's Lite, and News Café among many other companies.

When he is not writing or performing, Xavier is probably travelling somewhere in the world accompanied by his camera and a journal. You can follow his adventures on both his personal website and his *Facebook* page.

Bleeding Heart is his first novel.